Amidon Family

The Amidon Family

A RECORD OF THE DESCENDANTS OF

ROGER AMADOWNE

OF

REHOBOTH, MASS.

By FRANK E. BEST

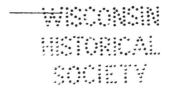

CHICAGO, ILL.
1904.
FRANK E. BEST, BOX 271.

Tradition has it that Roger Amadowne was a French Huguenot, who, after the revocation of the Edict of Nantes, was compelled to flee from France; that he went to England, where he remained for several years and then emigrated to America. No information has been obtained concerning the date and place of his birth or of his parentage.

On the records of Plymouth Colony and at Rehoboth his name is generally spelled Amadowne.

The majority of his descendants spell the name Amidon, while various branches of the family use the spellings Amadon, Amedon, Amidown, Ammidon and Ammidown.

An asterisk (*) preceding the number signifies that farther on under that number appears an account of the family of that individual.

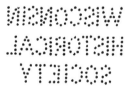

FRANK E. BEST

Genealogist

ANCESTRY TRACED
FAMILY HISTORY COMPILED
BOX 271

CHICAGO, ILLINOIS,

ROGER AMADOWNE.

The name of Roger Amadowne first appears at Salem, Massachusetts, in 1637.

"Att a meeting the 25th. of the 10th. moneth, 1637 being present Mr. Endicot, Mr. Connant, John Woodbury, John balch, Peeter Palfry, Jefry Massie, William Hathorne. It is agreed that the marsh & meadow Land that haue formerly layed in comon to this Towne shall now be appropriated to the Inhabitants of Salem, proportioned out vnto them according to heads of their families—To those that haue the greatest number an acre thereof & to those that haue least not aboue have an acre & to those that are betweene both 3 qrters of an acre, alwais provided & it is agreed that none shall sell away thier proportions of meadow, more or lesse, nor lease them onto any aboue 3 yeares, vnless they sell or lease out their howses wth their meadow."

Then follows a list of 224 names, in which list Roger Amadowne is the ninety-eighth and receives half an acre.

He is next found at Weymouth in 1640 as shown by the following from the town record:

"Sara daughter of Roger Amadowne born 10 (6) 1640."

The next mention is at Boston, in the list of births:

"Lida dau. Roger and Sara Amadowne 27, Feb. 1643.".

During his residence at Weymouth, the Rev. Samuel Newman was pastor of the church. In 1643 Rev. Newman, with a part of his congregation, formed the settlement at Rehoboth, near the Rhode Island line. In 1648 Roger Amadowne appears at Rehoboth, being the forty-third on the list of proprietors. The town of Rehoboth was afterwards divided and the older portion took the name of Seekonk.

The history of Rehoboth, by Bliss, says:

The town was built in a semi-circular form around what is now Seekonk common, with the meeting house and parsonage in the center. The semi-circle opened toward the Seekonk or Pawtucket river. This circle was afterward called the ring of the town.

Roger Amadowne's house was at the northeastern end of the semi-circle as shown by the following extract from the Rehoboth records:

"Oct. 18, 1660. William Sabine at a town meeting lawfully warned did agree with ye town to make ye mill bridge across Palmer's river and ye highway as far as ye foot of ye hill by Goodman Amadowne's, and to maintain it for forty a year, for twenty years and to have 4th. of his pay ready down."

This location is about one mile north east of the church in the present town of Seekonk.

On July 18, 1648, the records of Rehoboth show there was granted

3

"Roger Ammidowne a house lot between Walter Palmer's house lot and the mill."

By order of the Plymouth Court he was granted a tract of land June 3, 1662, and under date of June 7, 1665, the following:

"Fifty acrees of land is granted vnto Roger Amadowne, lying att a place called the Ten mile river, being a prte of that land which captaine Willett bought, lying on the bounds of Rehoboth; the said fifty acrees of land, with all and singulare the appurtenances belong therevnto, to appertaine to him, the said Roger Annadowne, to him and his heires assignee forever."

In 1658 he was granted more land and in 1671 had a grant of one hundred acres.

In 1657 his name appears in the list of freemen and in 1658 he first served on the coroner's jury, in which capacity he served several times.

Nothing is known of his first wife except that her name was Sarah and that she died at Rehoboth, June 20, 1668. He married for his second wife, December 27, 1668, Joanna, daughter of George and Jane Harwood. She survived him and died July 1, 1711.

The records do not give the date of his death but state that he was buried November 13, 1673. He probably died November 11, 1673, as the records show the following report of the coroner's jury:

"Wee, whose names are vnderwritten, being impannelled vpon a corrowner's inquest by the honored Mr. James Browne, Assistant, to sitt vpon the corpps of Roger Annadowne, deceased, occationed by some late striffe between his wife and him, hearing all euidences, pondering all cercumstances, and viewing the corpes, wee find noe wound nor bruise that might hasten his death.

"STEUEN PAINE, senr.
"THOMAS COOPER.
"WILLIAM SABIN.
"NICHOLAS PECKE.
"THOMAS COOPER, junr.
"ANTHONY PERREY.
"SAMUELL CARPENTER,
"JOHN PECKE.
"JONAH PALMER.
"JOHN MILLER, senr.
"BENJAMIN SABIN.
"HENERY SMITH.

"11th nouember, 1673, this verdict aboue written was giuen in vpon oath before mee. James Browne, Assistant."

The following is found showing the settlement of his estate:

"Wheras, Roger Amnadowne, of Rehoboth, late deceased, died intestate, for the more equall disposing of his estate, it is mutually concluded by and between Joanna Annadowne and John Coblech of Swansey, in the behalfe of Ebinezer, the eldest son of the said Annadowne and with the advise and consent of John Harrod of Patucksett, in the jurisdiction of Prouidence Plantations, brother vnto the said widdow Annadowne, and with the consent and approbation of the Court, that what remaines of the estate shalbe disposed of and settled as followeth:—

Viz: Impr, that twenty-four acrees of vpland and a peece of salt marsh belonging therevnto, lying att Wachamaucutt Necke, and fifty pounds commonage within the township of Rehoboth, and one acree of fresh meddow, lying att a place called the 40 acree meddow, shalbe and is settled and confirmed vnto and vpon the said Ebenezer Annadowne, to him and his heires and assigns for euer.

Alsoe, it is agreed and concluded by and between the pties aboue named, that one other acree of fresh meddow, lying att the aforesaid 40 acree meddow, be settled vnto and vpon Hannah Wheaton, the daughter of the said Roger Annadowne, wife vnto Jeremiah Wheaton, and likewise ten acres of vpland lying at Wachamaucutt Necke.

Furthermore, that John Johnson shall haue a coate of the said Roger Annadownes, vallued att two and twenty shillings, and a horse, harnis and cart vallued att eighteen shillings.

Finally, that the remainder of the whole estate, be it more or lesse, shall belong and appertaine vnto the said widdow Annadowne, prouided that att her decease, that the house, and land lying about the house, being twelve acrees, more or lesse, and fifty pounds commonage, and three or four acrees of vpland lying att Deare Hill, shall appertain vnto Phillip and Henery Annadowne, her children, in equall and like proportions, and prouided, that shee pay all such debts as are due and owing to any out of said estate.''

CHILDREN.
(By first wife.)

2—Ebenezer. The date of his birth or death has not been found. He is not given in the list of inhabitants of Rehoboth in 1689. In the History of Rehoboth, by Bliss, in a list of those who advanced money during King Philip's war appears the name of Eben Amidown as having advanced one shilling, six pence.

3—Sarah, born December 6, 1640, at Weymouth; no other record of her.

4—Lydia, born February 27, 1643, at Boston; no other record of her.

5—Hannah, born at Rehoboth, September 20, 1652. She married Jeremiah Wheaton, of Rehoboth, and had—
    i—Hannah, born July 3, 1666.
    ii—Jeremiah, born March 18, 1669.
    iii—John, born September 2, 1671.
    iv—Sarah, born September 29, 1673.
    v—Ebenezer, born March 7, 1677.
    vi—Nathaniel, born March 6, 1679.
    vii—Mehitable, born April 4, 1681.
    viii—Nathaniel, born March 6, 1683.
    Mrs. Hannah Wheaton died at Rehoboth, September 13, 1719.

(Second wife.)

*6—Philip, born at Rehoboth, January 26, 1670.

7—Henry, born at Rehoboth, January 24, 1671. He is given in the list of inhabitants of Rehoboth in 1689. No other record of him has been found.

8—Mehitable, born at Rehoboth, August 27, 1672. She married December 23, 1709, John Thompson, of Rehoboth.

6.

PHILIP AMIDOWN (ROGER[1]) was born at Rehoboth, January 26, 1670. He resided at Rehoboth until after the death of his first wife, when he removed to Mendon, Massachusetts. In 1704 his minister's rate at Mendon was one shilling and he had a share in the sixth division of the lands there in 1713. In 1717 he removed to Oxford,

Massachusetts, where he died March 15, 1747. He was a farmer and cooper. In 1720 he and his wife became members of the church at its organization in Oxford. In 1730 he served as Selectman and as Constable in 1735.

He married, first, at Rehoboth, May 27, 1698, Mehitable, daughter of Samuel and Mary (Millard) Perry. She was born at Rehoboth, April 30, 1680, and died there July 4, 1699. He married, second, September 16, 1700, Ithamar Warfield, who survived him. She was born March 28, 1676, daughter of Deacon John Warfield, of Mendon, and his third wife, Hannah Randall.

Will of Philip Amidown:

Will allowed May 12, 1747.

In the name of God, Amen, this sixteenth day of December in the year of our Lord one thousand seven hundred and **fourty** three, I, Philip Amidown of Oxford in the County of Worcester, in the province of the Massachusetts Bay in New England, yeoman, being advanced in years and in a weak and low condition. Do make this my last will & testament, as follows, viz:—First and principally I commit my soul into the hands of Almighty God, my Creator, hoping in his mercy thro the merits Death & Passion and prevailing intercession of Jesus Christ my Lord and Saviour and my body I desire may be decently interred at the discretion of my executor hereinafter named in faith of the resurrection of it at the last day and as touching such temporal estate as God has betrusted me with (after my just debts and funeral charges are paid) I will and bequeath the same as follows:—That is to say

Impr. I give and bequeath unto my beloved wife Ithamar Amidown the improvement use profit and incomes of one quarter part of my farm whereon now I dwell in quantity and quality, as also my house which we now occupy, and the equal half of my barn together with all my moveables of the within doors as well as without to be possessed and enjoyed by her during her natural life, and at her decease the said quarter part of my farm house and barn to be to my son Ephraim Amidown his heirs and assigns forever as his and their proper estate and inheritance, and my moveable estate and goods to be distributed as 'hereafter expressed in this my last will and testament.' Item,

I give and bequeath unto my sons Henry Amidown, Roger Amidown, Ichabod Amidown, Philip Amidown and John Amidown to each of them three pounds in Good public bills of credit or good current lawful money of New England, each and every pound equal to six shillings and eight pence in bills of credit of the new tenor of the said province to be paid to each of them for their respective heirs and assigns before or at the expiration of one year after my decease. Also my carpenter's tools to be divided equally between them, my said sons and their respective heirs and assigns having already given unto my said sons their full part & portion of all my estate real & personal.

Item. I give and bequeath unto the heirs of my son Ithamer Amidown three pounds of money as above specified to be paid to them their heirs and assigns at the expiration of one year after my decease. The said Ithamer Amidown having in his life time received his part & portion of my estate real and personal.

Item. I give and bequeath unto my daughter Mary Chamberlain three pounds in money as above specified to be paid to her and the heirs begotten of her body at the expiration of one year after my decease and one moiety of my household goods after the decease of my said wife to be possessed and enjoyed by her and her aforesaid as above expressed.

Item. I give and bequeath unto my daughter Hannah Wheelock three pounds to be paid unto her her heirs and assigns at the expiration of one year after my decease in money as above specified and also the other moiety of my household goods after the decease of my said wife, having already given to my said daughters their part & portion of my estate.

Item. I give, grant and devise unto my son Ephraim Amidown his heirs and assigns all my real and personal estate whatsoever together with all my buildings profits, incomes of my said real estate after the decease of my said wife Ithamar Amidown appointing and ordaining the said Ephraim Amidown sole executor of this my last will & testament and to pay all my just debts & legacies in manner as is above expressed.

In witness whereof I, the said Philip Amidown have hereunto put my hand and seal the day and year first hereinbefore written.

PHILIP AMIDOWN. (Seal)

Signed, sealed and delivered in the presence of us by the said Philip Amidown and by him declared to be his last will & testament.

BENJ. DAVIS,
DUNCAN CAMPBELL,
JOHN CAMPBELL.

Worcester, ss, Probate Office.

April 20, 1747. The Revd. Mr. John Campbell and Duncan Campbell two other witnesses to this within instrument personally appearing made oath that they saw Philip Amidown the testator sign and seal and heard him publish pronounce and declare the same instrument to be and contain his last will and testament and that when he did so he was of sound disposing mind according to those deponants best deeming & that then with Benjamin Davis the other witness set to their names as witnesses thereof at the same time in said testators presence.

Sworn before me John Chandler, Judg. Prob.

Oxford, May 12, 1745.

These lines may notify you that I am satisfied with the will of my husband.

to witness my hand.

her
ITHAMER X AMIDOWN.
mark

The old homestead owned by Philip Amidown in South Oxford now belongs to Franklin H. Clark. The transfers being as follows: April 24, 1717, Joseph Chamberlain to Philip Amidown; December 15, 1743, Philip Amidown to his son Ephraim, three-fourths with a new house; November 2, 1793, heirs of Ephraim Amidown to Elisha Davis; 1795, Elisha Davis to Joseph Davis; January 10, 1807, Joseph Davis to Abijah Davis; 1810, Abijah Davis to Silas Fitts; May 6, 1868, executor of estate of Silas Fitts to Sylvanus Robinson; August 1, 1868, Sylvanus Robinson to Mary J., wife of Abel M. Chaffee, who took down the old house and built the present one; April 6, 1884, Mary J. and Abel M.

Chaffee to George A. Kimball; June 16, 1885, George A. Kimball to Horace Shepardson; June 20, 1885, Horace Shepardson to Franklin H. Clark. The other quarter of the land owned by Philip Amidown is now owned by Lucinda Morse.

CHILDREN.
(First wife.)

*9—Henry, born February 8, 1699.

(Second wife.)

*10—Roger, born February 6, 1702.
*11—Ichabod, born May, 1704.
12—Mary, born March 30, 1706. She married, July 18, 1728, Benjamin Chamberlain and resided in Oxford.
*13—Philip, born in 1708.
*14—Ephriam, born in 1710.
*15—Ithamar, born April 25, 1712.
*16—John, born May 19, 1713.
17—Hannah, born February 2, 1717. She married Samuel Wheelock, of Hardwick, Mass. Their daughter Mary, born 1738, married Caleb Cheney, of Mendon. They resided in Milford, Mass., where he was Town Clerk, Selectman, and served in the Revolutionary Army with the rank of Lieutenant. They (Caleb and Mary Cheney) had twelve children, one of whom was an ancestor of Gen. A. B. Underwood, U. S. A.

9.

HENRY AMIDON (Philip², Roger¹), born at Rehoboth, February 8, 1699. He married at Mendon, March 31, 1718, Meltiah, daughter of Joseph and Hannah (Thurston) Cheney. She was born October 14, 1690, and died May 17, 1780. Henry Amidon was a farmer and lived in Oxford and Dudley until 1744, when he removed to Ashford, Connecticut, where he died March 5, 1778.

CHILDREN.

*18—Jacob, born February 28, 1720.
19—Mehitable, born January 15, 1723. She married, December 12, 1742, William Curtis, of Dudley. They had James and Henry and probably other children.
*20—Joseph, born February, 1725.
*21—Henry, born May 3, 1727.

10.

ROGER AMIDON (Philip², Roger¹), born February 6, 1702. He was a farmer and lived in Oxford. He married, first, October 27, 1731, Elizabeth, daughter of Thomas Hawkins; second, February 28, 1757, Mrs. Rachel Rice.

In January, 1759, he served in the company commanded by Captain Samuel Davis that marched for the relief of Fort William Henry.

CHILDREN.

22—Rachel, born September 28, 1732; died young.
23—Elizabeth, born July 18, 1734; married Joseph Kingsbury in 1760.
24—Roger, born November 11, 1736; died young.
*25—Jeremiah, born November 12, 1738.
26—Samuel, born June 18, 1741; died young.
*27—Samuel, born October 13, 1742.
28—Rachel, born February 20, 1744; married Benjamin Curray, of Douglas, in 1768.
*29—Roger, born May 12, 1747.

11.

ICHABOD AMIDON, (Philip², Roger¹), born in May, 1704. He was a farmer and resided in Mendon. He served as Selectman in 1756 and was on the Grand jury in 1758. In the records of the town he is called Lieutenant.

He married May 7, 1732, Margery, daughter of Jacob and Margery (Hayward) Aldrich, of Mendon. She was born March 14, 1714, and died in 1753.

CHILDREN.

30—Ichabod, born February 10, 1733. He died in 1818. No record of his marriage is found. Holmes Ammidown gave him as unmarried, but the records of Canton, Mass., show the intentions of marriage of Ichabod Amidon and Elizabeth Wales were published February 17, 1781.
31—Hannah, born May 28, 1735; died young.
32—Margery, born April 10, 1737; died young.
*33—Ebenezer, born March 2, 1741.
34—Margery, born May 25, 1743; married John Holden in 1761.
35—Mary, born May 5, 1747; married, October 23, 1770, Samuel Scarborough, of Pomfret, Conn.
*36—Philip, born April 22, 1749.
37—Hannah, born January 14, 1751; married, April 2, 1772, Ebenezer Scarborough, of Pomfret, Conn.
*38—Jacob, born September 15, 1753.

13.

PHILIP AMMIDOWN (Philip,² Roger¹), born in 1708. He was a farmer and lived in that part of Oxford which in 1754 became a part of Charlton and is now included in Southbridge. He died in 1779. He married Submit Ballard.

CHILDREN.

*39—Caleb, born August, 1736.
*40—Joseph, born August 14, 1741.
*41—Reuben, born September 13, 1747.

14.

EPHRIAM AMIDON (Philip*, Roger¹), born in 1710. He married, first, Hannah, daughter of John and Hannah Dean, of Dedham, March 10, 1736. His second wife was Hannah Smith, whom he married February 24, 1743. He was then of Dudley, but soon settled on the homestead in Oxford and was the administrator and principal heir of his father's estate.

His will was dated April 13, 1786, but was disapproved June 6, 1786, as it had but two witnesses, while the law required three. His wife, Hannah Smith Amidon, died September 14, 1807, aged ninety-three years.

CHILDREN.
(First wife.)

42—John, born November 25, 1736; probably died young.
43—Keziah, born April 4, 1739. She married first, in 1771, John Allen, of Oxford. They had one child, which died in infancy. He died in 1780 and she married Jonathan Bixby, of Oxford, in 1793.

(Second wife.)

*44—Noah, born October 19, 1743.
45—Hannah, born January 16, 1745; married Abel Ray and lived at Hinsdale, Vt., where she died December 24, 1814.
46—Abigail, born March 9, 1746; died unmarried at Oxford, December 24, 1818.
*47—Philip, born January 6, 1748.
*48—Ephraim, born February 9, 1749.
49—Dorcas, born November 10, 1750.
50—Hepsibah, born February 27, 1752; married Ephriam Town and lived at Newport, N. H.
51—Mehitable, born January 4, 1754; married Obediah Allen and lived in Oxford. They had Bathsheba, Cornelius, Darius, Elizabeth and Timothy.
52—Meribah, born January 15, 1756; married Ebenezer Robbins.

15

ITHAMAR AMADON (Philip,⁴ Roger¹), born April 25, 1712, at Mendon, Mass. In 1733 he purchased one hundred and forty-five acres of land in the eastern part of Oxford. In 1739 he sold a part of this to John Curtis, a part to his brother Henry Amidon and in 1740 the balance to his father. From the records it appears that he died before December, 1743, but the exact date is not known. He married Ruth Curtis, Jan. 5, 1736. In 1747 she was then of Woodstock, Conn., where she married Daniel Child.

CHILDREN.

*53—Ithamar.
*54—Ebenezer.

16.

JOHN AMIDON (Philip⁴, Roger¹), born at Mendon, Mass., May 19, 1713. He was a farmer and lived at Hardwick, Mass., where he died between March 15 and May 12, 1755. He married July 14, 1737, Sarah, daughter of Daniel Hastings.

CHILDREN.

55—Sarah, born April 3, 1738; died young.
56—Abigail, born April 25, 1740; died young.
57—Sarah, born July 7, 1742; married, in 1779, Jonathan Gilbert, of North Brookfield, Mass.
*58—John, born January 6, 1744.
59—Abigail, born May 31, 1747; married as second wife, March 27, 1777, Lemuel Cobb. They removed to Hardwick, Vt., and had John, born 1778; Lemuel, 1780; Elizabeth, born 1782, married Micajah Haskell, and Nabby, born 1789.
*60—Philip, born January 16, 1749.
61—Hannah, born October 25, 1752. She married, November 25, 1790, Seth Ruggles, and died October 26, 1791, leaving one child, Seth Amidon Ruggles.

18.

JACOB AMIDON (Henry,⁶ Philip,⁴ Roger¹), born February 28, 1720. He was a farmer and lived in Dudley until 1753, when he removed to Woodstock, Conn., where he was living in 1786. No record of his death is found at Woodstock and he may have removed to Wallingford, Vt.

He first married, December 27, 1744, Elizabeth Curtis, of Dudley. No record of their children, if any, nor date of her death have been found. He married, second, at Woodstock, June 10, 1773, Joanna Johnson.

CHILDREN.

62—John, born April 14, 1776.
63—Elizabeth, born February 15, 1778.
64—Irene, born April 11, 1786.

20.

JOSEPH AMIDON (Henry,⁶ Philip,⁴ Roger¹), born February, 1725. He was a farmer and resided at Ashford, Conn. About 1808 he removed to Onondaga county, New York, where he died November 27, 1810. He married Patience Chaffee. She died in 1816.

CHILDREN.

65—Eunice, born September 13, 1762; died August 9, 1834, unmarried.
66—Chloe, born April 10, 1764; died June 22, 1842. She married David Thomas and had a son, Asahel Thomas.
*67—Abel, born March 14, 1767.
68—Rhoda, born April 4, 1771; died June 22, 1845. She married Elisha Russell and their daughter Nancy married Gardner Amidon, 262.
69—Abner, born February 9, 1774; died October 24, 1804, unmarried.
*70—Asahel, born June 17, 1776.

71—Hannah, born October 5, 1778. She married Captain Amasa Chapman, of Ashford, Conn. They moved to Onondaga county in 1801, where she died April 14, 1851. Children—
  i—Adelia, married Samuel Amidon, 238.
  ii—Sabina, born August 21, 1800. She married Volney King, of Onondaga, and had four children—Volney L., George T. and Sabina, who married Rev. Thomas Haroun.
  iii—Abner, born September 30, 1798. He was Captain in militia in 1826. From 1828 to 1858 was Justice of the Peace and member of the Legislature in 1860. He died June 18, 1873.
  iv—Amasa.
  v—Zina.
  vi—Lois.
*72—Caleb, born July 12, 1781.
*73—Cheney, born September 3, 1783.
74—Meltiah, born March 22, 1787; died April, 1830. She married Joseph Wing.

21.

CAPTAIN HENRY AMIDON (Henry[3], Philip[2] Roger[1]), born at Oxford, Mass., May 3, 1727. He was a farmer and resided first at Pomfret, Conn., but after 1752 at Willington, Conn., where he died. He appears on the Lexington Alarm list from Willington as a private and served nine days. He was commissioned by Gov. Jonathan Trumbull, March 21, 1777, as Captain of the third company in the 22d regiment of Connecticut militia and served at New London and elsewhere. He married at Pomfret, Conn., Sept. 25, 1751, Sarah Doubledee (or Doubleday). She died at Willington, Conn., Jan. 8, 1794.

CHILDREN.

75—Jedediah, born May 15, 1752; died August 11, 1752.
*76—Jedediah, born 1753.
*77—Moses, born 1756.
*78—Jonathan, born 1757.
79—Mary, born 1762. She married Jonathan Flint and lived at Braintree, Vt., where she died August 26, 1840. They had Asaryl, 1785; Elisha, 1788; Joseph, 1789; Augustus, 1792; Anna, 1794; Sally, 1796, and Polly, 1798.
*80—Jacob, born March 5, 1764.
*81—William, born January 30, 1767.
*82—Henry, born February 9, 1769.
*83—Asaryl, born July 20, 1771.
84—Sarah, born February 9, 1774. She married Shubal Hall and removed to Onondaga county, New York, in 1799. She died March 27, 1841. Her children were Shubal, born 1796; Sallie, 1800, and George, born 1805, married Ruth West.

25.

JEREMIAH AMIDON (Roger[10], Philip[2], Roger[1]), born November 12, 1738. He was a shoemaker and lived in Oxford, where all his children were born. The name of his first wife was Bathsheba, nothing more known of her. He married second, February 23, 1769, Elizabeth Martin, of Douglas. She died October 10, 1826, and he, May 2, 1813.

CHILDREN.

35—Mary, born May 13, 1764 ; died young.
86—Bathsheba, born March 4, 1766 ; died young.
87—Elizabeth, born April 30, 1768 ; married David Leonard.

(Second wife.)

88—Lucy, born December 5, 1769 ; married Lemuel Moffitt.
*89—Isaac, born January 28, 1772.
90—Molly, born August 29, 1773 ; married Elisha Harwood.
91—Lois, born September 14, 1775 ; died young.
92—Sarah, born August 14, 1777 ; married Rufus Humphrey.
*93—Jeremiah, born March 31, 1779.
*94—Samuel, born January 28, 1781.
95—Lurania, born February 11, 1786 ; married Lyman Wetherell.

27.

LT. SAMUEL AMIDON (Roger[10], Philip[4], Roger[1]), born Oxford, Mass., October 13, 1742. He resided in Douglas and was school director in 1791.

During the Revolutionary war he served as follows: On the alarm of April 19, 1775, he enlisted in Capt, Samuel Read's company and served six days; was commissioned April 10, 1778, as First Lieutenant in Capt. Caleb Whiting's company in Col. Wood's (3d Worcester Co.) regiment and served as such in the expedition to Rhode Island June 19 to July 12, 1778. He resigned May 29, 1780, but in August of that year he again served for a short time in an expedition to Tiverton. He married, March 3, 1768, Ruth Wood.

CHILDREN.

*96—Jedediah, born 1769.
*97—Ezra, born February 2, 1771.
*98—Samuel.
99—Molly, born May 7, 1775 ; died March 16, 1861. She married John Walker and had nine children, as follows:
    i—Betsey Walker, died young.
    ii—Rufus Walker, married and had two sons, Emory and Rufus.
    iii—Benjamin Walker.
    iv—Polly Walker, married Joseph Hicks and had thirteen children—Emerson, Massena, Emily, Calvin, Cynthia, McKendre, Miranda, Harriet, Lemira, Welcome, Mary, and two unnamed.
    v—Roxy Walker, died young.
    vi—Content Walker, born January 15, 1804 ; married Samuel Stockwell and had eleven children, viz.:
        i—Samuel Welcome, died young.
        ii—Adaline, born 1824 ; married, first, William Phelps, and had two children, Francis W. and Ella Adaline ; married, second, Azariah E. Bliss and had Merrit E. and Ella W.
        iii—Lorenzo, born 1826 ; married Delise G. Brown and had a son, Elwyn L. Stockwell.
        iv—Samuel Welcome, died young.
        v—Norman, born 1831 ; married Abigail Steel and had Delia A. and George N.
        vi—Emory, born 1833 ; married, first, Berilla P. Brown and had Herbert C. and Delia ; married, second, Emily Wardwell and had Harry E.
        vii—Merrit, died young.

viii—Sarah Ann, born 1836; married Norton L.
    Brown and had Stell S. and Myrtie D.
ix—Mary Elizabeth, born 1838; married J. Frank-
    lin Brown and had six children—Frank ·H.,
    Emory W., Newton H., Herbert S., Gertrude
    K. and E. Clair.
x—Lucy Emaline, born 1841; died 1863.
xi—Cynthia Ellen, born 1843. She married, first,
    Moses M. Nichols and had Viola Ellen, born
    1863, who married Solomon Henry Amidon,
    705. Cynthia Ellen married, second, John J.
    DeWolf and had Clayton A., born 1865. She
    married, third, Timothy Negus and had Daisy
    E., Roy L., Halbert E. and Fred T.

vii—Cynthia Walker, born January 27, 1807. She married
    Calvin Baker and had eight children:
    i—Augustus Collins, born 1830; married and had
        Lewis W., Leslie C. and Harlan A.
    ii—Cynthia Lucretia, born 1832; married James
        Bullock and had Elmer J. and Nettie L.
    iii—Diantha Lestina, born 1834; married Daniel
        Carpenter and had Henry, Herbert, Frank
        and Martha L.
    iv—Lucy Caroline, born 1838; married Joseph J.
        Streeter and had Lillian C., Gertie May and
        Hiland J.
    v—Sophronia Emeline, born 1841; married Albert
        C. Bishop and had George, Oliver E. and
        Osland L.
    vi—Martha Francelia, born 1844; married, first,
        Franklin L. Todd and had Judson F. and Ar-
        thur D. She married, second, Amos Tucker
        and had Amos H.
    vii—Mary Cordelia, born 1844; married Walter F.
        Scott and had Alta V., Winfield B. and Susie.
    viii—Ellen Marinda, born 1850; married Samuel
        Woffendan and had Murray S., Frederick W.,
        Leon H. and Ruth E.

viii—Welcome, died young.
ix—Lucy, married Shepherd Dalrymple and had Sophrina,
    Ursula and Francis.

100—Ruth. She married Asa Whitney and died in 1840. They had five
    children:
    i—Lorenzo, married Lucy Caroline Jackson and had—
        i—Almira M., married Solomon Amidon Stone, son
            of Lucy Amidon, 323.
        ii—Ira Jackson.
        iii—Jane Lucretia, married F. J. Rice.
        iv—Harriet D., married Billing Millard and had
            Arthur, Jenny L., Lucy C. and Laura.
        v—Lucy Caroline, married William Conrad and had
            Harriet and Grace.
        vi—Emily Francelia, died young.
        vii—Emily Francelia, died young.
        viii—Lorenzo M., born 1848; married Ella Potter.
        ix—Chauncey John, born 1850; married Nettie
            Wells.
        x—George W., born 1852.
    ii—Almira Whitney, married Joel Houghton and had Chandler,
        Chauncey, Jane A., Warren, Wesley and Henry.
    iii—Chauncey, died young.
    iv—Asa.
    v—Ira, married and had Ira, McKendree, Ruth A., Chauncey
        L., Wesley, Warren, Ellen A., Lawrence, Clarence and
        Harriet.

101—Sybil. She married Benjamin Chatman and had Persis and Ben-
    jamin.
102—Rhoda. She married Wilson Chatman and had Merritt, Jonathan,
    Welcome, Susan and Sophronia.
103—Lois. She married John Whitney (brother of Asa) and had Worthy,
    Warren, William, Welcome, Wesley, Waters, Almira, Pliny, Ira
    and Ursula.

EDMOND EDDY AMIDON, 112

29.

ROGER AMIDON (Roger[10], Philip[3], Roger[1]), born in Oxford, Mass., May 12, 1747. His first wife was Elizabeth Shepherd, who was born in 1738. She first married a Mr. Rider and had five children. She and Roger Amidon were married in 1766 and resided in Douglas until about 1790, when they removed to Readsboro, Vermont, where she died January 27, 1819. He married, 2d, in Rowe, Mass., Ruth Eddy. She was born in 1784, and died August 10, 1860.

At the Lexington Alarm, Roger Amidon enlisted as a private in Capt. Benjamin Wallis' company, Col. Arnold's regiment, and served thirteen days. He died at Readsboro, Vt., May 31, 1825.

CHILDREN.

(First wife.)

*104—John, born November 26, 1766.
105—Rachel. She married Amos Cummings and had Lawton, Sylvia and Zelpha. Zelpha married Clark Burlingame, Shaftsbury, Vt.
106—Sally. She married Jedediah Briggs and lived at Arlington, Vt. They had Polly, married Solomon Gowdy; Sally, married Chester Buck; Nancy, married Mr. Squires; John, Thankful, Jedediah and Alvira.
107—Lucy. She married Jedediah Amidon, 96.
*108—Ralph, born May 3, 1772.
109—Eunice. She married Elijah Phelps and lived at Salina, N. Y. They had Chester, Clark, Simon, William and Edward.
*110—Solomon, born February 27, 1778.
111—Polly. She married Samuel Amidon, 98.

(Second wife.)

112—Edmund Eddy, born September 1, 1821. He resides, unmarried, at Rowe, Mass., where he was a merchant for nearly thirty years. He has served as Town Clerk and as Postmaster. He is one of the few men now living whose father served in the Revolutionary War.
113—Luther Wilson, born June 6, 1823. He married Mary C. Henshaw. They had no children and after her death he married again and lived at Charlton, Mass.

33.

EBENEZER AMIDON (Ichabod[11], Philip[3], Roger[1]), born at Mendon, Mass., March 2, 1741. He married Silence, daughter of William and Abigail (Sumner) Thayer, of Mendon, August 19, 1761. They resided in Dudley. He was a member of the School committee, 1770, 1771, 1774, 1782 and 1784; Surveyor of Highways, 1775, 1776 and 1787; in 1777 was on committee to provide for soldiers' families; 1781 on Committee of Correspondence; and in 1783 was Constable. In 1781 and 1783 on the records he is called Ensign Amidon. At the Lexington Alarm he marched as a private in Capt. Ebenezer Craft's company, Col. Larned's regiment and served twelve days. He served as private from March 14, 1776 to December 2, 1776 in Capt. David Reed's company and was Sergeant in Capt. Joseph Warner's company, Col. Ruggles' regiment, from August 17, 1777, to November 29, 1777.

CHILDREN.

114—Nancy. She married, first, October 13, 1785, William Larned, of Dudley, and second, William Barker. She died in 1819, leaving six children by her last husband. Myra A. Clifford, Auburndale, Mass., is a descendant.
*115—Alpheus, born November 14, 1768.
116—Margaret, born June 1, 1770.
117—Abigail, born September 13, 1772. She was not married in 1817, at which time she signed a deed.
118—Silvia, born June 4, 1775.
119—Ichabod, born January 26, 1780; lived at Hamilton, N. Y.
120—Ebenezer, born November 1, 1783. In 1803 he chose his mother for his guardian and in 1827 was living at Sand Lake, N. Y.
121—Samuel, born July 13, 1786.

36.

COL. PHILIP AMMIDOWN (Ichabod,[11] Philip,[4] Roger[1]), born at Mendon, Mass., April 22, 1749. He married, November 17, 1770, Sylvia Taft of Mendon. He resided in that town, was a member of the Congregational church and prominent in public affairs.

At the Lexington Alarm he marched as Sergeant in Capt. John Albree's company to Roxbury, April 19, 1775. On July 9, 1776, he was chosen First Lieutenant in Capt. Samuel Cragin's company in the Third Worcester county regiment and was on an expedition to Rhode Island in December, 1776, and January, 1777. From August 14, 1777, to November 29, 1777, was First Lieutenant in Capt. Peter Penniman's company, Col. Job Cushing's regiment. August 27, 1779, was commissioned Captain of the first company on Col. Nathan Tyler's (3d Worcester Co.) regiment and held that rank until March, 1781.

The History of Mendon shows his services in the town as follows:
1780, member of school committee.
1782, Town Treasurer.
1783, Town Treasurer and Town Clerk.
1784, Selectman and Town Clerk, and was also on a committee to consider a lottery scheme to raise funds for the purpose of repairing roads.
1787, was commissioned Lieutenant-Colonel of the Third Regiment Worcester County militia.
1789, had a tavern.
1790, on a committee to make new arrangement of the school districts.
1794, on committee to establish boundary between Mendon and Milford.
1797 and 1798, Selectman.
1798, 1799 and 1800, Representative to General Court.

CHILDREN.

*122—Otis, born December 30, 1771.
123—Sylvia, born May 27, 1773. She married, April 3, 1794, Hon. Jonathan Russell. He was born at Providence, R. I., February 27, 1771, and died at Milton, Mass., February 17, 1832. He graduated at Brown University in 1794 and practiced law until 1810, when he was appointed Charge d'Affaires at Paris and 1811 at London. In 1814 he was appointed a commissioner with Henry Clay, James A. Bayard, John Q. Adams and Albert Gallatin and as such signed the Treaty of Peace with England at

Ghent. He then served as Minister to Sweden until October, 1818, when he resigned and returned to Boston, where he engaged in business. He served as Representative in Congress from 1821 to 1825. His wife died at Providence, R. I., July 10, 1811. Children:

    i—Amelia E. Russell, born January 3, 1798; died young.
    ii—George Robert Russell, born May 5, 1800; died August 5, 1866. He graduated from Brown University in 1821, from which institution he received the degree of LL. D. in 1849. He married Sarah P. Shaw, of Boston, and resided at West Roxbury, Mass. Children:

        i—Elizabeth, born November 2, 1836; married Col. Theodore Lyman. He graduated from Harvard in 1855, served in the civil war and lives at Brookline, Mass.
        ii—Col. Henry Sturges Russell, born June 21, 1838. He graduated from Harvard in 1860, served in the civil war and was for a time in Libby prison. He married Mary Hathaway Forbes, and resides at Milton, Mass.
        iii—Anna Russell, born April 23, 1840. She married Prof. Alexander Agassiz, of Harvard University.
        iv—Emily Russell, born January 26, 1843; married Charles L. Pierson.
        v—Marion Russell, born November 14, 1846.
        vi—Robert Shaw Russell, born June 10, 1850.
        vii—Sarah Russell, born September 22, 1851.
    iii—Caroline A. Russell, born June 17, 1805. She married, first, Jazariah Ford, of Milton, Mass., and had five children. He died May 18, 1839, and she married, second, June 24, 1842, Francis Taft.
    iv—Anna Matilda Russell, born January 21, 1808. She married her cousin, Philip Ammidown, 336.

*124—Philip, born October 1, 1774.
125—Nancy, born May 25, 1776.
126—Stephen, born November 6, 1778; died at Providence, R. I.

38.

JACOB AMIDON (Ichabod,[11] Philip,[6] Roger[1]), born at Mendon, Mass., September 15, 1753. His name appears in the catalogue of Harvard among the graduates of the class of 1775. He enlisted early in the Revolutionary war and was at the battle of Bunker Hill. He was taken prisoner near New York city and was for twenty-eight months confined on board a prison ship.

In December, 1782, he purchased land in Chesterfield, N. H., where he engaged in trade and was Town Clerk from 1785 to 1799, and Selectman from 1785 to 1797. His name was placed on the pension roll in 1833.

He married Esther, daughter of Timothy and Rachel (Spencer) Ladd, of Chesterfield. She was born September 26, 1762, and died March 26, 1852. He died February 11, 1839.

CHILDREN.

127—Lucretia, born October, 1785; died unmarried.
128—Harriet, born June 7, 1788; died May 14, 1799.
129—Rachel, born May 16, 1791; died 1795.
*130—Otis, born April 26, 1794.
131—Rachel, born May 16, 1797; died August 1, 1807.
132—Jacob. Date of birth not given; died of yellow fever in Georgia about 1820.
133—Harriet, born 1804. She died unmarried, April 14, 1871.

39.

CALEB AMMIDOWN (Philip,¹¹ Philip,⁴ Roger¹), born August, 1736. He married, in Dudley, April 14, 1758, Hannah, daughter of Joseph and Mehitable Sabin, a descendant of William Sabin, of Rehoboth, Mass. They lived in that part of Charlton which is now in Southbridge. He died April 13, 1799, and she married, second, and as his second wife, Ebenezer Davis. She died March 20, 1820.

At the Lexington Alarm, April 19, 1775, he enlisted as Sergeant in the company commanded by Capt. Samuel Curtis. In December, 1776, and January, 1777, he served with the same rank in Capt. Abijah Lamb's company, and again under the same captain as Quartermaster Sergeant in July and August, 1780.

Hon. George Davis in ''A Historical Sketch of Sturbridge and Southbridge,'' says ''The writer in the former part of his life recollects very well hearing the elderly men speak of Mr. Ammidown as a man of notoriety and influence, and whose opinion was highly appreciated. More than once we have heard the following anecdote related of him: ''At some period in the earlier part of his life, he was the orderly sergeant of a militia company. It was thought expedient to memorialize the existing government, in some matter deemed important. To whom shall we apply to make the draft of the instrument to be sent? was a matter of consultation among the officers of the militia. The captain of the company, to which Mr. Ammidown belonged, proposed his orderly sergeant. Some surprise was manifested. It was concluded that Sergeant Ammidown should make the attempt. The object of the proposed memorial was stated to him. Mr. Ammidown, having procured pen, ink and paper, and making his lap, covered with his leather apron, his writing desk, went to work, and soon produced a document which exactly met their views.'' This instance is related to show his early aptness as a ready writer. We are informed by our venerable friend, Dea. John Phillips, of Sturbridge, who was well acquainted with Mr. Ammidown, that he was a man of extraordinary abilities. In important questions his judgment was highly valued. He speaks of him as a legislator, having few superiors in correct and comprehensive views. As a ready writer his pen was freely and profitably used in the legislature. Although not a very ready debater, he would frequently baffle those who were more learned, and more gifted in speaking. He was fond of collisions of this sort, as an occasion of pleasantry. A rude attack would receive such a retort as could not be comfortably enjoyed.''

The Hon. E. D. Ammidown has furnished us some additional particulars respecting his grandfather, Caleb Ammidown. As he was extensively known, and influential, although moving in the common walks of life, his business talents, as well as other traits of character, are worthy of remembrance. During the revolutionary struggle he was actively engaged in discharging various important trusts. After the close of the war, he represented the town of Charlton several years. This was one of the trying periods in our history. The state of affairs was such as required the strongest and most discreet men. Mr. Ammidown was one of the men who took an active part in bringing order out of confusion, and adjusting the discordant elements.

He was appointed to survey the confiscated lands, including a large part of Charlton and that section of country. Among his papers were to be seen numerous plans and maps of lands surveyed and lotted out by him.

He was a member of the Court of Sessions, a Court whose jurisdiction embraced many important matters within the limits of Worcester County. The duties of exciseman required an annual inventory
of the groceries sold in the county, and the imposition and collection
of a specific tax on the same. This was a very laborious office, including, as it did, the whole county of Worcester. It is evident that Mr.
Ammidown was a working as well as a calculating man. In summing
up the traits of his character, the most prominent were: Firmness,
resolution, integrity, perseverance and keen foresight. It was not
easy to impose upon him by any ingenious pretexts or specious preten-
sions.

Mr. Ammidown was plain in his dress, in his manners and in con-
versation, but not vulgar or profane. When such men as Mr. Ammidown are entrusted with public concerns, there is little danger but
they will be managed with discretion.''

CHILDREN.

*134—John, born April 5, 1759.
*135—Luther, born July 8, 1761.
*136—Calvin, born June 21, 1768.
137—Mehitable, born February 4, 1772. She married, as second wife,
 in September, 1799, Dr. James Wolcott, a prominent citizen of
 Charlton. They removed to Queechee, Vt. She died December
 23, 1842. They had one child—Henry Wolcott, born November
 2, 1804. He married, in 1847, Mary A. Carter.
138—Susannah, born March 15, 1775 ; died August, 1790.
139—Hannah, born August 14, 1779. She married, May 6, 1797, Zephaniah Brown, of Dudley. She died April 15, 1861. They had
 eleven children:
  i—John Windsor, born May 21, 1800 ; died April 25, 1815.
  ii—Hannah, born May 12, 1802 ; died October 16, 1835.
   She married Joseph C. Allen, of Sturbridge, and had
   one son.
  iii—Elmira, born August 2, 1804 ; married Henry Whiting,
   of Charlton, and had one daughter.
  iv—Caroline, born December 8, 1806 ; died October 2, 1808.
  v—Caroline, born February 9, 1809 ; married George Lines.
  vi—George, born May 27, 1811 ; married Eliza C. Ward.
  vii—Fidelia, born July 11, 1813 ; married Elbridge G.
   Blanchard, of Sturbridge, and had two children.
  viii—Julia Ann, born May 23, 1816 ; married Charles Carlisle,
  ix—Celia Ann, born July 18, 1818 ; died March 9, 1832.
  x—John W., born September 25, 1820.
  xi—Jane, born October 5, 1822.

40.

JOSEPH AMMIDOWN (Philip,[11] Philip,[4] Roger[1]), born August
14, 1741. He married Dorcas Carpenter of Woodstock, Conn. She was
born January 7, 1747, and died March 7, 1835. He was a farmer and
lived mostly in Charlton, but died near Troy, N. Y., May 14, 1821.

He enlisted at the Lexington Alarm, April 19, 1775, in the company
commanded by Capt. Samuel Curtis, and served eleven days, and he again
served in August, 1779, in Capt. Nathan Fales company.

CHILDREN.

*140—Cyrus, born October 4, 1765.
*141—Philip, born July 25, 1767.
142—Reuben, born September 23, 1768; died May 30, 1853. Mrs. Rees
      Rickerds, of Blackinton, Mass., is a granddaughter.
143—Hannah, born December 5, 1770; died May 10, 1843.
144—Mercy, born August 29, 1773; died May 23, 1850.
145—Sally, born September 29, 1775; died 1854; married John Dunbar.
*146—Joseph, born October 15, 1781.
147—Dorcas, born October 17, 1783; died March 21, 1812.
148—Ebenezer, born December 24, 1787.
149—Patty, born August 12, 1790.

41.

REUBEN AMMIDOWN (Philip,[11] Philip,[5] Roger[1]), born September 13, 1747. He was a farmer and resided in Dudley, where he died January 12, 1802. In 1776 he served as a private in Capt. Abijah Lamb's company, and in 1792 was a member of the school committee.

He married Olive Logan, who was born at Woodstock, Conn., August 8, 1771, and died March 26, 1840.

CHILDREN.

150—Mary, born November 17, 1771; died October 16, 1847.
151—Uranah, born September 18, 1773; died August 29, 1848. She mar-
      ried, in 1793, Henry Searls, of Charlton.
152—Walter, born October 5, 1775; died September 14, 1847.
*153—Jabez, born September 7, 1777.
*154—Rufus, born October 6, 1780.
155—Manre, born March 4, 1782; died October 8, 1848.
156—John, born April 25, 1784.

44.

NOAH AMIDON (Ephraim,[14] Philip,[5] Roger[1]), born at Oxford, October 19, 1743. He married, February 19, 1767, Abigail Putney of Oxford. He died November 9, 1769.

CHILDREN.

157—John, died young.
158—Calvin, born 1769. In 1793 was living at Pomfret, Conn., where
      he married, August 15, 1792, Martha Koufler.

47.

PHILIP AMIDON (Ephraim,[14] Philip,[5] Roger[1]), born at Oxford, January 6, 1748. He married, November 2, 1768, Eunice, daughter of John Shumway. About 1778 he removed to Chesterfield, N. H., and in 1783 to Fitzwilliam, N. H., where he had a mill. He died February 2, 1834, and his wife died August 25, 1837.

During the Revolutionary war he served from July 10, 1777, to December 22, 1777, in Capt. Ebenezer Newell's company, Col. Danforth Keyes' regiment, the service being mostly in Rhode Island.

CHILDREN.

159—Dorcas, born December 10, 1769. She married, May 20, 1788, Daniel Rice. They lived in Jaffrey, N. H., and had ten children. Her son, Laban Rice, kept hotel and she lived with him until her death, which occurred April 15, 1874, being over 104 years old. She was very active and retained her memory until the last.

*160—John, born 1771.

161—Roxalana, born February 3, 1774. She married Levi Haskell and had six children. After his death she married Abel Angier.

162—Lavinia, born 1776. She married, December 29, 1795, Abel Angier and had ten children.

163—Mary (Polly), born at Chesterfield, 1778. She married, April 5, 1801, Liberty Allen, of Shrewsbury, Mass., and had twelve children.

    i—Owen Warland, born 1801; died at Fredonia, N. Y., 1882.
    ii—Lucius Shumway, born 1802; died at Worcester, Mass., 1880. He was Representative to General Court, 1851-1855, and State Senator in 1858. He had one son, George L.
    iii—Augustus Amidon, born 1804; died at Shrewsbury, 1882. His daughter, Mrs. G. E. Sawtelle, lives at Shrewsbury.
    iv—Thankful Hortensia, born 1805; died 1876; married Artemas Perrin.
    v—Eunice Sophronia, born 1807; died 1850; married Leander Sawyer.
    vi—Mary Eliza, born 1809; died 1864; married John W. Barton.
    vii—Keziah Cleora, born 1811; died 1883; married Timothy Ellis.
    viii—Flora Rosaline, born 1813; died 1885; married A. F. Maynard.
    ix—Caroline Cynthia, born 1815; died 1861; married Thomas Rice.
    x—Liberty Gilman, born 1817; died 1892; served during the Civil War in Twenty-second Massachusetts Infantry.
    xi—James Appleton, born 1819; died 1852.
    xii—Henry E. W., born 1822; lives at Shrewsbury.

164—Eunice, born 1781; married Benjamin Sampson, Jr., in 1804.

165—Infant, born and died in 1785.

*166—Josiah, born August 9, 1787.

167—Cynthia, born 1789; married, August 10, 1809, John Jarvis Allen. They lived at Fitzwilliam, N. H., where she died December 24, 1865. Mr. Allen was born in 1789 and died in 1880. He was Selectman in 1815-1823, 1826-1829, 1832, 1835 and 1836. In 1833 and 1834 he was Representative. They had ten children:

    i—Edward Ervin, born 1809; died 1841.
    ii—Caroline, born 1811; died 1891; married Milton Chapin.
    iii—Infant, born and died 1813.
    iv—Keziah Amidon, born 1815; died 1877; married Almond Phillips.
    v—John Jarvis, born 1818; died 1884. He was Representative in 1849, 1850, 1857 and 1858.
    vi—Cynthia, born 1822; died 1823.
    vii—Cynthia, born 1823. Her second husband was Joseph Bowman, and in 1896 she lived at Troy, N. Y.
    viii—Henry W., born 1828; died 1828.
    ix—Ellen Maria, born 1830. She married, in 1850, John Warren Shirley and lived in Boston, Mass.
    x—Charles H., born 1832; died 1833.

168—Kezlah, born 1793; died October 10, 1833. She married November
20, 1816, Jubal Eldridge Allen. They resided at Fitzwilliam,
N. H., and had seven children—
    i—Mary, born 1817; died 1822.
    ii—Ann, born and died in 1818.
    iii—Julia, born 1819; died 1822.
    iv—Daphne, born 1822; died 1842.
    v—Mary Ann Julia, born 1823; died 1866; unmarried.
    vi—Jubal Eldridge, born 1827; died 1891; served in Company H, Thirty-third Massachusetts Regiment.
    vii—Henry Clay, born 1829; died 1895; served in Company A, Nineteenth Massachusetts Regiment.

48.

EPHRIAM AMIDON (Ephriam,[14] Philip,[6] Roger[1]), born February 9, 1749. He married December 17, 1772, Jane Robbins and re moved to Chesterfield, N. H., and afterwards to Londonderry, Vt., where he was living in 1793. In June, 1777, he served as a private in Capt. Oliver Cobleigh's company, Col. Ashley's regiment, which marched for the relief of Ticonderoga. Later in the same year he served in Capt. Kimball Carlton's company in Gen. Stark's brigade.

CHILDREN.

169—Hepsibah, born 1773.
170—Matilda, born 1775, and died at Chesterfield in 1777.
171—Abigail, born in 1777 at Chesterfield.

53.

ITHAMAR AMADON (Ithamar[14], Philip[6], Roger[1]). He married March 29, 1759, Tabitha, daughter of Daniel Green, of Woodstock, Conn. He settled in Granby, Mass., before 1763.

CHILDREN.

*172—Titus, born July 18, 1763.
*173—John, born May 2, 1766.

54.

EBENEZER AMADON (Ithamar,[15] Philip,[6] Roger[1]), born at Dudley, Mass. He married August 24, 1762, Sarah Flynn, of Woodstock, Conn., where he was living at that time. She was born May 26, 1743, and was a daughter of Richard and Sarah Flynn. In 1763 they removed to Goshen, Mass., living on a farm in the western part of the town, where he died later than 1807.

CHILDREN.

174—Azerba, born at Woodstock, Conn., March 1, 1763. She married
    Gersham Bates.
175—Sally, died unmarried.
176—Hannah. She married, February 15, 1808, John Wilder, of Ches-
    terfield, Mass.
*177—Ansel, born August 25, 1770.

58.

JOHN AMIDON (John¹⁰, Philip⁹, Roger¹), born at Hardwick,
Mass., January 6, 1744. He was a farmer and lived at Hardwick, where
he died October 25, 1825. He married (1st) February 4, 1771, Mercy
Allen. She was a daughter of Joseph Allen and was born April 19,
1746. She died February 9, 1808. He married (2d) December 14, 1809,
Mrs. Anna (Dean) Ruggles.

CHILDREN.

178—Chloe, born January 17, 1772; died September 11, 1842, unmarried.
179—Lydia, born August 26, 1774; died April 23, 1828, unmarried.
*180—John, born June 1, 1782.
*181—Elijah, born September 27, 1787.

60.

PHILIP AMIDON (John¹⁰, Philip⁹, Roger¹), born at Hardwick,
Mass., January 16, 1749. He served as a private in Capt. Ebenezer
Humphrey's Company, Col. Jacob Davis' Regiment, from July 30,
1780, to August 8, 1780, on an alarm at Rhode Island. He was a
farmer and lived in Hardwick, where he died August 11, 1796. He
married November 27, 1788, Rhoda, daughter of Shearjashub Goodspeed.
She was born in 1770 and died June 16, 1841.

CHILDREN.

182—Sarah (Susan), born 1789; died September 13, 1828, unmarried.
183—Alice, born 1791; died June 26, 1830. She married March 26,
    1822 (as second wife) Ichabod Dexter, of Hardwick, and had
    the following children:
    i—Hannah, born March 26, 1823; married in 1842 Lys-
        ander Powers, and had three children:
        i—Joel L., born 1843; was Assessor in Hardwick.
        ii—Frank.
        iii—Elmer D.
    ii—Sally, born May 6, 1825; married in 1845 James P.
        Fay, of Hardwick. He was a school teacher, Assessor
        and Justice of Peace. She had two children:
        i—George E.
        ii—John H.
    iii—Ruth, born May 30, 1827; married Zenas D. Tinney,
        Newburg, Me.
    iv—John Bangs, born July 30, 1829. He was adopted by
        his uncle, Elisha Bangs, and went to Springfield, Mo.,
        as a clerk. He afterwards became Mayor of that
        town and served in the army. Later he was appointed
        Postal Agent, Portland, Ore.

184—Hannah, born 1798; died September 2, 1844. She married December 19, 1814, Elijah Banga, Jr.
185—Sophronia, born 1793; died October 12, 1840. She married September 9, 1819, Stillman Clark, and had five children:
    i—Charles Stillman, born June 19, 1823. He married Sarah W. Newcomb, and had five children:
        i—Charles L.
        ii—George S.
        iii—Frederick W.
        iv—Frank D.
        v—Carrie M.
    ii—Rhoda Ann, born March 20, 1825; married Bela B. Paige.
    iii—Susan Sophronia, born August 16, 1826.
    iv—Sarah Amidon, born July 17, 1829; married Oren Gould.
    v—Alice, born 1836.

67.

ABEL AMIDON (Joseph[10], Henry[9], Philip[2], Roger[1]), born at Ashford, Conn., March 14, 1767, died in Onondaga county, New York, December 20, 1830.

CHILDREN.

186—Abel.
187—Abner.
(Mrs. Parsons says that Abner was the father of Miles B. Amidon, who was a corporal in Co. G, 149th New York Regiment, and was killed in the Army. She also says that Mrs. Stephen Hunt, of Navarino, New York, is a descendant of Abel.)

70.

ASAHEL AMIDON (Joseph,[10] Henry,[9] Philip,[4] Roger[1]), born at Ashford, Conn., June 17, 1776. He married Sally Tanner. He was a farmer and lived in Onondaga county, where he died, March 25, 1844.

CHILDREN.

188—Emily; married Lewis Amidon, 243.
189—Cheney.
190—Polly, born September 29, 1810; died February 19, 1886. She married in 1832 Daniel Owen and had four children:
    i—Esther, born November 8, 1834; married in 1854 Jay H. Griswold and lives at Central Square, New York.
    ii—Rev. Daniel D., born June 12, 1837; married in 1865 Ella S. Woodward and lives at Central Square, New York.
    iii—Alida, born March 28, 1840; died August 22, 1858.
    iv—Polly, born July 12, 1843; died young.
191—Hannah. She married, first a Maddock and second a Wessels.
192—Abel. He was a carpenter and married Martha M. Starr. They had no children.
193—Ruth; died unmarried.
194—Angelina A., born May 25, 1819. She married a Griffin and lives at South Onondaga, N. Y.
195—Joseph, died young.
196—Caroline; married Alonza Fuller.

72.

CALEB AMIDON (Joseph,[5] Henry,[4] Philip,[2] Roger[1]), born at Ashford, Conn., July 12, 1781. He married Anna Parker and lived in Onondaga Co., where he died April 16, 1810.

CHILDREN.

197—Miles, died in 1836. He married April 10, 1834, Martha Cleveland, who died November 10, 1835.
198—Abner.
199—Caleb.

73.

CHENEY AMIDON (Joseph[5], Henry[4], Philip[2], Roger[1]) born at Ashford, Conn., September 3, 1783. He was a farmer and was among the early settlers of Onondaga Co., New York. He married in 1818 Mary Reynolds. Her father was Benoni, a revolutionary soldier. She died in 1878. Cheney Amidon died in 1863.

CHILDREN.

200—Chloe Ann, born January 14, 1819; died March 13, 1868. She married June 13, 1838, Leonard P. Field, of South Onondaga, N. Y., and had the following children:
    i—Silas C., lives at South Onondaga, N. Y.
    ii—Hannah.
    iii—Charles H., served in the army.
    iv—Robert Emmett; lives at Tully, N. Y.
    v—Mary Matilda.
    vi—Alice.
    vii—Albert.
    viii—Leonard.
    ix—Abner.
    x—Philip.
201—Rhoda, born 1821; married Henry Amidon, 247.
*202—Philip Van Cortland, born 1823.
203—Eliza Cordelia, born 1825; died 1888. She married John Hildreth. Some of her children live at Charleston, Ill.
    i—Cheney.
    ii—Katuria.
    iii—Fanny.
    iv—Albert Gallatin.
    v—Nellie.
    vi—Henry.
204—Sarah Hutchings, born 1827; died 1855.
205—Helen Marr, born 1829; died 1897. She married George C. Nichols and lived at South Onondaga, N. Y. They had six children:
    i—Cheney.
    ii—Mary Elizabeth.
    iii—Florence Ella; married Dempster Browning and has two children: Lina and Flora.
    iv—Emerson Earl; married Emma Olney and has four children: Cheney, Dora, Clara and Daniel.
    v—Charles B.
    vi—George O.; married and has two children: Homer and Beulah.
206—Charles Barber, born 1833; died 1834.
*207—Outerbridge Horsey, born 1836.
208—Fanny Olivia, born 1840; married Perrin P. Parsons.
209—Mary Elizabeth, born 1842; married Thomas Joyce and has two children.
    i—Charles Henry; lived at South Onondaga, N. Y.
    ii—Chloe; married Walter Austin, Lyndon, Ill.

76.

CAPTAIN JEDEDIAH AMIDON (Capt. Henry,[11] Henry,[5] Philip,[8] Roger[1]), born in 1753, probably at Pomfret, Conn. He married June 11, 1778, Hannah Walker. She died May 16, 1813. He was a farmer and lived in Willington and Ashford, Conn. He served in the Revolutionary Army as follows:

Private on the Lexington alarm from the town of Willington, and served nine days.

Corporal, May 1, 1775, in Capt. Thomas Knowlton's Company, Third Continental Regiment, Col. Israel Putnam. This Company was stationed principally at Cambridge, Mass., and participated in the battle of Bunker Hill. His term of service expired December 16, 1775.

Sergeant, from June to December, 1776, in Capt. Parker's Company.

Captain, June 10, 1777, of the 10th Company, 22d Regiment, Conn., Militia. He was placed on the pension roll, September 14, 1833.

CHILDREN.

*210—Experience Johnson, born April 30, 1779.
.211—Abigail, born January 20, 1781.
212—Jedediah, born December 2, 1782; died February 19, 1783.
213—Hannah, born December 30, 1783; died March 14, 1826.
214—Ebenezer, born March 21, 1786; died May 29, 1803.
*215—Henry, born September 24, 1788.
216—Wealthy, born February 6, 1791; died August 14, 1798.
217—Horace, born July 27, 1793; died April 28, 1806.
*218—Horatio, born July 27, 1793.
219—Sally, born June 22, 1797; married David Wright.
220—Polly, born June 22, 1797; married Lyman Strong.
221—Jedediah, born March 2, 1800.

77.

MOSES AMIDON (Capt. Henry[21], Henry[3], Philip[5], Roger[1]), born in 1756, probably in Pomfret, Conn. He married at Willington, Conn., May 26, 1780, Sarah Davis. He was a farmer at Willington, where all of his children were born. He served in the Revolutionary army as follows:

Private from May 5, 1775, to December 17, 1775, in Capt. Solomon Willes' Company, 2d Continental Regiment. This company was stationed near Boston, and a portion of it was engaged in the battle of Bunker Hill. He also served in New York City and on Long Island as a private in Capt. Parker's Company from June, 1776, to December 25, 1776, and was engaged at the battle of White Plains, October 28, of that year. He served as sergeant from July 1, 1778, to March, 1779, in Capt. Hill's Company, Col. Samuel McClellan's Regiment, which served mostly in Rhode Island. He was placed on the pension roll in 1833, and at that time was living in Washington County, N. Y.

CHILDREN.

222—Davis, born January 16, 1783.
223—Polly, born February 6, 1785.
224—Annis, born April 12, 1787.
225—Elizabeth, born May 21, 1789. She is probably the Elizabeth
  Amidon who married November 7, 1813, Gordon C. Burnham, of
  Windsor, Conn.
*226—Nathaniel, born February 29, 1782.
*227—Samuel, born February 22, 1794.
*228—Moses, born May 29, 1796.
*229—Henry, born December 30, 1798.

78.

JONATHAN AMIDON (Capt. Henry[11], Henry[9], Philip[4], Roger[1]),
born in 1757, probably at Pomfret, Conn. He served in the Revolutionary War as follows:

Private from May 26, 1777, to June 10, 1778, in Capt. Perkin's
Company, in the 2d Conn. Regiment. This Regiment served along the
Hudson River, and in Nov. 1777, joined General Washington in Pennsylvania. In December of that year they were at the battle of White
Marsh and spent the winter at Valley Forge. He again enlisted in
the same regiment as a private, July 3, 1779, and served till January 15, 1780, the winter being spent at Morristown, N. J. He again
enlisted, June 7, 1781, in Capt. David Dorrance's Company, 5th Conn.
Regiment and served till December 31, 1781. He was placed on the
pension roll in 1819 and for some reason was dropped, but afterwards placed on the roll in 1832.

He married, January 29, 1784, at Willington, Keturah Holt. She
was born August 31, 1760, and died July 25, 1839. He was a farmer
and resided at Willington until about 1788, when he removed to Randolph, Vt., where he died April 15, 1838.

CHILDREN.

230—Hannah, born July 28, 1784; married Samuel Bruce, Northfield,
  Vt.
*231—Elijah, born July 1, 1786.
*232—Alfred Augustus, born May 16, 1789.
*233—Jacob, born September 26, 1791.
234—Diah, born March 18, 1794.
235—Mary, born August 18, 1796; died September 18, 1819.
236—Sarah, born May 16, 1800; died March 31, 1873. She married
  December 2, 1820, Walter Abbott, of Brookfield, Vt., and had
    i—Laura Lucinda, born April 6, 1822; died September
      28, 1839.
    ii—Orpha Lucinda, born June 2, 1824; died January 14,
      1849; married William S. Miller.
    iii—Owen Walter, born July 4, 1828; married Rebecca Lyon,
      and lives at Medford, Mass.
    iv—Mary Adeline, born July 10, 1835; married Marcus
      Peck, and lives at Brookfield, Vt.
    v—Emeline Laura, born September 7, 1838; died May 20,
      1857.
237—Lucinda, born August 18, 1804; died November 4, 1883. She married May 16, 1840, Solomon Tubbs. Their son, Andrew J. Tubbs,
  was born 1841 and lives at Moreton, Vt.

80.

JACOB AMIDON (Capt. Henry[11], Henry[3], Philip[2], Roger[1]), born at Willington, Conn., March 5, 1764. He served as a private in the Revolutionary army from August 12, 1782, to August 12, 1783, in Capt. Durkee's Company. In 1833 he was placed on the pension list. He married Hannah Pool, of Willington. In 1805 he removed to Onondaga County, N. Y., living near Navarino, where he died September 17, 1838.

CHILDREN.

*238—Samuel, born July 12, 1793.
*239—Jacob, born 1796.
*240—Elijah, born January, 1797.
*241—Leonard, born February 6, 1799.
242—Hannah; she married Ebenezer Comstock and their son, Jonathan
      C., lives at Cedarvale, N. Y.
*243—Lewis, born 1804.
*244—Moses, born December 20, 1808.
245—Lucinda. She married Thomas Vinton, and their son, Samuel
      Vinton, lives at Navarino, N. Y.
246—Philoma. She married Eli Anderson and had—
      i—Henry Eli, born August 18, 1843; died October 24, 1894.
      ii—Alma Philoma, born April 12, 1847. She married Janu-
        ary 1, 1868, Eugene A. Kenyon, and lives at South
        Onondaga, N. Y.
*247—Henry, born August 7, 1815.

81.

WILLIAM AMIDON (Capt. Henry,[11] Henry,[3] Philip,[2] Roger[1]), born at Willington, Conn., January 30, 1767. He married May 7, 1791, Prudence Thompson and about 1800 removed to Braintree, Vt. He was a school teacher for many years and at one time lived at Middlebury, Vt.

CHILDREN.

248—Almira; married Orin Orcott.
249—Sarah, born May 10, 1792.
250—Rial, born August 24, 1793.
*251—William, born May 13, 1795.
*252—Orin, born October 27, 1796.
253—Sabrina, born October 4, 1798. She married Rev. Benjamin Butler,
      a Methodist minister, living at one time at Middlebury, Vt.
254—Lodosia, born April 24, 1802.
255—John Thompson, born April 25, 1805; died young.
256—Prudence, born February 8, 1808.
*257—Edmund Sumner, born October 19, 1810.
258—Arcelia, born April 3, 1812; married about 1835 Solomon Dens-
      more, and lived at Painesville, Ohio.

82.

HENRY AMIDON (Capt. Henry[11], Henry[3], Philip[2], Roger[1]), born at Willington, Conn., February 9, 1769. He accompanied his brother, Jacob, to Onondaga county, where he settled on a farm and died soon afterwards.

CHILDREN.

259—Henry: lived at South Onondaga.
260—Freeman.
261—Cheney.
*262—Gardner, born May 27, 1800.

83.

ASARYL AMIDON (Capt. Henry[11], Henry[9], Philip[4], Roger[1]), born at Willington, Conn., July 20, 1771. He served in the War of 1812 and then removed to Belcherton, Mass., where he died February 7, 1833. He married, November 28, 1799, Aletheia Perry. She was born February 28, 1773 and died August 13, 1857.

CHILDREN.

*263—Asaryl, born September 26, 1800.
264—Aletheia, born July 23, 1802; died June, 1886.
265—Bridget, born July 28, 1804; died December 11, 1822.
266—Sally, born August 4, 1807. She married Porter Edwards and died at Willington, November 23, 1845, leaving a daughter, Sarah E., born November 7, 1845, and died April 6, 1861.
267—Samuel, born May 29, 1809. He married April, 1835, Harriet, daughter of Martin and Sally (King) Sedgwick. She was born June 29, 1827, and died July 12, 1889. He lived at Belcherton, where he died May 14, 1858. His widow removed to Springfield, Mass. They had no children, but adopted George Franklin Amidon. He now lives at Springfield, Mass., and has a son, George Samuel Amidon.
268—Polly, born November 9, 1811; died January 12, 1824.

89.

ISAAC AMIDON (Jeremiah[12], Roger[10], Philip[4], Roger[1]), born at Oxford, Mass., January 28, 1772. He was a shoemaker and lived mostly in Dudley, but died at Webster, Mass., August 21, 1859. He married in 1793, Hannah, daughter of Ebenezer Foster. She died April 3, 1840. Besides a daughter who died in infancy they had:
*269—Rufus, born October 4, 1794.

93.

JEREMIAH AMIDON (Jeremiah[12], Roger[10], Philip[4], Roger[1]), born at Oxford, Mass., March 31, 1779. He married, October 7, 1801, Abigal Harwood. She was born March 30, 1781 and died August 16, 1871. They resided in Charlton, Hardwick and Uxbridge, Mass., and removed to Swansey, N. H., in 1816, and in 1819 to Richmond, N. H., where he died December 14, 1865.

CHILDREN.

270—Maria; married Loami Green.
271—Abigal; married Luther C. Curtis.
*272—Cyril, born April 2, 1812.
*273—Martin, born August 21, 1818.
274—Betsey; married Sands Aldrich.
*275—Perley, born July 15, 1821.

94.

SAMUEL AMIDON (Jeremiah[31], Roger[10], Philip[6], Roger[1]), born January 28, 1781. He married August 28, 1809, Lucy, daughter of Deacon Ebenezer Humphrey. He was a shoemaker and lived in Oxford, Mass., where he died February 16, 1827. His family afterwards removed to Webster and his widow died at Springfield, Mass., July 28, 1865.

CHILDREN.

276—Rufus, born December 31. 1809.
*277—Isaac, born August 30, 1811.
*278—Jeremiah, born October 17, 1813.
279—Lucy Ann. born December 9, 1815. She married Smith Bruce, of Springfield, Mass., and had two children.
280—Louisa, born 1818; died unmarried in 1842.
281—Sarah, born February 19, 1819. She married October 9. 1841, Rufus Foster, Webster, Mass. They moved to Florida, 1888.
282—Infant, born 1824; died 1825.

96.

JEDEDIAH AMIDON (Lt. Samuel[31], Roger[10], Philip[6], Roger[1]), born at Douglas, Mass., in 1769. He married (1st) Hannah Walker and (2d) Lucy Amidon (107). He resided at Readsboro, Vt.

CHILDREN.
(First wife.)

*283—Abner.
284—Eunice. She married Mr. Littlefield, and had—
i—Hannah; married Mr. Keith, of Readsboro.
ii—Moses.
iii—Roxanna; married Parson Johnson.
vi—Samuel.

(Second wife.)
*285—Moses, born October 10, 1794.
*286—David, born September 10, 1797.
287—Hannah; married Gen. Elijah Bailey, of Bennington, Vt.; and had
i—Mary Ann.
ii—Caroline.
iii—Albert.
iv—Alfred.
v—Frank.
vi—Olive.
288—Esther; married (1) Stephen Esty, and had Lucy and Mary Ann. She married (2) Nathan Bullock.
289—Submit, born 1805; died unmarried.

97.

EZRA AMADON (Lt. Samuel[27], Roger[10], Philip[4], Roger[1]), born at Douglas, Mass., February 2, 1771. He married, August, 1791, Elizabeth Bailey. She was born October 2, 1773, and died August 12, 1861. In 1794 he was Selectman at Readsboro, Vt. He was a member and a minister of the Reformed Methodist Church, which was organized in 1814. He moved to Leon, N. Y., and organized the first church in that town. About 1850 he removed to Waupun, Wis., where he died March 30, 1860.

CHILDREN.

*290—Bailey, born August 2, 1792.
*291—Daniel, born May 20, 1795.
*292—Ezra, born July 11, 1796.
293—Betsey, born June 30, 1798; married Elias Carpenter.
294—Calvin.
295—Sally, born March 26, 1802; married John Carpenter. One of her sons, Monroe Carpenter, served in the army and died at Chattanooga, Tenn., and another son, Jefferson Carpenter, lives at Blue Earth City, Minn.
*296—Samuel, born January 18, 1804.
297—Ruth, born August 4, 1806; married Fuller Gould. A son, Samuel Gould, served in the army, and a daughter, Mrs. John McCune, lives at Waupun, Wis.
298—Polly, born April 17, 1808; married a Town, and her son, Wesley Town, lives at Waupun, Wis.
*299—Rev. Henry, born March 21, 1810.
300—Sylvanus.
*301—Jedediah, born November 29, 1813.
302—Lucy, born May 26, 1815; married Waterman Barrett. Her son, Oscar Barrett, lives at Sherbrook, N. D.
303—Hannah, born December 28, 1819; died unmarried.

98.

SAMUEL AMIDON (Lt. Samuel,[27] Roger,[10] Philip,[4] Roger[1]), married Polly Amidon[111] and besides seven children that died young they had:

CHILD.

*304—Preserved.

104.

JOHN AMIDON (Roger[22], Roger[10], Philip[4], Roger[1]), born at Douglas, Mass., November 26, 1766. He married Nancy Benson. He was a farmer and lived in Douglas and Southbridge; died 1857.

CHILDREN.

305—Solenda, born 1799; married Abraham Mason, Jr., and had seven children.
306—Samuel, born 1803; he married Widow Dudley, and lived in Douglas, where he died 1860.
307—Sally, born 1805; died young.
308—Sally, born 1807; died young.
309—John, born 1808; disappeared in 1834.
*310—William B., born 1811.

311—Asenith, born 1815; she married in Uxbridge, September 12, 1837,
Abijah Esty. He was a cotton and woollen manufacturer. They
lived at Millerville, Mass., and had five children, of which Amy
Ann, born April 12, 1847, married William H. Wilcox, and lived
at Blackstone, Mass.

108.

RALPH AMIDON (Roger⁵, Roger³, Philip², Roger¹), born at
Douglas, Mass., May 3, 1772. He lived at Readsboro, Vt., but died
in Michigan, October 31, 1856. He married Sally Brown, who was
born November 2, 1778. She died at Andover, N. Y., January 26, 1871.

CHILDREN.

312—Hannah; married (1) Nathan Bullock; (2) Dana Phelps. She
      died August 9, 1887.
*313—Russell, born June 26, 1801.
314—Rosina; married Tisdal Puffer.
*315—Smith, born 1800.
*316—Kingsley.
*317—Shepherd, born June 30, 1810.
318—Fidelia; married Jason Hunt, and lived at Andover, N. Y., where
      she died September, 1891.
*319—Jesse.
320—Sally; married George French.
321—Eliza; married in 1825, Ebenezer Hunt.
*322—Ralph W.

110.

SOLOMON AMIDON (Roger⁵, Roger³, Philip², Roger¹), born at
Douglas, Mass., February 27, 1778. He married, in 1797, Betsey Davi-
son. She was born at Conway, Mass., January 13, 1777, and died at
Rowe, Mass., August 30, 1861. He died August 30, 1847.

CHILDREN.

323—Lucy, born at Readsboro, Vt., November 9 1798, and died at Rowe,
      Mass., December 19, 1872. She married in June, 1825, Rev. Am-
      brose Stone, of Rowe, Mass., and had—
            i—Elizabeth D., born February 25, 1826; died March 9,
                  1826.
            ii—Lucy A., born June 11, 1827; died January 12, 1843.
            iii—Solomon Amidon, born January 29, 1829. He married
                  Almira Maria Whitney, a descendant of Samuel
                  Amidon, No. 27. He served as sergeant in the Fifty-
                  second Massachusetts Regiment. His chaplain said
                  that during the campaigning in Louisiana he was
                  never known to fall out on a march and frequently
                  carried the gun or equipment of some weaker com-
                  rade. He died December 1, 1874. Children:
                        i—Henry Solomon.
                        ii—William Royal; married in 1878 Agnes Mc-
                              Brayne, and had three children, Lillian May,
                              Lucy Almira, Royal Amidon. Residence,
                              New Britain, Conn.
                        iii—Frank Lorenzo; married Belle McKeney.
                        iv—Lizzie Jane.

iv—Royal Wells, born August 31, 1831. He served during
the war in a Massachusetts Regiment, and died September 11, 1868. He married in 1858 Caroline A.
Kendrick and had—
    i—Lucy Amidon, born 1852; married in 1883
Jonathan E. Davenport, Colrain, Mass.
v—Daniel S., born May 12, 1833; died January 28, 1866.
vi—Ambrose Pratt, born September 25, 1834; married in
1864 Sarah Reid Browning. He was Captain of a
company in the regiment of which his brother, Newton, was Colonel. He now resides in the South.
    i—Arthur Browning.
    ii—Frederick Carroll.
    iii—Royal Wells.
    iv—Myra Merrick.
    v—Walter Pratt.
    vi—Julian Dean.
    vii—Harry Amidon.
vii—Newton, born December 9, 1836. He studied law at the
outbreak of the Civil War and enlisted in the Fourth
Vermont Regiment as First Lieutenant and afterwards became Colonel of the Regiment. He was killed
at the battle of Wilderness, May 5, 1864.
viii—Martha Elizabeth, born July 27, 1839; died January 4,
1880. She married Lyman N. Clark and had six
children.
324—Clark, born at Readsboro, Vt., May 14, 1800; died May 20, 1800.
*325—Joseph, born May 5, 1801.
326—Solomon, born at Readsboro, Vt., February 27, 1803; died at
Rowe, Mass., May 31, 1892, unmarried. He was Selectman
1835, 1842 and 1850.
*327—Roger, born January 24, 1805.
*328—Daniel Davison, born November 18, 1806.
*329—Henry, born September 3, 1810.
*330—Elbert, born January 25, 1814.
331—Eliza, born at Rowe, Mass., May 30, 1816; died September 18,
1818.

115.

ALPHEUS AMMIDOWN (Ebenezer,[11] Ichabod,[11] Philip,[2] Roger[1]),
born at Mendon, Mass., November 14, 1768. He removed to Providence, R. I., and kept a hotel. He died there in 1861.

CHILDREN.

332—Ruth C.; married September 13, 1832, Whipple B. Mowry. Their
son, Banfield Mowry, lives at Woonsocket, R. I.
333—Sarah Ann; married December 31, 1847, Alpheus Tyning, of Smith-
field, R. I.

122.

OTIS AMMIDOWN (Col. Philip[11], Ichabod[11], Philip[2], Roger[1]),
born at Mendon, Mass., December 30, 1771, and died December 23,
1858, at Philadelphia, Pa. He married Abigail Russell, sister of Hon.
Jonathan Russell. They had no children. He was engaged in business for several years in the island of San Domingo and after his
return to the United States he went to Europe and was a merchant
in Paris. After the close of the French Revolution he was in Nor-

way, but returned to the United States in 1798. He removed to Philadelphia in 1813. In January, 1827, he became treasurer of the Lehigh Coal and Navigation Co., serving as such until a few days before his death. He was a ruling elder in the Presbyterian Church from 1818 till death.

124.

PHILIP AMMIDOWN (Col. Philip[18], Ichabod[11], Philip[8], Roger[1]), born at Mendon, Mass., October 1, 1774. He married, December 3, 1799, Elizabeth, daughter of Matthew and Martha (Eddy) Grice. She was born April 30, 1775, and died September 9, 1855. He resided in Boston, where all of his children were born except Sylvia, who was born at Hingham.

CHILDREN.

334—Philip Ellis, born 1800; died young.
335—Eliza, born September 6, 1802; married September, 1837, John Liscomb.
*386—Philip, born August 23, 1804.
337—Angelina, born October 30, 1807; married in 1838 Rev. William Howe, of Boston, Mass.
338—Melani, born August 23, 1809; married Rev. Joseph Parker, Boston, Mass.
339—Sylvia, born September 16, 1814; married in 1842 Rev. Henry Parker. She died in 1850 at Burlington, Vt.

130.

OTIS AMIDON (Jacob[18], Ichabod[11], Philip[8], Roger[1]), born at Chesterfield, N. H., April 26, 1794. He married, March 16, 1825, Nancy Cook, of Chesterfield. He resided at Chesterfield, N. H., and was Selectman, 1828 to 1831, and was Representative to the General Court in 1833, 1835, 1838 and 1856. He was a farmer and served several years as Justice of the Peace. He died July 22, 1866, at Hinsdale, N. H.

CHILD.

*340—Charles Jacob, born April 23, 1827.

134.

JOHN AMMIDOWN (Caleb[18], Philip[11], Philip[8], Roger[1]), born in Southbridge, Mass., April 5, 1759. He married, June 19, 1782, Olive Sanger, of Dudley. He lived in that part of Charlton which is now Southbridge. He had a large farm and was very active in town matters and in the organization of Southbridge. He served as Assessor in 1801 and died December 3, 1814.

CHILDREN.

*341—Caleb, born July 30, 1783.
*342—Otis, born January 1, 1785.
*343—Larkin, born March 13, 1787.
*344—Lewis, born September 24, 1789.
345—Susanna, born October 4, 1791; died February 20, 1825. She married April 23, 1817, M. John Haskell, and had two daughters.
*346—Adolphus, born October 5, 1793.
347—Callina, born April 2, 1797; died October 19, 1827. She married Moses Barnes and had a son, Moses.
*348—John, born December 13, 1799.
349—Olive, born July 25, 1802. She married in 1824 Francis S. Morse and had two daughters—
   i—Julia M., born February 18, 1826.
   ii—Callina, born February 3, 1828.
350—Julina, born January 30, 1805; died unmarried July 7, 1835.

135.

LUTHER AMMIDOWN (Caleb,[16] Philip,[11] Philip,[6] Roger[1]), born in Southbridge, July 8, 1761. He married (1st), December 23, 1789, Patty Holmes. She was born March 2, 1765; died December 23, 1794. He married (2d), May 11, 1796, Hannah, daughter of Josiah Hovey. She was born December 21, 1775; died February 15, 1857. He was a merchant and resided in Southbridge, where he also owned considerable land. He was Town Moderator several times and served as Assessor, Town Treasurer, etc. He died May 3, 1835.

CHILDREN.
(First wife.)

*351—Luther, born December 7, 1790.
352—Nancy, born August 31, 1792; died January 8, 1854, unmarried.

(Second wife.)

*353—Holdrige, born October 27, 1797.
*354—Oliver, born August 4, 1799.
*355—Holmes, born June 12, 1801.
356—Hannah, born January 18, 1806; died March 28, 1861. She married February 20, 1827, William Beecher, of Southbridge. He was Town Clerk in 1831 and 1832 and Representative in 1861. They had—
   i—William Ammidown, born July 10, 1828. He married (1) Hester Billings Thatcher, of Boston, and (2) Esther Ann Stenderon. He died in 1876.
   ii—Hannah Jane, born May 5, 1832; married in 1850 Rev. Oakman Sprague Stearns, Professor in the Newton Theological Institute. They had three children.
   iii—Nancy Ellen, born July 5, 1836; died young.

136.

CALVIN AMMIDOWN (Caleb[16], Philip[11], Philip[6], Roger[1]), born at Southbridge, June 21, 1768. He married January 31, 1791, Deborah Davis. She was born December 23, 1767, and died December 30, 1826. He was Representative in 1821. Hon. George Davis in "Historical Sketch of Sturbridge and Southbridge" says:

"We cannot allow ourselves to pass over in silence, Calvin Ammi-

down, Esq., son of Caleb Ammidown. The writer enjoyed his acquaint-
ance and frequent manifestations of his generous and benevolent heart.
He was ever ready to assist and encourage young men, if they were disposed to assist themselves.   Mr. Ammidown was one of the most
efficient men in procuring the incorporation of the town of Southbridge,
and in laying a foundation for its future growth and prosperity. He
was equally efficient in building up and sustaining the religious society
to which he belonged. The religious and civil state of things, when
the town was incorporated, was in its infancy, and required such men
as Mr. Ammidown to place it on a stable basis. To effect so desirable
an object, he spared no pains. He was ever ready with an open hand,
cheerful heart, and active personal efforts to promote any enterprise
which promised utility. He with his brother Luther furnished in 1811
the first wool manufactured for sale. A large proportion of the
expense of erecting the Congregational Church in Southbridge was
borne by him. In sustaining stated preaching he was equally liberal.
He never rushed precipitately into any project in contemplation, but
examined carefully and keenly bearings and consequences, before he
was ready to act. When his mind was made up he was not easily
diverted from his purpose. He carried out in life that firmness of
character which descended as a legitimate inheritance. Honest, high-
minded and possessing enlarged views, his controlling aim was to
promote the best interests of the community. Mr. Ammidown married
a daughter of Ebenezer Davis. By this connection his property was
considerably augmented, thereby enabling him to enlarge his business,
and to be more extensively useful. Mr. Ammidown was always actively
employed, either in his own concerns or in those of a public nature.
It is not improbable that he taxed his physical and mental powers too
severely, and thereby shortened the period of his usefulness. He discharged the duties of legislator, of a magistrate, and frequently of
an arbitrator in settling the disagreements of parties. In all these
trusts, no one doubted his ability or honesty. In his social habits,
cordial, agreeable and edifying, his company was always desirable.
Without any disparagement to others, it may truly be said, that no
man in Southbridge was exerting a more energetic and salutary influence than Calvin Ammidown, up to the time he was cut down in the
midst of his usefulness. Mr. Ammidown lived to witness the early
and promising growth of the town of which he was eminently one of
its fathers. He was, in person, a little above the ordinary size, possessing prominent features, and a countenance indicating firmness and intel-
ligence. In his death, all felt, especially in the community where he
was intimately known, a great public and private loss had been sus-
tained. Mr. Ammidown died January 5, 1825, in the 56th year of his
age.''

CHILDREN.

357—Cynthia, born September 20, 1793 ; died November 1, 1828. She
          married, March 14, 1815, Timothy Paige, Jr., of Hardwick, Mass.
          He was a lawyer and resided in Southbridge, where he died
          November 16, 1822.
                    CHILDREN.
                    i—Cynthia E., born December 4, 1815 ; died November 10,
                         1850.
                    ii—Juliette E., born April 14, 1817 ; died June 17, 1865. She
                         married Merrick Mansfield in July, 1842.
                    iii—Timothy, born February 22, 1819.
                    iv—Calvin Ammidown, born June 7, 1820. He married (first)
                         May 9, 1843, Mercy, daughter of Harold Dresser.
                         She died September 14, 1852, and he married (sec-

ond) February 20, 1856, Ellen M. (Schofield), widow
of James Shumway. She died February 21, 1899.
He was prominent in town affairs and was Representative in 1863. He died February 23, 1900.
358—Deborah, born June 21, 1795; died October 7, 1828. She married,
    January 1, 1816, Chester Dresser, of Southbridge. They had—
       i—Pamella, born November 2, 1816; married November,
          1842, Elijah Valentine.
       ii—Chester Ammidown, born September 2, 1828; married
          first, October 1. 1843, Mary C. Bartlett; second, Octo-
          ber 22, 1867, Mary N. McLaughlin, and third, April
          30, 1873, Mrs. Hannah M. Reynolds. He died August
          15, 1899.
       iii—George Albert, born August 5, 1821; married March 15,
          1843, Rosamond Kelly.
*359—Ebenezer Davis, born November 18, 1796.
360—Lydia, born January 14, 1799; died September 3, 1848. She mar-
    ried April 13, 1819, Dr. Samuel Hartwell, of Southbridge, and
    had—
       i—Samuel Cyrus, born March 28, 1820; married March
          18, 1844, Ellen Maria Plimton.
       ii—Calvin Ammidown, born January 13, 1826; died Novem-
          ber 23, 1828.
       iii—Lydia Louis, born August 28, 1830; died unmarried.

140.

CYRUS AMMIDOWN (Joseph[10], Philip[11], Philip[6], Roger[1]), born
in Charlton, now Stockbridge, Mass., October 4, 1765. He was a
farmer and died in Stockbridge, May 3, 1848. His first wife's name
was Ruth. She died October 26, 1790, and he married (2d) May 2, 1792,
Mercy Perry.

CHILDREN.

361—Ruth, born December 13, 1792; died in Stockbridge January 28,
    1868, unmarried.
362—Nancy, born February 17, 1794; died July 15, 1795.
363—Lydia, born May 26, 1795; married November 6, 1820, Alvin
    Powers.
*364—Jonathan Perry, born August 29, 1797.
365—Augusta, born July 5, 1798; died July 21, 1801.
366—Mercy, born November 18, 1799; died March 6, 1821.
*367—Joseph, born April 14, 1801.
*368—Cyrus, born March 28, 1804.
369—Polly, born November 26, 1806; died May 26, 1843.

141.

PHILIP AMIDON (Joseph[10], Philip[11], Philip[6], Roger[1]), born at
Charlton, Mass., July 25, 1767. He married, November 28, 1792,
Jerusha Smith. She was born December 2, 1768, and died February 1,
1845. They lived for a time at Keene, N. H., but moved to Albany
County, New York, where he died, December 26, 1835.

CHILDREN.

370—Infant, born January 17, 1794; died January 25, 1794.
371—Julia, born February 15, 1795; died May 1, 1799.
372—Lucretia, born June 28, 1797. She married July 28, 1823, Peter
      Dymond, and their son, Charles Dymond, lived at North Pem-
      broke, New York.
*373—Philip, born August 14, 1799.
374—Julia, born January 31, 1803; died June 16, 1840. She married
      a Mr. Horton.
375—Harriet, born June 17, 1805; died January 18, 1823. She mar-
      ried a Mr. Bronson and her daughter, Mrs. Alzina (George)
      Barber, lives at East Poenskill, New York.
376—Abigail A., born February 18, 1814; died April 17, 1833.

146.

JOSEPH AMIDON (Joseph[5], Philip[4], Philip[3], Roger[1]), born
at Charlton, Mass., October 15, 1781. He married Matilda Childs. He
was a farmer and moved to Sand Lake, New York, where he died,
November 23, 1846.

CHILDREN.

*377—Cyrus, born July 13, 1808.
*378—Martin.
379—Lura. She married, first, John Clopper, and, second, a Mr. Why-
      land.   Children:
        i—Philo Clopper, married Elizabeth Buell and lives at
            Hilton, New York.
       ii—Mary Whyland.
      iii—Sarah Whyland.
       iv—Julia Whyland.
        v—Alphonso Whyland.
       vi—Joseph Whyland.
380—Sophia, born November 29, 1814; married January 1, 1835, Seely
      Burritt and had—
        i—Dexter, born March 27, 1836; married Angeline Fowler.
       ii—Matilda, born August 13, 1838; married William Smith.
      iii—Melinda, born August 13, 1838; died November 25, 1838.
       iv—Celia, born February 27, 1841; married Marilla Monroe.
        v—Sarah, born May 27, 1843; died May 30, 1843.
       vi—Todema, born May 4, 1846; married Luther Collamer.
      vii—Joseph, born August 24, 1848; died February 27, 1852.
     viii—Cyrus, born December 10, 1851; married Ida Sage.
       ix—Hiram, born September 11, 1857; married Ella Winship.
*381—Dexter, born April 19, 1819.
382—Cenn.
383—Amelia.
384—Sarah.

153.

JABEZ AMIDON (Reuben[4], Philip[3], Philip[2], Roger[1]), born at
Dudley, Mass., September 7, 1777. When young he removed to Rome,
New York, where he married a Miss Chiles, and his children were born
there. Later he moved to Kenosha, Wisconsin, where he died in 1868.

CHILDREN.

385—Hollis. He lived in Washington, D. C., and represented the Agri-
      cultural Department at the Centennial, 1876. He died in Wash-
      ington, D. C., January 29, 1889.
386—Sophia; died young.
387—Sally; married Samuel Watson and died at the residence of her
      daughter Olive, in Chicago, about 1893.
*388—Reuben.

154.

RUFUS AMIDON (Reuben[41], Philip[11], Philip[4], Roger[1]), born at Dudley, Mass., October 6, 1780. He married Minerva Higgins; died October 26, 1820.

CHILDREN.

*389—Isaac Clark, born June 2, 1809.
*390—Francis H., born October 27, 1811.
391—Charles L., born December 5, 1814.
392—Valentine O., born September 5, 1817.

160.

JOHN AMIDON (Philip,[47] Ephraim,[14] Philip,[4] Roger[1]), born at Oxford, Mass., 1771. He married Roxalena Leach and lived at Claremont, N. H., until about 1805, when he removed to Canada.

CHILDREN.

393—Hortensia (Orra), born August 4, 1800, at Claremont. She married February 21, 1828, Enoch W. Gardner, of Hingham, Mass. She died at Hingham, January 7, 1876.
394—Ahial, born 1802. He lived at Fitzwilliam, N. H., where he died August 10, 1874.
395—Roxanna; she married Thomas Newman.

166.

JOSIAH AMIDON (Philip[47], Ephraim[14], Philip[4], Roger[1]), born at Fitzwilliam, N. H., August 9, 1787. In 1809 he settled at Troy, N. H., but about 1827 he returned to Fitzwilliam, where he died, July 6, 1846. He was a shoemaker. He married (1st) April 1, 1810, Lydia White. She was born May 8, 1788, and died January 15, 1827. He married (2d) May 9, 1839, her sister, Mary White.

CHILDREN.

396—Mary, born October 29, 1810. She married October 14, 1832, Gideon Bemus, of Westminster, Vt., and had—
    i—Lydia, born October 1, 1833.
    ii—Ruth, born March 5, 1836.
    iii—Josiah, born November 4, 1841.
    iv—Phebe, born November 4, 1841.
    v—Mary, born November 13, 1843.
*397—John, born November 4, 1813.
*398—Leander, born August 9, 1814.
399—Josiah, born February 20, 1816; died July 18, 1849.
400—Sarah A., born September 7, 1821. She married June 10, 1843, Jared Daniel Perkins. He was a watchmaker and lived at Bellows Falls, Vermont. They had one daughter, Addie Sarah, born March 25, 1844. She married in 1877, Lavant M. Reed.
401—Esther, born October 9, 1823; died December 4, 1879, at Worcester. She married Elbridge Aldrich.
402—Hannah, born August 26, 1825; married Daniel Damon.

172.

TITUS AMADON (Ithamar[51], Ithamar[16], Philip[4], Roger[1]), born at Granby, Mass., July 18, 1763. He married, Feb. 28, 1788, Sabra Gilbert. She was born May 12, 1776, and died May 13, 1852. He served in the Revolutionary army as follows:

He served five months and eleven days in the Tenth Massachusetts Regiment, and his discharge therefrom was dated at West Point, December 16, 1780. He again served in Capt. Abel King's Company, Col. Sears' Regiment, from August 20, 1781, to November 20, 1781, and was at Saratoga. He was placed on the pension roll in 1832. He was a farmer and resided at Wilbraham, Mass., where he died, March 19, 1846.

CHILDREN.

*403—Elial, born December 23, 1788.
404—Clarissa, born August 4, 1790; died January 24, 1827; she married in 1810 Jedediah Smith.
405—Lucy, born June 3, 1792.
406—Hepsibah, born March 2, 1794; died February 17, 1871.
407—Betsey, born June 22, 1795; died October 24, 1843. She married in 1813, Joel Moody, and their son, L. W. Moody, lives at New Haven, Conn.
408—Joel C., born March 30, 1797; died December 26, 1804.
409—Polly C., born December 24, 1798; died December 8, 1803.
410—Sophia, born November 13, 1800; died December 3, 1803.
*411—Titus, born July 7, 1803.
412—Sabra, born July 7, 1803; died May 10, 1816.
*413—Hollis G., born June 21, 1805.
414—Sophia, born June 27, 1807; died November 23, 1846. She married in 1827, Dexter Cross.
*415—Samuel Dexter, born July 4, 1809.

173.

JOHN AMIDON (Ithamar,[51] Ithamar,[16] Philip,[4] Roger[1]), born at Ellington, Conn., May 2, 1765. He married Sarah Adams, of Canterbury, Conn. He served from January 1, 1781, to April 1, 1781, in Capt. John Carpenter's Company. He was a farmer and lived in Wilbraham, Mass., where he died April 21, 1843.

CHILDREN.

*416—Abiram, born November, 1792.
417—Hannah (Ansa). She married August 20, 1807, Horatio Coomes, of Longmeadow. Mass. They had two daughters, Ada and Delia.
418—Ebenezer, born 1796. He was a shoemaker and lived in Wilbraham, where he died August 26, 1861. He married (first) Celia Lee and (second), in 1845, Mrs. Miriam Fowler. No children.
419—Lodicy. She never married and lived at Somers, Conn.
420—Eliza.
421—Joanna. She married in 1825 Dr. Levi Bliss, of Woodstock. He was born April 20, 1798, and died May 22, 1867.
   i—Samuel, born 1827; died while serving in Company C, Seventh Connecticut Volunteers at Beaufort, S. C., 1863.
   ii—Dr. Levi: served three years in Company C, Seventh Connecticut Volunteers; lives at East Woodstock, Conn.
   iii—Mary E.. died young.
   iv—David W., died young.

v—John L., lives in Minnesota; served in a Minnesota
    Regiment during the war.
vi—Permelia E., lives in Minnesota.
vii—Mary T., lives in Minnesota.
viii—Lyman B., born 1843; served in the Twentieth Massa-
    chusetts Volunteers and died, in Minnesota.
*422—John, born August 8, 1803.
*423—Lester.
424—Zenith (Asenith); married —— Porter.

177.

ANSEL AMADON (Ebenezer,[14] Ithamar,[18] Philip,[6] Roger[1]), born
at Goshen, Mass., August 25, 1770. He married, April 29, 1802, Susanna
Parker, of Goshen. He early became a member of the Baptist Church
at Goshen. In the spring of 1820 he removed to Stanford, Vt., where
he remained but a short time, and then removed to Petersburg, New
York, and soon to Pownal, Vt., where he continued to live. In the fall
of 1858 he visited his daughter, Mary, at Florida, Mass., and died there
of pneumonia, October 21, 1858. He was buried at North Adams, Mass.,
in the old cemetery. His widow lived with their son, Philander, until
her death, in 1868.

CHILDREN.

*425—Ariel, born December 20, 1802.
*426—Philander, born April 26, 1804.
427—Abel, born September 6, 1805; died unmarried February 13, 1876.
*428—Ansel, born October 13, 1807.
429—William Bowles, born December 6, 1808; died May 20, 1840.
*430—Melzar, born February 13, 1809.
431—Lucy, born November 10, 1811; married (first) at Pownal, Vt.,
    March 24, 1828, Alanson Smith. He was born January 22,
    1803, and died at Readsboro, Vt., August 6, 1860. They had—
    i—James Monroe, born January 1, 1829; died April 10,
        1829.
    ii—Seth Hurd, born August 7, 1830; died August 30, 1844.
    iii—Jane Janette, born March 31, 1833; died November 19,
        1874, at Readsboro, Vt. She married January 22,
        1854, Merritt M. Houghton. He was a Town Clerk,
        Town Treasurer, Selectman, Postmaster for many
        years, and Representative three times. She had—
        i—Edwin M., born September 23, 1853; died
          May 24, 1868.
        ii—Frederick H., born September 22, 1855; died
          January 30, 1860.
        iii—Willie C., born April 8, 1866; died December
          16, 1874.
    iv—Edwin Corliss, born March 1, 1835; died March 22, 1838.
    v—Francis Augustus, born December 22, 1844; died Novem-
        ber 8, 1863, at Ashtabula, Ohio.
    She married (second) October 1, 1863, Shubel Mowry. He
    died August 22, 1866, and she married (third) June 24, 1868,
    Chauncey Bishop, of Readsboro. He died January 16, 1882.
    She outlived all of her children and grandchildren. While visit-
    ing at the old home her brother, Henry, died February 10, 1894,
    and she died the next day, February 11, 1894.
*432—Richard Flynn, born December 22, 1812.
*433—Josiah, born July 14, 1814.
*434—Henry P., born August 8, 1816.
435—Mary, born December 20, 1817. She married April 1, 1843 (as
    second wife), Moses Walker Bliss, of Florida, Mass. He was
    born September 10, 1818, and died February 20, 1893. She died
    January 9, 1901.

i—Sherburn Lillie, born May 9, 1847; died September 26, 1849.
ii—Mary Lovica, born February 13, 1850. She married June 6, 1869, Sereno S. Tatcher, of Florida, Mass. They had one child, Carrie Lovica, born August 1, 1875; married 1895 Myron C. Harris.
iii—Frederick Byron, born March 4, 1860; married November 24, 1887, Bertha Evangeline Sherman.
*436—Samuel, born November 27, 1819.
437—Martha, born March 13, 1821. She married April 3, 1850, Daniel Hand Lillie, of Pownal, Vt. He was born December 8, 1822, and died November 28, 1896.
i—Frank Adelbert, born November, 29, 1860; married October 22, 1885, Nellie Helen Scriver. She was born November 20, 1863. They have five children:
i—Ralph Henry, born October 20, 1886.
ii—Lucy May, born December 24, 1888.
iii—Daniel Fred, born December 19, 1890.
iv—Everett S., born October 1, 1895.
v—Julia Martha Jane, born September 29, 1897.
vi—Abbie C., born July 20, 1900.
ii—Effie Martha, born September 3, 1862. She married at Hoosick Falls, N. Y., William Rogers.
*438—Perry Franklin, born January 8, 1824.
439—Lurania Melvina, born at Stanford, Vt., August 9, 1825. She married August 21, 1848, Daniel Southwick. He was born April 2, 1826, and died May 31, 1895. She died February 8, 1896. They had—
i—Ida Adele, born at Clarksburg, Mass., May 9, 1849; died September 26, 1888. She married September 28, 1865, George S. Stockwell, of Pownal, Vt. He served in Company B, Sixteenth Vermont Volunteers, and also in Company D, Sixty-first Massachusetts Volunteers. They had—
i—Ernest, born 1867; married 1895 Honora J. Bates and died in 1899.

180.

JOHN AMIDON (John,⁵⁵ John,¹⁸ Philip,⁴ Roger¹), born at Hardwick, Mass., June 1, 1782. He married, May 19, 1821, Sally Hutchinson. She died in 1875. He was a farmer and lived in Hardwick, where he died January 10, 1862.

CHILD.

*440—Philip, born 1822.

181.

ELIJAH AMIDON (John,⁵⁵ John,¹⁸ Philip,⁴ Roger¹), born at Hardwick, Mass., September 27, 1787. He married, May 18, 1818, Martha, daughter of Nathan Nye. She died in 1878. He was a deacon in the Congregational Church from 1824 to 1830. In 1834 he removed to Belchertown, Mass., and was deacon in the church until 1850, when he resigned. He died in Belchertown, June 7, 1857.

CHILDREN.

441—Mercy, born March 12, 1819; died May 22, 1845. She married in 1839 Luther White Burt, of Longmeadow, Mass. He was born July 4, 1812, and died March 25, 1846. They had two children, who both died young.

442—Martha, born October 30, 1820; died July 21, 1851.

443—John Allen, born February 13, 1822. He married (first) September 20, 1845, Eliza D., daughter of Friend M. Hamblett, of Longmeadow, Mass. She was born in 1824 and died in 1855 at Springfield, Mass. He married (second), in 1856, Mary Abby, daughter of Earl and Mary (Rudd) Woodworth. He lived at Springfield and Chicopee and died in Springfield, January 17, 1860.

444—Augustus B., born February 27, 1827. He was a tailor in Boston, where he died in 1870. He married March 17, 1850, Martha, daughter of John Haven, of Springfield, Mass.

202.

PHILIP VAN CORTLAND AMIDON (Cheney,[11] Joseph,[10] Henry,[5] Philip,[2] Roger[1]), born in 1823 and died in 1894. He married Laura Belding.

CHILDREN.

445—Isabel.

446—Fanny.

447—Cheney; married Sarah Brinkerhoff and lives at Marcellus, N. Y.

448—Edward.

449—Beauregard; lives at Marcellus, N. Y.

207.

OUTERBRIDGE HORSEY AMIDON (Cheney,[11] Joseph,[10] Henry,[5] Philip,[2] Roger[1]), born in 1836 and died in 1890. He married, first, Caroline Gleason. Besides a number of children, that died young, they had—

450—Nellie.

451—Cheney.

452—Ralph; lives at Syracuse, N. Y.

He married, second, Ella Stanton and had—

453—Robert.

454—William P.

455—Edward.

456—Rose.

210.

EXPERIENCE JOHNSON AMIDON (Jedediah,[14] Henry,[11] Henry,[5] Philip,[2] Roger[1]), born April 30, 1779, in Willington, Conn. He married Elizabeth Walker. He was a member of the Baptist Church and served in the war of 1812.

CHILDREN.

*457—Experience Johnson.
*458—John.
459—Daniel.
460—Matilda. She married about 1842 (as second wife) Hosea Vinton
       and had a son, John Vinton.
461—Hannah.
462—Louisa.

215.

HENRY AMIDON (Jedediah,⁶ Henry,⁵¹ Henry,⁴ Philip,² Roger¹),
born at Willington, Conn., September 24, 1788. He married, in 1811,
Clarissa, daughter of Ezra and Roxa (Kendall) Smith, of Ashford. She
was born in 1878 and died in 1873. He removed to Erie, Pa., and then to
Mottville, Mich., where he died in 1839.

CHILDREN.

463—Harriet, born in Ashford, Conn., and died at Orwell, O. She mar-
       ried, in 1844, Hiram Goddard, and had—
           i—Juliet.
           ii—Mervin.
           iii—Edwin.
465—Sophronia, died when 18 years old.
466—Mary, born March 12, 1822; died February 23, 1901, at Orwell,
       Ohio. She married February 12, 1846, Hiram Case and resided
       at Windsor, Ohio, and later at Orwell, Ohio. Children:
           i—Dr. Freeman Dwight Case, born December 16, 1846;
               married November 18, 1868, Amelia J. Barnard, and
               resides at Ashtabula, Ohio.
           ii—Frank Case, born July 2, 1849; married Theano Wattley
               and resides at Canton, Ohio.
           iii—Della Sophronia Case, born November 20, 1854; died
               April 19, 1882; married A. W. Decker, Cleveland,
               Ohio.
           iv—Fernando Cortez Case, born September 23, 1856; died
               September, 1862.
           v—Clara Antoinette Case, born February 4, 1860; died
               July, 1862.
467—George, born at Erie, Pa. He served in the Mexican War and
       died of consumption soon after his return from the army.
468—Roxa Ann, married Samuel Morse, of Canfield, Ohio, and had—
           i—Sarah, married Lucius Bingham, Orwell, Ohio.
           ii—Hattie, married Lewis Bethel, Kent, Ohio.

218.

HORATIO AMIDON (Jedediah,⁶ Henry,⁵¹ Henry,⁴ Philip,²
Roger¹), born at Ashford, Conn., July 27, 1793. He married, October
14, 1819, Marcia Strong. He was a farmer and lived in Willington,
Conn., where he died May 12, 1863.

CHILDREN.

469—Horatio Lyman, born December 25, 1825; died March 1, 1845.
470—Marcia Louisa, born September 26, 1829; died August 12, 1850.
471—Jedediah Sanford, born September 19, 1834; died April 8, 1838.
*472—Gilbert Eliphalet Strong, born August 20, 1836.

226.

NATHANIEL AMIDON (Moses,[11] Henry,[21] Henry,[3] Philip,[4] Roger[1]), born at Willington, Conn., April 29, 1792. His wife's name was Laura, and they lived mostly in Onondaga county, New York.

CHILDREN.

*473—Samuel.
474—Louisa.
*475—Chauncey.
*476—Nathaniel William, born April 18, 1822.
477—Moses H., lived at Dowagiac, Mich.
*478—George W.
*479—Thomas Jefferson, born June 17, 1837.
480—Harriet.

227.

SAMUEL AMIDON (Moses,[11] Henry,[21] Henry,[3] Philip,[4] Roger[1]), born at Willington, Conn., February 27, 1794. He married Clarissa Risley and lived at East Hartford, Conn.

CHILDREN.

481—Mary Ann. She married Willard Rowell and had—
    i—George; married Jennie Cooley.
    ii—Jerusha; married Frank Flower.
    iii—Frederick; died young.
482—Sarah. She married Nelson Gilbert and had—
    i—Elliot.
    ii—Clara.
483—Jerusha; died when sixteen years old.
*484—Frederick S., born May 30, 1824.
*485—Charles D., born 1827.

228.

MOSES AMIDON (Moses,[11] Henry,[21] Henry,[3] Philip,[4] Roger[1]), born at Willington, Conn., May 29, 1796. He accompanied his brother, Nathaniel, to Onondaga county, N. Y., and in 1823 went to Delanti (Stockton), New York, where he married the same year Laura, daughter of James and Elizabeth (Getchell) Deming. She was born in 1806 and died May 14, 1833, at Stockton. He had a distillery for some time at Stockton and in 1847 he went to Hamilton, Indiana, where he died August 29, 1850.

CHILDREN.

486—Henry, born January 4, 1825, at Stockton, N. Y. He went to Hamilton, Ind., in 1847. He enlisted in Company B, Twenty-ninth Indiana Volunteers and died of typhoid fever at Murfreesboro, Tenn., May 29, 1863. He is buried in the National cemetery at Stone River, Sec. G, grave 316. He never married.
*487—George, born Feb. 15, 1826.
*488—Seth, born April 15, 1827.
489—J. V. (daughter); died young.
*490—Aaron, born February 7, 1830.

491—Louisa, born August 9, 1831. About 1850 she was married at Hamilton, Ind., to Alexander Rhea. He served in the Civil War and later they removed to Greenville, Mich., where he died 1879. She lives at South Bend, Ind., with her daughter.
    i—Viola; married Mr. Sharp and had—
        i—Jesse.
        ii—Mabel.
    The name of Viola's second husband is not given.
    ii—Byron.

229.

HENRY AMIDON (Moses,[7] Henry,[21] Henry,[6] Philip,[2] Roger[1]), born at Willington, Conn., December 30, 1798. He lived at East Hartford, Conn., and married Delia, daughter of Linus and Hannah Hurlburt. She was born in 1800 and died September 30, 1865.

CHILDREN.

492—William, born October 19, 1824; died about 1874, unmarried. He served from April 12, 1847, to April 24, 1848, in the Ninth Infantry, U. S. A.
493—Frank, born February 22, 1828; lives unmarried at Unionville, Conn.
*494—Henry, born August 16, 1834.

231.

ELIJAH AMIDON (Jonathan,[18] Henry,[21] Henry,[6] Philip,[2] Roger[1]), born at Willington, Conn., July 1, 1876. He served in the War of 1812 and married in 1810 Rebecca Averill, of Randolph, Vt. They lived at Braintree, Vt., but he died November 7, 1863, in Bernardstown, Mass.

CHILDREN.

*495—William Henry Harrison, born August 12, 1813.
496—Maria; married Clapp Edwards, Weymouth, Mass.
497—Sarah F.; married Harvey Park, Munson, Mass.
*498—Elhanan Elijah, born January 22, 1820.
499—John Quincy; married Caroline Davis, and lives at East Haven, Vt.
500—Mary; married Warren Cameron, St. Johnsbury, Vt.
*501—Christopher Columbus.
502—Juliet; married Henry Park.
503—Chloe; married a Mr. Shepherd, of Northfield, Vt.

232.

ALFRED AUGUSTUS AMIDON (Jonathan,[18] Henry,[21] Henry,[6] Philip,[2] Roger[1]), born at Willington, Conn., May 16, 1789. In December, 1816, he married Bertha Stevens and moved to Onondaga county, N. Y., where he died December 8, 1817. He was a miller. His wife died at Barnard, Vt., April 19, 1837.

.CHILDREN.

504—Harriet R., born November 22, 1815; married February 11, 1838,
    Reuben B. Rand, of Royalton, Vt., and had—
      i—Preston A., born December 20, 1838; married Roberta
        Sawyer, Stockbridge, Vt.
      ii—Rosina A., born November 20, 1840; married A. C.
        Spalding, Royalton, Vt.
      iii—Benjamin A., born February 14, 1843; died June 1, 1867.
      iv—Alfred E., born June 3, 1844; married Emma Whipple;
        lives at Epson, N. H.
      v—Winfield S., born August 15, 1846; married Rachael
        Burnham.
      vi—Eldora H., born October 30, 1848; married S. W.
        Howard.
      vii—Alonzo A., born June 3, 1852; married Alice Prouty.
      viii—Frank, born December 1, 1854; married Amelia Adams.
      ix—Andrew B., born May 25, 1858; married Ellen Davis;
        died February 14, 1890.
*505—Augustus A., born July 10, 1818.

233.

JACOB AMIDON (Jonathan,[18] Henry,[11] Henry,[8] Philip,[2] Roger[1]),
born at Randolph, Vt., May 26, 1791. Married (1st) April 22, 1816,
Mercy Whitten. She died October 9, 1833, and he married (2d)
December 4, 1834, Armenia, daughter of Paul and Fanny (Udall) Richmond. She was born at Barnard, Vt., April 4, 1807, and died October
22, 1887. In 1824 he removed to Northfield, Vt., where he died March
5, 1866.

CHILDREN.

506—Olivia, born January 31, 1817. She married a Sturtevant, of Bris-
    tol, Vt.
507—Samuel, born August 19, 1819.
*508—Marshall, born February 21, 1823.
509—John, born February 9, 1825; died September 10, 1851.
510—Clarissa M., born June 25, 1827; married Erastus Chapman,
    Omaha, Neb.
511—George, born October 25, 1831; lives unmarried at Northfield, Vt.

(Second wife.)

512—Mercy C., born January 29, 1838; died October 4, 1845.
513—Newman D., born February 18, 1840. He died in the army De-
    cember 18, 1861.
514—Joan A., born August 22, 1841. She married Lavery Wakefield.
    He died while serving in the army. They had—
      i—Frances, born November 1, 1859.
      ii—Elmer E., born April 25, 1862; died July 12, 1885.
515—Adelina F., born December 9, 1843; married Frank Pratt, of
    Montpelier, Vt., and has a son Harry Pratt.

238.

SAMUEL AMIDON (Jacob,[19] Henry,[11] Henry,[8] Philip,[2] Roger[1]),
born at Willington, Conn., July 12, 1793. He married about
1818, Adelia, daughter of Amasa and Hannah (Amidon) Chap-

man. She was born at Ashford, Conn., April 26, 1796. About 1823 he
removed to Chautauqua County, but afterwards returned to Onondaga
county, N. Y., and died at South Onondaga, N. Y., 1871. He served
during the War of 1812.

CHILDREN.

*516—Alfred Leroy, born January 20, 1819.
517—Delia, born January 5, 1820; died 1891; married Samuel Kenyon
    and had Elizabeth, born 1840; died 1843.
518—Sarah T., born February 5, 1821; died 1877; married, in 1847,
    Henry Stewart and had—
        i—Josephine, born 1849; married in 1872, John Hay and has
            Henry and Duane.
        ii—Frank, born 1851.
        iii—Fred C., born 1852; married, in 1885, Fannie Kenyon,
            and had Harry, born and died in 1886.
        iv—George Herbert, born March 13, 1854; married, December
            19, 1884, Elizabeth Falls, and has—
                i—Henry James, born September 23, 1885.
                ii—Sarah Ann, born September 18, 1886.
                iii—Margaret Jane, born August 19, 1890.
                iv—George Alexander, born February 10, 1892.
                v—Mildred May, born May 23, 1895.
*519—Amasa Chapman, born April 26, 1823.
520—Celina, born June 10, 1827; died 1867; married, in 1850, Daniel
    Day and had—
        i—George Irving, born 1851; married Susan McManus and
            has Frank, Libbie, Irving, Flora and Arthur.
        ii—Emma, born 1855; died 1862.
        iii—Alice, born 1857; married Charles Clark and has Edward,
            James and Daniel. She married, second, James Mitten.
        iv—James, born 1860; died 1877.
        v—Sumer, born 1862; married and has Jessie, Alice, Beulah
            and Daniel.
        vi—Alfred, born 1865; married and has Emily and Sumner.
521—Amenza Fayette, born 1832. For his family, see after No. 1530.
522—Hannah, born August 12, 1835; married in 1856 Lorenzo Day and
    has—
        i—Lois E., born 1859; married Charles McManus, and has
            Laura, Grant, Robert, James, Fred, Edwin, Mamie, and
            Mabel.
        ii—Charles L., born 1861.
        iii—Jessie, born 1863; married Henry Knopp and has Lorenzo,
            Howard and Clifford.
        iv—Fred L., born 1865; married Olive Lee and has Inez,
            Winifred and Clara.
        v—Willis D., born 1869; married Susie Browning and has
            Mildred and Eunice.
523—Hester, born June 1837; died 1843.

239.

JACOB AMIDON (Jacob,[6] Henry,[5] Henry,[4] Philip,[2] Roger[1]),
born at Willington, Conn., 1796. He married Phebe Canada, and died
at Navarino, N. Y., in 1885.

CHILDREN.

524—Clarissa, born at Marcellus, N. Y.; married Sylvanus Henderson,
    and died at Dowegiac, Mich.
525—Climena; married Joshua A. Chaffee.
*526—Daniel.
*527—Orlow, born March 5, 1823.
528—William.
529—Mary I.; married Jason N. Holcomb, of Marcellus, N. Y. He
    died in 1868 and she died later at the residence of a daughter
    in Chicago, Ill.
530—Jacob; died unmarried.

531—Phebe A., born in 1832; married William Case, and lives at
    Navarino, N. Y.
532—Hannah; married Edward Wallace, Navarino, N. Y.
*533—Madison, born June 12, 1836.
534—Maryme, died unmarried.
*535—Perry.

240.

ELIJAH AMIDON (Jacob,[5] Henry,[4] Henry,[3] Philip,[2] Roger[1]),
born at Willington, Conn., January, 1797. He married Betsey Spalding
and lived for a while in Chautauqua county, New York, but removed
to Hayfield, Crawford county, Pa., where he died January 1, 1861.

CHILDREN.

*536—Hiram, born March 4, 1819
537—Mary Jane, born March 1, 1821; died April 11, 1850. She mar-
    ried Albert Whipple, of Hayfield, Pa. They had—
      i—Emma.
      ii—Mary.
      iii—Arminta.
      iv—Mary Alberta.
*538—Horace Starkwether, born March 12, 1824.
539—Maranda, born May 1, 1826; died Feb. 8, 1886. She married
    October 12, 1848, Abner Newton Keep, of Keepville, Pa., and
    had—
      i—Zachary Taylor, born October 10, 1849. He married,
        first, December 20, 1871, Eliza May Spaulding, who
        died July 30, 1886; and, second, October 18, 1888,
        Mrs. Anna (Tracy) Mills, who died August 12, 1903.
        He resides at Hendley, Neb. Children—
          i—Florence May, born July 11, 1898; married B.
            F. Moore, Beaver City, Neb., and has—
              i—Gertrude, born October 26, 1892.
              ii—Wendell Owen, born April 23, 1897.
              iii—Winfred Bertell, born May 4, 1899.
          ii—Alice Elnora, born January 16, 1875; married
            Frank S. Weatherwax, Hendley, Neb., and
            has—
              i—Lina, born July 17, 1896.
              ii—William Adelbert, born August 22, 1901.
          iii—Lloyd Abner, born November 28, 1889.
          iv—Earl Loe, born September 25, 1891.
          v—Shirley Dare, born May 26, 1893.
          vi—Sallie Best, born December 17, 1895.
          vii—John Oliver, born May 27, 1898.
          viii—Ethel Ruth, born May 27, 1900.
      ii—Ellen Louisa, born August 15, 1851. She married De-
        cember 26, 1882, Joshua Yeadon and resides at Keep-
        ville, Pa. Children—
          i—Ernest C. Keep, born October 9, 1873; married
            Bertha Leah Randall and resides at Albion,
            Pa., and has—
              i—Gladys, born August 15, 1895.
              ii—Ivan, born June 6, 1897.
              iii—Edna, born December 23, 1899.
              iv—Arthur William, born October 24, 1901.
          ii—Mary Jane Yeadon, born November 20, 1883;
            married September 26, 1903, Jerry Randall.
          iii—Emma Maranda Yeadon, born August 2, 1886.
          iv—Halgerda Yeadon, born October 14, 1889.
      iii—Emma A., born February 28, 1853; married November
        2, 1874, Lorenzo D. Brooks and resides at Keepville,
        Pa. Children—

   i—Frank Newton, born December 28, 1873; married Amie Clark and resides at Highlands, Cal., and has—

     i—Francis Lynn, born January 21, 1901.
     ii—Marlon Dow, born January 3, 1902.
     iii—Laura Iva, born April 14, 1903.

  ii—Arthur Lorenzo, born April 19, 1878, lives at Highland, Cal.
  iii—Ivie Fiorilla, born February 20, 1880; died August 9, 1881.
  iv—Lewis Newton, born August 7, 1882.
  v—Chester Alsinus, born December 27, 1884.
  vi—Robert Lee, born April 9, 1888.
  vii—Hazel Nell, born March 19, 1891.
  viii—Donald Best, born January 11, 1895.
  ix—Fern Fazetta, born July 4, 1897.

 iv—Frank Elijah, born September 8, 1855; married November 2, 1881, Ida May Kline, and lives at Hull, Iowa. Children—

   i—Margaret Maranda, born July 2, 1883; married Allen McManus and has Esther Fay, born January 12, 1904.
   ii—Paul Alsinus, born September 11, 1885.
   iii—Kester Leroy, born August 2, 1887.
   iv—Carlton Francis, born May 30, 1890.
   v—Willis Art, born February 3, 1893.
   vi—Inez May, born September 21, 1895.
   vii—Edward Clarence, born February 3, 1898.

 v—Polly Elizabeth, born October 28, 1857. She married, first, January 14, 1877, William R. Rea, who died October 13, 1881, and, second, January 29, 1890, Harvey S. Rexford. She died at Shiocton, Wis., March 1, 1899. Children—

   i—Nellie Edith *Rea*, born November 30, 1877.
   ii—Edna Alice *Rea*, born March 10, 1880; married May 14, 1904, Arthur A. Marquart, Chicago, Ill.
   iii—Edgar Charles *Rea*, born May 11, 1882.
   iv—Sanford Max Rexford, born August 8, 1892.
   v—Zella Fern Rexford, born May 16, 1896.

 vi—Sallie Lucinda, born August 18, 1860; married December 25, 1882, Frank Eugene Best, and resides in Chicago, Ill. Mrs. Best is the author of many poems and about one hundred published sacred songs.

 vii—George Alsinus, born January 29, 1863; married April 7, 1888, Irene L. Tracy and resides at Highlands, Cal. Children—

   i—Lyle Dighton, born May 22, 1889.
   ii—Inez Belle, born February 24, 1892.
   iii—Bertha Norma, born September 10, 1894.
   iv—Louis Tracy, born June 29, 1897.

 viii—Marsena Lewis, born December 14, 1864. He married, first, Emma Jane Gaut, who died in December, 1902, and, second, April 12, 1903, Matie Devore. He resides at Highlands, Cal. Children—

   i—Ralph Cecil, born May 12, 1890; died August 9, 1896.
   ii—Junie Marie, born June 15, 1892; died June 9, 1893.
   iii—Baby, born March 2, 1894; died May 13, 1894.
   iv—Mildred Lucenia, born July 9, 1893.

 ix—Dr. Hiram Asa, born February 2, 1867; married March 15, 1887, Rose Edna Tracy and has—

   i—Fenton Rea, born February 19, 1888.
   ii—Lina Belle, born March 3, 1889; died August 17, 1893.
   iii—Haskell Harold, born May 18, 1904.

540—Henry Denison, born February, 1828; died September 15, 1849.
*541—George Ross, born November 5, 1830.
*542—William Harvey, born October 9, 1833.

SALLIE KEEP BEST
(Daughter of Maranda Amidon, 539.)

543—Lucinda M., born May 6, 1839; died January 9, 1882. She married James A. Gaut and lived at Cambridge, Ill. They had—
    i—Harvey J.
    ii—Minnie.
    iii—Emma Jane; married M. Lewis Keep.
    iv—Ida.
    v—Lewis.
    vi—John.
    vii—Gertrude Lucinda.
*544—Lewis Rundel, born May 6, 1839.

241.

LEONARD AMIDON (Jacob,[40] Henry,[11] Henry,[4] Philip,[2] Roger[1]), born at Willington, Conn., February 5, 1799. He married (1st) Esther, daughter of John and Nancy (Wiggins) Smith. She was born at Fairfield, Conn., June 28, 1799, and died April 24, 1859. He married (2d) June, 1862, in Onondaga county, Cynthia Davis. He was a farmer and removed to Clymer, New York, in 1824. He died at Wayne, Erie county, Pa., July 4, 1872.

CHILDREN.

*545—Rev. John Smith, born September 2, 1821.
*546—Lorenzo D., born July 7, 1823.
*547—Lewis, born June 16, 1825.
548—Eliza.
*549—William, born March 12, 1830.
*550—George J., born December 24, 1831.
551—Mary A., born February 2, 1835. She married Chester Adams and had—
    i—Frank E.; lives at Ovid, Pa.
    ii—Dr. Melvin L.; lives at West New Brighton, N. Y.
552—Esther Elmira, born September 14, 1840; died January 28, 1883. She married, February 2, 1862, Rev. William H. Hodges, of Wayne, Erie county, Pa. He served in Company G., Fifteenth New York Volunteer Engineers. They had—
    i—Flora A., born April 1, 1863; married February 27, 1881, E. J. Baldwin, Hygrene, Colo.
    ii—Charles, born October 13, 1866; married, September 21, 1898, Alice Sturgeon and lives at Wayne.
    iii—Byron, born July 27, 1875; married, December 23, 1896, Nellie Patterson and lives at Wayne.

243.

LEWIS AMIDON (Jacob,[40] Henry,[11] Henry,[4] Philip,[4] Roger[1]) born at Wilmington, Conn., 1804. He married Emily, daughter of Asahel Amidon (70) and lived in Onondaga county, New York, where he died in 1876.

CHILDREN.

553—Joseph.
554—Sarah Jane: married George Sage, and lives at Hartington, Neb.
555—Mary; married a Comstock and lives at Cedarvale, N. Y.
556—Lewis. He served as corporal in Company D., 122d New York Regiment, and lives at Onondaga, N. Y.
557—Charity; married a Hull and lives at Cedarvale, N. Y.
558—Byron.
559—Frances.
560—Emily.

244.

MOSES AMIDON (Jacob,[10] Henry,[11] Henry,[8] Philip,[4] Roger[1]), born in Onondaga county, New York, December 20, 1808. He married, January 3, 1830, Sophia, daughter of Ephraim and Hannah (Gore) Starr. She was born February 5, 1807. He worked in a flour mill and died October 13, 1836.

CHILDREN.

561—Hannah J., born October 6, 1831; married November 5, 1858, Willard Stewart, and lives at South Granby, N. Y.
*562—Edson Danforth, born August 14, 1834.
563—Philona, born November 1, 1836; died September 13, 1839.

247.

HENRY AMIDON (Jacob,[10] Henry,[11] Henry,[8] Philip,[4] Roger[1]), born in Onondaga county, N. Y., August 7, 1815. He married (1st), July 4, 1839, Rhoda Amidon (201). She was born in 1821 and died in 1848. He married (2d) Rachel, daughter of Thomas and Eliza (Hall) Wilcox. She was born July 3, 1830, in Onondaga county, and died May 4, 1885. He lived at Concord, Mich., in 1897.

CHILDREN.

564—Helen Eliza; married Michael Belghen, of Jackson, Mich., and died March, 1892.
565—Adelaide; married Frank Cothren, Grand Rapids, Mich.
566—Moses; died when six months old.
567—Lois; married Orton Moseley, of Chicago and died April, 1892, leaving a son, Henry Moseley.
568—Polly; married Edward Miller, Syracuse, N. Y.

(Second wife.)

569—Hannah Eliza; born August 29, 1855; died February 6, 1874, unmarried.
570—Medora Luella, born October 18, 1857; died January 6, 1892. She married Henry C. Cochran, Hanover, Mich.
571—Zaidee, born June 22, 1860; she married James T. Cochran. They live at Concord, Mich., and have a son, Neil Cochran.

251.

WILLIAM AMIDON (William,[11] Henry,[31] Henry,[8] Philip,[4] Roger[1]), born at Willington, Conn., May 13, 1795. He married, in 1817, Charity, daughter of Caleb and Catherine (Haroun) Sweet. She was born August 4, 1779, and died March, 1855. He died at Perry, Ohio, in 1863.

CHILDREN.

572—Prudence, born May 1, 1820; married in 1843, John Gould McCormick and had—
    i—Rosetta.
    ii—Henry; lives at Chesaning, Mich.
    iii—George; lives at Chesaning, Mich.
*573—Henry Nelson; born December 22, 1821.
*574—William Dighton; born July 21, 1823.
575—Martha A., born 1826; she married, first, in 1843, Jared Ives,
  and, second, his brother, Jesse Ives. She had by first marriage:
    i—James.
    ii—Elenora.
    iii—John.
    iv—Jesse.
    They all live at Hastings, Minn.
*576—John Elliott, born March 26, 1828.
*577—Lucius P., born in 1829.
*578—Edmund Sumner, born May, 1831.

252.

ORIN AMIDON (William,[5][1] Henry,[2][1] Henry,[3] Philip,[2] Roger[1]),
born at Willington, Conn., October 27, 1796. He married, April 23, 1818,
Mrs. Hepsibah (Vinton) Bicknell of Dorchester, Mass. They lived at
Braintree, Vt.

CHILDREN.

579—Emeline, born November 23, 1818; she married, December 7, 1842,
  William Augustus Newcomb and lived at Middlebury, Vt. They
  had:
    i—Martin Luther, born September 16, 1843; died August
      14, 1868.
    ii—William Wallace, born January 8, 1847.
    iii—Iola D., born May 16, 1854.
580—Lorenzo, born 1821; died in 1832.
581—Waldo, born 1823; died in 1831.
582—Alonzo, born 1825; married Emeline Abbe.
583—Melissa, born 1827; married Newell Orcott.
584—Clarissa, born 1831; died 1832.
585—Clarissa, born 1833; married Henry Abbe.

257.

EDMUND SUMNER AMIDON (William,[5][1] Henry,[4][1] Henry,[3]
Philip,[2] Roger[1]), born October 10, 1810, at Braintree, Vt. He married,
August 21, 1835, at Perry, Ohio, Emeline Persis, daughter of Quincy
and Persis Barber. She was born February 15, 1816. In 1836 he removed to Sturgis, Mich., where he died May 6, 1878.

CHILDREN.

586—Mary Ann, born June 27, 1836; died January 22, 1853.
587—Adoline Orcelia, born January 28, 1838; she married William
  Culver and lives at Sturgis, Mich.
*588—Edmund Sumner, born January 5, 1840.
589—Persis Emeline, born November 26, 1841.
*590—Orrin Wallace, born June 5, 1843.
591—Laura Angeline, born January 5, 1846; died May 20, 1876. She
  married James Foster.
592—George Barber, born November 4, 1849; died July 27, 1851.
593—Ellen Jane, born February 6, 1853; died May 30, 1853.

262.

GARDNER AMIDON (Henry,⁵⁵ Henry,⁴⁴ Henry,³ Philip,² Roger¹), born in Onondaga county, N. Y., May 21, 1800. He married, in 1823, Nancy Russell. She was born in October, 1800, and died in August, 1856. She was a daughter of Elisha and Rhoda (Amidon) Russell. He lived at Bridgeport, N. Y., but afterwards removed to Hartford, Wis., where he died December, 1852.

CHILDREN.

*594—George.
*595—William Henry, born November 29, 1825.
*596—Elisha.
597—Jonathan.
598—David; lived somewhere in Michigan.
599—Charles; lives at Neilsville, Wis.
600—Janette.

263.

ASARYL AMIDON (Asaryl,⁴⁴ Henry,³³ Henry,² Philip,² Roger¹), born September 26, 1800, in Mansfield, Conn. He married, October 11, 1830, Aurelia McIntire. She was born April 9, 1809, in Thetford, Vt. He died at Belchertown, Mass., February 4, 1847, and his widow married in 1846, Foster Edwards. She died in 1871, in Belchertown.

CHILDREN.

*601—Samuel Gillett, born October 16, 1833.
*602—Edward Perry, born September 4, 1837.
603—John Alvin, born September 1, 1845; died November 24, 1847.

269.

RUFUS AMIDON (Isaac,⁴⁴ Jeremiah,³³ Roger,¹⁰ Philip,² Roger¹), born at Dudley, Mass., October 4, 1794. He married, May 27, 1821, Hannah, daughter of Capt. Thomas and Hannah (Morris) Learned. She was born May 13, 1794, and died July 27, 1891. He died in Webster, Mass., March 15, 1871.

CHILDREN.

604—Mary Lucy, born July 9, 1822; married November 25, 1846, Waldo Moses Healy and lives at Dudley, Mass.
    i—John Boyden, born June 15, 1850; died August 31, 1852.
    ii—Sally Cornelia, born June 29, 1853.
    iii—Elizabeth Learned, born November 29, 1854, and lives in Dudley, Mass.
605—Samuel Foster, born September 24, 1823; died August 29, 1825.
*606—Isaac Learned, born March 5, 1826.
*607—Thomas Morris, born August 27, 1827.
608—William Henry, born July 16, 1830. He is still living, but unmarried. He enlisted in 1861 and was taken prisoner. Since his return from the army his health has been very poor.

272.

CYRIL AMIDON (Jeremiah,⁴⁴ Jeremiah,¹⁵ Roger,¹⁰ Philip,⁶ Roger¹), born April 2, 1812. He married, November 27, 1834, Adeline, daughter of Richard Weeks. They lived at Richmond, N. H.

CHILDREN.

609—Alonzo, born April 19, 1835; died July 16, 1838.
*610—Frank, born June 16, 1837.
*611—Andrew, born February 14, 1840.
612—Julia, born July 4, 1843.
613—Henry, born April 28, 1845; married Lucy Coombs.
614—Estelle, born August 20, 1850; died September 21, 1865.

273.

MARTIN AMIDON (Jeremiah,⁴⁴ Jeremiah,¹⁵ Roger,¹⁰ Philip,⁶ Roger¹), born at Richmond, N. H., August 21, 1818. He married, first, Mila, daughter of Jonas and Polly (Field) Hunt. He married, second, March 31, 1865, Almira Lucinda Bigelow. He lived in Templeton, Mass., till about 1860, and then at Worcester, Mass., for a time. He afterwards removed to Swansey, N. H., where he died November 7, 1888.

CHILDREN.
(First wife.)

615—Charles, born March 25, 1845; married August 23, 1869, Susan
     C., daughter of Zelma and Chloe Barney. He resides at
     Worcester, Mass.
616—George, born June 21, 1854; died young.
617—Henry A., born September 26, 1854; died August 24, 1855.
618—Frederick Eugene, born May 9, 1856; married and lives in Worces-
     ter, Mass.

(Second wife.)

619—George, born January 5, 1867.
620—Martha M., born August 28, 1871.
621—Perlie E., born February 7, 1874.
622—Merton E., born December 3, 1876.

275.

PERLEY AMIDON (Jeremiah,⁴⁴ Jeremiah,¹⁵ Roger,¹⁰ Philip,⁶ Roger¹), born at Richmond, N. H., July 15, 1821. He married, November 29, 1843, Keziah, daughter of John Starky. He lived at Richmond, N. H.

CHILDREN.

623—Mary A., born February 26, 1845; married Orlan Whipple.
624—Edwin E., born September 29, 1848; married June 5, 1872, Anna
     J. Smith.
625—George E., died young.

277.

ISAAC AMIDON (Samuel,[14] Jeremiah,[13] Roger,[10] Philip,[4] Roger[1]), born at Oxford, Mass., August 30, 1811. He married Lois Howland, and lived at Killingly, Conn. It is stated that he had two sons, who served in the Civil War, one dying in the service, but correspondence has failed to bring out the names of these two sons.

278.

JEREMIAH AMIDON (Samuel,[14] Jeremiah,[13] Roger,[10] Philip,[4] Roger[1]), born at Oxford, Mass., October 17, 1813. He married Lucinda Corey and died in 1869 at Killingly, Conn.

CHILDREN.

626—Henry L. He served in the Fifteenth Massachusetts Infantry and was killed at Antietam, September 17, 1862.

283.

ABNER AMIDON (Jedediah,[14] Samuel,[17] Roger,[10] Philip,[4] Roger[1]), married Ruhama Cummings and had—

CHILDREN.

627—Mahala. She married Isaac S. Blanchard and had a son, Lysander B. Blanchard, who married Alice Whiting.
*628—Rufus.

285.

REV. MOSES AMIDON (Jedediah,[19] Samuel,[17] Roger,[10] Philip,[4] Roger[1]), born at Readsboro, Vt., October 10, 1794. He was admitted to the N. Y. (M. E.) Conference in 1814 and died March 21, 1830, at Durham, Green county, N. Y. His wife's name was Lucy.

CHILDREN.

629—William.
630—Moses.
631—Eliza. She married September 27, 1840, George P. Baldwin, West Dorset, Vt. They had—
  i—Daniel W.
  ii—Joseph.
  iii—Benjamin.
  iv—Pernelia.
  v—Maria.
632—Eliakim (?)

286.

DAVID AMIDON (Jedediah,¹⁸ Samuel,¹⁷ Roger,¹⁰ Philip,⁵ Roger¹), born at Readsboro, Vt., September 10, 1797. He married, February 7, 1822, Bertha Dunbar, and died February 14, 1868. He served as captain in the militia. His wife was born March 6, 1801, and died April 8, 1882.

CHILDREN.

633—Isiah J., born April 8, 1823; died November 12, 1846.
634—Moses, born September 12, 1825; lived at Los Angeles, Cal.
635—Charles H., born May 28, 1830; married in 1852 Louisa M. Yeomans, of Ashfield, Mass. She died at Greenfield, Mass., in 1854. He is an inventor and resides at Buffalo, N. Y.
636—David McKendre, born 1831; died April 11, 1833.
637—William McKendre, born July 17, 1834.
638—Sarah Jane, born October 28, 1836. She married October 8, 1858, John Taft, of Grafton, and had—
    i—Cora E., born June 20, 1859.
    ii—Charles Henry, born July 19, 1860; died April 26, 1870.
    iii—Lilly, born June 30, 1864; died July 21, 1864.
    iv—Will H., born April 24, 1866; married Sarah Jones and has Clifford E., Pauline E., Blanche G., Ruth D., Mildred V., and William A. A.
    v—Elmer C., born April 6, 1869.
639—Lucy Mahala, born December 9, 1838. She lives at Blackington, Mass. She married (first) January 21, 1856, William R. Robertson and had—
    i—Carrie B., born February 26, 1861; married January 15, 1877, Edward Humphreys and lives at North Adams, Mass.
She married (second) Stewart Lamon and had—
    ii—John H., born October 20, 1864.
    iii—Charles A., born March 29, 1866.
    iv—Walter S., born July 31, 1869; died 1870.
    v—Warren S., born July 31, 1869; died 1871.
    vi—Sarah Jane, born July 11, 1872.
    vii—William H., born July 8, 1874.
    viii—Raymond S., born September 22, 1876.
    ix—Ruth D., born October 3, 1877.
    x—Bertha, born April 26, 1878.
    xi—Archie F., born August 15, 1879.
640—Solomon H., born September 28, 1840; lives at Turners Falls, Mass.
641—Lydia R., born September 2, 1842; died July 11, 1843.

290.

BAILEY AMADON (Ezra,¹⁷ Samuel,¹⁷ Roger,¹⁰ Philip,⁵ Roger¹), born August 2, 1792. He married and had—

CHILDREN.

642—Ann.
643—Mary, married Titus Darling.
644—Henry, lived in Minnesota.

291.

DANIEL AMIDON (Ezra,[77] Samuel,[37] Roger,[16] Philip,[6] Roger[1]), born at Readsboro, Vt., May 20, 1795. He married, in 1819, Temperence Mary Strong, and removed to Ridgefield, Ohio, where he died September 19, 1820.

CHILD.

645—Mary Elizabeth, born August 22, 1820. She married November 12, 1839, William W. Steele and lived at Marysville, Ohio. He was Sheriff of Huron County. In 1846 they removed to Nauvoo, Ill., and in 1847 to Carthage, Ill., where he died in 1856. She now lives at De Graff, Ohio. They had—
　i—Arthur, born April 22, 1841; died June 5, 1841.
　ii—Leah Norah, born April 17, 1843; died July 25, 1843.
　iii—Cora Laura, born February 8, 1846; died July 7, 1847.
　iv—Myra Crete, born June 12, 1849. She married Benjamin F. Hudson and lives at De Graff, Ohio.
　v—Lydia Porter, born September 25, 1851; died July 25, 1852.

292.

EZRA AMIDON (Ezra,[77] Samuel,[37] Roger,[16] Philip,[6] Roger[1]), born at Readsboro, Vt., July 11, 1796. He married Clarissa Grover and removed to Cattaraugus county, N. Y.

CHILDREN.

*646—Lucius, born November 9, 1820.
647—Calvin, born December 4, 1831; lived at Bird. N. Y.
648—George B., born September 20, 1836; lived at Conewago Valley, N. Y.
649—Julia Ann; married Israel C. Warner and died July 24, 1840.

296.

SAMUEL AMADON (Ezra,[97] Samuel,[37] Roger,[16] Philip,[6] Roger[1]), born at Readsboro, Vt., January 18, 1804. He married, July 26, 1829, Lucretia Durfey. She was born September 1, 1811. He first settled in Cattaraugus county, N. Y., but in 1845 removed to Waupun, Wis., where he died February 1, 1892. He was a farmer and cattle buyer. He was a deacon in the Congregational Church.

CHILDREN.

650—Louise Rosina, born July 3, 1830; died August 22, 1892. She married January 1, 1849, Edwin W. Judd.
651—Sarah Jane, born February 29, 1832; died August 16, 1868. She married May 25, 1852, George Holmes.
*652—George Leroy, born April 2, 1834.
653—Augusta, born April 29, 1843. She married February 22, 1865, Charles H. Lindsley, Waupun, Wis., and has—
　i—Edward Amadon, born May 10, 1869.
　ii—Lucius Randall, born June 12, 1875; married June 22, 1901, Jennie Wentworth, and has—
　　i—Charles H., born December 5, 1902.
　iii—Archie Hazen, born June 12, 1875.
　iv—Clara Louise, born August 11, 1883.

299.

REV. HENRY AMADON (Ezra,⁸¹ Samuel,⁷⁷ Roger,¹⁰ Philip,⁶ Roger¹), born at Readsboro, Vt., March 21, 1810. He married, at Leon, N. Y., February 9, 1834, Emeline Blanchard. She died June 21, 1897. He removed to Waupun, Wis., in May, 1845, and died there in 1901. He was for many years a minister in the Wesleyan Methodist Church.

CHILDREN.

654—Martha Avasta, born at Leon, N. Y., October 17, 1834. She married November 23, 1854, David Canada Fairbank. He is a member of the Fairbank, Raymond & Co., Live Stock Commission Merchants, Union Stock Yards, St. Paul, Minn., and resides at Dodge Center, Minn. They had—
    i—Emma Amelia, born November 28, 1855. She married May 23, 1875, Dr. Isaac Hall Orcutt, Owatonna, Minn. They have a daughter, Alice Julia, born September 20, 1877.
    ii—Alice, born May 9, 1858. She married November 9, 1887, John Howard, Dodge Center, Minn. They have a son, Daniel Clyde, born January 8, 1889.
*655—William Percival, born October 14, 1843.

301.

JEDEDIAH AMADON (Ezra,⁸¹ Samuel,⁷⁷ Roger,¹⁰ Philip,⁶ Roger¹), born at Readsboro, Vt., November 29, 1813. His son—
656—Rollin; married Flora S., daughter of Charles and Hannah Pierce, and lives at Waupun, Wis. He served in the army.

304.

PRESERVED AMIDON (Samuel,⁸⁸ Samuel,⁸⁷ Roger,¹⁰ Philip,⁶ Roger¹), born ——. He married Susan Malissa Walsworth and lived at Readsboro, Vt., and later at Cherokee, Iowa, where his widow died January, 1901.

CHILDREN.

657—Elizabeth; married John Stow.
658—Ella; married —— Goldsborg.
659—Alvin.

310.

WILLIAM B. AMIDON (John,¹⁰⁴ Roger,⁵⁹ Roger,¹⁰ Philip,⁶ Roger¹), born at Douglas, Mass., 1811. He married, first, Celestia, daughter of Henry and Hannah Davidson. She died in Douglas, November 20, 1847, and he married, second, a Mrs. Jefferson. He was leader of the band in Douglas in 1840.

CHILDREN.
(First wife.)

*660—Capt. George H., born May 3, 1838.
661—Minerva, born December 11, 1839. She married June 26, 1866, Leonard C. Baldwin (or Belden). They had two children, Gertrude and George.
662—Victoria, born March 25, 1842; married June 23, 1861, Edward G. Hewett, of Sutton, Mass. They have a son, Henry.

(Second wife.)

663—William F., born February 13, 1852.

313.

RUSSELL AMIDON (Ralph,¹⁰⁸ Roger,²⁹ Roger,¹⁰ Philip,⁴ Roger¹), born at Readsboro, Vt., June 26, 1801. He married Esther Wilcox, December 24, 1825. They removed to Michigan, where he died June 8, 1887.

CHILDREN.

664—Hazard, born March 21, 1829; died March 21, 1858.
665—Eliza, born September 1, 1832; died October 22, 1890. She married June, 1852, Asa Wilcox.
*666—Andrew John, born February 19, 1834.

315.

SMITH AMIDON (Ralph,¹⁰⁸ Roger,²⁹ Roger,¹⁰ Philip,⁴ Roger¹), born at Readsboro, Vt., in 1800, and lived in Steuben county, N. Y. He married, first, Phoebe Wilcox, in 1821. She died in 1850 and he married, second, Lucy Granger.

CHILDREN.

667—Alameda.
668—Caleb S.; served in the army and his widow lives at Alfred, N. Y.
669—Mary A.
670—Eliza.
*671—Martin Van Buren, born November 3, 1837.
*672—Solomon B.
673—Phoebe A.
674—John L. He enlisted in Company B, Eighty-sixth New York Regiment and died in the service in 1862; aged 17.
675—Elsa D.
676—Elvisa A.

(Second wife.)

677—Melloday S., lives at Purdy Creek, N. Y.
678—Eunice.
679—Washington G.
680—Fanny F.
681—Abraham L.

316.

KINGSLEY AMIDON (Ralph,[10] Roger,[21] Roger,[10] Philip,[6] Roger[1]), married Jane Howell and a son—
682—Henry C., lives at Bishopville, N. Y.

317.

SHEPHERD AMIDON (Ralph,[104] Roger,[21] Roger,[10] Philip,[6] Roger[1]), born at Readsboro, Vt., June 30, 1810. He was deputy sheriff of Steuben county, N. Y., from 1841 to 1845. He was a farmer and shoemaker and served for many years as Justice of the Peace and was also Supervisor of the town of Hartsville, N. Y. He died at Purdy Creek, N. Y., April 27, 1866. He married, first, April 14, 1836, Lucy Carpenter. She was born August 26, 1817, and died June 18, 1849. He married, second, July 31, 1850, Betsey M. Razey, born in 1818 and died June 3, 1896.

CHILDREN.

683—Sylvia, born December 19, 1836; died July 18, 1849.
684—Ira, born August 31, 1838; died October 10, 1849.
*685—Albert, born August 23, 1840.
*686—Charles R., born September 11. 1842.
687—Densil, born at Greenwood, N. Y., September 18, 1844. He enlisted in Company B, Eighty-sixth New York Regiment. He was taken prisoner at The Wilderness in May, 1864, was confined in the Andersonville prison and died of consumption April 14, 1870.
688—Morris, born May 24, 1847; died April 3, 1852.

(Second wife.)

689—Sylvia C., born May 31, 1851. She married December 24, 1874, Calvin Slocum and lives at Andover, N. Y. They have a daughter, Rena, born in 1870.
690—Richard, born April 15, 1852; died December 24, 1856.
691—Shepherd Robert, born October 4, 1857; died December 21, 1865.

319.

JESSE AMIDON (Ralph,[104] Roger,[20] Roger,[10] Philip,[6] Roger[1]), married Matilda Dunlap and removed to Michigan, where he died June 4, 1886.

CHILDREN.

692—William.
693—Monroe; lives at New Lathrop, Mich.
694—Daughter; married Solomon Puffer, of New Lathrop, Mich.

322.

RALPH W. AMIDON (Ralph,[104] Roger,[20] Roger,[10] Philip,[6] Roger[1]) was a member of Co. B, 86th N. Y. Regt. and was killed at The Wilderness in May, 1864. He was married and had several children. His family removed West and a son—
695—Wesley; lives at Maple City, Mich.

325.

JOSEPH AMIDON (Solomon,[11] Roger,[27] Roger,[10] Philip,[5]
Roger[1]), born May 5, 1801, at Readsboro, Vt. He married at St.
Albans, Vt., December 31, 1832, Susan Stephens Newton. She was born
November 6, 1814, and died January 14, 1877. He died at Granville,
Ohio, September 20, 1891.

CHILD.

696—Elizabeth Davidson, born November 28, 1833, at St. Albans, Vt.
   She married November 22, 1853, Emory P. Andrews, a teacher
   at Rowe, Mass. They had—
      i—George Emory, born November 18, 1854; married Alice
         Mary Spence and has Robert Edmond, born October
         27, 1880.
      ii—Istenella Mae, born January 23, 1856; married Ernest
         F. Appy.
      iii—Joseph Erastus, born August 8, 1857.

327.

ROGER AMIDON (Solomon,[11] Roger,[27] Roger,[10] Philip,[5] Roger[1]),
born at Readsboro, Vt., January 24, 1805. He married, October 28,
1830, Emeline Carpenter. She was born at Rowe, Mass., March 18,
1807. He died at Springfield, Mass., October 26, 1879.

CHILDREN.

697—Susan N., born October 12, 1832; died January 5, 1869.
*698—William Cross, born October 7, 1836.
*699—Josiah Carpenter, born July 14, 1840.

328.

DANIEL DAVISON AMIDON (Solomon,[11] Roger,[27] Roger,[10]
Philip,[5] Roger[1]), born at Readsboro, Vt., November 18, 1806. He was
a farmer and lived in Rowe, Mass. He married, September 6, 1844,
Mary Fuller. She was born at Whitingham, Vt., October 27, 1819.

CHILDREN.

700—Elenor M., born September 28, 1845; married March 4, 1868,
   Alfred Reed, Whittingham, Vt.
701—Julia Franklin, born March 4, 1849. She married September 2,
   1872, Arthur Browning. He was born January 6, 1843; died
   May 2, 1882. They had—
      i—Frederic Amidon, born June 20, 1875.

329.

HENRY AMIDON (Solomon,[110] Roger,[38] Roger,[14] Philip,[4] Roger[1]), born at Rowe, Mass., September 3, 1810. He married, first, March 11, 1844, Rosetta M., daughter of Zadoc and Hannah Hale. She was born January 24, 1821, and died February 7, 1850. He married, second, March 5, 1856, Emeline S. Cross.

CHILDREN.

702 —Caroline Rosetta, born August 25, 1847. She married December 17, 1867, William B. Watts, of Springfield, Mass., and had—
    i—Harry Lorenzo, born December 5, 1868; married July 12, 1892, Dora Henrietta Rolshauser.
    ii—Fred Madison, born January 7, 1878.

(Second wife.)

703 —Mary Lizzie, born March 1, 1857. She married November 1, 1882, Charles King, and had—
    i—Sarah Lydia, born August 14, 1883.
    ii—Arthur Tyler, born November 20, 1884.
704 —Infant, born and died February, 1860.
*705 —Solomon Henry, born July 26, 1863.
705½—Newton Philo, born September 24, 1865.

330.

ELBERT AMIDON (Solomon,[110] Roger,[38] Roger,[14] Philip,[4] Roger[1]), born at Rowe, Mass., January 25, 1814. He was a farmer and removed to Deerfield, Mass., where he died December 21, 1893. He married, first, January, 1841, Emerine L. Wilson, of Heath, Mass. She died January 31, 1844, and he married, second, March 4, 1846, Martha, daughter of Noah Wells, of Rowe, Mass. She died May 10, 1866, and he married, third, May 26, 1868, Elizabeth, daughter of John Wilson. She died January 22, 1896.

CHILDREN.

706—Lucy Emerine, born January 10, 1843. She married February 20, 1864, David Henry, and resides at Deerfield, Mass.

(Second wife.)

707—Jeanette, born November 25, 1848; died November 27, 1878.
708—Margaret, born April 2, 1850; died October 31, 1882. She married September 17, 1873, E. C. Sequin.
709—Dr. Royal Wells, born August 7, 1853. He married November 25, 1885, Emma D. A. Field. He is a prominent physician in New York city.

336.

PHILIP AMMIDOWN (Philip,[114] Philip,[16] Ichabod,[11] Philip,[4] Roger[1]), born at Boston, Mass., August 23, 1804. He graduated at Harvard College. He married, June 12, 1833, his cousin, Anna Matilda Russell (daughter of Sylvia Amidon, 122). He died February 14, 1844, at Lowell, Mass.

CHILD.

*710—Philip Russell, born March 12, 1834.

340.

CHARLES JACOB AMIDON (Otis,[19] Jacob,[11] Ichabod,[11] Philip,[6] Roger[1]), born at Chesterfield, N. H., April 23, 1827. He married, May 11, 1851, Mary J. Harvey, of Chesterfield, N. H., and removed to Hinsdale, where he engaged in woolen manufacture, and where he died August 21, 1900. He served as postmaster, member of the Legislature and State Senator.

CHILDREN.

711—Philip Francis, born June 27, 1852. He married June 24, 1891, Annie E. Fuller, of Brattleboro, Vt. He now resides at Wilton, N. H.
712—Mary Elizabeth, born July 31, 1859; died September 1, 1888. She married October 28, 1886, Dr. R. B. Whitridge, of Boston, Mass.
713—Esther Maria, born February 4, 1862; died August 7, 1865.
714—William Otis, born November 25, 1864; lives at Hinsdale, N. H.

341.

CALEB AMMIDOWN (John,[114] Caleb,[11] Philip,[11] Philip,[6] Roger[1]), born at Southbridge, Mass., July 30, 1783. He married, December 1, 1807, Betsey Barrett. He was a farmer and lived in Southbridge, where he died in 1822.

CHILDREN.

715—Carlow, born 1812; died June 3, 1834.
716—Deliza; married in 1839 G. V. Alliard.

342.

OTIS AMMIDOWN (John,[114] Caleb,[11] Philip,[11] Philip,[6] Roger[1]), born at Southbridge, Mass., January 1, 1785. He lived in Southbridge and in the records is called Major. His wife's name was Sally May and she died February 28, 1855. He died December 19, 1827.

CHILDREN.

*717—Otis, born May 7, 1809.
*718—Elbridge, born 1813.

343.

LARKIN AMMIDOWN (John,[1][1][4] Caleb,[1][1] Philip,[1][1] Philip,[4] Roger[1]), born March 13, 1787, at Southbridge. He married Anna Shumway. He was a farmer and lived in Southbridge, where he died in 1873. He was postmaster in 1833, and Representative in 1831 and 1832.

CHILD.

719—Emeline S., born 1822; died February 16, 1875.

344.

LEWIS AMMIDOWN (John,[1][1][4] Caleb,[1][1] Philip,[1][1] Philip,[4] Roger[1]), born September 24, 1789, in Southbridge. He was a farmer and resided in Southbridge, where he died September 13, 1870. He married, April 30, 1820, Deborah Barnes. She died September 12, 1880.

CHILDREN.

720—Jane, born October 8, 1821; married September 27, 1842, Lucius H. Ammidown (736).
*721—Merrick, born December 21, 1823.
*722—Andros, born October 27, 1828.

346.

ADOLPHUS AMMIDOWN (John,[1][1][4] Caleb,[1][1] Philip,[1][1] Philip,[4] Roger[1]), born at Southbridge October 5, 1793. He was a farmer and veterinary surgeon and served as Selectman for several years. He died in Southbridge October 13, 1850. He married, January 13, 1820, Sally Maria Vinton. She was born October 7, 1798, and died February 2, 1878.

CHILDREN.

723—Infant, died young.
724—Harriet Eliza, born February 27, 1822; died October 22, 1847.
725—Caleb, born February 11, 1824; died December 16, 1854. He married Mary A., daughter of Edward Calvert.
726—Amelia, born July 24, 1826; maried April 20, 1848, Thomas Bottomley, Stonington, Conn.
727—Arinda, born December 14, 1828; died February, 1889; married (first) Cyrus P. D. Grosvenor; (second) Alonzo P. Jordan; (third) ——— Bennett.
728—Newton, born January 13, 1833; died February 11, 1834.
*729—George Angell, born July 15, 1835.
730—James M., born October 29, 1837; died December 29, 1841.
*731—Marcus Morton, born February 17, 1840.

348.

JOHN AMMIDOWN (John,[111] Caleb,[11] Philip,[11] Philip,[1] Roger[1]),
born at Southbridge, Mass., December 13, 1799. He married, November
18, 1828, Caroline Marcy. He was a farmer and lived in Southbridge.
He was a member of the Baptist Church and the leader of singing in
the church. Died May 3, 1848.

CHILDREN.

732—Caroline, born 1826; died July 8, 1898; married March 27, 1856,
    Leonard Streeter. They lived in Southbridge and had—
      i—Ada, born November 14, 1857; died June 21, 1880.
      ii—Emma C., born January 15, 1862; died June 23, 1864.
      iii—Mabel C., born December 26, 1871.
733—John, born 1829. He was a harnessmaker and lived in Springfield,
    Mass., where he died in May, 1899. He married January 7,
    1860, Czarina Plimpton Upham. She died February 8, 1902.

351.

LUTHER AMMIDOWN (Luther,[111] Caleb,[11] Philip,[11] Philip,[1]
Roger[1]), born at Southbridge, Mass., December 7, 1790. In the records
he is called Captain. He was a farmer and lived in Southbridge, where
he died October 5, 1877. He married, July 20, 1817, Adelaide, daughter of Jeremiah and Keziah (Freeman) Shumway. She was born September 15, 1794, and died August 6, 1866.

CHILDREN.

*734—Luther Shumway, born June 13, 1822.
 735—Andrew Fuller, born January 24, 1824. He died unmarried in
    1862. In 1859 he was appointed Navy Agent at Boston, the
    appointment being confirmed in the Senate, February 5, 1859.

353.

HOLDRIDGE AMMIDOWN (Luther,[111] Caleb,[11] Philip,[11]
Philip,[1] Roger[1]), born at Southbridge, Mass., October 27, 1797. He
married, November 25, 1818, Thankful Newell, and lived in Southbridge,
where he died March 24, 1862.

CHILDREN.

*736—Lucius Holdridge, born May 31, 1821.
 737—Adelia, born July 11, 1823; married November 3, 1842, Robert
    Henry Cole, of Southbridge, and had—
      i—Alfred E., born December 12, 1848.
      ii—Ella M., born April 22, 1846.

354.

OLIVER AMMIDOWN (Luther,[1][3][5] Caleb,[1][2] Philip,[1][1] Philip,[6] Roger[1]), born at Southbridge, Mass., August 4, 1799. He married, January 1, 1822, Harriet, daughter of Joshua Vinton, of Southbridge. She was born April, 1802, and died February 9, 1862. He was a merchant and died September 4, 1848.

CHILDREN.

738—Susan Maria, born September 5, 1822; married June 8, 1843, Rev. David B. Cheney. She died at Columbus, Ohio, August 18, 1850. They had—

    i—Harriet Elizabeth, born May 29, 1844; died January 8, 1846.

    ii—Frances Maria, born February 22, 1847. She married (first) Cassius M. Conro. He died in 1882. They had—

        i—Fanny M., born 1873.

        ii—Joseph A., born 1875.

    She married (second) Dr. R. F. Bennett, and lives at 4237 Indiana avenue, Chicago, Ill. Dr. Bennett died January 23, 1904.

    iii—Mary Ella, born September 27, 1848. She married in 1868 Franklin J. Clark, of Boston, Mass., and had—

        i—Mildred Ammidown Clark, born in 1871.

        ii—Frances J. Clark, died in infancy.

739—Avelina Harriet, born October 27, 1822; married September 28, 1843, Issacher Bates, of Macon, Ga., and had a son, Frank DeWitt Bates.

740—Caroline Melita, born February 27, 1827. She married November 4, 1847, Henry M. Emerson, of Salem, Mass.

741—Francis Oliver, born June 13, 1831; died August 9, 1832.

742—Oliver Franklin, born October 4, 1835. He married at Milford, Mass., July 4. 1858, Malvina M., daughter of Emory and Susan Barnard, of Harvard. He once lived at Milford, and was a tinner.

355.

HOLMES AMMIDOWN (Luther,[1][3][4] Caleb,[1][2] Philip,[1][1] Philip,[6] Roger[1]), born at Southbridge, Mass., June 12, 1801. He married, November 17, 1825, Seraph, daughter of Daniel Hodges, of Warren, Mass. He first engaged in business in Southbridge, where he resided until 1835. He was town clerk from 1828 to 1830. His health failing he went to Charleston, S. C., where he remained about one year and then returned to Southbridge. He was elected Representative in 1837 and soon removed to Boston. In 1835 he became a member of the firm of Ammidown-Bowman & Co., which soon became the firm of Holmes, Ammidown & Co., dealers in dry goods. In 1852 he became a member of the firm of Pierce, Lovejoy & Co., wholesale clothiers. He continued in this firm until about 1863, when he removed to New York City and established the dry goods firm of Ammidown, Lane & Co. He retired from business in 1870.

He spent a number of years in historical study and in 1877 he published "Historical Collections," in two volumes. He also published a pamphlet giving a partial account of the Amidon family. His business career was marked by great uprightness and he was very successful. He gave $25,000 to his native town for the purpose of establishing a library. The fine library building in Southbridge is a monument to his memory.

In the latter part of his life he generally spent his winters at St. Augustine, Fla., where he died April 3, 1883. His wife died May 25, 1888.

CHILDREN.

*743—Edward Holmes, born October 28, 1830.
744—Philip Henry, born May 16, 1833; resides at St. Augustine, Fla.
745—Charles Hovey, born October 23, 1837; died July 29, 1886. He married Anna Darling Gray, who died July 16, 1891.

359.

EBENEZER DAVIS AMMIDOWN (Calvin,⁵ Caleb,⁴ Philip,³ Philip,² Roger¹), born at Southbridge, Mass., November 18, 1796. He married May 12, 1816, Rebekah, daughter of Caleb and Mary (Plimpton) Fisher. She was born in New Salem, N. Y., July 16, 1798, and died in Boston February 20, 1878.

As a child his health was not good, and being an only son seems to have been favored in having his own way. That it did not spoil him shows he inherited good sense. At 14 years of age he was partner with Larkin, aged 23, son of John, and Luther, aged 20, son of Luther, in trade, 1810, in the "boy's store" as it was then styled, a one-story store 18 feet wide by 50 feet in length which stood in the north side of the main street in Southbridge. On the opposite side of this street Calvin Ammidown had built what was known all its existence as "The Columbian Building." In this he and his family lived while he had a store on the street floors. John, Luther and Calvin Ammidown continued business with each other to mutual satisfaction all their lives, but their sons saw best to separate their interests early in their youth, and continued the condition for the rest of their lives.

After the deaths of his father and sisters, Deborah and Cynthia, Ebenezer with his sister Lydia and her husband, Dr. Samuel Hartwell, provided for their children's future. The so-called Dresser Cotton Mill was erected in 1813, the Columbian Factory in 1821 (destroyed by fire 1844, December 6), the Central Mills in 1838, and the first cotton works were established at Westville, three miles up the river, in 1812. All these at one time Ebenezer D. operated. Born and brought up on a farm, but being of a slender constitution, he was not able to do hard work, and following his inclinations, employed himself in lighter mechanical matters of various kinds. He was ingenious and able from his native capacity to readily understand the intricacies of machinery. As said before, his father was a pioneer in the cotton manufacture in Southbridge, and at the time of his death had begun the business on a small scale. At his decease the prosecution of this new enterprise devolved upon the son, then a comparatively young man, in connection with Dr. Samuel Hartwell and Moses Plimpton. To this responsibility Mr. Ammidown applied himself with the energy and good judgment which always characterized his later efforts, and the result was the permanent establishment of the leading manufacture of the town. Mr. Holmes Ammidown in his history of Southbridge says that to him more than to any other person the place is indebted for the development of this industry. But the natural scope and bent of Mr. Ammidown's mind were by no means satisfied with a success in this direction. When railroading became established, in it he discerned at once an instrumentality which could be successfully used not only to increase general prosperity, but to benefit and build up his native town, in whose welfare he ever felt a special interest. He therefore entered heartily into that subject, acted as one of the board of commissioners about 1838 to locate and settle land claims on the Norwich and Worcester road; was foremost in projection of the Norfolk County (now New York, New Haven and Hartford) road and for a time its president, and was the main instrument in obtaining a charter for the Southbridge and Blackstone road. The new entrance into the city of Boston at Summer street over the South Boston flats was a scheme of his devising and was carried out mainly through his persistent efforts. And the land where now stands the Union Depot in Boston would have been bought by the railroads at a cheap price had his plans been carried out in 1859. In both houses of the State Legislature, to which he was repeatedly elected, he labored resolutely and perseveringly to effect his purpose. Nearly thirty years of his later life were chiefly devoted to this work, and the end was gained at last. He had reason to hope that he could see the fruit of his labor, but was not permitted this happiness. He died at 5:30 p. m., November 21, 1865, and on November 9, 1866, communication by rail between Southbridge and Boston was opened. He had a mind far-reaching in its range and therefore specially competent in the management of public affairs. As a magistrate, in which capacity he acted for a long time, doing much business, he was eminently successful and his decisions were rarely reversed by the higher courts. In private life Mr. Ammidown was most estimable, a true and wise friend and adviser, and possessed of a warm heart. Socially he was quiet and unobtrusive, and like the rest of that branch of his grandfather Davis' family ever too full of real work for much that was light and trifling, and though he had a keen sense of the ludicrous and a fund of dry wit, he was considered a sedate man. Says Mr. Linus Child, "He was always calm and collected, even in the most trying circumstances; was seldom off his guard and never manifested undue excitement. The undisturbed calmness with which he met the last hours of his life, when in perfect possession of all his faculties, he held his last interview with his family and gave his last counsels and directions, only indicated the same quiet and well-balanced mind which he had so constantly displayed throughout all the varying scenes of a long and useful life."

CHILDREN.

746—Mary Fisher, born August 23, 1817. She married September 15, 1840, Manning Leonard, of Southbridge. He was born June 1, 1814, and died July 31, 1885. She died May 31, 1892. Mr. Leonard was engaged in cotton manufacture from 1845 to 1863. He was Justice of the Peace from 1854 to 1885 and was also Selectman and Representative. They had—
    i—Dr. Charles Henry, born December 29, 1841. He served in Company A, Forty-fifth Massachusetts Regiment. He graduated from Yale College in 1865 and now lives in Providence, R. I. He married June 1, 1872, Mary Grace Beecher, and has three children, Mary Beecher, George Manning and Grace Fisher.

ii—Bernard Ammidown, born in the same room at "The Pines" in which his grandfather, Ebenezer D., died. His birth occurred July 25, 1844. Much of his early years was by his own inclination spent in the family of his maternal grandparents. His independent spirit showed early in life, but he was always amenable to every moral obligation which he owed to others. While in his third year in the Southbridge High School he showed his loyalty and patriotism by enlisting, August 28, 1862, in Company A, Forty-fifth Massachusetts Regiment, but to his lifelong regret his strength was not equal to his ambition to accompany his comrades to the front. He was so desirous of going later as to be examined, and being rejected he sent Levi B. Chase, of Sturbridge, a private in Company F, Fifty-first Regiment, to make his place good.

His business life was spent in Detroit, Michigan, engaged in the hardwood lumber trade; then in Cincinnati, Ohio, in manufacturing and selling stoves, and subsequently in a spice mill and grocery at Jackson, Michigan. During the last five and one-half years of his father's life, he spent with him, being interested in compiling a record of "Solomon Leonard and His Descendants," which was published in 1896. He married, first, Nellie Tucker Burr and had—

    i—Herman Burr, born August 22, 1872.
    ii—Russell Ammidown, born November 1, 1874.
    iii—Eleanor Tucker, born and died July 3, 1876.
    iv—Manning, born December 15, 1877.
    He married, second, Ermina Elizabeth Newton and they reside at DePere, Wisconsin.

iii—George Manning, born September 4, 1846; died September 8, 1863.
iv—Anna Rebekah, born April 8, 1849; resides at 5 Chestnut street, Boston, Mass.
v—Mary Frances, born August 2, 1851.
vi—Sarah Catherine, born December 16, 1854. She married William H. Green and lives at Grundy Centre, Iowa.
vii—David Fiske, born July 26, 1857; died May 31, 1864.

747—Ann, born November 24, 1819; died September 22, 1821.
748—Helen, born September 9, 1821. She married July 10, 1866 (as second wife) Merrick Mansfield, and died June 12, 1902.
749—Antoinette, born April 5, 1824; married November 26, 1844, Jonathan H. Barker, of Cincinnati, Ohio, and died February 16, 1890.
*750—Malcolm, born February 15, 1827.
751—Ann Frances, born February 6, 1829. She married December 15, 1851, Joseph Kinsey, of Cincinnati, Ohio, and died January 26, 1886.
752—Catherine Hartwell, born January 15, 1831; died April 18, 1856.
*753—Henry Clay, born November 7, 1833.

364.

JONATHAN PERRY AMMIDOWN (Cyrus,[148] Joseph,[46] Philip,[11] Philip,[4] Roger[1]), born August 29, 1797, in that part of Charlton which is now Southbridge, Mass. He was a farmer and lived in Southbridge, where he died October 9, 1840. He married, July 17, 1824, Sarah Rosebrook, daughter of William Moore. She was born at Union, Conn., February 9, 1800, and died April 17, 1847.

CHILDREN.

754 —Judson, born September 25, 1825; died August 6, 1843.
755 —Andrew J., born June 26, 1827; died August 27, 1843.
*756 —John Perry, born July 24, 1829.

756½—Pliny, born June 21, 1831; died February 4, 1833.
757 —Pliny M., born October 11, 1833; died October 11, 1839.
758 —Sarah B., born July 20, 1837; died unmarried June 20, 1859, at
        South Reading, Mass.
759 —Susan E., born December 10, 1839; died unmarried February 6,
        1856, at South Reading, Mass.

367.

JOSEPH AMMIDOWN (Cyrus,[140] Joseph,[48] Philip,[14] Philip,[4]
Roger[1]), born at Southbridge, Mass., April 14, 1801. He married Mary
A. Hammond December 7, 1826. He resided in Southbridge and was
town clerk at the time of his death, July 10, 1863. His wife died
July 20, 1885.

CHILDREN.

759½—Joseph M., born April 16, 1828; died September 24, 1829.
760 —Mary Josephine, born June 2, 1830; married March 15, 1853,
        Thomas Talbot, of Southbridge.
760½—James Melvin, born June 14, 1833; died April 20, 1893.
761 —Julia Melvina, born March 3, 1841. She married January 24,
        1864, Ephraim Booth, of Southbridge.

368.

CYRUS AMMIDOWN (Cyrus,[140] Joseph,[48] Philip,[14] Philip,[4]
Roger[1]), born at Southbridge, March 28, 1804. He married, February
26, 1829, Julia B. Marsh. She was born in 1809 and died October 8,
1852. He married (second), January 22, 1854, Laura Ann Dunbar. He
died in Southbridge in 1876.

CHILDREN.

762—Henry G., born 1830. He was a carpenter and lived in South-
        bridge. He married (first), August 30, 1853, Julia J. Dodge,
        and (second), December 12, 1867, Sarah P., widow of Lucius
        Leonard.
763—Edwin Cyrus, born August 7, 1842; died November 25, 1855.
764—George B., born 1836. He married October 7, 1857, Almira,
        daughter of Samuel Perrin, of Southbridge, Mass.
765—Louisa C., born 1839; died February 24, 1859.

373.

PHILIP AMIDON (Philip,[141] Joseph,[48] Philip,[14] Philip,[4] Roger[1]),
born at Keene, N. H., August 14, 1799. He lived for a time at Orange,
Mass., and then went to Batavia, N. Y., where he married, October 8,
1822, Sarah Child. She was born December 8, 1805, and died in 1867.
In 1825 they settled at East Pembroke, N. Y., where he died April 30,
1881.

CHILDREN.

*766—Otis, born December 24, 1823.
767—George, born and died August 22, 1825.
768—Harriet, born May 16, 1827; died January 21, 1834.
769—Malinda, born March 24, 1830; married January 1, 1849, Ichabod
    J. Case, and had—
        i—Marvin J., born November 24, 1849; died September
           10, 1851.
        ii—Helen L., born September 15, 1851.
        iii—Sarah A., born February 5, 1854.
        iv—Louis, born January 13, 1856.
        v—Philip J., born January 17, 1868.
*770—Marvin Child, born May 24, 1832.
771—Matilda J., born November 11, 1834; died July 17, 1874. She mar-
    ried April 5, 1852, Albert Cups, and had—
        i—Orra S., born July 24, 1855.
        ii—George, born August 23, 1858.
        iii—William, born June 18, 1863.
        iv—Nellie, born July 4, 1865.
        v—Bertie, born October 20, 1868.
        vi—Lura, born July 4, 1875.
*772—Albert, born January 2, 1837.
773—Harriet A., born December 27, 1839; married February 2, 1859,
    John Gowdy.
774—Sarah A., born July 15, 1842. She has been a teacher for a
    number of years and lives at East Pembroke, N. Y.
*775—Cyrus P., born May 19, 1845.

377.

CYRUS AMIDON (Joseph,[144] Joseph,[48] Philip,[14] Philip,[4]
Roger[1]), born July 13, 1808. He married, September 24, 1830, Uretta
Cropsey. She was born in 1810 and died September 14, 1859. They
lived at North Parma, N. Y., where he died December 14, 1847.

CHILDREN.

*776—Alfonso, born January 14, 1831.
777—Permelia Matilda, born June 22, 1833. She married (1st) Oc-
    tober 22, 1853, David Fossmire of North Parma. He died
    November 7, 1865. She married (2d) August 18, 1868, J. Boyd
    Dunlap of Rochester, N. Y.
        i—Will Knox Dunlap, born December 5, 1869. Is an elec
           trical engineer at the power house, Niagara Falls,
           N. Y.
        ii—Gertrude Dunlap, born June 25, 1871.
778—Joseph, born September 5, 1834; died February 16, 1835.
779—Otis, born June 7, 1836; died December 14, 1837.
*780—George W., born June 13, 1838.
781—Celia Frances, born October 15, 1843; died February 12, 1846.
782—Louisa Uretta, born September 16, 1846; died January 18, 1894,
    at Hiawatha, Kansas. She married December 2, 1864, John
    Simmons and they removed to Kansas in 1871.
        i—Cyrus; lives at Brookfield, Mo.
        ii—Boyd.
        iii—Alma.
        iv—Gertrude.
        v—Frank.
        vi—Lizzie.

378.

MARTIN AMIDON (Joseph,[144] Joseph,[49] Philip,[11] Philip,[5] Roger[1]), married July 12, 1833, Polly Burritt, and lived at Parma, N. Y.

CHILDREN.

783—Nelson, born 1840; married March 4, 1878, Delia Mosher and lives at Rochester, N. Y.
784—Elizabeth, born 1841; married February 21, 1861, Spencer Ketcham.
785—Hiram, born August 6, 1844; married January 1, 1862, Louisa Litchard.
786—Delephene, born August 31, 1848; married April 15, 1869, Curtis Fowler.
787—Cyrus, born May 27, 1850; married January 25, 1875, Julia Crary.
788—Giles, born July 22, 1853; married December 13, 1877, Nelly Mosher and lives at Davidson, Mich.

381.

DEXTER AMIDON (Joseph,[144] Joseph,[49] Philip,[11] Philip,[5] Roger[1]), born April 19, 1819. He married, May 1, 1839, Miranda Cropsey. She was born March 18, 1816, and died in January, 1898. They lived at North Parma, N. Y., where he died December 6, 1889.

CHILDREN.

789—Celia, born February 10, 1840; died December 21, 1860.
790—Dexter, born April 2, 1843; died July 8, 1846.
791—Frances, born June 2, 1845; married December 28, 1864, George Ingham, Hilton, N. Y.
792—William, born February 8, 1847; died March 31, 1852.
793—Italia, born December 21, 1849; married Deino Burritt, Hilton, N. Y.
*794—Warren W., born June 8, 1852.
*795—Oscar C., born November 21, 1854.

388.

REUBEN AMIDON (Jabez,[141] Reuben,[41] Philip,[11] Philip,[5] Roger[1]), born at Rome, N. Y. He went to Illinois about 1836 and settled at Plainfield, where he married Jane House. They afterwards took up a claim near Rock River, where she died in 1843.

CHILDREN.

796—May; died, aged 16.
797—Dwight; a carpenter and lives in Chicago.
798—Hollis H., born June 3, 1840. He served as Quartermaster Sergeant in Company C, Second Illinois Light Artillery, from January, 1863, to August 10, 1865. He married June 29, 1876, Laura M. Penoyer. She was born January 3, 1855, at Dover. Ohio, and was a daughter of Jonathan and Elizabeth Penoyer. They resided at Peoria, Ill., but in 1894 removed to Hemet, Cal.

389.

ISAAC CLARK AMIDON (Rufus,[5] Reuben,[4] Philip,[3] Philip,[2] Roger[1]), born June 2, 1809. He married Lydia Lester Miner and lived at Groton, Conn.

CHILD.

*799—Charles Eldridge, born December 1, 1846.

390.

FRANCIS H. AMIDON (Rufus,[5] Reuben,[4] Philip,[3] Philip,[2] Roger[1]), born October 27, 1811. He married Ann Hughes and resided at Jersey City, N. J., until 1847, when he removed to New York City, where he was engaged for many years as a wholesale hatter. He died July 14, 1886.

CHILDREN.

800—Mary Ann.
801—Minerva.
802—Sarah. She married (first) H. W. Hunt and (second) Dr. Douglas Bly, of Rochester, N. Y.
803—Josephine; married Reuben Ross, New York city.
804—Jane Louisa; married Joseph Thompson, New York city.
805—Victoria; married William Tucker, New York city.
806—Frances.
807—James Rufus, born in New York city, April 17, 1847. He was a member of the Seventh Regiment from 1865 to 1873. He married June 28, 1881, Georgianna M., daughter of George R. and Mary E. (Hyatt) Bunker, and resides at 29 West Fifty-eighth street, New York.

397.

JOHN AMADON (Josiah,[5] Philip,[4] Ephriam,[3] Philip,[2] Roger[1]), born November 4, 1813, at Troy, N. H. He married, October 20, 1840, Betsey B. Putney, of Chesterfield, N. H. She was born July 3, 1814, and died December 17, 1896. He was a blacksmith and lived at Fitzwilliam N. H. He enlisted, October 7, 1861, in Co. F, 6th N. H. Vols., and died at Hatteras Inlet, N. C., January 15, 1862.

CHILDREN.

808—Sarah Elizabeth, born July 1, 1841; married December 1, 1863, Joseph Foster Capron of Troy, N. H. He was the first man to enlist from the town of Troy, becoming a member of Company A, Second Regiment, April 25, 1861. He was disabled and discharged October 22, 1861, but re-enlisted December 16, 1863 in Company C. First Connecticut Cavalry, and served until June 12, 1865. He died at Troy, July 3, 1892.
 i—Dora E., born October 10, 1865; died June 5, 1873.
 ii—Grace Elizabeth, born December 19, 1872; married September 14, 1892, Frank J. Bemis. He is now postmaster at Madbury, N. H. They have—
  i—Harriet E., born May 11, 1895.
  ii—Franklin C., born October 21, 1897.
  iii—Ella Louise, born April 11, 1899.

*809—James Orlando, born September 10, 1842.
*810—Henry Josiah, born March 18, 1844.
*811—Frank Edward, born July 30, 1847.
*812—Charles H., born November 3, 1848.
 813—Ella Maria, born October 2, 1854. She married January 11, 1874,
     Julius E. Bemis, of Fitzwilliam, N. H., and has—
       i—Son, born December 20, 1875.
       ii—Henry H., born February 2, 1885.
       iii—Chester L., born August 14, 1886.
*814—George Frederick, born May 11, 1857.

398.

LEANDER AMIDON (Josiah,[5] Philip,[4], Ephriam,[3] Philip,[2] Roger[1]), born at Troy, N. H., August 9, 1814. He married, May 14, 1847, Sarah H. Randolph, and lived mostly at Bellows Falls, N. H. He died in Boston, Mass., December 12, 1878.

CHILDREN.

815—Clara Sarah, born February 18, 1850. She married October 20,
     1869, Warren Fay Ballou, of Bellows Falls, N. H., and had a
     daughter. Anna Paulina, born December 16, 1873.
816—Frederick, born February 25, 1852.
817—Alice, born September 25, 1856.
818—Henry, born July 31, 1858.

401.

ELIAL AMADON (Titus,[4] Ithamar,[3] Ithamar,[2] Philip,[2] Roger[1]), born at Wilbraham, Mass., December 23, 1878. He married (1st), September 25, 1811, Harriet Thompson. She died May 26, 1817, and he married (2d), May 31, 1818, Persis Stacy. He married (3d), November 15, 1826, Achasah Goodman. She died September 23, 1844, and he died September 27, 1828.

CHILDREN.

819—Susan Cordelia, born August 7, 1812. She married June 22, 1837,
     Lucius Nims, of Greenfield, Mass., where she died October 30,
     1890.
       i—Mary, born January 3, 1839 ; married Francis M. Thomp-
         son, Register of Probate, Greenfield, Mass., and had a
         son, Francis Nims Thompson, born August 26, 1872.
       ii—Henry Gilbert, born June 27, 1841.
       iii—Lucius, born April 14, 1844.
       iv—Della, born September 23, 1848.
       v—Thomas Hull, born April 7, 1851.
820—Henry Gilbert, born November 26, 1814 ; died September 25, 1839,
     unmarried, at Hawkinsville, Ga.
*821—Elial Thompson, born May 13, 1817.
822—Persis, born November 20, 1820 ; died February 22, 1826.
823—William Lucius, born August 2, 1822 ; died September 9, 1823.

411.

TITUS AMADON (Titus,[111] Ithamar,[22] Ithamar,[14] Philip,[4] Roger[1]), born at Wilbraham, Mass., July 7, 1803. He married, May 22, 1828, Eliza, daughter of Willard and Lois (Davis) Chaffee. She was born February 20, 1807, and died April 3, 1879. In 1820 he moved to Springfield, Mass., and worked most of the time for sixty years in the U. S. Armory. He served as Assessor, Overseer of the Poor, Selectman, Alderman and four terms as Representative to the State Legislature. He died in Springfield, May 9, 1889.

CHILDREN.

824—Edwin Bingley, born March 1, 1829; died June 5, 1858.
825—Frances Eliza, born May 26, 1831; died June 7. 1887. She married June 20, 1867, Henry Thrall, of Springfield.
*826—William Willard, born November 24, 1835.

413.

HOLLIS G. AMADON (Titus,[112] Ithamar,[22] Ithamar,[14] Philip,[4] Roger[1]), born June 21, 1805. He married June 3, 1833, Harriet White. He was a hatter at Springfield, Mass., where he died September 14, 1874.

CHILDREN.

827—George G., born 1842; died August 24, 1843.
828—Georgianna, born December 25, 1843.
829—Clara, born October 22, 1848; died May 29, 1849.

415.

SAMUEL DEXTER AMADON (Titus,[112] Ithamar,[22] Ithamar,[14] Philip,[4] Roger[1]), born at Wilbraham, Mass., July 4, 1809. He lived mostly in Palmer, Mass., and died in 1888. His wife's name was Laura.

CHILDREN.

*830—Charles L., born September 16, 1830.
831—Titus, born 1835; died 1838.
832—Sabria, born 1839; married August 4, 1856, James Maxwell, of Monson, Mass.
*833—Henry M., born 1839.
834—Roena Lucy, born 1841. She married December 22, 1866, Cyrus Clinton Day, a farmer, of Wilbraham. She died August 16, 1878.
835—Clara L., born 1843; married May 4, 1863, Charles Edson, of Wilbraham.
836—Ellen M., born 1844.
*837—Lucian Edgar, born March 20, 1848; married August 1, 1868, Mary Clay, of Monson, where he still resides.
838—Daughter, born October 20, 1851.

416.

ABIRAM AMIDON (John,[17] Ithamar,[5] Ithamar,[14] Philip,[2] Roger[1]), born November, 1792, in Wilbraham. He died April, 1864. His wife was Amy Adams. She was born October 14, 1792, and died August, 1876.

CHILDREN.

839—Philander, born March 21, 1816. He removed to Iowa, living somewhere near Sioux City.
840—Lusina, born February 20, 1818. She married about 1838 Emery Dunbar, of Hartford, Conn., and died about a year afterwards.
841—John, born June 30, 1820 ; died about 1823.
842—Caroline, born November 11, 1821 ; married about 1840 (as second wife), Emery Dunbar, and died in Norwich, Conn., October 1855.
*843—Rev. Sanford Newton, born July 4, 1823.
844—Ruth Harmony, born March 17, 1825 ; died in 1887. She married Rufus Abbe and had—
    i—Ruth.
    ii—Sanford.
    iii—Fred.
    iv—Frank.
    v—Caroline.
845—Celia L., born November 17, 1826 ; she died May 18, 1884. She married in 1845 Orin Goodrich, and lived at North Manchester, Conn.
846—Kesiah Amelia, born 1845, August 22, 1829, at Longmeadow, Mass. She married July 8, 1845, George, son of George W. and Elizabeth (Talcott) Griswold. She married (second) March 11, 1870, Henry, son of George and Amelia (Weldon) Jacobs. He served from March 10, 1862, to April 12, 1865, in Company D, Twelfth Connecticut Volunteers. He is a farmer and resides at Andover, Conn. Children—
    i—George Talcott Griswold, born April 1, 1848 ; married Louisa Niece and lived at Providence, R. I. They have a son, Frank Griswold.
    ii—Martha Elizabeth Griswold, born May 23, 1852. She married, first, John T. Cowles, and, second, Frank Brown.
    iii—Adelaide Rhoda Griswold, born November 18, 1861 ; died October 7, 1863.
    iv—Orin Philander Jacobs, born December 19, 1870.
847—Lester, born May 18, 1831. Lost at sea on a whaling vessel.
848—Orin, born July 10, 1833 ; died in 1851 at Marlboro, Mass.

422.

JOHN AMIDON (John,[17] Ithamar,[5] Ithamar,[14] Philip,[2] Roger[1]), born August 8, 1803, in Ellington, Conn. He married, April 6, 1836, Eliza Firman. He was a shoemaker and lived in Woodstock, Conn., where he died May 17, 1883.

CHILDREN.

*849—John Richard, born February 8, 1837.
850—Abigail, born April 19, 1838.
851—Mary Eliza, born February 28, 1840 ; died June 21, 1898. She married December 12, 1861, Alexander Field Stebbins and had—
    i—Lillian E., born February 19, 1865 ; died September 25, 1866.
    ii—Mary Lillian, born September 25, 1867.

852—James L., born March 12, 1842; died May 18, 1842.
*853—Jerome F., born August 8, 1844.
854—Martha Estella, born November 21, 1850; married February 14,
      1892, Rev. Alvin E. Goff, Springfield, Mass.
*855—Julius M., born November 3, 1853.

423.

LESTER AMIDON (John,[11] Ithamar,[11] Ithamar,[15] Philip,[4]
Roger[1]). Married (1st), November 13, 1832, at Woodstock, Conn.,
Hannah Colburn, and (2d) Mrs. Tabitha Adams, of Canterbury, Conn.,
August 5, 1842. She died in 1892 and he died in Canterbury, December 2, 1872.

CHILDREN.

856—Hannah, born July 21, 1835.
857—Abigial; a teacher; married a Stanton and lives at Rye, Ariz.
858—Martha.

425.

ARIEL AMADON (Ansel,[17] Ebenezer,[14] Ithamar,[15] Philip,[4]
Roger[1]), born at Goshen, Mass., December 20, 1802. He married
Weighty Carr. She was born March 22, 1800, and died March 1, 1878;
daughter of Abel Carr. He was a carpenter and lived in Pownal, Vt.,
where he died December 2, 1876.

426.

PHILANDER AMADON (Ansel,[17] Ebenezer,[14] Ithamar,[15] Philip,[4] Roger[1]), born at Goshen, Mass., April 26, 1804. He was a farmer
and lived at Pownal, Vt., and North Adams, Mass. He married (1st),
March 24, 1828, Mehitable Marble, daughter of Jonathan and Mehitable
(Bates) Luce. She was born at Chesterfield, Mass., March 22, 1809,
and died April 10, 1852, at North Adams, Mass. He married (2d),
June 18, 1853, Rebecca Fowler. She was born March 18, 1811, at
Chesterfield, Mass., and died April 24, 1891, at North Adams. He died
at North Adams, August 25, 1875.

CHILDREN.

*859—Ansel Lyman, born October 14, 1829.
*860—George Augustus, born January 1, 1831.
861—Samantha Maria, born June 13, 1833; at Pownal, Vt. She married, July 6, 1853, Spencer E. Phillips, and lives at Janesville,
      Wis.
      i—Wendell S., born April 7, 1854; married Belle A. Dickerman and has
           i—Hazel, born November 26, 1883.
           ii—Edmund S., born September 9, 1895.
           iii—Elizabeth B., born October 3, 1902.

ii—George H., born July 18, 1857 ; married Laura E. Horne
and has
    i—Westley G., born September 9, 1893.
    ii—Duane S., born November 8, 1901.
    iii—Ella, born June 10, 1867 ; died June 19, 1867.
*862—Leland Morgan, born October 7, 1836.
*863—Lewis Franklin, born December 20, 1838.
864—Martha Emeline, born March 3, 1841. She married, first, December 24, 1863, Jonathan Clegg, who died July 7, 1865 ; second, May 9, 1867, George W. Chamberlin, who died July 18, 1870 ; and, third, at Janesville, Wis., March 30, 1891, Edward Calf.

(Second wife.)

*865—Charles Fowler, born April 15, 1854.

428.

ANSEL AMADON (Ansel,[177] Ebenezer,[44] Ithamar,[15] Philip,[8] Roger[1]), born at Goshen, Mass., October 13, 1807. He married, December 19, 1830, Luretta Luce. She was born August 24, 1805, at Chesterfield, Mass., and died February 22, 1890. He was a carpenter and lived in Pownal, where he died May 2, 1892.

CHILDREN.

866—Harriet Ann, born 1831. She married in 1853 Sidney Abbott and died in 1855. They had—
    i—George Henry Abbott, born July 12, 1855 ; died November 27, 1884. He married March 3, 1881, Mary Hill, and had a son, Harry Abbott, born January 24, 1883, and lived at Greenwich, N. Y.
867—Mary Jane, born October 18, 1833. She married Daniel Watson October 30, 1859, and died September 26, 1882, at Atlantic, Iowa. They had—
    i—William Ansel Watson, born December 23, 1867 ; married August 21, 1895, Nettie Myrtle Olds ; lived at Hopland, California, and had a daughter, Laura Irene, born April 29, 1896.
    ii—Daniel Francis, born December 26, 1869. His last address was 40 Milepost, Alaska.
    iii—John Valentine, born December 20, 1871 ; died March 23, 1872
868—Henry Ansel, born in 1837. He was a member of Co. K, 4th Vt. Vols., and was killed at the battle of the Wilderness, in May, 1864.
*869—Francis Eldridge, born November 15, 1840.
870—Susan Maria, born at Pownal, Vt., October 28, 1843 ; married, August 22, 1865, William Canfield, and died August 28, 1873. They had—
    i—Henry, born March 12, 1866.
    ii—Emmons, born October 16, 1868 ; died 1875.
871—Lucy Abigail, born March 18, 1846 ; married, September 19, 1868, Emery Robert Carey, born May 5, 1840, and died August 16. 1888. He served during the war in Co. I, 57th Mass., and in Co. K, 61st N. Y. Regt. They have—
    i—Edwin Volney, born June 13, 1869 ; died March 26, 1891 ; married Harriet Green.
    ii—Frederick Francis, born May 9, 1871.
    iii—Loretta Mary, born October 9, 1875 ; married George H. Salls, Dalton, Mass., October 10, 1898, and has Ralph Edmond, born January 12, 1900.
872—Edward Lyman, born January 20, 1849 ; died August 13, 1872, at Clarksburg, Mass.

430.

MELZAR AMADON (Ansel,[177] Ebenezer,[64] Ithamar,[15] Philip,[6] Roger[1]), born February 13, 1809, at Goshen, Mass. He married Susan Matterson, of Shaftsbury, Vt., and removed to Ohio, where he soon died.

432.

RICHARD FLYNN AMADON (Ansel,[177] Ebenezer,[64] Ithamar,[15] Philip,[6] Roger[1]), born at Goshen, Mass., December 22, 1812. He married (1st) Judith M., daughter of John Trussell, May 24, 1835. She was born March 30, 1817, and died at Nicholville, N. Y., December 24, 1872. He married (2d), November 22, 1873, Nancy, daughter of Patrick Shales. He was a farmer and resided at Nicholville, where he died May 2, 1882.

CHILDREN.

*873—Loyal Richard, born June 21, 1837.
 874—Oscar T., born February 18, 1843 : died March 16. 1843.
 875—Wealtha L., born September 27, 1845. She married, October 22. 1863, Milton Lockwood, and died October 3, 1886.   Children—
    i—Annis, born June 29, 1865.   She married, in 1886, James P. Snider. They had a son, James P., Jr., born November 2, 1888 ; died November 26, 1893.
    ii—Frank R., born October 31, 1867 ; died March 28, 1872.
    iii—Burton T., born June 3, 1870 ; lived in Chicago, Ill.
    iv—Ella Izoria, born June 9, 1876 ; died April 26, 1882.
    v.—R. Pearl, born May 1, 1878 ; died August 7, 1888.
 876—Frank T., born December 19. 1847 ; died July, 1881, in London, England. He married at Auburn, N. Y., December 18, 1874, Ella Frost.
 877—Izoria Loretta, born December 8, 1853 ; married, October 3, 1881, Robert N. Harrison, and lives at Everett, Wash.

(Second wife.)

878—Verdie Belle, born November 15, 1875.
879—Rose May, born August 18, 1877.

433.

JOSIAH AMADON (Ansel,[177] Ebenezer,[64] Ithamar,[15] Philip,[6] Roger[1]), born July 14, 1814, at Goshen. He married at Pownal, Vt., January 18, 1839, Lucy, daughter of Thomas Banister, a Revolutionary soldier. She was born October, 1820; died 1880. He was a blacksmith. He died at Pownal, October 6, 1843.

CHILDREN.

880—Alice Charlane, born December 20, 1839 ; died February 5, 1872. She married Lyman Lillie and had—
    i—George Melvin, born June 22, 1862. He married, March 31, 1885, Wilhelmina Cook Reid, born in Scotland. He is a street car conductor at Pittsfield, Mass., and has four children—Melvin Lyman, Ralph Reid, Jennie Ethel, Harold Claude.
    ii—Almer L., born April 14, 1865 ; married, November 9. 1886, Lucinda C. Phillips; lives at Pownal, Vt., and has two children—George Myron and Ethel Irene.
    iii—Hattie Celestia, born March 8, 1867 ; married November 28, 1883, Albert Perry Bryant (grandnephew of Wm. Cullen Bryant), and has six children—Alice Lillian, Florence Almira, Albert Perry, James Henry, Maud Luella, Nellie Lousia.
    iv—Louise E., born November 1, 1869 ; married, January 1, 1886, James Albert Cheesbro, Pownal, Vt., and has two children—Fred and Ray.
881—Thomas J., born April 2, 1842 ; died August 12, 1862.

434.

HENRY P. AMADON (Ansel,[177] Ebenezer,[64] Ithamar,[18] Philip,[6] Roger[1]), born August 8, 1816, at Goshen, Mass. He married, April 18, 1841, Nancy Mason, of Pownal, Vt. She died October 23, 1903. He was a farmer and owned his father's homestead until his death, which occurred February 10, 1894.

CHILDREN.

882—Myra Ann, born December 23, 1841 ; married Charles Magee, of Stanford, Vt., and had—
    i—Hattie.
    ii—Libby ; married Frank Perham, Pownal, Vt.
*883—Christopher M., born September 15, 1846.
884—Egbert, born August 12, 1851 ; died December 5, 1860.
*885—Herbert, born November 4, 1858.

436.

SAMUEL AMADON (Ansel,[177] Ebenezer,[64] Ithamar,[18] Philip,[6] Roger[1]), born November 27, 1819. He learned the calico printing trade, at which he worked for many years. He married, in 1843, Fanny, daughter of Luke and Salina (Alexander) Flood. She was born in 1822. He died at North Adams, Mass., June 7, 1899.

CHILDREN.

*886—Ernest Alexander, born August 23, 1844.
887—Alina Lucena, born January 27, 1846. She married, November 27, 1866, William F. Forrester. They reside in Troy, N. Y., and have—
    i—Fanny, born December 13, 1867. She married, at Colon, South America, December 17, 1897, Charles Swett.
888—Samuel, born September 20, 1857 ; died young.

438.

FRANKLIN PERRY AMADON (Ansel,[111] Ebenezer,[34] Ithamar,[13] Philip,[4] Roger[1]), born at Petersburg, N. Y., January 8, 1824. He married, March 18, 1854, Eliza Mason, Pownal, Vt. He now lives at North Adams, Mass.

CHILDREN.

*889—Dr. Arthur F., born September 10, 1858.
890—Cally M., born September 22, 1862; died April 25, 1865.
*891—Dr. Alfred Mason, born May 21, 1867.
892—Walter Elijah, born January 31, 1870, at North Adams, Mass. He married, October 4, 1890, Maude E. Keyser.

440.

PHILIP AMIDON (John,[100] John,[33] John,[14] Philip,[4] Roger[1]), born at Hardwick, Mass., in 1822. He married, November 30, 1848, Sarah A. Warner. He was a farmer and lived at New Braintree, Mass., where he died in 1875.

CHILDREN.

*893—John Edwin, born November 1, 1850.

457.

EXPERIENCE JOHNSON AMIDON (Experience Johnson,[210] Jedediah,[78] Henry,[21] Henry,[9] Philip,[4] Roger[1]). He married Prudence Webster. He was a farmer and lived for a time at Sturbridge, Mass.

CHILDREN.

894—Maryetta Elizabeth; married Albert Jacobs.
895—Samuel Experience. He married Amy Josephine Keach, and for a time lived at Quinebaug, Conn., and later at Willimantic, Conn.
896—Ellen Antoinette, born December 4, 1845; married Charles Cummings.
897—Hannah Josephine, born October 15, 1848.
898—Jenny Prudence.

458.

JOHN AMIDON (Experience Johnson,[210] Jedediah,[78] Henry,[33] Henry,[9] Philip,[4] Roger[1]). He married Nancy Southworth and had

CHILDREN.

899—Charles M.
900—Frank.
901—Carrie M. She married Charles Havens and lives at Wethersfield, Conn.

464.

HENRY AMIDON (Henry,[14] Jedediah,[12] Henry,[11] Henry,[5] Philip,[4] Roger[1]). He married Mary Rickert and moved from Mottville, Mich., to Dubuque, Ia., in 1846. He went to California in 1849 and died in 1851 at American Bar, a mining camp.

CHILDREN.

*902—John Rickert, born May 29, 1840.
903—Mary ; married about 1888, John Nelson Barber.
904—Sophronia ; married Jerome J. Matthews, St. Louis, Mo.

472.

GILBERT ELIPHALET STRONG AMIDON (Horatio,[14] Jedediah,[12] Henry,[11] Henry,[5] Philip,[4] Roger[1]), born at Willington, Conn., August 20, 1836; married, November 11, 1868, Julia Sophia Whiton. He is a lumber dealer and lives at East Willington, Conn.

CHILDREN.

*905—Charles Sanford, born November 9, 1869.
906—Mary Louise, born May 11, 1871. She married John William Armitage.
907—Gilbert Whiton, born August 23, 1872.
908—Robert Strong, born June 8, 1875.
909—Lillian, born March 11, 1877.
910—Andrew Huntington, born March 16, 1879.
911—Harlan Page, born May 8, 1881.
912—Abigail Delight, born July 22, 1884.
913—Henry Nathan, born December 7, 1887.

473.

SAMUEL AMIDON (Nathaniel,[124] Moses,[77] Henry,[21] Henry,[5] Philip,[4] Roger[1]). He was born at Onondaga Hollow, N. Y.; married Maria Rockwell and resided at Plymouth, Ashtabula County, Ohio.

CHILD.

*914—Ira W., born August 9, 1839.

475.

CHAUNCEY AMIDON (Nathaniel,[124] Moses,[77] Henry,[21] Henry,[5] Philip,[4] Roger[1]). He resides at Plymouth, Ohio, or Ashtabula, Ohio. Particulars as to his family not obtained, but he had—

CHILDREN.

915—Mattie ; married a DeGroodt.
916—Estelle ; married a Colby.

476.

NATHANIEL WILLIAM AMEDON (Nathaniel,[111] Moses,[77] Henry,[11] Henry,[3] Philip,[2] Roger[1]), born at Hebron, N. Y., April 18, 1822. He was a farmer and resided in Hebron, where he died August 27, 1891. He married Phoebe, daughter of William and Ruth (Getty) Munson. She was born February 13, 1836, and still lives at Hebron, N. Y.

CHILDREN.

917—Julietta, born September 1, 1845; died May 28, 1865.
*918—William Franklin, born September 13, 1848.
919—Caroline Clarimon, born October 25, 1852; died December 25, 1878. She married in May, 1872, Samuel Robrins, of Peru, Vt.
*920—Asiel Sheldon, born December 25, 1854.
921—John Nathaniel, born July 30, 1856; died May 22, 1863.
922—George Herman, born February 4, 1860; died July 17, 1881.
923—Lora Alvira, born February 28, 1862; died June 30, 1890. She married in July, 1885, H. William Lee, of Cambridge, N. Y.
924—Nathaniel John, born February 20, 1865; died February 13, 1866.

478.

GEORGE W. AMIDON (Nathaniel,[111] Moses,[77] Henry,[11] Henry,[3] Philip,[2] Roger[1]). Married, July 1, 1855, Jane Emily, daughter of Gideon and Emily (Webster) Estes. She was born in Pompey, N. Y., January 25, 1835.

CHILDREN.

*925—Frances O., born March 27, 1856. She married January 25, 1876. Obed Nichols, of South Onondaga, N. Y. and has—
    i—Lotta, born Dec. 12, 1876.
    ii—Mattie, born June 14, 1879.
*926—Gideon E., born June 1, 1858.
927—Charles W., born Oct. 9, 1869.
928—Viola E., born Sept. 9, 1871.
929—Albert L., born Nov. 6, 1873.
930—Edwin G., born June 27, 1875.
931—Moses H., born May 25, 1882; died Feb. 10, 1883.

479.

THOMAS JEFFERSON AMIDON (Nathaniel,[111] Moses,[77] Henry,[11] Henry,[3] Philip,[2] Roger[1]), born in Onondaga County, N. Y., June 17, 1837. About 1855 he removed to Plymouth, Ohio, and married, July 3, 1863, Alvia M. Richards, and lives at Charlotte, Mich.

CHILDREN.

932—Alice L., born at Plymouth, Ohio, Feb. 16, 1865. She married (1st) June 4, 1881, Charles L. Kimball.
    i—Ira C., born Nov. 23, 1882.
    ii—Iva L., born Feb. 13, 1884.
    iii—Alfred J., born August 4, 1885; died July 26, 1886. She married (2d) July 20, 1889, Lucius Cooper of Charlotte, Mich.
933—Alta M., born Aug. 11, 1868; married March 11, 1836, James W. Hill, of Charlotte, Mich., and had—
    Rowland J., born Dec. 9, 1889.
934—Asa J., born at St. John, Mich., Dec. 26, 1874.

484.

FREDERICK S. AMIDON (Samuel,[5] Moses,[4] Henry,[3] Henry,[2] Philip,[4] Roger[1]), born at East Hartford, Conn., May 30, 1824. He married Dorothy J. Kingsbury.

CHILDREN.

*935—Charles Kingsbury, born March 26, 1846.
936—Alice C., born March 2, 1849; married (1st) June 2, 1869, John H. Johnson of Brookfield, Mass., and (2nd) April 1, 1873, Samuel T. Frothingham, of Boston, Mass.
*937—Frederick S., born March 2, 1854.
938—Frank W., born Jan. 2, 1856; he lives at Newtonville, Mass.

485.

CHARLES D. AMIDON (Samuel,[5] Moses,[4] Henry,[3] Henry,[2] Philip,[4] Roger[1]), born at East Hartford, Conn., in 1827. He married Martha B. Hills and lived in Hartford, where he died March 26, 1876. He served in a Connecticut regiment during the Civil War for three years.

CHILD.

939—Frederick S.; a carpenter of Hartford, Conn.

487.

GEORGE AMIDON (Moses,[5] Moses,[4] Henry,[3] Henry,[2] Philip,[4] Roger[1]), born February 15, 1826, at Stockton, N. Y. In 1847 he moved to Hamilton, Ind., and about 1870 to Six Lakes, Montcalm County, Michigan. He served in the Mexican War and throughout the Civil War in Company B, 29th Indiana Volunteers. He was twice married. His second wife was a Mrs. Taylor, by whose son he was shot at Six Lakes in 1878.

CHILDREN.

940—Guy P., born April 1, 1853; died, Oct. 6, 1854.
(Second wife.)
941—William.
942—Fred.
943—Edward.
944—Lyda.

488.

SETH AMIDON (Moses,[5] Moses,[4] Henry,[3] Henry,[2] Philip,[4] Roger[1]), born April 5, 1827, at Delanti (Stockton), N. Y. When 10 or 12 years old he was bound out to Mr. Chapman, of Mantua, Portage County, Ohio, where he lived until he was of age. He settled at Hamilton, Indiana, in 1849, and worked at his trade—wagonmaker and carpenter. He married there January 5, 1857, Jeanette, daughter of Nelson and Lauretta (Trowbridge) Earll. She was born at Hannibal, N. Y., August 14, 1832, and died at Bryan, Ohio, April 3, 1877. About 1878 he moved to Lake View, Mich., where he died July 5, 1884.

CHILDREN.

945—Frank E., born Dec. 16, 1857; died, Aug. 28, 1858.
*946—Fred Arwin, born Sept. 19, 1859.
*947—Lee Earll, born Feb. 4, 1865.

490.

AARON AMIDON (Moses,[111] Moses,[11] Henry,[21] Henry,[9] Philip,[8] Roger[1]), born February 7, 1830, at Stockton, N. Y. In 1847 he moved to Hamilton, Ind., and later to Lake View, Mich. He was a farmer and mechanic. He served throughout the Civil War in Company M, 1st Regiment Michigan Engineers, and died September 4, 1894, at Wirth, Arkansas. He married (1st) Cordelia Maria, daughter of Henry and Ruth Carnes. She was born July 5, 1839, at Milford, Mich., and died December 30, 1872, at Cato, Mich. He married (2d), May 3, 1874, Mrs. Betsey Jane (McKeough) Dunsmore.

CHILDREN.

*948—Frank Elihu, born Dec. 11, 1866.
*949—Fred Aaron, born February 7, 1868.

(Second wife.)

950—William A., born January 25, 1875; now engaged in sheep business, Rock Springs, Wyoming.
951—Alvin, born December 14, 1877.
952—Anna, born December 14, 1877; she married February 28, 1897, William Wirth of Wirth, Arkansas and has William Aaron Wirth, born December 20, 1897.

494.

HENRY AMIDON (Henry,[111] Moses,[11] Henry,[21] Henry,[9] Philip,[8] Roger[1]), born at Hartford, Conn., August 16, 1834. He married Harriet, daughter of Joseph and Lois Bliss, of Unionville, Conn.

CHILDREN.

953—Nelly.
954—Hattie.
955—Jenny.
*956—William Henry, born in 1859.

495.

WILLIAM HENRY HARRISON AMIDON (Elijah,[111] Jonathan,[18] Henry,[11] Henry,[8] Philip,[2] Roger[1]), born at Braintree, Vt., August 12, 1813. He removed to Gilmanton, Wis., in 1858 and later to Dover, Wis., where he died April 20, 1896. He married, March 10, 1840, Louisa, daughter of Joel and Louisa Mann. She was born at Randolph, Vt., March 1, 1820.

CHILDREN.

957—Alma Ann, born at Marshfield, Vt., November 6, 1841. She married March 6, 1859, George Sprague of Brunswick, Wis.
    i—Clarence G., born June 21, 1867.
    ii—Mary A., born June 3, 1873. She married December 24, 1890, Clinton Moses of Brunswick, Wis.
*958—Henry Marshall, born March 10, 1843.
959—Myra Corinne, born at Northfield, Vt., December 29, 1848; died February 6, 1875. She married September 7, 1867, Uriah Fisk of Dover, Wis., and had—
    i—Nina, born February 15, 1868; died young.
    ii—Seth, born June 23, 1869; married August 10, 1892, Annie Bidney and lives at Naples, Wis.
    iii—Alma L., born November 17, 1871; married July 15, 1892, Royal Cooley, Brunswick, Wis.
    iv—Hannah C., born October 7, 1873; married July 3, 1892, Ray Loomis, Gilmanton, Wis.
*960—Myron Hale, born February 22, 1855.

498.

ELHANAN ELIJAH AMIDON (Elijah,[111] Jonathan,[18] Henry,[11] Henry,[8] Philip,[2] Roger[1]), born at Randolph, Vt., January 22, 1820. He married January 9, 1845, Lucretia Smith and lived at Brookfield, Vt. He was choirmaster in the Congregational Church for over 30 years. He died at Lowell, Mass., April 14, 1896.

CHILDREN.

961—Ellen A., born April 10, 1848; married January 25, 1866, Hollis O. Claflin, Brookfield, Vt.
    i—Elmer Forrest.
    ii—Bertha Lena.
962—Julian R., born October 31, 1855; married September 11, 1888, Carrie A. Smith and lives at Hartford, Vt.
963—Minnie B., born August 23, 1857; she married, first, in 1880, Lewis C. Young and, second, June 20, 1899, George Adams, of Lowell, Mass.
964—Guy E., born February 29, 1860; died September 19, 1862.
965—Josie, born May 5, 1864; died May 5, 1864.
966—Jessie, born May 5, 1864; died June 16, 1865.

501.

CHRISTOPHER COLUMBUS AMIDON (Elijah,[111] Jonathan,[18] Henry,[11] Henry,[8] Philip,[2] Roger[1]). He married Olive Kibbe, and lived at St. Johnsbury, Vt. He had a son.
967—O. C., who lived at St. Johnsbury, Vt.

505.

AUGUSTUS A. AMIDON (Alfred Augustus,[111] Jonathan,[18] Henry,[11] Henry,[4] Philip,[2] Roger[1]), born July 10, 1818, at Barnard, Vt. He married Sophronia Mason and removed to Coldwater, Mich., where he died several years ago. He was a cabinetmaker and leader in the Baptist choir, and held several local offices.

CHILDREN.

968—Sarah, born July 3, 1847; married May 30, 1868, Thomas B. Russell of Coldwater, Mich. He served as lieutenant in the Ninth Michigan regiment.
969—Daughter, married John L. Keep of Coldwater, Mich.
970—Daughter; married G. W. Klock of Coldwater, Mich.
971—A. A.; he lived at one time at Kansas City.

508.

MARSHALL AMIDON (Jacob,[111] Jonathan,[18] Henry,[11] Henry,[4] Philip,[2] Roger[1]), born at Northfield, Vt., February 21, 1823. He married (1st) in 1840 Phoebe, daughter of Alfred and Marcia (Brown) Bridges. She was born in 1823 and died in 1858. The name of his second wife was not given and he married (3d) in 1898 Isabelle, daughter of Joseph and Linah (Pipe) Steele. He served in Company I, 16th New York Regiment, from 1861 to 1863. He is a farmer and lived at Northfield, Vt.

CHILDREN.

972—Henry, born 1847; left home in 1873 and has not been heard from since.
973—Ellen, born 1850; married in 1868 Edwin Andrews, of Berlin, Vt.
*974—John, born August 10, 1853.
975—Sarah, born 1854; died 1866.
976—Fred, born 1856; died 1862.

516.

ALFRED LEROY AMIDON (Samuel,[1111] Jacob,[48] Henry,[11] Henry,[4] Philip,[2] Roger[1]), born at South Onondaga, New York, January 20, 1819. In 1823 he removed to Clymer, N. Y., with his parents, but returned to Onondaga County in 1855. He was a miller and lived at 163 Mark Avenue, Syracuse, N. Y. He married, January 8, 1852, Charlotte Louise, daughter of Daniel and Susan (Fuller) Eaton. She was born September 3, 1827, and died March 18, 1893. He died October 14, 1902.

CHILDREN.

977—Clarence Alfred, born April 25, 1855; died December 22, 1863.
978—Willis Linwood, born June 12, 1857; died September 17, 1858.
979—Alice Louise, born, June 1, 1861; lives at Syracuse, N. Y.
980—Charles Ernest, born April 25, 1865.

519.

AMASA CHAPMAN AMIDON (Samuel,[111] Jacob,[41] Henry,[21] Henry,[9] Philip,[4] Roger[1]), born February 26, 1823, in Chautauqua County, N. Y. He moved to Onondaga County with his parents in 1832. He married, in April, 1847, Almira, daughter of Amos and Hannah (Warner) Griffin. She was born December 14, 1831. In 1870 he removed to Toledo, Iowa, where he died in 1901. He was a carpenter and joiner.

CHILDREN.

981—Mary Elizabeth, born September 17, 1853; married December 24, 1873, Levi Mohler, Garwin, Iowa.
*982—Charles Amasa, born June 26, 1855.
983—Willis Volney, born July 7, 1863; married July 7, 1887, Ollie Whitely and lives at Larchwood, Iowa.
984—Henry Stuart, born September 26, 1870; married January 2, 1890, Hattie M. Crilley and lives at Toledo, Iowa.

526.

DANIEL AMIDON (Jacob,[111] Jacob,[41] Henry,[21] Henry,[9] Philip,[4] Roger[1]), born in Onondaga County, N. Y., but removed to Virginia before 1860, and resided at Dumfries.

CHILDREN.

985—Mary; married in 1863, Lt. W. Kemp Tabb of Dumfries, Va.

527.

ORLOW AMIDON (Jacob,[111] Jacob,[41] Henry,[21] Henry,[9] Philip,[4] Roger[1]), born in Onondaga, N. Y., March 5, 1823. He married, January 8, 1843, Ruamah, daughter of Daniel and Minerva (Hall) Canada. She was born June 8, 1821, at Marcellus, N. Y. He removed to Michigan in 1860 and lived at Battle Creek, where he died April 28, 1902.

CHILDREN.

986—Olive Eugenia, born January 19, 1845; married December 24, 1862, Abram Minges, Battle Creek, Mich.
987—Mary Ann, born January 12, 1847; died September 9, 1870; married December 1, 1866, Henry D. Ward, Battle Creek, Mich., and had
  i—Jessie, born February 23, 1869; married, February 8, 1898, Frank R. Cowles.
  ii—Mary A., born September 9, 1870.

528.

WILLIAM AMIDON (Jacob,[111] Jacob,[41] Henry,[21] Henry,[9] Philip,[4] Roger[1]), born about 1826. He married Clarinda Jackson and died at Navarino, N. Y. His son
988—Myron, married Harriet E. Gilbert and lives at Navarino, N. Y.

533.

MADISON AMIDON (Jacob,[8] Jacob,[6] Henry,[5] Henry,[4] Philip,[2] Roger[1]), born at Onondaga, N. Y., June 12, 1836. He married, February 11, 1857, Sarah C., daughter of Josiah and Susan Henderson. She was born May 7, 1836, in Onondaga County. In 1875 he removed to Minnesota and in 1887 to Westport, Mo., where he now lives.

CHILDREN.

989—Willis Monroe, born February 4, 1858; married January 1, 1881, Lydia Hoffstetler.
990—Frank Delos, born July 3, 1862.
991—Hattie Deette, born December 19, 1867; died May 28, 1887.
992—Lina May, born October 1, 1871; died November 10, 1883.
993—Lena Maud, born October 1, 1871; died October 15, 1872.
994—Lilly Belle, born May 27, 1875; married December 15, 1897, Emmet Spenill, Dallas, Mo.

535.

PERRY AMIDON (Jacob,[8] Jacob,[6] Henry,[5] Henry,[4] Philip,[2] Roger[1]), born at Onondaga, N. Y., about 1840. He married Adelle Delano. They have two sons living at Cleveland, Ohio, names not given.

536.

HIRAM AMIDON (Elijah,[10] Jacob,[6] Henry,[5] Henry,[4] Philip,[2] Roger[1]), born in Onondaga County, N. Y., March 4, 1819. He was a farmer and cheesemaker and lived mostly at Hayfield and Rundell, Pa. He married, April 14, 1853, Mary Cordelia, daughter of Lewis and Martha (Curtis) Rundell. She was born August 5, 1829, and died February 3, 1893. He died at Keepville, Pa., August 24, 1890.

CHILDREN.

995—Martha K., born May 15, 1854. She married August 8, 1880, Dwight A. Curtis and lives at Northeast, Pa.
*996—Charles F., born September 10, 1856.
*997—William Harvey, born September 2, 1860.
998—Helen E., born July 21, 1863; died March 7, 1868.
999—Addie M., born September 21, 1870; she married December 7, 1892, Dallas M. DeWolf of Albion, Pa., and has
   i—Evie, born November 16, 1893.
   ii—Alice, born November 19, 1895.
   iii—Laura Estella, born August 8, 1897.
   iv—Lina Mary, born July 4, 1899.

537.

HORACE STARKWETHER AMIDON (Elijah,[10], Jacob,[6] Henry,[5] Henry,[4] Philip,[2] Roger[1]), born in Chautauqua County, N. Y., March 12, 1824. He married, August 20, 1848, Ruth E., daughter of Eliab and Ruth (Spencer) Skeel. She was born in Chautauqua County, N. Y., January 9, 1830, and died April 1, 1902. He was a farmer and lived in Hayfield, Pa., where he died November 18, 1882.

CHILDREN.

1000—Mary Elizabeth, born May 29, 1849; she married (1st) April 11, 1867, Harvey L. Carr. He died August 21, 1879, and she married (2d) William Watson. Children:
  i—Horace Eleazer, born September 13, 1868; married June 12, 1891, Nettie Stringfellow. They live at Cleveland, Ohio, and had:
    1—Dorothy, born August 14, 1896; died February 9, 1898.
  ii—David D., born June 17, 1870† married August 14, 1895, Maggie Okelf and lives at Cleveland, Ohio. His wife died January 24, 1898.
  iii—Lyman Leroy, born November 17, 1871; married June 15, 1898, Rose Urban and lives at Cleveland, Ohio.
  iv—Fred Clair, born October 8, 1874; lives at Little's Corners, Pa.
  v—Myrtle Belle, born August 24, 1876.
  vi—Harry L., born January 24, 1880; died April 1, 1882.
1001—Sarah Elmira, born July 7, 1850. She married June 22, 1875, John P. Carrier and lives at Rundell, Pa.
  i—Mary Emily, born February 11, 1877; married March 15, 1895, Jay D. Hadsell, and has:
    1—Clair Jay, born December 26, 1895.
  ii—Sylvia C., born March 25, 1883; died March 29, 1883.
  iii—Fenn W., born May 6, 1890.
1002—Lucy Belle, born May 25, 1852. She married, March 4, 1883, Joseph E. Chase, Summerhill, Pa. Children:
  i—Elsie, born September 18, 1884.
  ii—William Horace, born April 2, 1898.
1003—Lydia A., born November 3, 1853; married, October 8, 1884, David Wilson, Hayfield, Pa.
  i—Ruth Amidon, born March 29, 1886.

541.

GEORGE ROSS AMIDON (Elijah,[144] Jacob,[15] Henry,[11] Henry,[4] Philip,[2] Roger[1]), born in Chautauqua County, N. Y., November 5, 1830. He married, October 2, 1856, Lucevia Wells, daughter of John and Rachael (Trace) Cole. She was born January 26, 1832. He was a farmer and carpenter and served as sergeant in Company H, 169th Pennsylvania Regiment. He lived near Rundell, Pa., where he died December 17, 1892.

CHILDREN.

*1004—Orrin Alpheus, born July 4, 1857.
1005—Lewis Albert, born July 4, 1857; died August 10, 1857.
1006—Jenny Bell, born December 7, 1864; married, August 4, 1887, A. L. Thompson, Drakes Mills, Pa. Children:
  i—Mildred Floy, born September 17, 1888.
  ii—Leslie Lincoln, born September 23, 1890.
  iii—Mabel Elda, born September 10, 1892.
  iv—Elizabeth Gertrude, born November 20, 1894.
  v—Lena Belle, born October 20, 1901.
1007—Nettie, born November 3, 1866. She married, January 10, 1889, H. H. Devore, Coons Corners, Pa. Children:
  i—Pearl Lucevia, born October 11, 1890.
  ii—Robert George, born March 11, 1892.
  iii—Glen Hollis, born May 3, 1894.
  iv—Florence Mabel, born June 29, 1896.
  v—Forest, born December 16, 1900.
  vi—Mildred, born August 1, 1902.
*1008—John Edward, born November 25, 1870.
1009—Mae R., born December 28, 1875. She married, January 24, 1895, Eddie Doolittle of Coneaut, Ohio, and has
  i—Carl Nelson, born January 27, 1896.
  ii—Edna Lucile, born May 3, 1899.

542.

WILLIAM HARVEY AMIDON (Elijah,[148] Jacob,[46] Henry,[11] Henry[5], Philip,[2] Roger[1]), born October 9, 1833. He enlisted in September, 1861, in Company E, 111th Pennsylvania Regiment, but was discharged July, 1862, as being consumptive. In 1864 he went to Oregon, via Isthmus of Panama. He now resides at Montesano, Washington. He taught school for several years and served as probate judge. He married, February 13, 1868, Mary E. Mace.

CHILDREN.

1010—Elmer Leroy, born April 22, 1870. He married Frankie Bush and resides at Tacoma, Wash.
1011—Ossian Frank, born November 20, 1871.
1012—Sara Ella, born July 4, 1874; is a stenographer at Seattle, Wash.

544.

LEWIS RUNDELL AMIDON (Elijah,[148] Jacob,[46] Henry,[11] Henry,[5] Philip,[2] Roger[1]), born at Hayfield, Pa., May 6, 1839. He was a farmer and served for several years as justice of the peace and school director. He married (1st), July 3, 1862, Caroline, daughter of Samuel and Rosannah (Bradish) Russell. She was born in 1843 and died May 8, 1872. He married (2d), December 29, 1874, Amanda, daughter of Parker T. and Catherine (Baker) Allee. She was born in Hayfield, August 9, 1841, and died July 17, 1898. He married (3d) in 1899 Mrs. Alice Barnes. He died at Buffalo, N. Y., February 17, 1901.

CHILDREN.

1013—Gertrude, born August 19, 1863; married, December 17, 1885, J. Harry McClure, and lives at Newport, Ohio. Children:
    i—Marea, born September 3, 1890.
    ii—J. Stewart, born December 25, 1891.
*1014—Frank, born June 27, 1865.
1015—Russell, born March 27, 1872.

(Second wife.)

1016—Louise, born May 14, 1876; married, March 7, 1897, Jesse French of Mayfield, Pa., and has
    i—Dalpha Catherine, born December 7, 1897.
1017—Albert Ray, born February 13, 1878.
1018—Clifton Elmer, born March 13, 1880.
1019—Clarence, born May 31, 1883; died May 31, 1883.

545.

REV. JOHN SMITH AMIDON (Leonard,[141] Jacob,[46] Henry,[11] Henry,[5] Philip,[2] Roger[1]), born in Chautauqua County, N. Y., September 2, 1821. He married, September 4, 1882, Charlotte A. Curtis. He was for many years minister in the United Brethren Church. He died October 3, 1898, at Corry, Pa.

CHILDREN.

1020—Eugene C., lives at Corry, Pa.
1021—Nelson J., lives at Northeast, Pa.
*1022—Charles Fremont, born August 17, 1856.
1023—Fanny.
1024—Effie; married a Hopkins and has a daughter, Mary E.

546.

LORENZO D. AMIDON (Leonard,[141] Jacob,[40] Henry,[11] Henry,[4] Philip,[2] Roger[1]), born in Onondaga County, N. Y., July 7, 1823. He was a carpenter and cabinet maker and removed to Wisconsin July 10, 1848, where he married (1st), in 1850, Olive Starkwether. She died in 1874 and he married (2d), April 3, 1879, Fanny Lord, of Afton, Wis. In 1850 he moved to Brooklyn, Wis., where he died February 22, 1895.

CHILDREN.

1025—Henry, born 1852; died 1854.
*1026—William A., born August 19, 1854.
1027—Francis, born 1858; died 1860.
1028—Watson Eddy, born 1859; died young.
1029—Wilbur Eddy, born 1860; died young.
1030—Esther A., born May 18, 1864.
1031—Ella L., born June 18, 1866.
1032—Emma L., born April 3, 1868.

(Second wife.)

*1032 (a)—Gilbert, born March 31, 1880.
1032(b)—Byron, born October 10, 1881.

547.

LEWIS AMIDON (Leonard,[141] Jacob,[40] Henry,[11] Henry,[4] Philip,[2] Roger[1]), born at Clymer, N. Y., June 16, 1825. He married, March 29, 1849, Martha M., daughter of Benjamin and Hannah (Backus) Hagar. She was born May 2, 1829. He served in Company F, 152d Pennsylvania (3d Artillery) from March 7, 1863, to November, 1865. He was a farmer and lived at Clymer, where he died March 1, 1896.

CHILDREN.

*1033—Arthur A., born May 17, 1850.
1034—Alice Adell, born September 8, 1852; married, January 1, 1872, George Beebe, Clymer, N. Y., and has—
    i—Clarence, born April, 1873.
    ii—Arthur, born September, 1881.
1035—Florence L., born May 18, 1855; married, January 1, 1880, William Green. He was born in 1854, is a farmer and lives at Marvin, N. Y. Children:
    i—Earl L., born April 28, 1880.
    ii—Forrest, born May 9, 1882.
    iii—Iva B., born November 29, 1884.
    iv—Charley, born December, 1888.
    v—Ethel, born March, 1893.
1036—Benjamin Moses, born February 7, 1859; died April 27, 1894. Married, November 28, 1882, Stella Wallace.

1037—Elma Arvilla, born May 25, 1861. She married, April 20, 1879,
      William Schermerhorn. He was born September 5, 1855, and
      died June 6, 1886. She still lives at Jamestown, N. Y., and has
          i—Loyd B., born August 25, 1880; married, October 16,
             1901, Edith May Martin, and has
                 i—William Lee, born April 4, 1904.
         ii—Lyle C., born September 28, 1883.
        iii—Willard C., born July 18, 1886.
*1038—Edgar Backus, born July 2, 1862.
1039—Fred Zacus, born May 2, 1870; resides at Clymer, N. Y.

549.

WILLIAM AMIDON (Leonard,[5] Jacob,[4] Henry,[3] Henry,[2]
Philip,[1] Roger[1]), born March 12, 1830. He married, May 29, 1853,
Mary Jane, daughter of William and Mary (Griswold) Thompson. She
was born June 1, 1835. He was a farmer and member of the United
Brethren Church and lived at Clymer, N. Y. He enlisted in the 3d
Pennsylvania Heavy Artillery and died at Baltimore, Md., November,
1865. He is buried in the National Cemetery at Loudon Park, Grave
No. 1818.

CHILDREN.

1040—Mary Jeanette, born March 21, 1860. She married, July 24, 1881,
      Barnard Johann Van Braak. He died August 10, 1892. She
      lives at Jaquins, N. Y., and has
          i—Mary Bernardine, born March 21, 1883.
         ii—William Bernard, born January 21, 1885.
        iii—James Johann, born March 25, 1892.
*1041—Leonard William, born December 23, 1861.
*1042—Thompson Smith, born July 27, 1864.

550.

GEORGE J. AMIDON (Leonard,[5] Jacob,[4] Henry,[3] Henry,[2]
Philip,[1] Roger[1]), born at Clymer, N. Y., December 24, 1831. Married
(1st), August 11, 1855, Isabel J. Adams, and (2d) at Lee, Mass., 1877,
Rosa A. Roberts, of Stockbridge, Mass. He graduated at the Spen-
cerian Business College, Cleveland, Ohio, in 1878 and for several years
was a teacher of penmanship at Pittsfield, Mass. Later he was a farmer
at Northeast, Pa., and died at Brooklyn, N. Y., December 27, 1899.

CHILDREN.

1043—Edwin A., born October 27, 1857; married, June 1, 1881, Mary
      Tanner and resides at Westfield, N. Y.
*1044—Clark L., born May 21, 1859.
1045—Cassius M., born March 18, 1862; married in 1889, Nettie B.
      Jaques and resides at Cheshire, Mass.
1046—Lucy Belle, born August 7, 1868; married, December 25, 1886,
      Willie S. Lewis, Wayne, Pa. He died April 2, 1904.
1047—Geordia Alberta, born February 6, 1873; married, December 24,
      1896, James Gulliford, Erie, Pa., and died January 18, 1904.

562.

EDSON DANFORTH AMIDON (Moses,[144] Jacob,[48] Henry,[11] Henry,[5] Philip,[2] Roger[1]), born in Onondaga County, N. Y., August 14, 1834. He left Onondaga County in 1855 and went to Michigan. He served in Company B, 13th Michigan Regiment, from October 19, 1861, to August 8, 1865. He now resides at Muskegon Heights, Mich. He married, December 8, 1878, Laura Etta Henderson.

CHILDREN.

1048—Ruby Etta, born October 19, 1880.
1049—Pearl Sophia, born July 31, 1882.
1050—Harry Ray, born January 20, 1885.
1051—Elizabeth Marie, born June 14, 1887.
1052—Winnie Ruth, born December 11, 1891.

573.

HENRY NELSON AMIDON (William,[181] William,[41] Henry,[11] Henry,[5] Philip,[2] Roger[1]), born December 22, 1821. He married, May 13, 1845, Mary Ette Barker. She died in 1895. He lived at Painesville, Ohio, but now resides in Cleveland, Ohio. All of his children were college graduates.

CHILDREN.

1053—Andrew Augustus, born March 19, 1846. He died August 29, 1889. In 1871 he married Loverne Root. He was a lawyer in Painesville, Ohio.
1054—Alice A., born June 1, 1848. She married, June 25, 1868, Rev. James Calkins Cannon. She graduated from High School at Painesville and then went to Hiram College, where she graduated. She was for several years school teacher in Ohio and Mississippi. She now resides at Lakewood, Ohio.
    i—James Amidon. He is married; resides in Chicago, Ill., and has a son, James Lloyd.
    ii—Henry Levin; graduated at Adelbert College; spent a year at Harvard and now is teaching in Washington, D. C.
    iii—Nelson Augustus.
1055—Dr. Rebecca S., born April 3, 1856; resides at Cleveland, O.
1056—Nelly M., born October 8, 1857; teacher at Cleveland, Ohio.
1057—Dr. Henry Nelson, born October 3, 1858; married Vania J. Smith, and lives at Painesville, Ohio.
1058—Samuel Barker, born May 3, 1862; married, November, 1893, Alice Noyes. He is a lawyer at Wichita, Kan.

574.

WILLIAM DIGHTON AMIDON (William,[181] William,[41] Henry,[11] Henry,[5] Philip,[2] Roger[1]), born at Perry, Ohio, July 21, 1823. He married in 1848, Caroline Cotton and lived at Madison, Ohio, where he died in 1887.

CHILDREN.

1059—James ; died young.
1060—William.
1061—Nelly.
1062—Frank.
1063—Dell.

576.

JOHN ELLIOTT AMIDON (William,[111] William,[11] Henry,[11] Henry,[1] Philip,[1] Roger[1]), born at Perry, Ohio, March 26, 1828. He married in 1848 Adeline Gage and lived at Painesville, Ohio, where he died in 1894.

CHILDREN.

1064—Adeline. She married Julius Brindle and lives at Madison, O.
    i—Daisy.
    ii—Catherine.
    iii—Arthur.
1065—Catherine. She married Charles Luce of Painesville, Ohio.

577.

LUCIUS P. AMIDON (William,[111] William,[11] Henry,[11] Henry,[1] Philip,[1] Roger[1]), born at Perry, Ohio, in 1829. He married (1st), in 1851, Martha Glines Sinclair. She was born June 9, 1834, and died February 20, 1853. He married (2d), Maria Ives and resided at Perry, Ohio, where he died in 1874.

CHILDREN.

1066—Martha ; married Samuel Foster of Madison, Ohio.
    i—Wilbur.
    ii—Emma.

(Second wife.)

1067—Emma ; married Frank Montgomery, Adrian, Mich.
1068—Mary ; married Benjamin Hoskins, Geneva, Ohio.
1069—Cora ; married Charles Chapel, Ashtabula, Ohio.

578.

EDMUND SUMNER AMIDON (William,[111] William,[11] Henry,[11] Henry,[1] Philip,[1] Roger[1]), born at Perry, Ohio, May, 1831. He married (1st) Matilda Stearns, Geneva, Ohio, and (2d) Ann Richmond. He lives at Geneva, Ohio.

CHILDREN.

1070—Waldo ; died young.
1071—Ernest ; married and resides at Geneva, Ohio.
1072—Willis ; married and resides at Geneva, Ohio.
1073—Ina.

588.

EDMUND SUMNER AMIDON (Edmund Sumner,[111] William,[11] Henry,[11] Henry,[4] Philip,[2] Roger[1]), born at Sturgis, Mich., January 5, 1840. He married (1st), April 24, 1864, Esther Almeda, daughter of Alfred and Mary Ann (Hovey) Todd. She was born August 11, 1842, and died July 7, 1874. He married (2d), April 7, 1886, Harriet Birch Haffner. He served as First Sergeant in Company E, 19th Michigan Infantry, from August 8, 1862, to July 20, 1863, when he was discharged for disabilities received in the service. He resides at Sturgis, Mich. He was a member of the state legislature in 1895.

CHILDREN.

1074—Florence Almeda, born April 4, 1868; graduated from the Medical department of the University of Michigan in 1895. From 1895 to 1897 she was House Physician, Northwest Hospital, Minneapolis, Minn. She married May 19, 1898, Dr. Oscar Kelsey, son of Calvin Clinton and Frances (Kelsey) Richardson. He was born December 19, 1867, in Faystown, Vt. They reside in Minneapolis, Minn. Child:
    i—Dorothy Amidon Richardson, born August 6, 1900.
1075—Alfred Todd, born April 18, 1870. He is a printer and resides in Chicago, Ill. He married Viola Schafer.
*1076—Edmund Poyneer, born January 3, 1874.

590.

ORRIN WALLACE AMIDON (Edmund Sumner,[111] William,[11] Henry,[11] Henry,[4] Philip,[2] Roger[1]), born at Sturgis, Mich., June 5, 1843. He married, January 21, 1865, Mary Willard and lives at Elkhart, Ind.

CHILDREN.

*1077—Albro C., born November 27, 1868.
*1078—William Sumner, born July 24, 1875.

594.

GEORGE AMIDON (Gardner,[111] Henry,[11] Henry,[11] Henry,[4] Philip,[2] Roger[1]), born at Bridgeport, N. Y. He married Dorcas Bartlett and died in 1864 from exposure while serving in the army.

CHILDREN.

*1079—David R., born February 2, 1848.
1080—Walter L., born March 10, 1853.

595.

WILLIAM HENRY AMIDON (Gardner,[111] Henry,[11] Henry,[11] Henry,[4] Philip,[2] Roger[1]), born at Bridgeport, N. Y., November 29, 1825. He married, August 20, 1848, Emogene Dodge and lives at Hartford, Wis.

CHILDREN.

1081—Mary E., born March 17, 1851 ; married John Conrad.
1082—Angeline Melissa, born August 4, 1852 ; married Edward Stacy.

596.

ELISHA AMIDON (Gardner,[112] Henry,[11] Henry,[11] Henry,[3] Philip,[2] Roger[1]). He married Augusta Butler and lives at Hartford, Wis.

CHILDREN.

1083—Chester Gardner, born April 22, 1850. He married April 15, 1873, Elisa Cook and lives at Hartford, Wis.
*1084—Willard R., born April 18, 1856.
*1085—Ur, born September 10, 1859.

601.

SAMUEL GILLETT AMIDON (Asaryl,[112] Asaryl,[11] Henry,[11] Henry,[3] Philip,[2] Roger[1]), born at Belchertown, Mass., October 16, 1833. He removed to Minnesota in 1855 and married Sarah Ann McIntyre, March 2, 1857. In 1862 he served in Company B, 19th Wisconsin Volunteers. He resided at Houston, Minn., where he died April 16, 1883.

CHILDREN.

*1086—William Nelson, born December 30, 1857.
*1087—Edmund Perry, born April 4, 1865.

602.

EDWARD PERRY AMIDON (Asaryl,[112] Asaryl,[11] Henry,[11] Henry,[3] Philip,[2] Roger[1]), born at Belchertown, Mass., September 4, 1837. He married, May 10, 1860, Sophia Olive, daughter of Asa and Orlinda Shumway. She was born March 7, 1840, in Palmer, Mass. He died at Belchertown, November 12, 1874, and she now lives at Worcester, Mass.

CHILDREN.

1088— Fayette Asaryl, born July 13, 1862. He married June 16, 1895, Lucy Ella Higgins. He has a provision market in Providence, R. I., and another in Worcester, Mass., where he resides.

606.

ISAAC LEARNED AMIDON (Rufus,[112] Isaac,[11] Jeremiah,[11] Roger,[12] Philip,[2] Roger[1]), born at Dudley, Mass., March 5, 1826. He married, December 26, 1853, Jane Lydia, daughter of Milton George. He was a shoemaker in Webster.

CHILDREN.

1089—Ida Ella, born September 8, 1854; married December 23, 1889, Thomas Arthur Forsyth of Prince Edward Island.
1090—Edwin Learned, born July 6, 1856; married August 9, 1887, Alice Fletcher of Milwaukee, Wis.
1091—Eleanor Judith, born September 6, 1858; married in 1883, George F. Davis, of North Brookfield, Mass., and had a daughter, Eleanor May, born October 10, 1884.
*1092—Herbert Isaac, born August 2, 1860.
1093—Clarence Adelbert, born January 2, 1863; died January 20, 1890.
1094—Lizzie Hannah, born January 3, 1871; married June 2, 1898, Frederick Henry Lane of North Brookfield, Mass.

607.

THOMAS MORRIS AMIDON (Rufus,[18] Isaac,[11] Jeremiah,[10] Roger,[10] Philip,[2] Roger[1]), born at Dudley, Mass., August 27, 1827. He married at Worcester, August 17, 1854, Maria, daughter of Benajah and Maria Ricker. She resides at Webster, Mass.

CHILD.

1095—Emma Gertrude, born September 9, 1855; married Prentiss Leonard, in 1876 and died, leaving a daughter.

610.

FRANK AMIDON (Cyril,[12] Jeremiah,[11] Jeremiah,[10] Roger,[10] Philip,[2] Roger[1]), born at Richmond, N. H., June 16, 1837. Married (1st), January 21, 1863, Hattie, daughter of Silas and Diancy (Naramore) Whipple. She was born in 1844 and died in 1876. He married (2d), November 14, 1881, Lydia O., daughter of Calvin Barnes.

CHILDREN.

1096—Hattie J.
1097—Eney R., born May 9, 1863; died young.
1098—Emma E., born June 16, 1867; died young.

(Second wife.)

1099—Infant, born January 17, 1883.

611.

ANDREW AMIDON (Cyril,[12] Jeremiah,[11] Jeremiah,[10] Roger,[10] Philip,[2] Roger[1]), born at Richmond, N. H., February 14, 1840. He married Silvia, daughter of Zerah C. Goddard.

CHILDREN.

1100—William, born April 3, 1872.
1101—Daisy B., born July 30, 1877.

628.

RUFUS AMIDON (Abner,[1] Jedediah,[1] Samuel,[1] Roger,[1] Philip,[1] Roger[1]). He married (1st) Theresa H. Walworth, and (2d) Susie M. Gould.

CHILDREN.

*1102—John H.
1103—Anna M.; married Oscar A. Carpenter and lives at Readsboro, Vt.
      i—Effie A.; married Henry A. Ward.
      ii—John.
      iii—Judson.
      iv—Hallock.
      v—Molly.

(Second wife.)

1104—Lottie T.; married Charles Bishop. .
1105—William C.

637.

WILLIAM McKENDRE AMIDON (David,[1] Jedediah,[1] Samuel,[1] Roger,[1] Philip,[1] Roger[1]), born at Readsboro, Vt., July 17, 1834. He married in 1854 Frances Perry and lives at Millers Falls, Mass.

CHILDREN.

1106—Louisa, born May 16, 1855; married Dr. A. V. Bowker, Athol, Mass.
1107—Katie, born September 23, 1857.
1108—Anna, born November 14, 1861; married in 1884 Emory Brown (a descendant of Samuel Amidon 27).
      i—Earl Amidon.
1109—Perry, born October 24, 1868; lives at Millers Falls, Mass.

646.

LUCIUS AMIDON (Ezra,[1] Ezra,[1] Samuel,[1] Roger,[1] Philip,[1] Roger[1]). He was born November 9, 1820. He resided at Leon, N. Y., and later at South Brooklyn, Ohio.

CHILD.

1110—Truman G., born at Leon, N. Y., 1848.

652.

GEORGE LEROY AMADON (Samuel,[14] Ezra,[11] Samuel,[7] Roger,[4] Philip,[4] Roger[1]), born in Cataraugus County, N. Y., April 2, 1834. He married, April 3, 1856, Althea A., daughter of A. P. and Hannah (Champlin) Boardman. He is a farmer and lives at Waupun, Wis.

CHILDREN.

1111—Gertrude S., born April 20, 1858; married W. V. Whitney and resides at Rosendale, Mo.
1112—George W., born November 22, 1861; died May 9, 1890.
1113—John B., born May 1, 1869; died September 5, 1870.

655.

WILLIAM PERCIVAL AMADON (Henry,[14] Ezra,[11] Samuel,[7] Roger,[4] Philip,[4] Roger[1]), born at Leon, N. Y., October 14, 1843. Married, August 22, 1862, Ellen B., daughter of David H. and Betsey (Harmon) Fairbank. She was born at Pomfret, N. Y., September 12, 1845. He served as a musician in the army and was engineer for the pumping works, Waupun, Wis., where he died, March 22, 1904.

CHILDREN.

1114—Ellen Avasta.
1115—Marion Grant.

660.

CAPT. GEORGE H. AMIDON (William B.,[15] John,[14] Roger,[18] Roger,[10] Philip,[4] Roger[1]), born at Douglas, Mass., May 3, 1838. He enlisted in Company I, 4th Vermont Regiment, August 21, 1861; was promoted to Second Lieutenant January 19, 1862, and to First Lieutenant, Company G, July 19, 1862; became Captain Company E, September 23, 1862. He was wounded at the battle of the Wilderness in 1864 and again at the battle of Cedar Creek, October 17, 1864. He was breveted Major June 9, 1865, and mustered out July 13, 1865. He married, November 6, 1866, Anna M., daughter of Edwin S. and Mary (Cummings) Ball, of Dudley, Mass. He was a shoemaker and lived at Oxford, Mass., where he died January 4, 1871.

CHILD.

1116—Etta M. She married Anson Davis.

666.

ANDREW JOHN AMIDON (Russell,[111] Ralph,[108] Roger,[18] Roger,[10] Philip,[4] Roger[1]), born February 13, 1834. He married, September 2, 1854, Mary J. Reed and lives at New Lathrop, Mich.

CHILDREN.

*1117—George, born June 27, 1856.
1118—Nelly, born August 1, 1857. She married November 9, 1878, Lester Cantley, and had—
    i—Edna, born July 13, 1881.
    ii—Floyd, born March 11, 1885.
*1119—Frances Marion, born October 9, 1859.
*1120—Charles, born April 5, 1862.
*1121—William Frank, born April 19, 1863.
*1122—Henry, born October 19, 1867.

671.

MARTIN VAN BUREN AMIDON (Smith,[115] Ralph,[105] Roger,[59] Roger,[18] Philip,[5] Roger[1]), born at Hornellsville, N. Y., November 3, 1837. He married January 12, 1862, Sarah, daughter of Harry and Catherine (Brower) Head. She was born September 7, 1836. He served in Battery L, 16th N. Y. Regiment, from December 5, 1863, to August 21, 1865. He is a farmer and lives at Hornellsville, N. Y.

CHILDREN.

1123—Addie May, born April 22, 1863; married August 23, 1882, James Larrow, Hornellsville, N. Y.
1124—George Grant, born May 3, 1864; married August 25, 1883, Belle H. Jacobs.
1125—John Tyler, born December 10, 1867; married December 12, 1895, Alma Razey.
1126—Walter Caleb, born March 11, 1870.
1127—Hattie Elsie, born November 3, 1873; married June 6, 1897, Fred Bennett, Hornellsville, N. Y.
1128—Jessie Ella Bell, born December 12, 1879; married December 24, 1899, Monroe Woodworth, Hornellsville, N. Y.

672.

SOLOMON B. AMIDON (Smith,[115] Ralph,[105] Roger,[59] Roger,[18] Philip,[5] Roger[1]). He served in Company F, 86th N. Y. Regiment; was married and moved to Hoisington, Kan., where he died April 9, 1899.

CHILDREN.

1129—Arthur.
1130—Daughter.

685.

ALBERT AMIDON (Shepherd,[117] Ralph,[105] Roger,[59] Roger,[18] Philip,[5] Roger[1]), born at Hartsville, N. Y., August 23, 1840. He enlisted September 10, 1861, in Company B, 86th N. Y. Volunteers; was wounded at Gettysburg, July 2, 1863, and again at the battle of the Wilderness, May 6, 1864, his lower jaw being broken and one-half of left side jaw shot out. He receives a pension of $24 per month and lives at Purdy Creek, N. Y. He married, July 6, 1872, Prudy M. Puffer. She was born August 10, 1838.

CHILDREN.

1131—Roy Tisdale, born August 6, 1874.
1132—Fritz George, born January 23, 1876.

686.

CHARLES R. AMIDON (Shepherd,[11] Ralph,[10] Roger,[8] Roger,[4] Philip,[2] Roger[1]), born at Greenwood, N. Y., September 11, 1842. He was a merchant and served several years as supervisor and justice of the peace. He served during the war in the 6th N. Y. Cavalry. He married, February 2, 1866, Jane Webb and died at Purdy Creek, April 2, 1893.

CHILDREN.

*1133—Charles Henry, born June 28, 1867.
*1134—Ward D., born April 25, 1871.

698.

WILLIAM CROSS AMIDON (Roger,[117] Solomon,[110] Roger,[8] Roger,[4] Philip,[2] Roger[1]), born at Rowe, Mass., October 7, 1836. He married, October 8, 1856, Carrie D. Hamilton and removed to Springfield, Mass., where he was employed in the United States Armory. He died September 28, 1896.

CHILDREN.

1135—Emma Shephard, born September 29, 1857; died January 27, 1859.
1136—Herbert Roger, born August 23, 1859; died November 20, 1873.
*1137—Edgar Hamilton, born September 2, 1869.
1138—Mabel Minerva, born November 2, 1871; died February 23, 1872.

699.

JOSIAH CARPENTER AMIDON (Roger,[117] Solomon,[110] Roger,[8] Roger,[4] Philip,[2] Roger [1]), born July 14, 1840. He married, June 30, 1860, Jenny Smith Twichell and resides at Petersham, Mass. He served for a time in a Massachusetts regiment during the Civil War.

CHILDREN.

1139—Dora Emaline, born March 28, 1861; married August 25, 1876,
  Charles S. Coolidge, and has—
   i—Burt Carpenter, born May 26, 1877.
   ii—Roger Earl, born March 16, 1885.
*1140—William H., born October 30, 1863.
1141—Susan Rebecca, born October 29, 1866; married January 30, 1889,
  Louis F. Legare and has
   i—Harold A., born January 23, 1897.
*1142—Josiah Edgar, born September 4, 1868.

705.

SOLOMON HENRY AMIDON (Henry,[111] Solomon,[114] Roger,[12] Roger,[10] Philip,[6] Roger[1]), born at Rowe, Mass., July 26, 1863. Married, August 23, 1885, Viola E. Nichols (a descendant of Samuel Amidon, 27).

CHILDREN.

1143—Harry Nichols, born April 28, 1890.
1144—Earle Clifton, born August 11, 1892.
1145—Lucy Ellen, born May 20, 1895.
1146—Fred Emory, born October 6, 1897.

710.

PHILIP RUSSELL AMMIDOWN (Philip,[111] Philip,[114] Philip,[16] Ichabod,[11] Philip,[6] Roger[1]), born at Lowell, Mass., March 12, 1834. He was a merchant and lived principally in Cambridge, Mass., but died at Norwich, Conn., March 12, 1897. He married (1st) Susan Pickering, April 10, 1861, daughter of Emery and Susan (Pickering) Bemus. She died November 4, 1870, and he married (2d) April 26, 1879, Nelly Adele, daughter of David M. Bissell.

CHILDREN.

*1147—Russell Philip, born January 17, 1862.
1148—Alfred Pickering, born January 4, 1864; married December 26, 1889, Eva Raymond and lives in Boston, Mass.
1149—Alice Angie, born 1870; died 1870.

(Second wife.)

1150—Harry Russell, born 1880.

717.

OTIS AMMIDOWN (Otis,[112] John,[114] Caleb,[16] Philip,[11] Philip,[6] Roger[1]), born at Southbridge, Mass., May 7, 1809. Married (1st), October, 1837, Mrs. Lena Sayles, daughter of Paul T. and Lilis Kimball, of Stockbridge, Mass. She died July 11, 1838, and he married (2d) Anna Lovejoy Chaffee. He removed to Gilsun, N. H., in 1838, and in 1851 to Westmoreland, N. H., where he died July 18, 1888.

CHILDREN.
(Second wife.)

*1151—Amasa Otis, born December 31, 1843.
1152—Eldridge Putnam, born May 11, 1846.
1153—Sarah Anna, born February 3, 1848; died August 28, 1897; married April 22, 1871, Horatio S. Black. They had:
    1—Frank Sumner, born March 11, 1874; died September 22, 1881.
1154—George Washington, born May 8, 1850; died May 17, 1864.
1155—Abbie Stella, born at Willington, Conn., May 12, 1852; died Southbridge, Mass., August 17, 1854.
1156—Callina Morse, born Southbridge, Mass., Feb. 28, 1855; lives at East Westmoreland, N. H.

718.

ELBRIDGE AMMIDOWN (Otis,[8] John,[6] Caleb,[5] Philip,[4] Philip,[2] Roger[1]), born at Southbridge, Mass., in 1813 and died there October 28, 1891. He married Mary Jane Eddy, who was born November 28, 1833, and died May 10, 1902.

CHILD.

1156 (a)—Edward Cleveland, born November 15, 1859.

721.

MERRICK AMMIDOWN (Lewis,[6] John,[5] Caleb,[4] Philip,[3] Philip,[2] Roger[1]), born at Southbridge, Mass., December 21, 1823; married, April 11, 1843, Lucy Ann Cheney, of Auburn, Mass. She died at Denver, Col., September 18, 1899. He kept a hotel and grocery in Providence, Rhode Island, until 1861 and later removed to Eustis, Neb., where he died February 5, 1895.

CHILDREN.

1157—Frank Lewis, born October 14, 1845; died September 22, 1861.
*1158—Charles Merrick, born September 6, 1861.

722.

ANDROS AMMIDOWN (Lewis,[6] John,[5] Caleb,[4] Philip,[3] Philip,[2] Roger[1]), born at Southbridge, Mass., October 27, 1828. He married, February 8, 1851, Susan E. Brown, of Newton, Mass. She was born April 8, 1830, and died in Southbridge, February 27, 1879. He lived at Milford, Mass.

CHILDREN.

1159—Herbert Munro, born September 14, 1853 ; died December 31, 1853.
1160—Emma Celinda, born February 16, 1860 ; died May 6, 1864.
*1161—Eugene Lewis, born May 29, 1869.

729.

GEORGE ANGELL AMMIDOWN (Adolphus,⁶⁸⁸ John,¹¹⁴ Caleb,⁴⁹ Philip,¹⁸ Philip,⁶ Roger¹), born July 15, 1835. He married, November 9, 1857, Maryetta, daughter of Isaac Prouty, of Worcester. He was a shoemaker at Southbridge, Mass.

CHILD.

1162—Etta Marla, born January 3, 1859.

731.

MARCUS MORTON AMMIDOWN (Adolphus,⁶⁸⁸ John,¹¹⁴ Caleb,⁴⁹ Philip,¹⁸ Philip,⁶ Roger¹), born at Southbridge, Mass., February 17, 1840. He lived for a while at Worcester and then removed to Boston, where he now resides at 4345 Washington Street. He is a machinist and inventor. He married, May 2, 1873, Matilda Elizabeth Higgins. She was born May 2, 1858, in Montreal, Canada.

CHILDREN.

1163—Albert Morton, born February 9, 1874 ; married June 29, 1896,
      Edith Reed. He graduated from the English High School and
      is at present a civil engineer.
1164—Lillian Gertrude, born July 15, 1876 ; died November 1, 1895.
1165—Eva Blossom, born May 20, 1879 ; a graduate of Mount Holyoke
      College.
1166—Edward Holmes, born May 9, 1882.
1167—Mabel Marlon, born March 9, 1885.
1168—Blanch Maude, born January 6, 1888.
1169—Walter Lewis, born April 8, 1890.
1170—Louis Vinton, born August 31, 1892.
1171—George Leslie, born January 3, 1897.

734.

LUTHER SHUMWAY AMMIDOWN (Luther,⁶⁶¹ Luther,¹⁸⁸ Caleb,⁴⁹ Philip,¹⁸ Philip,⁶ Roger¹), born at Southbridge, Mass., June 23, 1822. He was a merchant in that place and died January 16, 1897. He married, November 22, 1843, Mary Lucy, daughter of John and Lucy (Stone) Russell. She was born May 17, 1823.

CHILDREN.

1172—Albert Holmes, born August 7, 1846. He graduated from Harvard
    College in 1868 and is a lawyer at 206 Broadway, N. Y. He
    resides at Orange, N. J.
1173—Mary Adelaide, born February 4, 1852; married June 1, 1872, E.
    H. Ammidown, 743.

736.

LUCIUS HOLDRIDGE AMMIDOWN (Holdridge,[''''] Luther,[''''] Caleb,[''] Philip,['] Philip,[*] Roger[1]), born at Southbridge, Mass., May 31, 1821. He was a silversmith and died at Southbridge, Mass., in 1853. He married Jane, daughter of Lewis Ammidown (344), September 27, 1842. She died in Southbridge, November 26, 1898.

CHILD.

*1174—Lucius Edwin, born September 9, 1852.

743.

EDWARD HOLMES AMMIDOWN (Holmes,[''''] Luther,[''''] Caleb,[''] Philip,['] Philip,[*] Roger[1]), born at Southbridge, Mass., October 28, 1830. He graduated from Harvard in 1853; was in business in New York City for several years and now resides in Seattle, Wash. He married, June 1, 1872, Mary Adelaide Ammidown (1173).

CHILDREN.

1175—Russell Hodges, born June 18, 1873; died June 10, 1874.
1176—Philip Holmes, born May 13, 1875.

750.

LT. MALCOLM AMMIDOWN (Ebenezer Davis,[''''] Calvin,[''''] Caleb,[''] Philip,['] Philip,[*] Roger[1]), born at Southbridge, Mass., February 15, 1827. He attended the schools in his native town and in 1850 went to Oregon, where he remained two years, locating at Salem and being employed as a surveyor by the U. S. government. In 1852 he returned to Southbridge and the year 1853 was spent at Charlton in the employ of the Boston and Albany railroad. Again returning to Southbridge he engaged in farming for several years, when in company with his brother, Henry C., purchased the Columbian Mills. In 1860 was elected Selectman and served until his enlistment, July 6, 1862, in Company H, 34th Massachusetts Regiment, of which company he was elected second Lieutenant. The citizens of Stockbridge presented him with a handsome sword, belt and sash. He served with his company until the battle of Newmarket, May 15, 1864, when he was taken prisoner. He died of yellow fever at Charleston, S. C., October 1, 1864. Malcolm

Ammidown Post, No. 168, G. A. R., of Southbridge, was named in his honor. He married, January 13, 1858, Mary Louise, daughter of Grosvenor and Fanny (Walker) Lamb. She was born August 3, 1837, and died September 2, 1894.

CHILDREN.

1177 —Fanny Lamb, born October 13, 1858.
1177(a)—Ebenezer Davis, born July 24, 1860.
1177(b)—Lucian Malcolm, born January 5, 1863 ; died September 18, 1870.

753.

HENRY CLAY AMMIDOWN (Ebenezer Davis,[169], Calvin,[124] Caleb[17], Philip[15], Philip[6], Roger[1]), born at Southbridge, Mass., November 7, 1833. He married, July 1, 1857, Mary Towne, daughter of Liberty and Catherine (Thurston) Litchfield. She was born in Oxford, February 22, 1833, and now resides in Boston, Mass.

He was for a time with the firm of Blanchard, Converse & Co., of Boston, and later was superintendent of the Central Manufacturing Co., of Stockbridge. He was associated with his brother Malcolm in the Columbian Mills, becoming the sole owner after the death of his brother. Later he sold this property and engaged in the manufacture of spectacles. He died while on a visit for his health at Guilford Center, Vt., June 28, 1869.

CHILDREN.

1178—Catherine Helen, born June 26, 1858 ; married September 8, 1880, Dr. Henry Fiske Leonard. He resides in Boston, and is a professor in Harvard University. They have a son, Edward Henry, born May 4, 1884.
1178(a)—Mary Jeannette, born July 10, 1862 ; died October 25, 1862.

756.

JOHN PERRY AMMIDON (Jonathan P.,[144] Cyrus,[149] Joseph,[45] Philip,[15] Philip,[6] Roger[1]), born at Southbridge, Mass., July 24, 1829. He moved to Lowell, Mass., in 1847, where he was engaged in business for several years, but is now a merchant in Baltimore, Md. For more than thirty years he has been a ruling elder in the Presbyterian Church. He married, June 17, 1851, Sarah E., daughter of Clark and Lucy (Dane) Crombie. She was born at New Boston, N. H., August 26, 1829.

CHILDREN.

1179—Lizzie Crombie, born January 22, 1853 ; died January 28, 1862.
1180—Daniel Clark, born January 28, 1857.
1181—John P., born April 13, 1864 ; died April 18, 1870.
1182—Frederick Brooks, born December 13, 1869 ; died June 29, 1870.

766.

OTIS AMIDON (Philip,[111] Philip,[141] Joseph,[46] Philip,[13] Philip,[5] Roger[1]), born in Batavia, N. Y., December 24, 1823. He married, October 7, 1847, Grace Cooley. She was born May 5, 1820, in Yates county, N. Y. He was a farmer and lived in Pembroke, N. Y., where he died September 29, 1864.

CHILDREN.

1183—Sarah A., born July 5, 1848; died July 30, 1848.
1184—Mary J., born March 3, 1850; married December 23, 1875, Julius Inglasbee and had
    i—Frank, born September 14, 1876.
    ii—Eugene, born January 26, 1878.
1185—George E., born June 11, 1852.
1186—Alice J., born September 28, 1855.
1187—Elmer O., born April 9, 1861.

770.

MARVIN CHILD AMIDON (Philip,[111] Philip,[141] Joseph,[46] Philip,[13] Philip,[5] Roger[1]), born May 24, 1832, in Pembroke, N. Y. He married, October 26, 1854, Susan Fishell. She was born October 25, 1835. They live at Pembroke, N. Y.

CHILDREN.

1188—Frank, born February 5, 1858; married November 1, 1878, Emma Tucker.
1189—John, born November 28, 1871.

772.

ALBERT AMIDON (Philip,[111]. Philip,[141] Joseph,[46] Philip,[13] Philip,[5] Roger[1]), born January 2, 1837. Married, March 12, 1868, Nancy Baker. She was born February 4, 1852. They lived at Pembroke, N. Y.

CHILDREN.

1190—Bertie, born May 24, 1869.
1191—Warren E., born March 26, 1871.
1192—Vesta P., born October, born October 24, 1876.

775.

CYRUS P. AMIDON (Philip,[111] Philip,[141] Joseph,[46] Philip,[13] Philip,[5] Roger[1]), born May 19, 1845. He married, October 10, 1867, Mary Brown. She was born June 20, 1848.

CHILD.

1193—Nelly, born July 15, 1868.

776.

ALFONSO AMIDON (Cyrus,[177] Joseph,[144] Joseph,[48] Philip,[13] Philip,[4] Roger[1]), born at North Parma, N. Y., January 14, 1831. He married, December 16, 1850, Sarah Jennings. She was born January 20, 1832. They lived at Albion, Mich., where he died May 23, 1892.

CHILDREN.

1194—Estella, born September 20, 1853; died July 12, 1854.
1195—Adelmar, born May 14, 1855; married July 29, 1884, Lizzie Cook. lives at Albion, Mich.
1196—Sarah Uretta, born August 24, 1857; married June 30, 1881, Martin Burns and has
    i—Floyd, born 1883.
    ii—Willie, born 1888.
1197—Bell, born April 16, 1861; married December 11, 1880, Fred Fox.
    i—Charles, born 1881.
    ii—Fred, born 1884.
    iii—Blanche, born 1887.
    iv—Robert, born 1889.
    v—Hiller, born 1896.
1198—Mattie, born September 1, 1866; married September 12, 1888, Robert Staples. They have:
    i—Perry, born 1890.
    ii—Lawrence, born 1895.
1199—Grace, born August 11, 1874; died August 24, 1874.

780.

GEORGE W. AMIDON (Cyrus,[177] Joseph,[144] Joseph,[48] Philip,[13] Philip,[4] Roger[1]), born at North Parma, N. Y., June 13, 1838. In 1860 he went to California and worked in the mines until 1873. Since then he has been a commercial traveler and in 1897 was located at Portland, Ore.

CHILDREN.

1200—Cyrus S., born November 27, 1858; went to California in 1875 and in 1897 was a merchant at Alameda, Cal.
1201—H. Boyd, born November 19, 1875, at San Jose, Cal.; in 1897 was a student in the university at Alameda, Cal.

794.

WARREN W. AMIDON (Dexter,[181] Joseph,[144] Joseph,[48] Philip,[13] Philip,[4] Roger[1]), born at North Parma, N. Y., June 8, 1852. He married, February 4, 1874, Olivia Lawrence. He is a farmer and lives at Hilton, N. Y.

CHILD.

1202—Fay W., born at North Parma, January 13, 1878; graduated from the Brockport Normal School and is engaged in teaching.

795.

OSCAR C. AMIDON (Dexter,[191] Joseph,[144] Joseph,[49] Philip,[18] Philip,[4] Roger[1]), born at North Parma, N. Y., November 21, 1854. He married, October 27, 1881, Hattie A. Slade and resides at Hilton, N. Y.

CHILDREN.

1203—Merle D., born April 14, 1885.
1204—Gladys L., born July 27, 1892.

799.

CHARLES ELDRIDGE AMIDON (Isaac Clark,[199] Rufus,[144] Reuben,[41] Philip,[13] Philip,[4] Roger[1]), born at Groton, Conn., December 1, 1845. He removed to Mauch Chunk, Pa., in September, 1862. From June 30 to August 10, 1863, he was a member of Company A, 34th Regiment, Pennsylvania Militia. He married, October 16, 1877, Ada, daughter of Elwen and Sarah Ann (Leslie) Dauer, of Lehighton, Pa. She was born October 12, 1853. He now resides at 3307 North Sixteenth Street, Philadelphia, Pa. He is an elder in the Presbyterian Church and is connected with the general office of the Lehigh Valley Coal Company.

CHILD.

1205—Herbert Elwen, born January 14, 1882.

809.

JAMES ORLANDO AMADON (John,[197] Josiah,[146] Philip,[47] Ephraim,[14] Philip,[4] Roger[1]), born at Fitzwilliam, N. H., September 10, 1842. He enlisted, April 25, 1861, in the 2d N. H. Regiment. He married, March 2, 1871, Susie Bryant, and lived at Keene, N. H., for a time, and later at New London, Conn.

CHILDREN.

1206—Robert S., born August 24, 1872.
1207—Mary Lulie, born September 10, 1874; married, July 30, 1898, Charles W. Herrington, and died at Peterboro, N. H., January 23, 1904.
1208—Henry H., born August 13, 1876.
1209—Annie K., born February 11, 1878.
1210—James G., born January 18, 1881.
1211—Fred P., born November 17, 1882.

810.

HENRY JOSIAH AMADON (John,[107] Josiah,[100] Philip,[47] Eph-raim,[14] Philip,[5] Roger[1]), born at Fitzwilliam, N. H., March 18, 1844. He served in Company F, 6th Regiment, N. H. Volunteers, from November 28, 1861, to November 27, 1864. He was wounded at Spottsylvania, in May, 1864. During his term of service he was engaged in 23 battles and was one of the few who survived the wreck of the steamer West Point on the Potomac. He died July 27, 1867.

811.

FRANK EDWARD AMADON (John,[107] Josiah,[100] Philip,[47] Eph-raim,[14] Philip,[5] Roger[1]), born at Richmond, N. H., July 30, 1847. He served from March 1, 1865, to July 29, 1865, in Company I, 18th N. H. Regiment. He married, November 4, 1872, Sarah Agnes Wright. She was born February 15, 1851, at Keene, N. H. They lived for a time in Troy, N. H., but now at Keene.

CHILD.

1212—Howard John, born May 24, 1880.

812.

CHARLES H. AMADON (John, Josiah, Philip, Ephraim, Philip, Roger), born at Fitzwilliam, N. H., November 3, 1848. He enlisted in the 1st N. H. Cavalry Regiment as a waiter for Col. Edwards, in May, 1864, and served near Richmond and in the Shenandoah Valley under Generals Custer and Sheridan. He was mustered out July 13, 1865. His life at sea began in 1867, since which time he has been constantly in the service, either in the navy or in the merchant marine. His first service was on the United States ship Onward. After his term of enlistment on that vessel he went into the merchant service, where he remained for 10 years, visiting India, China and South America and other countries. He again enlisted in the navy and has served continually for 20 years. He was on the Hartford, Admiral Farragut's flagship, going to the Pacific, through the straits of Magellan, taking a scientific party to the Caroline Islands to study an eclipse. He was then transferred to the Alert, which made a trip to China, where he remained for quite a time. He was stationed on the Vandalia, but a day before that vessel started for Samoa, where it was wrecked in a hurricane, he was transferred to the Mohican, which took him to Mare Island. He was soon transferred to the Adams, which vessel was sent to Samoa, after the wreck of the Vandalia. In 1891 he joined the Olympia, when she first went into commission, and continued on that vessel until after the capture of Manila. During the battle at Manila he was in charge of the 8-inch magazine forward. The temperature of that room was 140 degrees. He spoke in the greatest terms of admiration for Admiral Dewey. After his return from Manila in 1900 he was assigned to the Wabash.

814.

GEORGE FREDERICK AMADON (John,[111] Josiah,[100] Philip,[8] Ephraim,[14] Philip,[6] Roger [1]), born at Fitzwilliam, N. H., May 11, 1857. He married, June 12, 1879, Clara C. Webber, and lives at South Framingham, Mass.

CHILDREN.

1213 —Paul Herbert, born March 31, 1881.
1214 —Frederick Webber, born July 21, 1883.
1215 —Helen Louise, born March 25, 1887.
1216 —John J. Herald, born May 9, 1889.
1217 —Frank Philip, born October 21, 1894.
1217½—Elizabeth Lucinda, born January 17, 1902.

821.

ELIAL THOMPSON AMADON (Elial,[401] Titus,[172] Ithamar,[89] Ithamar,[15] Philip,[6] Roger[1]), born at Wilbraham, Mass., May 13, 1817. In 1844 he was at Springfield, Mass., where he married, August 6, 1844, Julia M., daughter of Jesse and Rachael Collins. She was born in 1824. He later removed to Illinois, where he was a farmer and served for a time in an Illinois regiment. He died at Caeldonia, Ill., February 21, 1862.

CHILDREN.

1218—Charles, born December 2. 1850.
1219—William Fisher, born July 13. 1852.

826.

WILLIAM WILLARD AMADON (Titus,[411] Titus,[172] Ithamar,[89] Ithamar,[15] Philip,[6] Roger[1]), born at Springfield, Mass., November 24, 1835. He was a druggist in Springfield for several years, when his health failing he moved to West Springfield, where he still resides, engaged in market gardening. He married, April 26, 1859, Frances A., daughter of William Bordurtha. She was born May 2, 1836; died February 9, 1899.

CHILDREN.

1220—Fred A., born September, 1862; died young.
1221—Ada B., born 1863; married in 1882 R. W. Cartter, West Springfield, Mass.

830.

CHARLES L. AMIDON (Samuel Dexter,[411] Titus,[172] Ithamar,[89] Ithamar,[15] Philip,[6] Roger[1]), born at Palmer, Mass., September 16, 1830. He married, November 22, 1858, Mrs. Jeanette Brown, and resided at Monson, Mass. He served from February 10, 1864, to July 25, 1865, in the 12th Massachusetts Battery.

CHILD.

1222—Fred C., born May 22, 1870; married Grace Chapman and lives at Lowell, Mass.

833.

HENRY M. AMIDON (Samuel Dexter,[11] Titus,[11] Ithamar,[11] Ithamar,[11] Philip,[4] Roger[1]), born at Palmer, Mass., in 1839. He married, May 24, 1856, Martha A. Glazier, of Leverett, Mass. He was a farmer at Amherst and died in the army, August 26, 1864. His widow afterward married Charles Williams.

CHILD.

1223—Harriet E., born 1864; died July, 1866.

837.

LUCIEN EDGAR AMADON (Samuel D.,[11] Titus,[11] Ithamar,[11] Ithamar,[11] Philip,[4] Roger[1]), born in Wilbraham, Mass., March 20, 1848. He married, August 1, 1868, Mary Jane Clay, and died April 19, 1886.

CHILDREN.

1224—Henry Clinton, born June 23, 1869; died December 19, 1889.
1225—Edwin Titus, born March 10, 1872. He served in Battery I, First Massachusetts Artillery, in the Spanish War in 1898, and now resides at Brockton, Mass.
*1226—Samuel Elliott, born May 15, 1874.
1227—Clara May Rowena, born May 1, 1878; lives at Warren, Mass.
1228—Charles Carpenter, born November 22, 1881; died December 18, 1884.

843.

REV. SANFORD NEWTON AMIDON (Abiram,[11] John,[11] Ithamar,[11] Ithamar,[11] Philip,[4] Roger[1]), born at East Windsor, Conn., July 4, 1823. He married, April 4, 1847, Elizabeth Ann, daughter of Oliver and Sarah (Pierson) Nichols. She was born November 27, 1828, at Glastonbury, Conn. He was a minister of the M. E. Church for many years, and lived at 7 Sylvan Avenue, New Haven, Conn., where he died April 28, 1901.

CHILDREN.

1229—Celia Ann, born January 4, 1848; died March 30, 1850.
1230—Martha Jane, born August 4, 1849; died September 29, 1850.
1231—Orrin Philander, born March 16, 1852; died May 6, 1862.
1232—Marcus William, born May 16, 1857; drowned at sea April 21, 1876.
1233—Sarah Emma, born July 27, 1866. She taught school for several years, but is now a stenographer and resides at New Haven, Conn.

849.

JOHN RICHARD AMIDON (John,[49] John,[17] Ithamar,[5] Ithamar,[14] Philip,[6] Roger[1]), born at Ellington, Conn., February 8, 1837. He married, April 14, 1859, Mary C. Tiffany, Southbridge, Mass. He was a traveling salesman and lived for some time at Toledo, O.

CHILD.

1234—Salem Richard, born March 2, 1860.

853.

JEROME F. AMIDON (John,[49] John,[17] Ithamar,[5] Ithamar,[14] Philip,[6] Roger[1]), born at Ellington, Conn., August 8, 1844. He married, March 17, 1866, Martha (or Maryetta), daughter of Henry and Hannah Bliss, of North Woodstock, Conn. He died May 14, 1867, at Hubbardstown, Mass.

CHILDREN.

1235—John J. F., born August 25, 1866, in Dudley, Mass.
1236—Ella Estella, born October 14, 1867, at Woodstock.

855.

JULIUS M. AMIDON (John,[49] John,[17] Ithamar,[5] Ithamar,[14] Philip,[6] Roger[1]), born at Ellington, Conn., November 3, 1853. He married, December 4, 1884, at Worcester, Mass., Fanny M. Clark. He is a farmer and lives at North Woodstock, Conn.

CHILD.

1237—Walter J., born October 27, 1885, in Worcester, Mass.

859.

ANSEL LYMAN AMADON (Philander,[49] Ansel,[17] Ebenezer,[5] Ithamar,[14] Philip,[6] Roger[1]), born at Pownal, Vt., October 14, 1829. He married at North Adams, Mass., January 1, 1852, Nancy Maria, daughter of David and Maria (Stearns) Caneday. She was born at Buffalo, N. Y., December 5, 1834, and now resides at North Adams. He served in Company M, 1st Massachusetts Heavy Artillery, from 1863 until his death, April 2, 1865.

CHILDREN.

1238—Nelly Maria, born March 11, 1854; married January 1, 1881, Fred J. Harrington.
    i—Everett A., born April 18, 1883, at North Adams.
1239—Lillian Marble, born September 19, 1856; married September 15, 1886, Ira S. Ball. He was born March 30, 1851, at Lee, Mass. He is a telegraph operator. Children:
    i—Marion Helena, born January 10, 1889.
    ii—Raymond Henry, born November 20, 1890.
    iii—Edward Calf, born April 11, 1892.
    iv—Howard Ira, born May 9, 1894.
1240—Moses Leoland, born August 4, 1861; married October 31, 1891, Mary Adeline Connig. She was born at Clinton, Mass., April 23, 1863. He is a bookkeeper at North Adams, Mass.

860.

GEORGE AUGUSTUS AMADON (Philander,[7] Ansel,[6] Ebenezer,[5] Ithamar,[4] Philip,[2] Roger[1]), born at North Adams, Mass., January 1, 1831. Married, June 4, 1863, Emeline, daughter of Martin and Elizabeth (Wilkinson) Miller. She was born June 1, 1839, at Poestenkil, N. Y. He is a carpenter and lives at North Adams, Mass.

CHILDREN.

*1241—Wilford Philander, born November 3, 1866.
1242—Elmer Martin, born March 11, 1875.

862.

LELAND MORGAN AMIDON (Philander,[7] Ansel,[6] Ebenezer,[5] Ithamar,[4] Philip,[2] Roger[1]), born at Pownal, Vt., October 7, 1836. He removed to Wisconsin and enlisted, September 7, 1861, in Company G, 10th Regiment, Wisconsin Infantry, and re-enlisted December 7, 1863. He was appointed Corporal, July 1, 1864, and November 5, 1864, was transferred to Company D, 21st Wisconsin Infantry. December 29, 1864, he was appointed Sergeant and transferred to the 3d Wisconsin Regiment. He was mustered out July 18, 1865. He married, June 11, 1870, at Irving, Wis., Sarah M., daughter of George and Debbey (Snider) Calkins. She was born March 25, 1852. They live at Melrose, Wisconsin.

CHILDREN.

1243—Ida Samantha, born May 2, 1872; died May 14, 1880.
*1244—Tenney D., born September 7, 1876. See last page.

863.

LEWIS FRANKLIN AMADON (Philander,[7] Ansel,[6] Ebenezer,[5] Ithamar,[4] Philip,[2] Roger[1]), born at North Adams, Mass., December 20, 1838. He married, October 12, 1865, Lucy Elizabeth, daughter of Andrew and Jane (Bowen) Cook. She was born at Middle Granville, N. Y., October 28, 1841. He enlisted in the 10th Massachusetts Infantry, Company B, and afterward served in Company L, 1st Massachusetts Cavalry. He was wounded at the battle of Fair Oaks in 1862 and again at the battle of the Wilderness in 1864. He was a prisoner in Libby Prison for five months. He is a farmer at North Adams and has served as a member of the City Council.

CHILD.

1245—Lena Mehitable, born July 31, 1866; married August 21, 1890, Edward Kendrick Jones.

865.

CHARLES FOWLER AMADON (Philander,[***] Ansel,[***] Ebenezer,[**] Ithamar,[**], Philip,[*] Roger[1]), born at North Adams, Mass., April 15, 1854. He resided at Nashua, N. H., but is now at Cleveland, Ohio. He married, April 5, 1882, Maud Lillie, daughter of Henry A. and Ann (Walker) Tower. She was born at North Adams, Mass., July 12, 1865.

CHILDREN.

1246—Clarence Henry, born June 3, 1885.
1247—Florence May, born December 15, 1886.

869.

FRANCIS ELDRIDGE AMADON (Ansel,[***] Ansel,[***] Ebenezer,[**] Ithamar,[**] Philip,[*] Roger[1]), born November 15, 1840. He married, September 19, 1864, Eliza Ann, daughter of John J. and Emily Amelia (Ford) Greenslet. She was born November 5, 1840, at Bennington, Vt.

CHILDREN.

1248—George Frank, born October 8, 1866; died September 8, 1886.
1249—Lura Hattie, born January 26, 1869; married September 18, 1898, Jay Potter Armstrong, Bennington, Vt. He is a carpenter and lived in Troy, N. Y., 1873, but removed to Bennington, Vt.
1250—Jenny Carpenter, born September 14, 1871; married January 20, 1894, Isaac Henry Sanborn, Jr., of Bennington, Vt., and has—
   i—Richard Wall, born July 21, 1895.
   ii—Dorothy Esther, born June 2, 1898.
   iii—Mary Alice, born February 7, 1902.
1251—Alice Belle, born July 22, 1875; married March 20, 1895, Joseph Stockwell, Jr. They live at Bennington, Vt., and have—
   i—Frank Everett, born January 3, 1896.
   ii—Rodney Joseph, born August 5, 1899.
   iii—Oliver Bernard, born November 29, 1901.
   iv—Raymond Ansel, born July 23, 1903.
1252—Emily Ford, born April 4, 1878; married January 27, 1904, Simeon F. Crosier, Pownal, Vt.

873.

LOYAL RICHARD AMADON (Richard Flynn,[418] Ansel,[177] Ebenezer,[44] Ithamar,[18] Philip,[4] Roger[1]), born at Lawrence, N. Y., June 21, 1837. He removed to Fergus Falls, Minn., in 1881. In 1898 he removed to Bennettville, Minn. He married, July 5, 1863, Martha H., daughter of Almon A. and Fanny M. (Clough) Fisk.

CHILDREN.

*1252—Fulton V., born November 29, 1863.
  1254—Lettie, born August 28, 1868 ; married January 1, 1884, William
     J. Farrell, Fergus Falls, Minn.
      i—William Amadon, born May 22, 1885.
      ii—Victor, born April 9, 1887.
      iii—Helen Beatrice, born February 10, 1889.
  1255—Guy S., born January 21, 1877

883.

CHRISTOPHER MASON AMADON (Henry P.,[414] Ansel,[177] Ebenezer,[44] Ithamar,[18] Philip,[4] Roger[1]), born at Pownal, Vt., September 15, 1846. He married, February 24, 1869, Abby Serina Morgan.

CHILDREN.

  1256—Rachel Ella, born February 28, 1873 ; died November 15, 1877.
*1257—Egbert Henry, born November 24, 1876.
*1258—Benjamin Franklin, born August 15, 1879. See last page.
  1259—Henry, born July 10, 1886.

885.

HERBERT PERRY AMADON (Henry P.,[414] Ansel,[177] Ebenezer,[44] Ithamar,[18] Philip,[4] Roger[1]), born at Pownal, Vt., November 4, 1858. He married, April 7, 1880, Freelove Kimball.

CHILDREN.

  1260—Florence Luella, born March 12, 1881 ; died March 22, 1884.
  1261—Mina Eliza, born May 18, 1886.
  1262—Lorena Louisa, born June 26, 1889.

886.

ERNEST ALEXANDER AMADON (Samuel,[414] Ansel,[177] Ebenezer,[44] Ithamar,[18] Philip,[4] Roger[1]), born August 23, 1844. He married, January, 1865, Harriet Augusta, daughter of Roger and Maria (Douchey) Flood. She was born February 18, 1849. They lived at Lowell, Mass.

CHILDREN.

1263—Roger A. Flood, born May 16, 1866; died February 15, 1895.
1264—Bessie Alice, born April 19, 1870; married at Bennington, July
      28, 1891; Edward S. Parmenter, and has—
          i—Raymond, born January, 1898.
1265—Samuel Edgar, born August 7, 1872.
1266—Alene Harriet, born July 22, 1875.

889.

DR. ARTHUR FRANK AMADON (Franklin Perry,[111] Ansel,[177] Ebenezer,[44] Ithamar,[15] Philip,[8] Roger[1]), born at Pownal, Vt., September 10, 1858. He graduated from Williams College in 1881 and from Dartmouth Medical School in 1891. He married, November 25, 1886, Mary E. Whitcombe, of Boston, Mass. He then removed to Springfield, Mo., where his three children were born. After teaching at Monson and Pepperell, Mass., and Putnam, Conn., and as professor of mathematics, Drury College, Springfield, Mo., he began the practice of medicine in Boston, Mass., residing in Melrose, Mass.

CHILDREN.

1267—Arthur Franklin, born November 14, 1887.
1268—Ruth, born February 20, 1889.
1269—Frank Whitcombe, born January 17, 1891.

891.

DR. ALFRED MASON AMADON (Franklin Perry,[111] Ansel,[177] Ebenezer,[44] Ithamar,[15] Philip,[8] Roger[1]), born at North Adams, Mass., May 21, 1867. He graduated from Williams College in 1889 and from Dartmouth Medical School in 1897. He taught at Monson and Williamstown, Mass., and was professor of mathematics at Purdue University, Lafayette, Ind. He married, October 12, 1899, Bertha B. Smith, Hanover, Conn., and settled in Dorcester, Mass., for the practice of medicine.

CHILD.

1269a—Bertha Smith, born May 8, 1901.

893.

JOHN EDWIN AMIDON (Philip,[448] John,[144] John,[44] John,[14] Philip,[8] Roger[1]), born at Braintree, Mass., November 1, 1850. He married, December 19, 1875, Lucy J. Lamb. He lived at Braintree in 1897.

CHILDREN.

1270—Elmer Warner, born March 15, 1877.
1271—Carrie May, born April 8, 1880.

902.

JOHN RICKERT AMIDON (Henry,[***] Henry,[***] Jedediah,[*] Henry,[**] Henry,[*] Philip,[*] Roger[1]), born at Mottville, Mich., May 29, 1840. He accompanied his parents to Dubuque in 1846 and in 1855 he went to Shullsburg, Wis. He served four and one-half years in the 3d Wisconsin Regiment. He removed to St. Paul, Minn., where he married, February 15, 1872, Nancy, daughter of Caleb and Clarissa Potwin. She was born at Shullsburg, Wis., June 16, 1839. He spent the winter of 1872 at Blairstown, Ia., and in November, 1873, removed to Cedar Rapids, Ia., where he now resides and is a banker.

CHILDREN.

1272—Clara Bell, born December 31, 1872; died March, 1873.
1273—Mary Irene, born December 1, 1874. She graduated from the University of Michigan in 1898.
1274—Kitty, died young.
1275—Helen Bertha, born May 19, 1882.

905.

CHARLES SANFORD AMIDON (Gilbert E. S.,[***] Horatio,[***] Jedediah,[**] Henry,[**] Henry,[*] Philip,[*] Roger[1]), born at Willington, Conn., November 9, 1869. He married Alice May Holt and has

CHILDREN.

1276—Raymond Holt, born February 20, 1896.
1277—Frank Rupert, born February 13, 1897.
1278—Mildred Julia, born May 10, 1899.

914.

IRA W. AMIDON (Samuel,[***] Nathaniel,[***] Moses,[**] Henry,[**] Henry,[*] Philip,[*] Roger[1]), born at Plymouth, Ohio, August 9, 1839. He married, March 10, 1864, Laura A. Klumph and is a merchant at Ashtabula, Ohio.

CHILDREN.

1279—Florence A., born January 21, 1866; married October 3, 1888, Frank W. Wagner, and resides at Ashtabula, Ohio.
1280—Anna L., born October 13, 1869; married June 17, 1891, Fred K. Lewis, of Ashtabula, Ohio.
1281—Samuel I., born May 7, 1871; died August 16, 1900.

918.

WILLIAM FRANKLIN AMEDON (Nathaniel William,[478] Nathaniel,[298] Moses,[77] Henry,[21] Henry,[9] Philip,[4] Roger[1]), born at Hebron,. N. Y., September 13, 1848. He married, in May, 1871, Augusta Robbins. He lived at Manchester Centre, Vt., where he died, September 5, 1899. His mother writes that he has seven children; the oldest son was married and had children, but the names are not given.

920.

ASIEL SHELDON AMEDON (Nathaniel William,[478] Nathaniel,[298] Moses,[77] Henry,[21] Henry,[9] Philip,[4] Roger[1]), born at Hebron, N. Y.,. December 25, 1854. He married, in January, 1877, Emma Taylor, and lived at Manchester Centre, Vt. His mother writes that he has six children, but the names are not given.

926.

GIDEON E. AMIDON (George W.,[479] Nathaniel,[298] Moses,[77] Henry,[21] Henry,[9] Philip,[4] Roger[1]), born at Cass, Mich., June 1, 1858.. He married, May 27, 1880, Bertha E., daughter of Charles Quirk, Onondaga, N. Y.

CHILD.

1282—Lena E., born June 1, 1881.

935.

CHARLES KINGSBURY AMIDON (Frederick S.,[494] Samuel,[117] Moses,[77] Henry,[21] Henry,[9] Philip,[4] Roger[1]), born at East Hartford, Conn., March 26, 1846. He enlisted in 1863 in the 4th Massachusetts. Cavalry, and served for two years. During that time he was Orderly at the headquarters of the 24th Army Corps. He married, April 28, 1873, Kate Kendrick. He is engaged in real estate business at 45 Milk Street, Boston, Mass.

CHILDREN.

1283—Edward Kendrick, born October 20, 1877. He married November 1, 1897, Daisy Mary Baldwin; resides in Boston and is a banker.
1284—Charles Kingsbury, born 1876.

937.

FREDERICK S. AMIDON (Frederick S.,[444] Samuel,[137] Moses,[77] Henry,[31] Henry,[9] Philip,[4] Roger[1]), born at East Hartford, Conn., March 2, 1854. He served nine months in the 42d Massachusetts Infantry. He married, October 1, 1881, Lena Matthews, and lives in Boston, Mass.

CHILDREN.

1285—Willie M., born June 21, 1882.
1286—Frank, born March 11, 1885.
1287—Ralph, born September 4, 1886.

946.

FRED ARWIN AMIDON (Seth,[444] Moses,[222] Moses,[77] Henry,[31] Henry,[9] Philip,[4] Roger[1]), born September 19, 1859, at Hamilton, Ind. He married, November 14, 1885, at Lakeview, Mich., Ellen Edelpha, daughter of Moses and Betsey Jane (McKeough) Dunsmore. She was born October 31, 1867, in Orange Township, Ionia County, Mich. For several years Mr. Amidon was engaged in farming and storekeeping at Wirth, Ark., and later was engaged in sheep raising in Colorado. Since 1902 he has resided at Chelon, Wash.

CHILDREN.

1288—Earl Seth, born September 24, 1886, at Lakeview, Mich.
1289—Mabel Jessie, born April 3, 1892.

947.

LEE EARLL AMIDON (Seth,[444] Moses,[223] Moses,[77] Henry,[31] Henry,[9] Philip,[4] Roger[1]), born February 4, 1865, at Hamilton, Ind. On the death of his mother in 1877 he was placed on a farm at Ainger, Ohio, with Mr. and Mrs. Henry A. Watt, by whom he was educated. Here he attended and later for three years taught the district school. From 1887 to 1890 he attended Wooster University, Wooster, Ohio, changing from there to Michigan University, where he graduated in the classical course (A.B.) in 1892. From 1892 to 1897 Mr. Amidon was superintendent of schools at West Bend, Wisconsin. The year 1897-8 was spent in post-graduate work at Harvard University, from which he graduated (A.M.) in 1898. Since then he has been superintendent of city schools at Iron Mountain, Mich. On June 17, 1893, at Ainger, Ohio, Mr. Amidon was married to Viola, daughter of Volney and Martha (Kimmell) Powers, of Ainger, Ohio. She was born at Ainger, November 30, 1868, and is a lineal descendant of Walter Power, of Concord, Mass. (1654). Mrs. Amidon graduated from the Angola (Ind.) Normal College in 1892.

948.

FRANK ELIHU AMIDON (Aaron,[8] Moses,[7] Moses,[6] Henry,[5] Henry,[4] Philip,[2] Roger[1]), born at Greenville, Mich., December 11, 1866. He married, August 12, 1891, Bertha Anna, daughter of James Harvey and Jane Elizabeth Weeks. He lives at Greenville, Mich.

CHILD.

1290—Vera May, born March 17, 1897.

949.

FRED AARON AMIDON (Aaron,[8] Moses,[7] Moses,[6] Henry,[5] Henry,[4] Philip,[2] Roger[1]), born at Greenville, Mich., February 7, 1868. He married, June 19, 1892, Ella May, daughter of Alfred Clement and Isadore Emma Johnson. She was born February 1, 1873, in Grattan, Kent County, Mich. He is a carpenter by trade and resides in Weidman, Mich.

CHILDREN.

1291—Cordelia May, born February 10, 1893.
1292—Harvey A., born October 20, 1894.
1293—Bessie Isadore, born December 31, 1896.

956.

WILLIAM HENRY AMIDON (Henry,[6] Henry,[5] Moses,[4] Henry,[3] Henry,[2] Philip,[2] Roger[1]), born at Unionville, Conn., in 1859. He married and lives in Hartford, Conn.

CHILDREN.

1294—Howard William, born 1893.
1295—Frank Edward, born 1895.
1296—Edna May, born 1896.

958.

HENRY MARSHALL AMIDON (William H. H.,[6] Elijah,[5] Jonathan,[4] Henry,[3] Henry,[2] Philip,[2] Roger[1]), born at Northfield, Vt., March 10, 1843. He served two years in Company G, 2d Wisconsin Cavalry. He lives at Dover, Wis. He married (1st), January 16, 1863, Julia O., daughter of David and Louisa (Pierce) Lockwood. She was born January, 1842; died December 7, 1866. He married (2d), May 1, 1871, Fanny F. Anderson.

CHILDREN.

1297—Annie J., born October 28, 1865; married November 15, 1879, Gus.
    Myers, Dover, Wis.
1298—Hattie L., born November 22, 1866. She graduated at the State
    Normal School, River Falls, Wis., and was for four years super-
    intendent of the Pepin County Schools. She married August
    7, 1889, Alexander A. Peck, of Durand, Wis.

(Second wife.)

1299—Clayton H., born March 24, 1872.
1300—Elverton M., born December 27, 1873.
1301—Ida M., born February 4, 1876.
1302—Alma R., born October 29, 1878. She married June 15, 1897,
    Wilbur Holbrook, Dover, Wis.
1303—Goldie F., born March 4, 1884.
1304—Leslie H., born March 6, 1887.
1305—Mabel M., born May 26, 1891.
1306—Walter H., born November 2, 1895.

960.

MYRON HALE AMIDON (William H. H.,[411] Elijah,[311] Jona-
than,[79] Henry,[31] Henry,[9] Philip,[9] Roger[1]), born at Braintree, Vt., February 22, 1855. He married, August 26, 1894, May Kremm, of Dover,
Wis.

CHILD.

1307—Eugenia, born August 26, 1898.

974.

JOHN AMIDON (Marshall,[408] Jacob,[311] Jonathan,[79] Henry,[33]
Henry[9], Philip,[9] Roger[1]), born at Northfield, Vt., August 10, 1853. He
married, December 1, 1874, Mary Eastman. She was born May 14,
1854. He is a farmer and lives at Lawrenceville, N. Y.

CHILDREN.

1308—Ora, born September 17, 1876; married August 15, 1898, Lulu
    Copps.
1309—Mina, born February 10, 1879.
1310—Emma, born December 5, 1886.

982.

CHARLES AMASA AMIDON (Amasa Chapman,[519] Samuel,[219]
Jacob,[99] Henry,[34] Henry,[9] Philip,[9] Roger[1]), born in Onondaga
County, N. Y., June 26, 1855. He married, August 21, 1881, Mattie E.
Mettlen. He is a farmer and lives at Garwin, Iowa.

CHILDREN.

1311—Grace, born November 8, 1886.
1312—Walter Mettlen, born September 8, 1895.
1313—Russell Chapman, born February 2, 1897.
1314——————, born June 24, 1899.

996.

CHARLES F. AMIDON (Hiram,[***] Elijah,[***] Jacob,[**] Henry,[**] Henry,[*] Philip,[*] Roger[1]), born at Hayfield, Pa., September 10, 1856. He married, April 6, 1882, Mabel, daughter of Samuel and Permelia (Smith) Roberts. She was born at Rundell, Pa., June 28, 1861. In April, 1890, he removed to Northeast, Pa., and is a salesman and engaged in fruit growing.

CHILDREN.

1315—Forrest F., born April 19, 1883; died December 14, 1886.
1316—Carl C., born May 3, 1885; died May 28, 1885.
1317—Millicent, born May 5, 1886.
1318—Paul E., born January 23, 1889.
1319—Amy Dorris, born December 10, 1891.
1320—Florence M., born May 10, 1894.
1321—Don Leroy, born December 15, 1897.
1322—Charles Roice, born March 13, 1902.

997.

WILLIAM HARVEY AMIDON (Hiram,[***] Elijah,[***] Jacob,[**] Henry,[**] Henry,[*] Philip,[*] Roger[1]), born at Hayfield, Pa., September 2, 1860. He married, April 3, 1884, Dell, daughter of Corydon and Joanna (Radle) Alderman. She was born at Keepville, Pa., January 23, 1860. They now reside at Lorain, Ohio.

CHILDREN.

1323—Hazel D., born November 26, 1885.
1324—Hugh C., born May 1, 1891.
1325—Bruce W., born December 2, 1892.
1326—Margaret, born December 9, 1894.
1327—Gertrude, born February 20, 1897.

1004.

ORRIN ALPHEUS AMIDON (George Ross,[***] Elijah,[***] Jacob,[**] Henry,[**] Henry,[*] Philip,[*] Roger[1]), born at Rundell, Pa., July 4, 1857. He married, October 17, 1884, Tyla G. Giles, of Edinboro, Pa. He is a farmer and resides at Edinboro and is secretary of the board of trustees of the State Normal School at that place, having served as president of the same for four years.

CHILDREN.

1328—George Hudson, born January 11 1885. Member Senior Class
    State Normal School in 1904.
1329—Guy Albert, born September 24, 1886. Member Junior Class
    State Normal School, 1904.
1330—Roy Carl, born September 2. 1889.
1331—Ethel Elizabeth, born August 2, 1891.
1332—Angie Louise, born January 8, 1895.

1008.

JOHN EDWARD AMIDON (George Ross,[441] Elijah,[248] Jacob,[48] Henry,[14] Henry,[6] Philip,[2] Roger[1]), born at Rundell, Pa., November 25, 1870. He married, December 26, 1895, Lilly Jaynes, and resides at Edinboro, Pa.

CHILDREN.

1333—Annie Maria, born August 2, 1896.
1334—Georgie Lucile, born December 17, 1901.

1014.

FRANK AMIDON (Lewis Rundell,[444] Elijah,[248] Jacob,[48] Henry,[14] Henry,[6] Philip,[2] Roger[1]), born at Hayfield, Pa., June 27, 1865. He married, December 17, 1896, Ella Carpenter, and lives at Sisterville, W. Va.

CHILD.

1335—Ida, born October, 1897.

1022.

CHARLES FREMONT AMIDON (Rev. John Smith,[449] Leonard,[241] Jacob,[48] Henry,[21] Henry,[6] Philip,[2] Roger[1]), born at Clymer, N. Y., August 17, 1856. He graduated from Hamilton College in 1882. After graduation he went to Fargo, N. D., and was principal of the High School for one year. He then studied law with Hon. Alfred Thomas, United States District judge for North Dakota and began to practice in January, 1887. He served as City Attorney of Fargo several terms. In 1893 he was appointed a member of the commission to revise the Statute and Code of North Dakota, and the present revision of 1895 is the work of that commission. On August 31, 1896, he was appointed by President Cleveland, United States District Judge for the District of North Dakota, which appointment was confirmed by the Senate, February 18, 1897. The Times-Herald, Chicago, Ill., in noticing the appointment, said ''Judge Amidon has the highest testimonials that can possibly be desired to his character, learning and ability from the bar and the people of North Dakota. He is in every way qualified for the position.'' He married, November 15, 1892, Beulah Richardson, daughter of Samuel and Elizabeth T. (Richardson) McHenry. She was born at Point Pleasant, Pa., November 7, 1866.

ARTHUR A. AMIDON, 1033

CHILDREN.

1336—Beulah Elizabeth, born August 19, 1894.
1337—Charles Curtis, born December 7, 1895.
1338—John McHenry, born April 27, 1898.

1026.

WILLIAM A. AMIDON (Lorenzo D.,[141] Leonard,[141] Jacob,[19] Henry,[21] Henry,[4] Philip,[4] Roger[1]), born at Brooklyn, Wis., August 19, 1854. He married at Madison, Wis., 1887, Addie W. Roe. She died in 1897 and he died at some point in Dakota, 1893. He left three children, whose names were not furnished.

1032a.

GILBERT AMIDON (Lorenzo D.,[141] Leonard,[141] Jacob,[19] Henry,[21] Henry,[4] Philip,[4] Roger[1]), born at Brooklyn, Wis., March 3, 1880. He married, July 23, 1901, Jessie L. Larson and resides at Brooklyn, Wis.

CHILD.

1339—Hazel May, born October 3, 1902.

1033.

ARTHUR A. AMIDON (Lewis[147], Leonard[141], Jacob[19], Henry[21], Henry[4], Philip[4], Roger[1]), born at Clymer, N. Y., May 17, 1850. He married (1st) May 29, 1872, Edith I., daughter of Peter and Cora (Smith) Gron. She was born May 22, 1851, at Grossafal, Sweden. She died December 11, 1879, and he married (2d) February 11, 1881, Hannah, daughter of Andrew and Mary (Simpson) Gron. She was born October 24, 1851. In 1881 he moved to Jonesville, Va., and engaged in lumber business, but returned to Clymer in 1883. In 1884 he removed to Jamestown, N. Y., where he still resides. He is a contractor and builder and also engaged in mercantile business. He is a trustee in the M. E. Church and has served as alderman in Jamestown, and as president of the board of public works of that city.

CHILDREN.

1340—Byron Peter, born July 3, 1873; died July 8, 1873.
1341—Myron August, born July 3, 1873; died July 8, 1873.
1342—Cora Belle, born October 30, 1875; married August 26, 1903, Manfred M. Sadler, of Russell, Pa.

(Second wife.)

1343—Levi Lewis, born April 17, 1883; married December 24, 1903, Eva M. Schopp, of Jamestown, N. Y.
1344—Otto Melvin, born February 26, 1885.
1345—Pearlie Maud, born December 12, 1886.
1346—Minnie, born September 3, 1892; died October 6, 1892.
1347—Nelly Viola, born December 30, 1894.

1038.

EDGAR BACKUS AMIDON (Lewis[7], Leonard[6], Jacob[5], Henry[4], Henry[3], Philip[2], Roger[1]), born at Clymer, N. Y., July 2, 1862. He married Emma Prescott September 4, 1897, and lives at Findley Lake, N. Y.

CHILD.

1348—Ruth Evelyn, born November 16, 1898.

1041.

LEONARD WILLIAM AMIDON (William[6], Leonard[5], Jacob[4], Henary[3], Henry[3], Philip[2], Roger[1]), born at Clymer, N. Y., December 23, 1861. He married (1st) November 16, 1888, Blanche King. She died June 9, 1895, and he married (2d) December 24, 1896, Cora L. Austin. He died at Corry, Pa., July 14, 1904.

CHILDREN.

1349—Mabel Blanche, born June 23, 1889.
1350—Franklin William, born December 9, 1891.

(Second wife.)

1351—Leonard Lee, born November 18, 1897.

1042.

THOMPSON SMITH AMIDON (William[6], Leonard[5], Jacob[4], Henry[3], Henry[3], Philip[2], Roger[1]), born at Clymer, N. Y., July 27, 1864. He married November, 1886, Mabel Loch, and lives at Minneapolis, Minn. He has four children, the name of only two being given.
1352 —Dorcas.
1352a—Lester.

1044.

CLARK L. AMIDON (George J.[5], Leonard[4], Jacob[3], Henry[2], Henry[3], Philip[2], Roger[1]), born May 21, 1859. He married, September 9, 1887, Lilly B. Schermerhorn, and resides at Clymer, N. Y.

CHILDREN.

1353—Linnie May, born March 14. 1889.
1354—Isabella, born June 21, 1893.
1355—Blanche Amanda, born May 12, 1898.

1076.

EDMUND POYNEER AMIDON (Edmund S.,[5][6][7] Edmund S.,[5][6][7] William[4][1], Henry[3][1], Henry[3], Philip[2], Roger[1]), born at Sturgis, Mich., January 3, 1874. He married at Tacoma, Wash., October 5, 1902, Ethelyn Shaw, and resides at Everett, Wash.

CHILD.

1356—Almeda Marie, born December 6, 1903.

1077.

ALBRO C. AMIDON (Orin Wallace[5][6][7], Edmund Sumner[5][6][7], William[4][1], Henry[3][1], Henry[3], Philip[2], Roger[1]), born at Elkhart, Ind., November 27, 1868. He married, November 12, 1890, Maud Truax.

CHILDREN.

1357—Merle T., born December 3, 1891.
1358—Otis W., born November 6, 1893.
1359—Harry C., born February 14, 1896.
1360—Hazel, born February 14, 1896; died July 15, 1896.
1361—Rollo P., born March 15, 1898.

1078.

WILLIAM SUMNER AMIDON (Orin Wallace[5][6][7], Edmund Sumner[5][6][7], William[4][1], Henry[3][1], Henry[3], Philip[2], Roger[1]), born at Elkhart, Ind., July 24, 1875. He married, December 25, 1897, Fanny Doremus, and lives at Elkhart, Ind.

CHILD.

1362—George Wallace, born October 3, 1898.

1079.

DAVID R. AMIDON (George[5][6][7], Gardner[5][6][7], Henry[3][1], Henry[3][1], Henry[3], Philip[2], Roger[1]), born at Hartford, Wis., February 2, 1848. He married, May 27, 1880, Rebecca Tucker. He is a farmer and lives at Ono, Wis.

CHILD.

1363—Leon, born September 24, 1882.

1084.

WILLARD R. AMIDON (Elisha[6], Gardner[5], Henry[4], Henry[3], Henry[2], Philip[2], Roger[1]), born at Hartford, Wis., April 18, 1856. He married, April 12, 1884, Laura Allen. She was born April 1, 1859, at Albany, Wis. He lives at Hartford, Wis., is a jeweler and has served as alderman.

CHILDREN.

1364—Irene, born January 12, 1886.
1365—Ethel, born December 15, 1887.
1366—Ransom, born August 19, 1889.

1085.

UR AMIDON (Elisha[6], Gardner[5], Henry[4], Henry[3], Henry[2], Philip[2], Roger[1]), born at Hartford, Wis., September 10, 1859. He married, November 4, 1886, Hattie May, daughter of Chester W. and Mary E. (Meldrum) Turner. She was born at Hartford, Wis., March 23, 1866. He is a jeweler and lives at Hartford, Wis.

CHILDREN.

1367—Harry Ur, born September 18, 1889.
1368—Grace Turner, born November 27, 1892.

1086.

WILLIAM NELSON AMIDON (Samuel G.[5], Asaryl[4], Asaryl[3], Henry[2], Henry[2], Philip[2], Roger[1]), born at Dedham, Minn., December 30, 1857. He married, October 11, 1880, Florence Robertson, and resides at Houston, Minn. He began teaching school when 19 years old, and has served as county surveyor.

CHILDREN.

1369—Perry Nelson, born March 25, 1882.
1370—Norma, born June 5, 1892.

1087.

EDMUND PERRY AMIDON (Samuel G.[5], Asaryl[4], Asaryl[3], Henry[2], Henry[2], Philip[2], Roger[1]), born at Houston, Minn., April 9, 1865. He married, March 21, 1893, Mabel Julia Briggs, and resides at Houston, Minn.

CHILDREN.

1371—Muriel Mabel, born March 1, 1894.
1372—Edna Phyllis, born October 27, 1895.
1373—Helen Dorris, born July 5, 1897.
1374—Paul Samuel, born April 10, 1899.

1092.

HERBERT ISAAC AMIDON (Isaac Leonard[6], Rufus[5], Isaac[4], Jeremiah[3], Roger[1°], Philip[2], Roger[1]), born at Webster, Mass., August 2, 1860. He married, November 23, 1883, Jessie Smith, of North Brookfield, Mass.

CHILD.

1375—Effie Ida, born July 8, 1884.

1102.

JOHN H. AMIDON (Rufus[11°], Abner[6], Jedediah[8], Samuel[7], Roger[1°], Philip[2], Roger[1]). He married, (1st) Mary S. Houghton; (2d) Jenny F. Tyler, and lives at Greenfield, Mass.

CHILD.

1376—Fred T., born October 26, 1869.

1117.

GEORGE AMIDON (Andrew John[6], Russell[11], Ralph[1°], Roger[2], Roger[1°], Philip[2], Roger[1]), born at New Lathrop, Mich., June 27, 1856. He married Ellen Farrar and died November 2, 1886.

CHILDREN.

1377—Clarence, born August 2, 1882.
1378—Mertie, born June 6, 1885.

1119.

FRANCIS MARION AMIDON (Andrew John[6], Russell[11], Ralph[1°], Roger[2], Roger[1°], Philip[2], Roger[1]), born at New Lathrop, Mich., October 9, 1859. He married, December 20, 1891, Mary Abenethy, and lives at Inland, Mich.

CHILDREN.

1379—George, born August 9, 1893.
1380—Thurman, born February 16, 1895.
1381—Alice Mabel, born September 16, 1896.

1120.

CHARLES AMIDON (Andrew John[6], Russell[11], Ralph[1°], Roger[2], Roger[1°], Philip[2], Roger[1]), born at New Lathrop, April 5, 1862. He married, April 6, 1885, Laura Dunlap, and lives at Greyling, Mich.

CHILD.

1382—Ray, born May 2, 1899.

1121.

WILLIAM FRANK AMIDON (Andrew John[8], Russell[7], Ralph[6], Roger[5], Roger[4], Philip[2], Roger[1]), born at New Lathrop, Mich., April 19, 1863. He married, April 16, 1892, Hattie Perry, and lives at Latin, Mich.

CHILDREN.

1383—Maud, born February 15, 1893.
1384—Willie, born October 11, 1896.

1122.

HENRY AMIDON (Andrew John[8], Russell[7], Ralph[6], Roger[5], Roger[4], Philip[2], Roger[1]), born at New Lathrop, Mich., October 19, 1867. He married (1st) Maggie Cooper; (2d) Lizzie Walsh.

CHILDREN.

1385—Elegan, born October 4, 1888.

(Second wife.)

1386—Charles R., born March 12, 1899.

1133.

CHARLES HENRY AMIDON (Charles R.[6], Shepard[5], Ralph[4], Roger[3], Roger[2], Philip[2], Roger[1]), born at Purdy Creek, N. Y., June 28, 1867. He married Margaret Page, and lives at Canisteo, N. Y.

CHILD.

1387—Roy, born 1890.

1134.

WARD D. AMIDON (Charles R.[6], Shepard[5], Ralph[4], Roger[3], Roger[2], Philip[2], Roger[1]), born at Purdy Creek, N. Y., April 25, 1871. He married Mary Clark, and lives at Purdy Creek, N. Y.

CHILDREN.

1388—Alzina.
1389—Floyd.
1390—Catherine.
1391—Son, born December, 1899.

1137.

EDGAR HAMILTON AMIDON (William C.*⁴⁴, Roger*²⁷, Solomon¹¹⁰, Roger⁸⁰, Roger¹⁰, Philip⁴, Roger¹), born at Springfield, Mass., September 2, 1869. He married, October 22, 1890, Bessie May, daughter of William J. and Amy J. (Blake) Priest. She was born December 12, 1871. He lives at Springfield, Mass., and is proprietor of the Baggage Express Co.

CHILD.

1392—Hazel May, born November 7, 1891.

1140.

WILLIAM H. AMIDON (Josiah Carpenter*⁴⁴, Roger*²⁷, Solomon¹¹⁰, Roger⁸⁰, Roger¹⁰, Philip⁴, Roger¹), born at Petersham, Mass., October 30, 1863. He married, (1st) February 16, 1892, Lottie Eliza ———. She died in 1894. He married (2d) October 5, 1897, Martha L. Smith.

CHILDREN.

1393—Infant, died 1894.

(Second wife.)

1394—Mildred Jenny Martha, born June 26, 1898.

1442.

JOSIAH EDGAR AMIDON (Josiah Carpenter*⁴⁴, Roger*²⁷, Solomon¹¹⁰, Roger⁸⁰, Roger¹⁰, Philip⁴, Roger¹), born at Petersham, Mass., September 4, 1868. He married (1st) October 12, 1887, Mary McAuley; (2d) August 5, 1896, Blanche Bolton, and died in 1898.

CHILDREN.

1395—Clarence Roderick, born July 25, 1889.

(Second wife.)

1396—Edgar B., born July 9, 1897.

1147.

RUSSELL PHILIP AMMIDOWN (Philip Russell[11], Philip[10], Philip[9], Philip[8], Ichabod[3], Philip[2], Roger[1]), born at Cambridge, Mass., January 17, 1862. He married, June 16, 1884, Frances Alice, daughter of Jonathan Edward and Frances (Thomas) Ott. She was born at Halifax, N. S., October 9, 1864. He is a carpet salesman and lives at North Cambridge, Mass.

CHILD.

1397—Philip Russell, born November 24, 1884.

1151.

AMASA OTIS AMIDON (Otis[17], Otis[10], John[14], Caleb[10], Philip[11], Philip[2], Roger[1]), born at Gilsun, N. H., December 31, 1843. He served in Co. E of the 15th N. H. Volunteers from November 15, 1862, to August 13, 1863. He married, September 4, 1866, Sara C. Black, and lives at East Westmoreland, or Keene, N. H.

CHILDREN.

*1398—Lucius Edgar, born September 19, 1870.
1399—Emma Carrie, born February 3, 1876. She married, September 4, 1894, Henry Blanchard, of Keene, N. H., and they have Bessie Emma, born November 24, 1895.
1400—Nelly May, born February 2, 1883.

1158.

CHARLES MERRICK AMMIDOWN (Merrick[11], Lewis[14], John[14], Caleb[10], Philip[11], Philip[2], Roger[1]), born at Providence, R. I., September 6, 1861. In 1897 he removed to Eustis, Neb., and engaged in real estate business. He married, February 26, 1884, Lucy I. Cheney.

CHILDREN.

1401—Stanley C., born April 14, 1892.
1402—Ruth Arvilla, born October 29, 1898.

1161.

EUGENE LEWIS AMMIDOWN (Andros[11], Lewis[14], John[14], Caleb[10], Philip[11], Philip[2], Roger[1]), born at Southbridge, Mass., May 29, 1869. He married and has
1403—Doris, born August 15, 1897.

1174.

LUCIUS EDWIN AMMIDOWN (Lucius H.[114], Holdridge[111], Luther[113], Caleb[19], Philip[17], Philip[9], Roger[1]), born at Southbridge, Mass., September 9, 1852. He married, July 11, 1884, Flora B. Allen, and now resides at Southbridge.

CHILD.

1404—Harry Frank, born May 1, 1885.

1226.

SAMUEL ELLIOTT AMADON (Lucien E.[117], Samuel D.[111], Titus[117], Ithamar[19], Ithamar[15], Philip[9], Roger[1]), born May 15, 1874. He married Kate Dixon and lives in South Boston, Mass.

CHILD.

1405—Edwin Elliott, born July 24, 1898.

1241.

WILFORD PHILANDER AMADON (George Augustus[190], Philander[119], Ansel[117], Ebenezer[19], Ithamar[15], Philip[9], Roger[1]), born at North Adams, Mass., November 3, 1866. He married, September 12, 1888, Cora Ann, daughter of Jerome B. and Bernice (Rice) Tinney. She was born at North Adams, Mass., October 17, 1867.

CHILD.

1406—Addison Elmer, born June 27, 1897.

1253.

FULTON V. AMIDON (Loyal Richard[119], Richard Flynn[113], Ansel[117], Ebenezer[19], Ithamar[15], Philip[9], Roger[1]), born at Fergus Falls, Minn., November 29, 1863. He married, June 28, 1888, Hilda J. Whilt, daughter of Joseph Whilt. She was born March 2, 1871. He is a farmer and lives at Bennettville, Minn.

CHILDREN.

1407—John Fisk, born November 11, 1889; died December 2, 1889.
1408—Neal, born March 9, 1891.
1409—Alfred Grove, born October 5, 1893; died November 9, 1893.
1410—Margery, born April 28, 1896.
1411—Iris, born October 27, 1898.

1257.

EGBERT HENRY AMADON (Christopher M,[555], Henry P.[454], Ansel[117], Ebenezer[46], Ithamar[16], Philip[4], Roger[1]), born November 24, 1876, at Pownal, Vt. He married, December 29, 1897, Lottie Hathaway, of Pownal, Vt.

CHILD.

1412—Harold Egbert, born April 27, 1898.

1398.

LUCIUS EDGAR AMIDON (Amasa O.[1141], Otis[117], Otis[449], John[114], Caleb[16], Philip[11], Philip[4], Roger[1]), born at East Westmoreland, N. H., September 19, 1870. He married, April 1, 1891, Ella M. Herrick, and resides at Keene, N. H.

CHILD.

1413—Roy Herrick, born April 4, 1895.

1414.

JACOB AMADON (possibly a son of Jacob[14]), married Chloe Ives, and resided at Wallingford, Vt.; where he died about 1820.

CHILDREN.

1415—Ives.
*1416—Horatio Gates, born April 25, 1803.
1417—Aurelia; married —— Rose and a son, J. O. Rose, lives at Hicksville, Ohio.
1418—Eliza; married Edwin Axtell, and lived at Watertown, N. Y.
*1419—John, born 1808.

1416.

HORATIO GATES AMADON (Jacob[1414]), born at Wallingford, Vt., April 25, 1803. He removed to Westfield, Mass., in 1824; to St. Lawrence, N. Y., in 1828, and in 1830 enlisted in the United States army. In 1833 he married Charlotte Johnson and removed to Williams Co., Ohio, in 1844. His wife died in 1846, and he died July 9, 1884, in Milford Tp., Defiance Co., Ohio.

CHILDREN.

*1420—Morton A.
*1421—Henry.
*1422—John.
1423—Aurelia N.; married Augustus S. Lease, of Ann Arbor, Mich.

1419.

JOHN AMADON (Jacob[1414]), born in 1808. He married Nancy Fodder, and died at Watertown, N. Y., in 1892.

CHILDREN.

1424—George, born 1834; married in 1858, Ada Blodgett. He died while
  in the army in 1863.
*1425—Edward C., born September 10, 1841.
1426—Mary M.; married —— Palmer.
1427—Louisa; married Freeman Morgan, Elgin, Ill.
1428—Aurelia; married Ed. Rounds, Watertown, N. Y.

1420.

MORTON A. AMADON (Horatio G.[1418], Jacob[1414]), married. Nancy Luce and lived at Edgerton, Ohio.

CHILDREN.

1429—Edwin.
1430—Horace.

1421.

HENRY AMADON (Horatio G.[1418], Jacob[1414]), born at Herman, St. Lawrence Co., N. Y., May 8, 1840. He served as Corporal in Co. E, 21st Ohio Vols., and has been Township Clerk, Treasurer and Justice of the Peace. He married, in 1868, Harriet Celestia Wilcox and lives at Hicksville, Ohio.

CHILDREN.

1431—Madora M., born September 10, 1869; died May 3, 1891.
1432—Guy Wilcox, born June 8, 1872.
1433—Otho Gates, born November 7, 1874.
1434—Addie E., born May 21, 1877.
1435—John Augustus, born November 1, 1879.
1436—George Alfred, born May 3, 1883; died November 18, 1899.
1437—Henry Earl, born November 4, 1888; died October 30, 1891.

1422.

JOHN AMADON (Horatio[1418], Jacob[1414]), married Dorliska Crary and lives in Toledo, Ohio.

CHILDREN.

1438—Aurelia.
1439—Adell.
1440—John Clyde.
1441—Walter Donald.

1425.

EDWARD C. AMADON (John[141], Jacob[114]), born in Pierpont Tp., St. Lawrence Co., N. Y., September 10, 1841. During the Civil War he served in Co. F, 47th Indiana Vols. For some years he was in business in Elgin, Ill., and in Chicago. He is now in the Soldiers' Home, Danville, Ill. He married (1st) May 6, 1867, Eliza Bonge, and (2d), May 4, 1887, Clara Smith.

CHILDREN.

1442—Ralph J., born September 20, 1868.
1443—Jessie K., born April 10, 1870.
1444—George, born March 4, 1890.
1445—Ruby, born December, 1891.

1446.

JOHN AMIDON (probably John[144]), lived in Rensselaer Co., N. Y. He was a member of the Baptist Church and had two sons and three daughters. One son was
*1447—Darius.

1447.

DARIUS AMIDON (John[1444]) was a lumberman and lived thirteen miles east of Troy, where he died in 1884. He married Evaline Pollock.

CHILDREN.

1448—Frank, served three years in Col. Swain's Reg't.
1449—Philip, served in Seventh N. Y. Heavy Artillery and was killed at Cold Harbor.
*1450—Walter D.
1451—Mary.
1452—Charles.
1453—William.
1454—George.

1450.

WALTER D. AMIDON (Darius[1447], John[1444]). He served in Co. G, 192d N. Y. Infy., and was wounded while on picket duty at Summit Point, Va. He married, March 12, 1877, Lizzie Gunthaur, and lives at Bleecher, N. Y.

CHILDREN.

1455—Ella D.
1456—Harry W.
1457—Ida B.
1458—Clara E.
1459—Leonard.

1460.

SIMEON AMIDON (possibly a brother of Darius above). His wife's name was Abiah and they lived in New York State. They had

CHILD.

*1461—John Goss, born September, 1828.

1461.

JOHN GOSS AMIDON (Simeon[1460]), born September, 1828. He was a stage driver and a volunteer soldier in the Indian wars in Oregon. He married, March 18, 1854, Mary L. Woodward, and later lived in California.

CHILDREN.

1462—Simeon J., born in Oregon, March 18, 1855; lives at Oakland, Cal.
1463—Frances H., born in Oregon April 10, 1856; married Fred Jenkins, Alameda, Cal.
1464—Flora E., born in California, March 18, 1858; married Frank Hammett, Salinas, Cal.
1465—William H., born September 26, 1860.
1466—Charles E., born September 15, 1864; lives in Oakland, Cal.
1467—Fred J., lives in San Francisco, Cal.
1468—Manerva.

1469.

AHIMAAZ AMIDON (son of Eunice Amidon[1469]), born at Readsboro, Vt., July 16, 1809. He married, November 4, 1832, Fanny Kimball. In 1843 he removed to Shaftsbury, Vt. He died at Dexter, Iowa, February 21, 1886.

CHILDREN.

*1470—Albert, born January 21, 1835.
1471—Allen T., born July 2, 1837; died March 22, 1848.
1472—Truman, born November 12, 1841; died February 12, 1864.
1473—Freelove K., born May 11, 1843; married H. H. Harrington, Dexter, Ia. ·
1474—Mary F., born September 1, 1847; married M. Percy, Dexter, Ia.
1475—Jane H., born April 15, 1849; married, first, M. Woodward and second, F. M. Buckles, What Cheer, Ia.
1476—Emily A., born Dec. 8, 1854; married E. D. Percy.

1470.

ALBERT AMIDON (Ahimaaz[1469]), born at Pownal, Vt., January 21, 1835. He married, December 12, 1859, Jane Perkins, and lives at Shaftsbury, Vt.

CHILDREN.

1477—Letta, born May 6, 1860; married S. Centro, White Creek, N. Y.
1478—Elmer, born December 19, 1862; married Miss Green and lives
      at Shaftsbury, Vt.
1479—Truman, born December 2, 1866; married Anna Dyer and lives at
      Shaftsbury, Vt.

1480.

LEONARD AMIDON, born at Charlton, Mass, 1804. His wife's
name was Roxana. He died at West Stockbridge, Mass., June 3, 1851.

CHILDREN.

1481—Eliza Fowler, born October 9, 1845.
1482—Payson, born November 3, 1847; died October 31, 1848.

1483.

WILLIAM H. AMIDON, of 1026 Walnut St., Chicago, born near
Syracuse, N. Y., June 13, 1840.

CHILDREN.

1484—Clarence Earl, born June 28, 1866.
1485—William H., born February 20, 1869.
1486—Francis E., born August 15, 1873.
1487—Corinna, born May 18, 1879.
1488—Rex Irving, born April 14, 1881.

The compiler was unable to obtain more information concerning
the following:

1489—Abbie Amidon; married in 1881, Francis Carpenter, of Chester, Vt.
1490—Noah Amidon; name appears on Belcherton (Mass.) tax list, 1810.
1491—Susan E. Amidon, at Lowell, Mass., 1848; had name changed to
      Susan E. Walker.
1492—John Amadon, of New Ireland, P. Q., Canada; married February
      11, 1840, Abigail Kimball.
1493—Harriet Amidon, in 1813, married William Norton, of Charlestown,
      Mass.
1494—Ephriam R. Amidon, a carpenter at Westmoreland. N. H.; mar-
      ried Emily Ann Allen. She was born in 1841 and died in 1880.
      (From Massachusetts State Records.)
1495—George W. Amidon, in 1874 was married at Worcester, Mass., and
      lived at 14 Crown St., in 1897.
1496—Alice Fredelene Amidon, born at Worcester, Mass., in 1878.
1497—Ralph C. Amidon, born at Worcester, Mass., in 1880.
1498—Sylvester Amidon, born at Worcester, Mass., in 1880.
1499—Caroline M. Amidon, died at Worcester, Mass., in 1869.
1500—Willie M. Amidon, lived at Worcester, Mass., in 1897 at 58 Irv-
      ing St.
1501—William S. Amidon, lived at Worcester, Mass., in 1897 at 34 Col-
      lier St.
1502—Benjamin Amadon, of Adams, Mass., born at Readsboro, Vt., in
      1843; married at Adams, Mass., April 24, 1865, Fanny Dunn.
1503—James S. Amidon, born in Douglas, Mass., 1837; married in West
      Boylston, Mass., Aug. 28, 1867, Ella A. Russell.
1504—Victoria Amidon, born at Lanesboro, Mass., in 1867.
1505—Charles W. Amidon, born Oxford, Mass., 1870, and died 1870.

1506—George L. Amidon, born Oxford, Mass., 1869, and died in 1872.
1509—Nellie D. Amidon, born Oxford, Mass., 1869.
1508—Burrie E. Amidon, born Oxford, Mass., 1864.
1509—Etta Laura Amidon; married in Shelburne, Mass., in 1884.
1510—Anna J. Amidon; married in Amherst, Mass., in 1875.
1511—Gad A. Amidon; was married at Holden, Mass., in 1871.
1512—Widow Irene Amidon, of Sturbridge; married July 9, 1794,
    Daniel Aldrich.

These names obtained from Directories, and all were written to, but no response received:

1513—George W. Amadon, publisher "Review and Herald," Battle Creek,
    Mich.
1514—Claude Amadon, Battle Creek, Mich.
1515—John Amadon, a student in high school, Dowagiac, Mich., 1856.
1516—Mary Amadon, a student in high school Dowagiac, Mich.
1517—Joseph P. Amidon, in 1895 lived at Decatur, Ill.
1518—Dell F. Amidon, in 1895 lived at Decatur, Ill.
1519—Dana Amidon, in 1895 lived at Flint, Mich.
1520—Rebecca Amidon (widow of Sylvander), Flint, Mich.
1521—Dyre D. Amidon, Richfield, Mich.
1522—William W. Amidon, Davidson, Mich.
1523—Ward G. Amidon, Richfield, Mich.
1524—E. J. Amidon, Cilo, Mich.
1525—Charles Amidon, Rome, N. Y.
1526—Earl Amidon, Merrill, Wis.
1527—Charles H. Amidon, San Jose, Cal.
1528—Edward Amidon, San Jose, Cal.
1529—Charles Amidon, 27 Preble St., Cleveland, O.
1530—William J. Amidon, 27 Preble St., Cleveland, O.

RECEIVED TOO LATE TO APPEAR IN PROPER PLACE.

521.

AMENZA FAYETTE AMIDON (Samuel[7], Jacob[6], Henry[5], Henry[4], Philip[2], Roger[1]), born in 1832. He married, in 1856, Martha Hull. He enlisted in Co. I, Twelfth New York Volunteers, and was wounded at the second battle of Bull Run. He lives near Syracuse, N. Y.

CHILDREN.

1531—Abner Jerome, born October 28, 1858; married Anna Thorpe and
    lives at Camillus, N. Y.
1532—Marriam, born 1861; died 1863.
*1533—Porter, born October 29, 1863.
*1534—Elmer, born 1865.
*1535—Fenton W., born January 7, 1868.
1536—Lucy, born 1870; married Barney Randall and has Clarence, Gladys
    and Alvarette.
1537—Flora, born 1872; married Frank Williams and has Burdette,
    Blanche, Alola, Corinne and Mildred.

1533

PORTER AMIDON (son of Amenza F., 521), born at South Onondaga, N. Y., October 29, 1863. He married, February 3, 1886, Eva B. Wilcox, and lives at Cardiff, N. Y.

CHILDREN.

1538—Blaine F., born March 24, 1891.
1539—Blanche F., born April 30, 1894.
1540—Frank F., born April 15, 1896.
1541—Belle I., born December 15, 1897.
1542—C. Jerome, born April 20, 1900.
1543—Porter H., born December 6, 1901.
1544—Jay J., born December 20, 1903.

1534.

ELMER AMIDON (son of Amenza F.[111]). Married Hannah
Adams and has—

CHILDREN.

1545—Herbert.
1546—May.
1547—Eva.
1548—Harvey.
1549—Stella.
1550—Martha.

1535.

FENTON W. AMIDON (son of Amenza F., 521), born at South
Onondaga, N. Y., 1868. He married, March 10, 1892, Maud A.
French, and lives at Lafayette, N. Y.

CHILDREN.

1551—Emma G., born February 22, 1893.
1552—Oscar E., born June 7, 1895; died April 30, 1896.
1553—Nelly M., born November 13, 1897; died July 26, 1898.
1554—Leon M., born October 29, 1900.

1244.

TENNEY D. AMIDON (son of Leland M., 862), born at Irving,
Wis., September 7, 1876. He married, March 14, 1900, at Winona,
Minn., Inga Larkin, and has:
1555—Leon Leroy, born January 29, 1901.

1258.

BENJAMIN FRANKLIN AMADON (son of Christopher M., 883),
born at Pownal, Vt., August 15, 1879. He married, at Bennington, Vt.,
September 19, 1900, Julia, daughter of Eris and Mary Ellen (Greenslet) Hicks, and has:
1556—Ernest Forrest, born November 15, 1901.

I

AMIDON.

(All Spellings of the Name.)

A. A., 971.
Aaron, 490.
Abbie, 1489.
Abbie Stella, 1155.
Abel, 67, 186, 192, 427.
Abigail, 46, 56, 59, 117, 171, 211, 271, 850, 857.
Abigail A., 376.
Abigail Delight, 912.
Abiram, 416.
Abner, 69, 187, 198, 283.
Abner Jerome, 1531.
Abraham L., 661.
Ada B., 1221.
Addie E., 1434.
Addie M., 999.
Addie May, 1123.
Addison Elmer, 1406.
Adelaide, 565.
Adelia, 737.
Adeline, 1064.
Adeline F., 515.
Adele, 1439.
Adelmar, 1195.
Adoline Orcelia, 587.
Adolphus, 346.
Ahimaaz, 1469.
Ahial, 394.
Alameda, 667.
Albert, 685, 772, 1470.
Albert Holmes, 1172.
Albert L., 929.
Albert Morton, 1163.
Albert Ray, 1017.
Albro C., 1077.
Alene Harriet, 1266.
Alethela, 264.
Alfonso, 776.
Alfred Augustus, 232.
Alfred Grove, 1409.
Alfred Leroy, 516.
Alfred Mason, 891.
Alfred Pickering, 1148.
Alfred Todd, 1075.
Alice, 183, 817.
Alice A., 1054.
Alice Adell, 1034.
Alice Angie, 1149.
Alice Belle, 1251.
Alice C., 936.
Alice Charlane, 880.
Alice Fredelene, 1496.
Alice J., 1186.
Alice L., 932.
Alice Louise, 979.
Alina Lucena, 887.
Alina Mabel, 1381.
Allen T., 1471.

Alma Ann, 957.
Alma R., 1302.
Almeda Marie, 1356.
Almira, 248.
Alonzo, 582, 609.
Alpheus, 115.
Alta M., 933.
Alvin, 659, 951.
Alzina, 1388.
Amasa Chapman, 519.
Amasa Otis, 1151.
Amelia, 383, 726.
Amenza Fayette, 521.
Amy Doris, 1319.
Andrew, 611.
Andrew Augustus, 1053.
Andrew Fuller, 735.
Andrew Huntington, 910.
Andrew J., 755.
Andrew John, 666.
Andros, 722.
Angelina, 337.
Angeline A., 194.
Angeline Melissa, 1082.
Angie Louise, 1332.
Ann, 642, 747.
Ann Frances, 751.
Anna, 952, 1108.
Anna J., 1510.
Anna L., 1280.
Anna M., 1103.
Annie J., 1297.
Annie K., 1209.
Annie Maria, 1333.
Annis, 224.
Ansel, 177, 428.
Ansel Lyman, 859.
Antoinette, 749.
Arcella, 258.
Ariel, 425.
Arinda, 727.
Arthur, 1129.
Arthur A., 1033.
Arthur F., 889.
Arthur Franklin, 1267.
Asahel, 70.
Asa J., 934.
Asaryl, 83, 263.
Asenith, 311, 424.
Asiel Sheldon, 920.
Augusta, 365, 653.
Augustus A., 505.
Augustus B., 444.
Aurelia, 1417, 1428, 1438.
Aurelia N., 1423.
Aveline Harriet, 785.
Azerba, 174.

Bailey, 290.
Bathsheba, 86.
Beauregard, 449.
Belle, 1197.
Belle I., 1541.
Benjamin, 1502.
Benjamin Franklin, 1258.
Benjamin Moses, 1036.
Bertha Smith, 1269a.
Bertie, 1190.
Bessie Alice, 1264.
Bessie Isadore, 1293.
Betsey, 274, 293, 407.
Beulah Elizabeth, 1336.
Blaine F., 1538.
Blanche F., 1539.
Blanche Amanda, 1355.
Blanche Maud, 1168.
Bridget, 265.
Bruce W., 1325.
Burrie E., 1508.
Byron, 558, 1032a.
Byron Peter, 1340.

Caleb, 39, 72, 199, 341, 725.
Caleb 8., 668.
Callie M., 890.
Callina, 347.
Callina Morse, 1156.
Calvin, 136, 158, 294, 647.
Carl C., 1316.
Carlow, 715.
Caroline, 196, 732, 842.
Caroline Clarimon, 919.
Caroline M., 1499.
Caroline Melitta, 740.
Caroline Rosetta, 702.
Carrie M., 901.
Carrie May, 1271.
Cassius M., 1045.
Catharine, 1065, 1390.
Catharine Hartwell, 752.
Catharine Helen, 1178.
Celia, 789.
Celia Ann, 1229.
Celia Frances, 781.
Celia L., 845.
Celina, 520.
Cenn, 382.
Charity, 557.
Charles, 597, 615, 1120, 1218, 1452, 1525, 1529.
Charles Amasa, 982.
Charles Barber, 206.
Charles Carpenter, 1228.
Charles Curtis, 1337.
Charles D., 485.
Charles Eldridge, 799.
Charles E., 1466.
Charles Ernest, 980.
Charles F., 996.
Charles Fowler, 865.
Charles Fremont, 1022.
Charles H., 635, 812, 1527.
Charles Henry, 1133.
Charles Hovey, 745.
Charles Jacob, 340.
Charles Kingsbury, 935, 1284.
Charles L., 391, 830.
Charles M., 899.
Charles Merrick, 1158.
Charles R., 686, 1386.
Charles Royce, 1322.

Charles Sanford, 905.
Charles W., 927, 1525.
Chauncey, 475.
Cheney, 73, 189, 261, 447, 451.
Chester Gardner, 1083.
Chloe, 66, 178, 508.
Chloe Ann, 200.
Christopher Columbus, 501.
Christopher Mason, 883.
C. Jerome, 1542.
Clara, 829.
Clara Bell, 1272.
Clara E., 1458.
Clara L., 835.
Clara May Rowena, 1227.
Clara Sarah, 815.
Clarence, 1019, 1377.
Clarence Adelbert, 1093.
Clarence Alfred, 977.
Clarence Earl, 1484.
Clarence Henry, 1246.
Clarence Roderick, 1395.
Clarissa, 404, 524, 584, 585.
Clarissa M., 510.
Clark, 324.
Clark L., 1044.
Claude, 1514.
Clayton H., 1299.
Clifton Elmer, 1018.
Climena, 525.
Cora, 1069.
Cora Belle, 1342.
Cordelia May, 1201.
Corinna, 1487.
Cynthia, 167, 357.
Cyril, 272.
Cyrus, 140, 368, 377, 787.
Cyrus P., 775.
Cyrus S., 1200.

Daisy B., 1101.
Dana, 1519.
Daniel, 291, 459, 526.
Daniel Clark, 1180.
Daniel Davison, 328.
Darius, 1447.
David, 286, 598.
David McKendre, 636.
David R., 1079.
Davis, 222.
Dayton G., 1557.
Deborah, 358.
Delephene, 786.
Della, 517.
Deliza, 716.
Dell, 1063.
Dell F., 1518.
Denzil, 687.
Dexter, 381, 790.
Diah, 234.
Don Leroy, 1321.
Dora Emeline, 1139.
Dorcas, 49, 147, 159, 1352.
Doris, 1403.
Dwight, 793.
Dyre D., 1521.

Earl, 1526.
Earl Clifton, 1144.
Earl Seth, 1288.
Ebenezer, 2, 33, 54, 120, 148, 214, 418.

Ebeneser Davis, 359, 1177a.
Edgar B., 1396,
Edgar Backus, 1038.
Edgar Hamilton, 1137.
Edmund Eddy, 112.
Edmund Perry, 1087.
Edmund Poyneer, 1076.
Edmund Sumner, 257, 578, 588.
Edna May, 1296.
Edna Phyllis, 1372.
Edson Danforth, 562.
Edward, 448. 455, 943, 1528.
Edward C., 1425.
Edward Cleveland, 1156½.
Edward Holmes, 743, 1161.
Edward Kendrick, 1283.
Edward Learned, 1090.
Edward Lyman, 872.
Edward Perry, 602.
Edwin, 1429.
Edwin A., 1043.
Edwin Bingley, 824.
Edwin Cyrus, 763.
Edwin E., 624.
Edwin Elliott, 1405.
Edwin G., 930.
Edwin Titus, 1225.
Effie, 1024.
Effie Ida, 1375.
Egbert, 884.
Egbert Henry, 1257.
E. J., 1524.
Elbert, 330.
Elbridge, 718.
Elbridge Putnam, 1152.
Elegan, 1385.
Eleanor Judith, 1091.
Elenor M., 700.
Elhanan Elijah, 498.
Eliakim, 632.
Elial, 403.
Elial Thompson, 821.
Elijah, 181, 231, 240.
Elisha, 596.
Eliza, 321. 331. 335, 420, 548, 631, 665, 670. 1418.
Elizabeth 23, 63, 87. 225, 657, 784.
Elizabeth Davison, 696.
Elizabeth Lucinda. 1217½.
Elizabeth Maria. 1051.
Eliza Cordelia, 203.
Eliza Fowler, 1481.
Ella, 658.
Ella D., 1455.
Ella Estelle, 1236.
Ella L., 1031.
Ella Maria, 803.
Ellen, 973.
Ellen A., 961.
Ellen Antoinette, 886.
Ellen Avasta, 1114.
Ellen Jane, 593.
Ellen M., 836.
Elmer, 1478, 1534.
Elmer Leroy, 1010.
Elmer Martin, 1242.
Elmer O., 1187.
Elmer Warner, 1270.
Elsa D., 675.
Elrisa A., 676.
Elverton M., 1300.
Emeline, 579.
Emeline S., 719.

Emily, 188, 560.
Emily A., 1476.
Emily Ford, 1252.
Emma, 1067. 1310.
Emma Arvilla, 1087.
Emma Celinda, 1160.
Emma Carrie, 1399.
Emma E., 1098.
Emma G., 1551.
Emma Gertrude, 1095.
Emma L., 1032.
Emma Shephard, 1135.
Eney R., 1097.
Ephriam, 14, 48.
Ephriam R., 1494.
Ernest, 1071.
Ernest Alexander, 886.
Ernest Forrest, 1556.
Estella, 1194.
Estelle, 614, 916,
Esther, 288, 401.
Esther A., 1030.
Esther Elmira, 552.
Esther Maria, 713.
Ethel, 1365.
Ethel Elizabeth, 1331.
Etta Laura, 1509.
Etta M., 1116.
Etta Maria, 1162.
Eugene C., 1020.
Eugene Lewis, 1161.
Eugenia, 1307.
Eunice, 65, 109. 164, 284, 678.
Eva, 1547.
Eva Blossom, 1165.
Experience Johnson, 210, 457.
Ezra, 97, 292.

Fanny, 446. 1023.
Fanny F., 680.
Fanny Lamb, 1177.
Fanny Olina, 208.
Fayette Asaryl, 1088.
Fay W., 1202.
Ferton, 1535.
Fidelia, 318.
Flora, 1537.
Flora E. 1464.
Florence A., 1279.
Florence Almeda. 1074.
Florence L., 1035.
Florence Luella. 1260.
Florence M., 1320.
Florence May, 1247.
Floyd, 1389.
Forest F., 1315.
Frances, 559, 791, 806.
Frances Eliza, 821.
Frances H., 1463.
Frances O., 925.
Francis, 1027.
Francis E., 1486.
Francis Eldridge, 869.
Francis H., 390.
Francis Marion, 1119.
Francis Oliver, 741.
Frank, 493. 610, 900, 1014, 1062, 1188, 1286, 1448.
Frank Delos, 990.
Frank E., 945.
Frank Edward, 811, 1295.
Frank Elihu, 948.

Frank F., 1540.
Frank Lewis, 1157.
Franklin William, 1350.
Frank Philip, 1217.
Frank Rupert, 1277.
Frank T., 876.
Frank W., 938.
Frank Whitcombe, 1269.
Fred, 942, 976.
Fred A., 1221.
Fred Aaron, 949.
Fred Arwin, 946.
Fred C., 1222.
Fred Emory, 1146.
Frederick, 816.
Frederick Brooks, 1182.
Frederick Eugene, 618.
Frederick S., 484, 937, 939.
Frederick Webber, 1214.
Fred J., 1467.
Fred P., 1211.
Fred T., 1376.
Fred Zacus, 1089.
Freelove K., 1473.
Freeman, 260.
Fritz George, 1132.
Fulton V., 1253.

Gad A., 1511.
Gardner, 262.
Geordie Alberta, 1047.
George, 467, 487, 511, 504, 616, 619, 767, 1117, 1379, 1424, 1444, 1454.
George Agnell, 729.
George Alfred, 1486.
George Augustus, 860.
George B., 648, 764.
George Barber, 592.
George E., 625, 1185.
George Frank, 1248.
George Franklin, 267.
George Frederick, 814.
George G., 827.
George Grant, 1124.
George H., 660.
George Herman, 922.
George Hudson, 1328.
George J., 550.
George L., 1506.
George Leroy, 652.
George Leslie, 1171.
George Ross, 541.
George Samuel, 267.
George W., 478, 780, 1112, 1495, 1513.
George Wallace, 1362.
George Washington, 1154.
Georgiana, 828.
Georgie Lucile, 1384.
Gertrude, 1018, 1327.
Gertrude S., 1111.
Gideon E., 926.
Gilbert, 1032a.
Gilbert E. S., 472.
Gilbert Whiton, 907.
Giles, 788.
Gladys L., 1204.
Goldie F., 1303.
Grace, 1199, 1311.
Grace Turner, 1368.
Guy Albert, 1329.

Guy E., 964.
Guy P., 940.
Guy S., 1255.
Guy Wilcox, 1432.

Hannah, 5, 17, 31, 37, 45, 61, 71, 139, 143, 176, 184, 191, 213, 230, 242, 287, 303, 312, 356, 402, 417, 461, 522, 532, 856, 1025.
Hannah J., 561.
Hannah Josephine, 897.
Harlan Page, 911.
Harold, 1412.
Harriet, 128, 133, 375, 463, 480, 768, 1493.
Harriet A., 773.
Harriet Ann, 866.
Harriet E., 1123.
Harriet Eliza, 567, 724.
Harriet R., 504.
Harry C., 1359.
Harry Frank, 1404.
Harry Nichols, 1143.
Harry Ray, 1050.
Harry Russell, 1150.
Harry Ur., 1367.
Harry W., 1456.
Harvey, 1548.
Harvey A., 1292.
Hattie, 954.
Hattie Deette, 991.
Hattie Elsie, 1127.
Hattie J., 1096.
Hattie L., 1298.
Hazard, 664.
Hazel, 1360.
Hazel D., 1323.
Hazel May, 1339, 1392.
H. Boyd, 1201.
Helen, 748.
Helen Bertha, 1275.
Helen Dorris, 1373.
Helen E., 998.
Helen Eliza, 564.
Helen Louise, 1215.
Helen Marr, 205.
Henry, 7, 9, 21, 82, 215, 229, 247, 259, 299, 329, 464, 486, 494, 613, 644, 818, 972, 1122, 1259, 1421.
Henry A., 617.
Henry Ansel, 868.
Henry C., 682.
Henry Clay, 753.
Henry Clinton, 1224.
Henry Denison, 540.
Henry Earl, 1437.
Henry G., 762.
Henry Gilbert, 820.
Henry H., 1208.
Henry Josiah, 810.
Henry L., 626.
Henry M., 833.
Henry Marshall, 958.
Henry Nathan, 913.
Henry Nelson, 573, 1058.
Henry P., 434.
Henry Stuart, 984.
Hepsibah, 50, 169, 406.
Herbert, 1545.
Herbert Elwen, 1205.
Herbert Isaac, 1092.
Herbert Munro, 1159.

Herbert Perry, 885.
Herbert Roger, 1136.
Hester, 523.
Hiram, 536, 781.
Holdridge, 353.
Hollis, 385.
Hollis G., 413.
Hollis H., 798.
Holmes, 355.
Horace, 217, 1430.
Horace Starkwether, 538.
Horatio, 218.
Horatio Gates, 1416.
Horatio Lyman, 469.
Hortensia, 393.
Howard John, 1212.
Howard William, 1294.
Hugh C., 1324.

Ichabod, 11, 30, 119.
Ida, 1335.
Ida B., 1457.
Ida Ellis, 1089.
Ida M., 1301.
Ida Samantha, 1243.
Ina, 1073.
Ira, 684.
Ira W., 914.
Irene, 64 1364, 1512.
Iris, 1411.
Isaac, 89, 277.
Isaac Clark, 389.
Isaac Learned, 606.
Isabel, 445.
Isabella, 1354.
Isiah J., 633.
Italia, 793.
Ithamer, 15, 53.
Ives, 1415.
Izoria Loretta, 877.

Jabez, 153.
Jacob, 18, 38, 80, 132, 233, 239, 530, 1414.
James, 1059.
James G., 1210.
James L., 852.
James M., 730.
James Melvin, 760½.
James Orlando, 809.
James Rufus, 807.
James S., 1503.
Jane, 720.
Jane H., 1475.
Jane Louise, 804.
Janette, 600.
Jay J., 1544.
Jeanette, 707.
Jedediah, 75, 76, 96, 212, 221, 301.
Jedediah Sanford, 471.
Jenny, 955.
Jenny Belle, 1006.
Jenny Carpenter, 1250.
Jenny Prudence, 898.
Jeremiah, 25, 93, 278.
Jerome F., 853.
Jerusha, 483.
Jesse, 319.
Jessie, 966.
Jessie Ella Belle, 1128.
Jessie K., 1445.

Joan A., 514.
Joanna, 421.
Joel C., 408.
John, 16, 42, 58, 62, 104, 134, 156, 157, 160, 173, 180, 309, 348, 397, 422, 458, 507, 733, 841, 974, 1189, 1419, 1422, 1446, 1492, 1515.
John Allen, 443.
John Alvin, 603.
John Augustus, 1435.
John B., 1113.
John Clyde, 1440.
John Edward, 1608.
John Edwin, 893.
John Elliott, 576.
John Fisk, 1407.
John Goss, 1461.
John H., 1102.
John J. F., 1235.
John J. H., 1216.
John L., 674.
John McHenry, 1338.
John Nathaniel, 921.
John P., 1181.
John Perry, 756.
John Quincy, 499.
John Richard, 849.
John Rickert, 902.
John Thompson, 255.
John Tyler, 1125.
Jonathan, 78, 597.
Jonathan Perry, 364.
Joseph, 20, 40, 146, 195, 325, 367, 553, 778.
Josephine, 803.
Joseph M., 759½.
Joseph P., 1517.
Josiah, 166, 399, 433.
Josiah Carpenter, 699.
Josiah Edgar, 1142.
Josie, 965.
Judson, 754.
Julia, 371, 374, 612.
Julia Ann, 649.
Julia Franklin, 701.
Julia Melvina, 761.
Julian R., 961.
Juliet, 502.
Julietta, 917.
Julina, 350.
Julius M., 855.
J. V., 489.

Katie, 1107.
Kelly, 1274.
Keziah, 43, 168.
Keziah Amelia, 846.
Kingsley, 316.
Kitty, 1274.

Larkin, 343.
Laura Angeline, 591.
Lavinia, 162.
Leander, 398.
Lee Earll, 947.
Leland Morgan, 862.
Lena E., 1282.
Lena Maud, 993.
Lena Mehitable, 1245.
Leon, 1363.
Leonard, 241, 1459, 1480.

Leonard Lee, 1351.
Leonard William, 1041.
Leon Leroy. 1555.
Leon M., 1554.
Leslie H., 1304.
Lester, 423, 847.
Lettie, 1254, 1477.
Levi Lewis, 1343.
Lewis, 243, 344, 547, 556.
Lewis Albert, 1005.
Lewis Franklin, 863.
Lewis Rundel, 544.
Lillian, 909.
Lillian Gertrude. 1164.
Lillian Marble. 1239.
Lilly Belle, 994.
Lina May, 992.
Linnie May, 1353.
Lizzie Crombie, 1179.
Lizzie Hannah. 1094.
Lodicy, 419.
Lodosia, 254.
Lois, 91, 103, 567.
Lora Alvira, 923.
Lorena Louisa, 1262.
Lorenzo, 580.
Lorenzo D., 546.
Lottie T., 1104.
Louisa, 280, 462, 474, 491, 1106, 1427.
Louisa C., 765.
Louise, 1016.
Louise Rosina, 650.
Louise Uretta, 782.
Louis Vinton, 1170.
Loyal Richard, 873.
Lucian Edgar, 837.
Lucian Malcolm. 1177b.
Lucinda, 237, 245.
Lucinda M., 543.
Lucius, 646.
Lucius Edgar, 1398.
Lucius Edwin, 1174.
Lucius Holdridge, 736.
Lucius P., 577.
Lucretia, 127, 372.
Lucy, 88, 107, 302, 323, 405, 431, 1536.
Lucy Abigail, 871.
Lucy Ann, 279.
Lucy Bell, 1002, 1046.
Lucy Ellen, 114b.
Lucy Emerine, 706.
Lucy Mahala, 639.
Lura, 379.
Lura Hattie. 124v.
Lurania, 95.
Lurania Melvina, 439.
Lusina, 840.
Luther, 135, 351.
Luther Shumway, 734.
Luther Wilson, 113.
Lyda, 944.
Lydia, 4, 179, 360, 363.
Lydia A., 1003.
Lydia R., 641.

Mabel Blanche, 1349.
Mabel Jessie. 1289.
Mabel M., 1305.
Mabel Marion, 1167.
Mabel Minerva, 1138.
Madison, 533.

Madora M., 1481.
Mae R., 1009.
Mahala, 627.
Malcolm, 730.
Malinda, 769.
Mamre, 155.
Manerva, 1468.
Maranda, 539.
Marcia Louisa, 470.
Marcus Morton, 731.
Marcus William, 1232.
Margaret, 116, 708, 1326.
Margery, 32, 34, 1410.
Maria, 270, 496.
Marion Grant, 1115.
Marriam, 1532.
Marshall, 508.
Martha, 437, 442, 858, 1066, 1550.
Martha A., 575.
Martha Avasta. 654.
Martha Emeline, 864.
Martha Estella, 854.
Martha Jane, 1230.
Martha K., 995.
Martha M., 620.
Martin, 273, 878.
Martin Van Buren. 671.
Marvin Child, 770.
Mary, 12, 35, 79, 85, 150, 163, 235, 396, 435, 466, 500, 555, 643, 903, 985, 1068, 1451, 1516.
Mary A., 551, 623, 669.
Mary Adelaide, 1173.
Mary Ann, 481, 586, 800, 987.
Mary E., 1081.
Mary Elisa, 851.
Mary Elizabeth, 209, 645, 712, 981, 1000.
Maryetta Elizabeth, 894.
Mary F., 1474.
Mary Fisher, 746.
Mary I., 529.
Mary Irene, 1273.
Mary J., 1184.
Mary Jane, 537, 867.
Mary Jeanette, 1040, 1178a.
Mary Josephine. 760.
Mary Lizzie, 703.
Mary Louise, 906.
Mary Lucy, 604.
Mary Lulie, 1207.
Mary M., 1426.
Maryme, 534.
Matilda, 170, 460.
Matilda J., 771.
Mattie, 915, 1198.
Maud, 1383.
May, 796, 1546.
Medora Luella, 570.
Mehitable, 8, 19, 51, 137.
Melani, 338.
Melissa, 583.
Melloday S., 677.
Meltiah, 74.
Melzar, 430.
Mercy, 144, 366, 441.
Mercy C., 512.
Meribah, 52.
Merle D., 1203.
Merle T., 1357.
Merrick, 721.
Mertie, 1378.
Merton E., 622.
Mildred Jenny M., 1394.

Mildred Julia, 1278.
Miles, 197.
Miles B., 187.
Millicent, 1317.
Mina, 1309.
Mina Eliza, 1261.
Minerva, 661, 801.
Minnie, 1346.
Minnie B., 963.
Molly, 90, 99.
Monroe, 693.
Morris, 688.
Morton A., 1420.
Moses, 77, 228, 244, 285, 566, 630, 634.
Moses H., 477, 931.
Moses Leoland, 1240.
Muriel Mabel, 1371.
Myra Ann, 882.
Myra Corinne, 959.
Myron, 988.
Myron August, 1341.
Myron Hale, 960.

Nancy, 114, 125, 352, 362.
Nathaniel, 226.
Nathaniel John, 924.
Nathaniel William, 476.
Neal, 1408.
Nelly, 450, 953, 1061, 1118, 1193.
Nelly D., 1507.
Nelly M., 1057, 1553.
Nelly Maria, 1288.
Nelly May, 1400.
Nelly Viola, 1347.
Nelson, 783.
Nelson J., 1021.
Nettie, 1007.
Newman D., 513.
Newton, 728.
Newton Philo, 705½.
Norma, 1370.
Noah, 44, 1490.

O. C., 967.
Olive, 349.
Olive Eugenia, 986.
Oliver, 354.
Oliver Franklin, 742.
Olivia, 506.
Ora, 1308.
Orin, 252, 848.
Orlow, 527.
Orrin Alpheus, 1004.
Orrin Philander, 1231.
Orrin Wallace, 590.
Oscar C., 795.
Oscar E., 1552.
Oscar F., 874.
Ossian Frank, 1011.
Otho Gates, 1433.
Otis, 122, 130, 342, 717, 762, 779.
Otis W., 1358.
Otto Melvin, 1344.
Outerbridge Horsey, 207.

Patty, 149.
Paul Herbert, 1213.
Paul R., 1318.
Paul Samuel, 1374.

Payson, 1482.
Pearl Sophia, 1049.
Pearlie Maud, 1345.
Percis, 822.
Percis Emeline, 589.
Perley, 275.
Perlie E., 621.
Permelia Matilda, 777.
Perry, 535, 1109.
Perry Franklin, 438.
Perry Nelson, 1369.
Phebe A., 581.
Philander, 426, 839.
Philip, 6, 13, 36, 47, 60, 124, 141, 336, 373, 440, 1449.
Philip Ellis, 334.
Philip Francis, 711.
Philip Henry, 744.
Philip Holmes, 1176.
Philip Russell, 710, 1397.
Philip Van C., 202.
Philoma, 246, 563.
Phoebe A., 673.
Pliny, 756½.
Pliny M., 757.
Polly, 111, 190, 220, 223, 268, 295, 369, 568.
Polly C., 409.
Porter, 1553.
Porter H., 1543.
Preserved, 304.
Prudence, 256, 572.

Rachel, 22, 28, 105, 129, 131.
Rachel Ella, 1256.
Ralph, 108, 452, 1287.
Ralph C., 1497.
Ralph J., 1442.
Ralph W., 322.
Ransom, 1366.
Ray, 1382.
Raymond Holt, 1276.
Rebecca, 1520.
Rebecca S., 1056.
Reuben, 41, 142, 388.
Rex Irving, 1488.
Rhoda, 68, 102, 201.
Rial, 250.
Richard, 690.
Richard Flynn, 482.
Robert, 453.
Robert S., 1206.
Robert Strong, 908.
Roena Lucy, 834.
Roger, 1, 10, 24, 29, 327.
Roger, A. F., 1263.
Rollin, 656.
Rollo P., 1361.
Rose, 456.
Rose May, 879.
Rosina, 314.
Roxalana, 161.
Roxana, 395.
Roxa Ann, 458.
Roy, 1387.
Royal Wells, 709.
Roy Carl, 1330.
Roy Herrick, 1413.
Roy Tisdale, 1181.
Ruby, 1445.
Ruby Etta, 1048.
Rufus, 154, 269, 276, 628.

Russell, 313, 115.
Russell Chapman, 1313.
Russell Hodges, 1175.
Russell Philip, 1147.
Ruth, 100, 103, 297, 361, 1268.
Ruth Arvilla, 1402.
Ruth C., 332.
Ruth Evelyn, 1348.
Ruth Harmony, 844.

Sabra, 412, 832.
Sabrina, 253.
Salem Richard, 1234.
Sally, 106, 145, 175, 219, 266, 295, 307, 308, 320, 387.
Samantha Maria, 861.
Samuel, 26, 27, 94, 98, 121, 227, 238, 267, 296, 306, 436, 473, 507, 888.
Samuel Barker, 1055.
Samuel Dexter, 415.
Samuel Edgar, 1265.
Samuel Elliott, 1226.
Samuel Experience, 895.
Samuel Foster, 605.
Samuel Gillett, 601.
Samuel I., 1281.
Sanford Newton, 843.
Sara Ella, 1012.
Sarah, 3, 55, 57, 84, 92, 182, 236, 249, 281, 384, 482, 518, 802, 968, 975.
Sarah A., 400, 774, 1183.
Sarah Ann, 333.
Sarah Anna, 1153.
Sarah B., 758.
Sarah Elizabeth, 808.
Sarah Elmira, 1001.
Sarah Emma, 1233.
Sarah F., 497.
Sarah Hutchings, 204.
Sarah Jane, 554, 638, 651.
Sarah Uretta, 1196.
Seth, 488.
Shephard, 317.
Shepherd Robert, 691.
Silvia, 118.
Simeon, 1460.
Simeon J., 1462.
Smith, 315.
Solenda, 305.
Solomon, 110, 326.
Solomon B., 672.
Solomon H., 640.
Solomon Henry, 705.
Sophia, 380, 386, 410, 414.
Sophronia, 185, 465, 904.
Stanley C., 1401.
Stella, 1549.
Stephen, 126.
Submit, 289.
Susan, 182.
Susan Cordelia, 819.
Susan E., 759, 1491.
Susan Maria, 738, 870.
Susan N., 697.
Susannah, 138, 345.
Susan Rebecca, 1491.
Sybil, 101.
Sylvanus, 300.
Sylvester, 1498.
Sylvia, 123, 339, 683.
Sylvia C., 689.

Tenny D., 1244.
Thomas J., 881.
Thomas Jefferson, 479.
Thomas Morris, 607.
Thompson Smith, 1042.
Thurman, 1380.
Titus, 172, 411, 831.
Truman, 1472, 1472.
Truman O., 1116.

Ur, 1085.
Uranah, 151.
Valentine O., 392.
Vera Mav, 1290.
Verdie Belle, 878.
Vesta P., 1192.
Victoria, 662, 805, 1505.
Viola E., 928.

Waldo, 581, 1070.
Walter, 152.
Walter Caleb, 1126.
Walter D., 1450.
Walter Donald, 1441.
Walter Elijah, 892.
Walter H., 1306.
Walter J., 1237.
Walter L., 1080.
Walter Lewis, 1169.
Walter Mettler, 1312.
Ward D., 1134.
Ward G., 1523.
Warren E., 1191.
Warren W., 794.
Washington G., 679.
Watson Eddy, 1028.
Wealtha L., 875.
Wealthy, 216.
Wesley, 695.
Wilbur Eddy, 1029.
Wilford Philander, 1241.
Willard R., 1084.
William, 81, 251, 310, 492, 528, 547, 629, 692, 792, 941, 1060, 1102, 1453.
William A., 950, 1026.
William Bowles, 429.
William C., 698, 1105.
William Deighton, 574.
William F., 663.
William Fisher, 1219.
William Frank, 1121.
William Franklin, 918.
William H., 1240, 1465, 1483, 1485.
William Harvey, 542, 997.
William Henry, 595, 608, 956.
William Henry Harrison, 495.
William J., 1530.
William Lucius, 823.
William McKendre, 637.
William Nelson, 1086.
William Otis, 714.
William P., 454.
William Percival, 655.
William S., 1501.
William Sumner, 1078.
William W., 1522.
William Willard, 826.

Willie, 1384.
Willie M., 1285, 1500.
Willis, 1072.
Willis Linwood, 978.
Willis Monroe, 989.
Willis Volney, 983.

Winnie Ruth, 1052.

Zaidee, 571.
Zenith, 424.

II

OTHER NAMES.

Abbe, Caroline, 844.
" Emeline, 582.
" Frank, 844.
" Fred, 844.
" Henry, 585.
" Rufus, 844.
" Ruth Caroline, 844.
" Sanford, 844.
Abbott, Emeline Laura, 236.
" George Henry, 866.
" Harry, 866.
" Laura Lucinda, 236.
" Mary Adeline, 236.
" Orpha Lucinda, 236.
" Owen Walter, 236.
" Sidney, 866.
" Walter, 236.
Abenethy, Mary, 1119.
Adams, Amelia, 504.
" Amy, 414.
" Chester, 551.
" Frank E., 551.
" George, 963.
" Hannah, 1534.
" Isabel J., 550.
" Melvin L., 551.
" Sarah, 173.
" Mrs. Tabitha, 421.
Agassiz, Alexander, 123.
Alderman, Dell, 997.
Aldrich, Elbridge, 401.
" Margery, 11.
" Sands, 274.
Allee, Amanda, 544.
Allen, Ann, 168.
" Augustus Amidon, 163.
" Bathsheba, 51.
" Caroline, 167.
" Caroline Cynthia, 163.
" Charles H., 167.
" Cornelius, 51.
" Cynthia, 167.
" Daphne, 168.
" Darius, 51.
" Edward Ervin, 167.
" Elizabeth, 51.
" Ellen Maria, 167.
" Eunice Sophronia, 163.
" Flora B., 1174.
" Flora Rosaline, 163.
" George L., 163.
" Henry Clay, 168.
" Henry E. W., 163.
" Henry W., 167.
" James Appleton, 163.
" John, 43.
" John Jarvis, 167.
" Joseph C., 139.
" Jubal Eldridge, 168.
" Julia, 168.
" Keziah Amidon, 167.
" Keziah Cleora, 163.

Allen, Laura, 1084.
" Liberty, 163.
" Liberty Gilman, 163.
" Lucius Shumway, 163.
" Mary, 168.
" Mary Ann Julia, 168.
" Mary Eliza, 163.
" Mercy, 58.
" Obediah, 51.
" Owen Warland, 163.
" Thankful Hortensia, 163.
" Timothy, 51.
Alliard, G. V., 716.
Anderson, Alma Philoma, 246.
" Eli, 246.
" Fanny F., 958.
" Henry Eli, 246.
Andrews, Edwin, 973.
" Emory P., 696.
" George Emory, 696.
" Istenella Mae, 696.
" Joseph Erastus, 696.
" Robert Edmund, 696.
Angier, Abel, 161, 162.
Appy, Ernest F., 696.
Armitage, John William, 906.
Armstrong, Jay Potter, 1249.
Austin, Cora L., 1041.
" Walter, 209.
Averill, Rebecca, 231.
Axtell, Edwin, 1418.

Bailey, Albert, 287.
" Alfred, 287.
" Caroline, 287.
" Elijah, 287.
" Elizabeth, 97.
" Frank, 287.
" Mary Ann, 287.
" Olive, 287.
Baker, Augustus C., 99.
" Calvin, 99.
" Cynthia L., 99.
" Diantha Lestina, 99.
" Ellen Marinda, 99.
" Harlan A., 99.
" Leslie C., 99.
" Lewis W., 99.
" Lucy Caroline, 99.
" Martha Francelia, 99.
" Mary Cordelia, 99.
" Nancy, 772.
" Sophronia E., 99.
Baldwin, Benjamin, 631.
" Daisy Mary, 1283.
" Daniel W., 631.
" E. J., 552.
" George, 661.
" George P., 631.
" Gertrude, 661.
" Joseph, 631.

Baldwin, Leonard C., 661.
" Maria, 631.
" Pernelia, 631.
Ball, Anna M., 660.
" Edward Calf, 1239.
" Howard Ira, 1239.
" Ira S., 1239.
" Marion Helena, 1239.
" Raymond Henry, 1239.
Ballard, Submit, 13.
Ballou, Anna Paulina, 815.
" Warren Fay, 815.
Bangs, Elijah, Jr., 184.
Banister, Lucy, 431.
Barber, Emeline Persis, 257.
" Alzina, 375.
" John Nelson, 903.
Barker, Mary Ette, 573.
" William, 114.
" Jonathan H., 749.
Barnard, Amelia J., 466.
" Malvina M., 742.
Barnes, Mrs. Alice, 544.
" Deborah, 342.
" Lydia O., 610.
" Moses, 347.
Barney, Susan C., 615.
Barrett, Betsey, 339.
" Oscar, 302.
" Waterman, 302.
Bartlett, Dorcas, 594.
" Mary C., 358.
Barton, John W., 163.
Bates, Frank DeWitt, 739.
" Gershom, 174.
" Honora J., 437.
" Issacher, 739.
" Solomon, 174.
Beebe, Arthur, 1034.
" Clarence, 1034.
" George, 1034.
Beecher, Hannah Jane, 356.
" Mary Grace, 746.
" Nancy Ellen, 356.
" William, 356.
" William Ammidown, 356.
Beighen, Michael, 564.
Belding, Laura, 202.
Bemis, Chester L., 813.
" Ella Louisa, 808.
" Frank J., 808.
" Franklin C., 808.
" Harriet E., 808.
" Henry H., 813.
" Julius E., 813.
Bemus, Josiah, 396.
" Gideon, 396.
" Lydia, 396.
" Mary, 396.
" Phebe, 396.
" Ruth, 396.
" Susan Pickering, 710.
Bennett, Fred, 1127.
Benson, Nancy, 104.
Best, Frank E., 539.
Bethel, Lewis, 468.
Bicknell, Mrs., Hepsibah, 252.
Bidney, Annie, 959.
Bigelow, Almira Lucinda, 273.
Bingham, Lucius, 468.
Bishop, Albert C., 99.
" Charles, 1104.
" Chauncey, 431.

Bishop, George, 99.
" Oliver E., 99.
" Osland L., 99.
Bissell, Nelly Adele, 710.
Bixby, Jonathan, 43.
Black, Frank S., 1153.
" Horatio S., 1153.
" Sara C., 1151.
Blanchard, Bessie Emma, 1399.
" Elbridge G., 139.
" Emeline, 299.
" Henry, 1399.
" Isaac S., 627.
" Lysander D., 627.
Bliss, Azariah E., 99.
" David W., 421.
" Ella W., 99.
" Frederick Byron, 435.
" Harriet, 494.
" John L., 421.
" Levi, 421.
" Lyman B., 421.
" Martha, 853.
" Mary E., 421.
" Mary Lovica, 435.
" Mary T., 421.
" Merrit E., 99.
" Moses Walker, 435.
" Pemelia E., 421.
" Samuel, 421.
" Sheburn Lillie, 435.
Blodgett, Ada, 1424.
Blye, Douglas, 802.
Boardman, Althea A., 652.
Bolton, Blanche, 1142.
Bonge, Eliza, 1425.
Booth, Ephraim, 761.
Bordurtha, Frances A., 826.
Bottomley, Thomas, 726.
Bowker, A. V., 1106.
Bowman, Joseph, 167.
Bridges, Phoebe, 508.
Briggs, Alvira, 106.
" Jedediah, 106.
" John, 106.
" Mable J., 1087.
" Nancy, 106.
" Polly, 106.
" Sally, 106.
" Thankful, 106.
Brindle, Arthur, 1064.
" Catherine, 1064.
" Daisy, 1064.
" Julius, 1064.
Brinkerhoff, Sarah, 447.
Bronson, Mr., 375.
Brooks, Arthur L., 539.
" Chester A., 539.
" Donald B., 539.
" Fern F., 539.
" Francis L., 539.
" Frank N., 539.
" Hazel N., 539.
" Ivie F., 539.
" Laura I., 539.
" Lewis N., 539.
" Lorenzo D., 539.
" Marion D., 539.
" Robert L., 539.
Brown, Berilla P., 139.
" Caroline, 139.
" Celia Ann, 139.
" Delise G., 99.

Brown, Earl A., 1108.
"   E. Clair, 99.
"   Elmira, 139.
"   Emory, 1108.
"   Emory W., 99.
"   Fidelia, 139.
"   Frank, 846.
"   Frank H., 99.
"   George, 139.
"   Gertrude K., 99.
"   Hannah, 139.
"   Herbert S., 99.
"   Jane, 139.
"   Jeanette, 830.
"   J. Franklin, 99.
"   John Windsor, 139.
"   John W., 139.
"   Julia Ann, 139.
"   Mary, 775.
"   Myrtle D., 99.
"   Newton H., 99.
"   Norton L., 99.
"   Sally, 108.
"   Stell S., 99.
"   Susan E., 722.
"   Zephaniah, 139.
Browning, Arthur, 701.
"   Dempster, 205.
"   Flora, 205.
"   Frederic Amidon, 701.
"   Lina, 205.
"   Sarah Reid, 323.
"   Susie, 522.
Bruce, Samuel, 230.
"   Smith, 279.
Bryant, Albert Perry, 880.
"   Alice L., 880.
"   Florence A., 880.
"   James H., 880.
"   Maud L., 880.
"   Nellie L., 880.
"   Susie, 809.
Buck, Chester, 106.
Buckles, F. M., 1475.
Buell, Elizabeth, 379.
Bullock, Elmer J., 99.
"   James, 99.
"   Nathan, 288, 312.
"   Nettie L., 99.
Bunker, Georgianna M., 807.
Burlingame, Clark, 105.
Burnett, R. F., 738.
Burnham, Gordon C., 225.
"   Rachel, 504.
Burns, Floyd, 1196.
"   Martin, 1196.
"   Willie, 1196.
Burr, Nelly Fisher, 746.
Burritt, Celia, 380.
"   Cyrus, 380.
"   Delno, 793.
"   Dexter, 380.
"   Hiram, 380.
"   Joseph, 380.
"   Matilda, 380.
"   Melinda, 380.
"   Polly, 378.
"   Sarah, 380.
"   Seely, 380.
"   Todema, 380.
Burt, Luther White, 441.
Bush, Frankie, 1010.

Butler, Augusta, 596.
"   Benjamin, 253.

Calf, Edward, 864.
Calkins, Sarah M., 862.
Calvert, Mary A., 725.
Cameron, Warren, 500.
Canada, Phoebe, 239.
"   Ruamah, 527.
Caneday, Nancy Maria, 859.
Canfield, Emmons, 870.
"   Henry, 870.
"   William, 870.
Cannon, Henry Levin, 1054.
"   James Amidon, 1054.
"   James Calkins, 1054.
"   James Lloyd, 1054.
"   Nelson Augustus, 1054.
Cantley, Edna, 1118.
"   Floyd, 1118.
"   Lester, 1118.
Capron, Dora E., 808.
"   Grace Elizabeth, 808.
"   Joseph Foster, 808.
Carey, Edwin Volney, 871.
"   Emery R., 871.
"   Fred Francis, 871.
"   Loretta Mary, 871.
Carlisle, Charles, 139.
Carnes, Cordelia Maria, 490.
Carpenter, Daniel, 99.
"   Dorcas, 40.
"   Effie A., 1103.
"   Elias, 293.
"   Ella, 1014.
"   Emeline, 327.
"   Frank, 99.
"   Hallock, 1103.
"   Henry, 99.
"   Herbert, 99.
"   Jefferson, 295.
"   John, 295, 1103.
"   Judson, 1103.
"   Lucy, 317.
"   Martha L., 99.
"   Mary Alice, 1250.
"   Molly, 1103.
"   Monroe, 295.
"   Oscar A., 1103.
Carr, David D., 1000.
"   Dorothy, 1000.
"   Fred Clair, 1000.
"   Harry L., 1000.
"   Harvey L., 1000.
"   Horace Eleazer, 1000.
"   Lyman Leroy, 1000.
"   Myrtle Belle, 1000.
"   Weighty, 423.
Carrier, Fenn W., 1001.
"   John P., 1001.
"   Mary Emily, 1001.
"   Sylvia C., 1001.
Carter, Mary A., 137.
Cartter, R. W., 1221.
Case, Clara A., 466.
"   Fernando C., 466.
"   Della S., 466.
"   Frank, 466.
"   Freeman Dwight, 466.
"   Helen L., 769.
"   Hiram, 466.
"   Ichabod J., 769.

Case, Louis, 769.
  "   Marvin J., 769.
  "   Philip J., 769.
  "   Sarah A., 769.
  "   William, 531.
Centro, C., 1477.
Chaffee, Anne Lovejoy, 717.
  "   Eliza, 409.
  "   Joshua A., 525.
  "   Patience, 20.
Chamberlain, Benjamin, 12.
  "   George W., 864.
Chapel, Charles, 1060.
Chapin, Milton, 167.
Chapman, Abner, 71.
  "   Adelia, 71, 238.
  "   Amasa, 71.
  "   Erastus, 510.
  "   Grace, 1222.
  "   Louis, 71.
  "   Sabina, 71.
  "   Zina, 71.
Chase, Elsie, 1002.
  "   Joseph E., 1002.
  "   William Horace, 1002.
Chatman, Benjamin, 101.
  "   Jonathan, 102.
  "   Merritt, 102.
  "   Persis, 101.
  "   Sophronia, 102.
  "   Susan, 102.
  "   Welcome, 102.
  "   Wilson, 102.
Cheney, Caleb, 17.
  "   David B., 738.
  "   Harriet Elizabeth, 738.
  "   Frances Maria, 738.
  "   Lucy Ann, 721.
  "   Lucy I., 1158.
  "   Mary Ellen, 738.
  "   Meltiah, 9.
Cheesbro, Fred, 880.
  "   James A., 880.
  "   Ray, 880.
Child, Daniel, 15.
  "   Sarah, 371.
Childs, Matilda, 146.
  "   Miss, 153.
Claflin, Bertha L., 961.
  "   Elmer F., 961.
  "   Hollis O., 961.
Clark, Alice, 185.
  "   Carrie M., 185.
  "   Charles, 520.
  "   Charles L., 185.
  "   Charles Stillman, 185.
  "   Daniel, 520.
  "   Edward, 520.
  "   Fanny M., 855.
  "   Frances J., 738.
  "   Frank D., 185.
  "   Franklin J., 738.
  "   Frederick W., 185.
  "   George S., 185.
  "   James, 520.
  "   Lyman N., 823.
  "   Mary, 1134.
  "   Mildred A., 738.
  "   Rhoda Ann, 185.
  "   Sarah Amidon, 185.
  "   Stillman, 185.
  "   Susan Sophronia, 185.
Clay, Mary J., 837.

Clegg, Jonathan, 864.
Cleveland, Martha, 197.
Clifford, Myra A., 114.
Clopper, John, 379.
  "   Philo C., 379.
Cobb, Elizabeth, 59.
  "   John, 59.
  "   Lemuel, 59.
  "   Nabby, 59.
Cochran, Henry C., 570.
  "   James T., 571.
  "   Nell, 571.
Colburn, Hannah, 421.
Cole, Alfred E., 737.
  "   Ella M., 737.
  "   Lucevia Wells, 541.
  "   Robert Henry, 737.
Collamer, Luther, 380.
Collins, Julia M., 821.
Comstock, Ebenezer, 242.
  "   Jonathan C., 242.
Connig, Mary Adeline, 1240.
Conrad, Grace, 100.
  "   Harriet, 100.
  "   John, 1081.
  "   William, 100.
Conro, Cassius M., 738.
  "   Fanny M., 738.
  "   Joseph A., 738.
Cook, Eliza, 1083.
  "   Lizzie, 1195.
  "   Lucy Elizabeth, 863.
  "   Nancy, 130.
Cooley, Grace, 766.
  "   Jennie, 481.
  "   Royal, 959.
Coolidge, Burt Carpenter, 1139.
  "   Charles S., 1139.
  "   Roger Earl, 1139.
Coombs, Lucy, 613.
Coomes, Ada, 417.
  "   Della, 417.
  "   Horatio, 417.
Cooper, Lucius, 982.
  "   Maggie, 1122.
Copps, Lulu, 1308.
Corey, Lucinda, 278.
Cothren, Frank, 565.
Cotton, Caroline, 574.
Cowles, Frank E., 987.
  "   John T., 846.
Crary, Dorliska, 1422.
  "   Julia, 787.
Crilley, Hattie M., 984.
Crombie, Sarah E., 756.
Cropsey, Miranda, 379.
  "   Uretta, 395.
Crosier, Simeon F., 1252.
Cross, Dexter, 414.
  "   Emeline S., 329.
Culver, William, 587.
Cummings, Amos, 105.
  "   Charles, 896.
  "   Lawton, 105.
  "   Ruhama, 283.
  "   Sylvia, 105.
  "   Zelpha, 105.
Cups, Albert, 771.
  "   Bertie, 771.
  "   George, 771.
  "   Lura, 771.
  "   Nellie, 771.

Cups, Orra S., 771.
"   William, 771.
Curray, Benjamin, 28.
Curtis, Charlotte A., 545.
"   Dwight A., 995.
"   Elizabeth, 18.
"   Henry, 19.
"   James, 19.
"   Luther C., 271.
"   Ruth, 15.
"   William, 19.

Dalrymple, Francis, 99.
"   Shepherd, 99.
"   Sophrina, 99.
"   Ursula, 99.
Damon, Daniel, 402.
Darling, Titus, 643.
Dauer, Ada, 799.
Davenport, Jonathan E., 323.
Davidson, Celestia, 310.
Davis, Anson, 1116.
"   Caroline, 499.
"   Cynthia, 241.
"   Deborah, 186.
"   Eleanor May, 1091.
"   Ellen, 504.
"   George F., 1091.
"   Sarah, 77.
Davison, Betsey, 111.
Day, Alfred, 520.
"   Alice, 520.
"   Arthur, 520.
"   Beulah, 520.
"   Charles L., 522.
"   Clara, 522.
"   Cyrus C., 834.
"   Daniel, 520.
"   Emily, 520.
"   Emma, 520.
"   Eunice, 522.
"   Flora, 520.
"   Frank, 520.
"   Fred L., 522.
"   George I., 520.
"   Inez, 522.
"   Irving, 520.
"   James, 520.
"   Jessie, 522.
"   Libbie, 520.
"   Lois E., 522.
"   Lorenzo, 522.
"   Mildred, 522.
"   Sumner, 520.
"   Willis D., 522.
"   Winifred, 522.
Dean, Hannah, 14.
Decker, A. W., 466.
Delano, Adelle, 535.
Deming, Laura, 228.
Densmore, Solomon, 258.
Devore, Florence Mabel, 1007.
"   Forest, 1007.
"   Glen Hollis, 1007.
"   H. H., 1007.
"   Matie, 589.
"   Mildred, 1009.
"   Pearl Lucevia, 1007.
"   Robert George, 1007.
De Wolf, Alice, 999.
"   Clayton A., 99.
"   Dallas M., 999.

De Wolf, Evie, 999.
"   John J., 99.
"   Laura Estella, 999.
"   Lina Mary, 999.
Dexter, Hannah, 183.
"   Ichabod, 183.
"   John Bangs, 183.
"   Ruth, 183.
"   Sally, 183.
Dixon, Kate, 1226.
Dodge, Emogene, 593.
"   Julia J., 762.
Dickerman, Belle A., 861.
Doolittle, Carl Nelson, 1009.
"   Eddie, 1009.
"   Edna Lucile, 1009.
Doremus, Fanny, 1078.
Doubledee, Sarah, 21.
Dresser, Chester, 358.
"   Chester Ammidown, 358.
"   George A., 358.
"   Mercy, 357.
"   Pamella, 358.
Dudley, Widow, 306.
Dunbar, Bertha, 286.
"   Emery, 840-842.
"   John, 145.
"   Laura Ann, 866.
Dunlap, Gertrude, 777.
"   J. Boyd, 777.
"   Laura, 1120.
"   Matilda, 319.
"   Will Knox, 777.
Dunn, Fanny, 1502.
Dunsmore, Betsey Jane, 490.
"   Ellen Edelpha, 946.
Durpey, Lucretia, 296.
Dyer, Anna, 1479.
Dymond, Charles, 372.
"   Peter, 372.

Earll, Jeannette, 488.
Eastman, Mary, 974.
Eaton, Charlotte Louise, 516.
Edson, Charles, 835.
Edwards, Clapp, 496.
"   Foster, 269.
"   Porter, 266.
"   Sarah E., 266.
Eddy, Ruth, 29.
Ellis, Timothy, 163.
Emerson, Henry M., 740.
Estes, Jane Emily, 478.
Esty, Abijah, 311.
"   Amy Ann, 311.
"   Lucy, 288.
"   Mary Ann, 288.
"   Stephen, 288.

Fairbank, Alice, 654.
"   David Canada, 654.
"   Ellen B., 655.
"   Emma Amelia, 654.
Falls, Elizabeth, 518.
Farrar, Ellen, 1117.
Farrell, Helen Beatrice, 1254.
"   Victor, 1254.
"   William Amadon, 1254.
"   William J., 1254.
Fay, George E., 183.
"   James P., 183.
"   John H., 183.

Field, Abner, 200.
" Albert, 200.
" Alice, 200.
" Charles H., 200.
" Emma D. A., 709.
" Hannah, 200.
" Leonard, 200.
" Leonard P., 200.
" Mary Matilda, 200.
" Philip, 200.
" Robert Emmett, 200.
" Silas C., 200.
Firman, Eliza, 420.
Fishell, Susan, 770.
Fisher, Rebekah, 357.
Fisk, Alma L., 959.
" Hannah C., 959.
" Martha H., 873.
" Nina, 959.
" Seth, 959.
" Uriah, 959.
Fletcher, Alice, 1090.
Flint, Anna, 79.
" Asaryl, 79.
" Augustus, 79.
" Elisha, 79.
" Jonathan, 79.
" Joseph, 79.
" Polly, 79.
" Sally, 79.
Flood, Fanny, 434.
" Harriet Augusta, 886.
Flower, Frank, 481.
Flynn, Sarah, 54.
Fodder, Nancy, 1419.
Forbes, Mary Hathaway, 123.
Ford, Jazariah, 123.
Forrester, Fanny, 887.
" William F., 887.
Forsyth, Thomas Arthur, 1089.
Fossmire, Davis, 777.
Foster, Emma, 1066.
" Hannah, 89.
" James, 591.
" Rufus, 281.
" Samuel, 1066.
" Wilbur, 1066.
Fowler, Angeline, 380.
" Curtis, 786.
" Mrs. Miriam, 418.
" Rebecca, 424.
Fox, Blanche, 1197.
" Charles, 1197.
" Fred, 1197.
" Hiller, 1197.
" Robert, 1197.
French, Dalpha Catherine, 1016.
" George, 320.
" Jesse, 1016.
" Maud A., 1535.
Frost, Ella, 876.
Frothingham, Samuel T., 936.
Fuller, Alonza, 196.
" Annie E., 711.
" Mary, 328.

Gage, Adeline, 575.
Gardner, Enoch W., 393.
Gaut, Emma J., 539, 543.
" Gertrude L., 543.
" Harvey, 543.

Gaut, Ida, 543.
" James A., 543.
" John, 543.
" Lewis, 543.
" Minnie, 543.
George, Jane Lydia, 606.
Gilbert, Clara, 482.
" Elliot, 482.
" Harriet E., 988.
" Jonathan, 57.
" Nelson, 482.
" Sabra, 172.
Giles, Tyla G., 1004.
Glazier, Martha A., 833.
Gleason, Caroline, 207.
Goddard, Edwin, 463.
" Hiram, 463.
" Juliet, 463.
" Melvin, 463.
" Silvia, 611.
Goff, Alvin E., 854.
Goldsberg, ——, 658.
Goodman, Achasah, 401.
Goodrich, Orin, 845.
Goodspeed, Rhoda, 60.
Gould, Fuller, 297.
" Oren, 185.
" Samuel, 297.
" Susie M., 628.
Gowdy, John, 773.
" Solomon, 106.
Granger, Lucy, 315.
Gray, Anna D., 745.
Green, Charley, 1035.
" Earl L., 1035.
" Ethel, 1035.
" Forrest, 1035.
" Harriet, 877.
" Iva B., 1035.
" Loami, 270.
" Tabitha, 53.
" William, 1035.
" William H., 746.
Greenslit, Emily Amelia, 869.
Griffin, Almira, 519.
Grice, Elizabeth, 124.
Griswold, Adelaide Rhoda, 846.
" Frank, 846.
" George, 846.
" George Talcott, 846.
" Jay H., 190.
" Martha Elizabeth, 846.
Gron, Edith I., 1033.
" Hannah, 1033.
Grosvenor, Cyrus P. D., 727.
Grover, Clarissa, 292.
Gulliford, James, 1047.
Gunthaur, Lizzie, 1450.

Hadsell, Clair Jay, 1001.
" Jay D., 1001.
Haffner, Harriet Birch, 588.
Hagar, Martha, 547.
Hale, Rosetta M., 329.
Hall, George, 84.
" Sallie, 84.
" Shubal, 84.
Hamblett, Eliza D., 443.
Hamilton, Carrie D., 698.
Hammett, Frank, 1464.
Hammond, Mary A., 365.
Haroun, Thomas, 71.

Harrington, Everett A., 1238.
"   H. H., 1473.
"   Fred J., 1238.
Harris, Myron C., 435.
Harrison, Robert N., 877.
Hartwell, Calvin A., 360.
"   Lydia Louise, 360.
"   Samuel, 360.
"   Samuel Cyrus, 360.
Harvey, Mary J., 338.
Harwood, Abigail, 93.
"   Elisha, 90.
"   Joanna, 1.
Haskell, M. John, 345.
"   Levi, 161.
"   Micajah, 59.
Hastings, Sarah, 16.
Hathaway, Lottie. 1257.
Haven, Martha, 444.
Havens, Charles, 901.
Hawkins, Elizabeth, 10.
Hay, Duane, 518.
"   Henry, 518.
"   John, 518.
Head, Sarah, 671.
Healy, John Boyden, 604.
"   Elizabeth Learned, 604.
"   Sally Cornelia, 604.
"   Waldo Moses, 604.
Henderson, Laura Etta, 562.
"   Sarah C., 533.
"   Sylvanus, 524.
Henry, David, 706.
Henshaw, Mary C., 113.
Herrick, Ella M., 1398.
Herrington, Charles W., 1207.
Hewett, Edward G., 662.
"   Henry, 662.
Hicks, Calvin, 99.
"   Cynthia, 99.
"   Emerson, 99.
"   Emily, 99.
"   Harriet, 99.
"   Joseph, 99.
"   Julia, 1258.
"   Lemira, 99.
"   McKendre, 99.
"   Mary, 99.
"   Massena, 99.
"   Miranda, 99.
"   Welcome, 99.
Higgins, Lucy Ella, 1088.
"   Matilda Elizabeth, 781.
"   Minerva, 154.
Hildreth, Albert Gallatin, 203.
"   Cheney, 203.
"   Fanny, 203.
"   Henry, 203.
"   John, 203.
"   Katuria. 203.
"   Nellie, 203.
Hill, James W., 933.
"   Mary, 866.
"   Rowland J., 933.
Hills, Martha B., 485.
Hodges, Byron, 552.
"   Charles, 552.
"   Flora A., 552.
"   Seraph, 353.
"   William H., 552.
Hoffstetler, Lydia, 989.
Holbrook, Wilbur. 1302.
Holcomb, Jason N., 529.

Holden, John, 34.
Holmes, George, 651.
"   Patty, 135.
Holt, Alice May, 905.
"   Keturah, 78.
Hopkins, Mary E., 1024.
Horne, Laura E., 861.
Horton, Mr., 374.
Hoskins, Benjamin, 1068.
Houghton, Chandler, 100.
"   Chauncey, 100.
"   Edwin M., 431.
"   Frederick H., 431.
"   Henry, 100.
"   Jane A., 100.
"   Joel, 100.
"   Mary S., 1102.
"   Merritt M., 431.
"   Warren, 100.
"   Wesley, 100.
"   Willie C., 431.
House, Jane, 386.
Hovey, Hannah, 135.
Howard, Daniel Clyde, 654.
"   John, 654.
"   S. W., 504.
Howe, William, 337.
Howell, Jane, 316.
Howland, Lois, 277.
Hudson, Benjamin, 645.
Hughes, Ann, 388.
Hull, Martha, 521.
Humphrey, Lucy, 94.
"   Rufus, 92.
Humphreys, Edward, 639.
Hunt, Ebenezer, 321.
"   H. W., 802.
"   Jason. 318.
"   Mila, 275.
"   Mrs. Stephen, 67.
Hurlburt, Della, 229.
Hutchinson, Sally, 180.

Ingham, George, 791.
Inglasbee, Eugene, 1184.
"   Frank, 1184.
"   Julius, 1184.
Ives, Chloe. 1414.
"   Elenora. 575.
"   James, 575.
"   Jared, 575.
"   Jesse, 575.
"   John, 575.
"   Maria, 577.

Jacobs, Albert, 894.
"   Belle H., 1124.
"   Henry, 846.
"   Orin Philander, 846.
Jackson, Almira M.
"   Clarinda, 528.
"   Lucy Caroline, 100.
Jacques, Nettie B., 1045.
Jaynes, Lilly, 1008.
Jefferson, Mrs., 310.
Jenkins, Fred, 1463.
Jennings, Sarah, 776.
Johnson, Charlotte, 1416.
"   Ella May, 949.
"   Joanna, 18.
"   John H., 936.
"   Parson, 284.

Jones, Edward Kendrick, 1245.
" Sarah, 638.
Jordan, Alonzo P., 727.
Joyce, Charles Henry, 209.
" Chloe, 209.
" Thomas, 209.
Judd, Edwin W., 650.

Keach, Amy J., 895.
Keep, Abner N., 539.
" Alice E., 539.
" Arthur W., 539.
" Bertha N., 539.
" Carlton F., 539.
" Earl L., 539.
" Edna, 539.
" Edward C., 539.
" Ellen L., 539.
" Emma, A., 539.
" Ernest C., 539.
" Ethel Ruth, 539.
" Fenton R., 539.
" Florence M., 539.
" Frank E., 539.
" George A., 539.
" Gladys, 539.
" Haskell Harold, 539.
" Hiram A., 539.
" Inez B., 539.
" Inez M., 539.
" Ivan, 539.
" John L., 960.
" John O., 539.
" Junie M., 539.
" Kester L., 539.
" Lina B., 539.
" Lloyd A., 539.
" Lois T., 539.
" Lyle D., 539.
" Margaret M., 539.
" Marsena L., 539.
" Mildred L., 539.
" Paul A., 539.
" Polly E., 539.
" Ralph C., 539.
" Sallie Best, 539.
" Sallie Lucinda, 539.
" Shirley Dare, 539.
" Willis A., 539.
" Zachary T., 539.
Keith, ——, 284.
Kelly, Rosamond, 358.
Kendrick, Caroline A., 323.
" Kate, 835.
Kenyon, Elizabeth, 517.
" Eugene A., 246.
" Fannie, 518.
" Samuel, 517.
Ketcham, Spencer, 784.
Keyser, Maude E., 892.
Kibbee, Olive, 501.
Kimball, Alfred J., 932.
" Charles L., 932.
" Fanny, 1469.
" Freelove, 885.
" Ira C., 932.
" Iva L., 932.
" Lena, 717.
King, Arthur Tyler, 703.
" Blanche, 1041.
" Charles, 703.
" George T., 71.

King, Sabina, 71.
" Sarah Lydia, 703.
" Volney, 71.
" Volney L., 71.
Kingsbury, Dorothy J., 484.
" Joseph, 23.
Kinsey, Joseph, 751.
Kline, Ida M., 539.
Klock, G. W., 970.
Klumph, Laura A., 914.
Knapp, Clifford, 522.
" Henry, 522.
" Howard, 522.
" Lorenzo, 522.
Koufler, Martha, 158.
Kremm, May, 960.

Ladd, Esther, 38.
Lamb, Lucy H., 893.
" Mary L., 750.
Lamon, Archie L., 639.
" Bertha, 639.
" Charles A., 639.
" John H., 639.
" Raymond S., 639.
" Ruth D., 639.
" Sarah Jane, 639.
" Stewart, 639.
" Walter S., 639.
" Warren S., 639.
" William H., 639.
Lane, Frederick Henry, 1094.
Larned, William, 114.
Larkin, Inga, 1244.
Larrow, James, 1123.
Larson, Jessie L., 1032A.
Lawrence, Olivia, 794.
Leach, Roxalena, 160.
Learned, Hannah, 269.
Lease, Augustus S., 1423.
Lee, Celia, 418.
" H. William, 923.
" Olive, 522.
Lagare, Harold A., 1141.
" Louis F., 1141.
Leonard, Anne Rebekah, 746.
" Bernard Ammidown, 746.
" Charles Henry, 746.
" David Fiske, 746.
" David, 87.
" Edward Henry, 753.
" Eleanor Tucker, 746.
" George Manning, 746.
" Grace Fisher, 746.
" Henry Fiske, 753.
" Herman Burr, 746.
" Manning, 746.
" Mary Beecher, 746.
" Mary Frances, 746.
" Prentiss, 1095.
" Russell Ammidown, 746.
" Sarah Catherine, 746.
" Sarah P., 762.
Lewis, Fred K., 1280.
" Willie S., 1046.
Lichard, Louisa, 785.
Lillie, Abbie C., 437.
" Abner L., 880.
" Daniel Fred, 437.
" Daniel Hand, 437.
" Effie Martha, 437.
" Ethel Irene, 880.

Lillie, Everett S., 437.
"   Frank Adelbert, 437.
"   George Melvin, 880.
"   George Myron, 880.
"   Haroll Claude, 880.
"   Hattie Celestia. 880.
"   Jennie Ethel, 880.
"   Julia Martha, 437.
"   Louise E., 880.
"   Lucy May, 437.
"   Lyman, 880.
"   Melvin Lyman, 880.
"   Ralph Henry, 437.
"   Ralph Reid, 880.
Lindsley, Archie H., 653.
"   Charles H., 653.
"   Clara L., 653.
"   Edward A., 653.
"   Lucius R., 653.
Lines, George, 139.
Liscomb, John, 335.
Litchfield, Mary Towne, 753.
Loch, Mabel, 1042.
Lockwood, Annis, 875.
"   Burton T., 875.
"   Frank R., 875.
"   Ella Izoria, 875.
"   Julia O., 958.
"   Milton, 875.
"   R. Pearl, 875.
Logan, Olive, 41.
Loomis, Ray, 957.
Lord, Fanny, 546.
Luce, Charles, 1065.
"   Luretta, 426.
"   Mehitable Marble, 424.
"   Nancy, 1420.
Lyman, Theodore. 123.
Lyon, Rebecca, 236.

Mace, Mary E., 542.
McAuley, Mary, 1142.
McBrayne, Agnes, 323.
McClure, J. H., 1013.
"   J. Stewart, 1013.
"   Marea, 1013.
McCormick, George. 572.
"   Henry, 572.
"   John Gould, 572.
"   Rosetta, 572.
McCune, Mrs. John, 297.
McHenry, Beulah Richardson, 1022.
McIntire, Aurelia. 263.
McIntyre, Sarah Ann, 601.
McKeney, Belle, 323.
McLaughlin, Mary N., 358.
McManus, Allen, 539.
"   Charles, 522.
"   Edwin, 522.
"   Esther F., 539.
"   Fred. 522.
"   Grant, 522.
"   James, 522.
"   Laura. 522.
"   Mabel. 522.
"   Mamie. 522.
"   Robert, 522.
"   Susan, 520.
Maddock. ——, 191.
Magee, Charles, 882.
"   Hattie, 882.
"   Libby, 882.

Mann, Louisa, 495.
Mansfield, Merrick, 357, 748.
Marcey, Caroline, 346.
Marquart. Arthur A., 539.
Marsh, Julia B., 366.
Martin, Edith M., 1037.
"   Elizabeth, 25.
Matterson, Susan, 428.
Matthews, Jerome J., 904.
"   Lena, 937.
Mason, Abraham, Jr., 305.
"   Eliza. 436.
"   Nancy, 482.
"   Sophronia, 505.
Maxwell, James, 832.
Maynard, A. F., 163.
Mettlen, Mattie E., 982.
Millard, Arthur, 100.
"   Billing, 100.
"   Jenny L., 100.
"   Laura, 100.
"   Lucy C., 100.
Miller, Edward, 568.
"   Emeline, 860.
"   William S., 236.
Mills, Anna T., 539.
Miner, Lydia L., 387.
Minges, Abram, 986.
Mitten, James, 520.
Moffitt, Lemuel, 88.
Mohler, Levi, 981.
Monroe, Marilla, 380.
Montgomery, Frank, 1067.
Moody, Joel, 407.
"   L. W., 407.
Moore, B. F., 539.
"   Gertrude, 539.
"   Sarah R., 363.
"   Wendell O., 539.
"   Winfred B., 539.
Morgan, Abby, 883.
"   Freeman, 1427.
Morse, Callina, 349.
"   Francis S., 349.
"   Hattie, 468.
"   Julia M., 349.
"   Samuel, 468.
"   Sarah, 468.
Moses, Clinton, 957.
Moseley, Henry, 567.
"   Orton. 567.
Mosher, Della, 783.
"   Nelly, 788.
Mowry, Banfield, 332.
"   Shubel, 431.
"   Whipple B., 332.
Munson, Phoebe, 476.

Negus, Daisy E., 99.
"   Halbert E., 99.
"   Fred T., 99.
"   Roy L., 99.
"   Timothy, 99.
Newcomb, Iola D., 579.
"   Martin Luther, 579.
"   Sarah W., 185.
"   William Augustus, 579.
"   William Wallace, 579.
Newell, Thankful, 351.
Newman, Thomas, 395.
Newton, Ermina Elizabeth, 746.
"   Susan Stephens, 325.

Nichols, Beulah, 205.
" Charles B., 205.
" Cheney, 205.
" Clara, 205.
" Daniel, 205.
" Dora, 205.
" Elizabeth Ann, 843.
" Emerson Earl, 205.
" Florence Emma, 205.
" George C., 205.
" George O., 205.
" Homer, 205.
" Lotta, 925.
" Mary Elizabeth, 205.
" Mattie, 925.
" Moses M., 99.
" Obed, 925.
" Viola B., 99, 705.
Niece, Louisa, 846.
Nims, Delia, 819.
" Henry G., 819.
" Lucius, 819.
" Mary, 819.
" Thomas Hull, 819.
Noyes, Alice, 1055.
Nye, Martha, 181.

Okeif, Maggie, 1000.
Olds, Nettie Myrtle, 867.
Orcott, Newell, 583.
Orcutt, Alice Julia, 654.
" Isaac Hall, 654.
Ott, Frances Alice, 1147.
Owen, Alida, 190.
" Daniel, 190.
" Daniel D., 190.
" Esther, 190.
" Polly, 190.

Page, Margaret, 1133.
Paige, Bela B., 185.
" Calvin A., 357.
" Cynthia E., 537.
" Juliette E., 357.
" Timothy, Jr., 357.
Park, Harvey, 497.
" Henry, 502.
Parker, Anna, 72.
" Henry, 359.
" Joseph, 358.
" Susanna, 177.
Parmenter, Edward S., 1264.
" Raymond, 1264.
Parsons, Perrin P., 206.
Patterson, Nellie, 552.
Peck, Alexander A., 1298.
" Marcus, 236.
Perham, Frank, 882.
Penoyer, Laura M., 798.
Percy, E. D., 1476.
" M., 1474.
Perkins, Addie Sarah, 400.
" Jane, 1470.
" Jared Daniel, 400.
Perrin, Almira, 764.
" Artemas, 163.
Perry, Aletheia, 83.
" Frances, 637.
" Hattie, 1121.
" Mehitable, 6.
" Mercy, 140.

Phelps, Chester, 109.
" Clark, 109.
" Dana, 312.
" Edward, 109.
" Elijah, 109.
" Ella Adaline, 99.
" Francis W., 99.
" Simon, 109.
" William, 99, 109.
Phillips, Almond, 167.
" Duane S., 861.
" Edward S., 861.
" Elizabeth B., 861.
" Ella, 861.
" George H., 861.
" Hazel, 861.
" Jerome, 861.
" Spencer, 861.
" Wendell S., 861.
" Westley G., 861.
Pierce, Flora S., 656.
Pierson, Charles L., 123.
Plymton, Ellen M., 360.
Pollock, Evaline, 1447.
Pool, Hannah, 80.
Potter, Ella, 100.
Potwin, Nancy, 902.
Powers, Elmer, 363.
" Elmer D., 183.
" Frank, 183.
" Viola, 947.
" Joel L., 183.
" Lysander, 183.
Pratt, Frank, 515.
" Harry, 515.
Prescott, Emma, 1038.
Priest, Bessie May, 1137.
Prouty, Alice, 504.
" Maryetta, 729.
Puffer, Prudy M., 685.
" Solomon, 694.
" Tisdale, 314.
Putney, Abigail, 44.
" Betsey B., 393.

Quirk, Bertha E., 926.

Rand, Alfred E., 504.
" Alonzo A., 504.
" Andrew B., 504.
" Benjamin A., 504.
" Eldora H., 504.
" Frank, 504.
" Preston A., 504.
" Reuben B., 504.
" Rosina A., 504.
" Winfield S., 504.
Randall, Alvarette, 1536.
" Barney, 1536.
" Bertha L., 539.
" Clarence, 1536.
" Gladys, 1536.
" Hannah, 6.
" Jerry, 539.
Randolph, Sarah H., 396.
Ray, Abel, 45.
Raymond, Eva, 1148.
Razey, Alma, 1125.
" Betsey M., 317.
Rea, Edgar C., 539.
" Edna A., 539.
" Nellie E., 539.
" William R., 539.

Reed, Alfred, 700.
" Edith, 1163.
" Lavant M., 400.
" Mary J., 666.
Reid, Wilhelmina R., 880.
Rexford, Harvey S., 539.
" Max, 530.
" Zella F., 539.
Reynolds, Hannah M., 358.
" Mary, 73.
Rhea, Alexander, 491.
" Byron, 491.
" Viola, 491.
Rice, Daniel, 159.
" F. J., 100.
" Laban, 159.
" Thomas, 163.
Rider, —, 29.
Risley, Clarissa, 227.
Ricker, Maria, 607.
Rickerds, Rees, Mrs., 142.
Rickert, Mary, 464.
Richards, Alvira M., 479.
Richardson, Dorothy A., 1074.
" Oscar Kelsey, 1074.
Richmond, Ann, 578.
" Armenia, 233.
Robbins, Augusta, 918.
" Ebenezer, 52.
" Jane, 48.
" Samuel, 919.
Roberts, Mabel, 996.
" Ross, 550.
Robertson, Carrie B., 639.
" Florence, 1086.
" William R., 639.
Rockwell, Maria, 473.
Roe, Addie W., 1026.
Rogers, William, 457.
Rolhauser, Dora Henrietta, 702.
Root, Luverne, 1053.
Rose, J. O., 1417.
Ross, Reuben, 803.
Rounds, E., 1428.
Rowell, Frederick, 481.
" George, 481.
" Jerusha, 481.
" Willard, 481.
Ruggles, Mrs. Anna, 58.
" Seth, 61.
" Seth Amidon, 61.
Rundell, Mary Cordelia, 536.
Russell, Abigail, 122.
" Amelia E., 123.
" Anna, 123.
" Anna Matilda, 123, 334.
" Caroline, 544.
" Caroline A., 123.
" Elisha, 68.
" Elizabeth, 123.
" Ella A., 1503.
" Emily, 123.
" George Robert, 123.
" Henry Sturges, 123.
" Jonathan, 123.
" Marian, 123.
" Mary Lucy, 734.
" Nancy, 68, 262.
" Robert Shaw, 123.
" Sarah, 123.
" Thomas H., 968.

Sabin, Hannah, 39.
Sadler, Manfred M., 1342.
Sage, George, 554.
" Ida, 380.
Sails, George H., 871.
" Ralph E., 871.
Sampson, Benjamin, Jr., 164.
Sanborn, Dorothy Esther, 1250.
" Isaac Henry, 1250.
" Richard Wall, 1250.
Sanger, Olive, 134.
Sawtelle, Mrs. G. E., 163.
Sawyer, Leander, 163.
" Roberta, 504.
Sayles, Mrs. Lena, 717.
Scarborough, Ebenezer, 37.
" Samuel, 35.
Schafer, Viola, 1075.
Schermerhorn, Lilly B., 1044.
" Loyd B., 1037.
" Lyle C., 1037.
" William C., 1037.
" William, 1037.
" William L., 1037.
Schofield, Ellen M., 357.
Schopp, Eva M., 1343.
Scott, Alta V., 99.
" Walter F., 99.
" Susie, 99.
" Winfield B., 99.
Scriver, Nellie Helen, 437.
Searls, Henry, 151.
Sedgwick, Harriet, 267.
Sequim, E. C., 708.
Shales, Nancy, 430.
Sharp, Jessie, 491.
" Mabel, 491.
Shaw, Ethelyn, 1076.
" Sarah P., 123.
Shepherd, Mr., 503.
" Elizabeth, 29.
Sherman, Bertha Evangeline, 435.
Shirley, John Warren, 167.
Shumway, Adelaide, 349.
" Anna, 341.
" Eunice, 47.
" Olive Sophia, 603.
Simmons, Alma, 782.
" Boyd, 782.
" Cyrus, 782.
" Frank, 782.
" Gertrude, 782.
" John, 782.
" Lizzie, 782.
Sinclair, Martha Glines, 577.
Skeel, Ruth E., 587.
Slade, Hattie A., 795.
Slocum, Calvin, 689.
" Rena, 689.
Smith, Alanson, 431.
" Anna J., 624.
" Bertha B., 891.
" Carrie A., 962.
" Clara, 1425.
" Clarissa, 215.
" Edwin C., 431.
" Esther, 241.
" Francis A., 431.
" Hannah, 14.
" James Monroe, 431.
" Jane Janette, 431.

Smith, Jedediah, 404.
" Jerusha, 141.
" Jessie, 1092.
" Lucretia, 498.
" Martha L., 1140.
" Seth Hurd, 431.
" Vania J., 1058.
" William, 380.
Snider, James P., 875.
" James P., Jr., 875.
Southwick, Daniel, 439.
" Ida Adell, 439.
Southworth, Nancy, 456.
Spalding, A. C., 504.
" Betsey, 240.
" Eliza M., 539.
Spence, Alice Mary, 696.
Spenill, Emmet, 994.
Sprague, Clarence G., 957.
" George, 957.
" Mary A., 957.
Squires, ——, 106.
Stacy, Edward, 1082.
" Persis, 401.
Stanton, Ella, 207.
Staples, Lawrence, 1198.
" Perry, 1198.
" Robert, 1198.
Starkwether, Olive, 546.
Starky, Keziah, 275.
Starr, Martha M., 192.
" Sophia, 244.
Stearns, Matilda, 578.
" Oakman Sprague, 356.
Stebbins, Alexander Field, 857.
" Lillian E., 851.
" Mary Lillian, 851.
Steel, Abigail, 99.
Steele, Arthur, 645.
" Cora Laura, 645.
" Isabelle, 508.
" Leah Nora, 645.
" Lydia Porter, 645.
" Myra Crete, 645.
" William W., 645.
Stenderson, Ester Ann, 356.
Stevens, Bertha, 232.
Stewart, Frank, 518.
" Fred, 518.
" George A., 518.
" George H., 518.
" Henry, 518.
" Henry J., 518.
" Josephine, 518.
" Margaret J., 518.
" Mildred M., 518.
" Sarah A., 518.
" Willard, 561.
Stockwell, Adaline, 99.
" Cynthia Ellen, 99.
" Delia A., 99.
" Della, 99.
" Elwyn L., 99.
" Emory, 99.
" Ernest, 439.
" Frank Everett, 1251.
" George N., 99.
" George S., 439.
" Harry E., 99.
" Herbert C., 99.
" Joseph, Jr., 1251.
" Lorenzo, 99.
" Lucy Emaline, 99.

Stockwell, Merrit, 90.
" Mary Elizabeth, 99.
" Norman, 99.
" Oliver B., 1251.
" Raymond A., 1251.
" Rodney Joseph, 1251.
" Samuel, 99.
" Samuel Welcome, 99.
" Sarah Ann, 99.
Stone, Ambrose, 323.
" Ambrose Pratt, 323.
" Arthur Browning, 323.
" Daniel S., 323.
" Elizabeth D., 323.
" Frank Lorenzo, 323.
" Frederick Carroll, 323.
" Harry Amidon, 323.
" Henry Solomon, 323.
" Julian Dean, 323.
" Lillian May, 323.
" Lizzie Jane, 323.
" Lucy A., 323.
" Lucy Amidon, 323.
" Lucy Almira, 323.
" Martha Elizabeth, 323.
" Myra Merrick, 323.
" Newton, 323.
" Royal Amidon, 323.
" Royal Wells, 323.
" Solomon Amidon, 100, 323.
" Walter Pratt, 323.
" William Royal, 323.
Stow, John, 657.
Streeter, Ada, 732.
" Emma C., 732.
" Gertie May, 99.
" Hiland J., 99.
" Joseph J., 99.
" Leonard, 732.
" Lillian C., 99.
" Mabel C., 732.
Stringfellow, Nettie, 1000.
Strong, Lyman, 220.
" Marcia, 218.
" Temperance Mary, 291.
Sturgeon, Alice, 552.
Sturtevant, Mr., 507.
Sweet, Charity, 251.
Swett, Charles, 887.

Tabb, W. Kemp, 985.
Taft, Blanche G., 638.
" Charles Henry, 638.
" Clifford E., 638.
" Cora E., 638.
" Elmer C., 638.
" Francis, 123.
" John, 638.
" Lilly, 638.
" Pauline E., 638.
" Sylvia, 36.
" Will H., 638.
Talbot, Thomas, 760.
Tanner, Mary, 1043.
" Sally, 70.
Taylor, Emma, 922.
" Mrs., 487.
Thatcher, Carrie Lovica, 435.
Thatcher, Hester Billings, 356.
" Sereno S., 435.
Thayer, Silence, 33.

Thomas, Asahel, 66.
"   David, 66.
Thompson, A. L., 1006.
"   Elizabeth Gertrude, 1006.
"   Francis M., 819.
"   Francis Nima, 819.
"   Harriet, 401.
"   John, 8.
"   Joseph, 804.
"   Lena Belle, 1006.
"   Leslie Lincoln, 1006.
"   Mabel Elda, 1006.
"   Mary Jane, 549.
"   Mildred Floy, 1006.
"   Prudence, 81.
Thorpe, Anna, 1531.
Thrall, Henry, 821.
Tiffany, Mary C., 849.
Tinney, Cora Ann, 1241.
"   Zenas D., 183.
Todd, Arthur D., 99.
"   Esther Almeda, 588.
"   Franklin L., 99.
"   Judson F., 99.
Tower, Maud Lillie, 865.
Town, Ephriam, 50.
"   Wesley, 298.
Tracy, Anna, 539.
"   Irene L., 539.
"   Rose E., 539.
Truax, Maud, 1077.
Trussell, Judith M., 430.
Tubbs, Andrew J., 237.
"   Solomon, 237.
Tucker, Amos, 99.
"   Amos H., 99.
"   Emma, 1188.
"   Rebecca, 1079.
"   William, 805.
Turner, Hattie May, 1085.
Twining, Alpheus, 333.
Twitchell, Jenny Smith, 699.
Tyler, Jenny F., 1102.

Underwood, A. B., 17.
Upham, Czarina P., 733.
Urban, Rose, 1000.

Valentine, Elijah, 358.
Van Braak, Bernard Johann, 1040.
"   James Johann, 1040.
"   Mary B., 1040.
"   William Bernard, 1040.
Vinton, Harriet, 352.
"   Hosea, 460.
"   John, 460.
"   Sally Maria, 344.
"   Samuel, 245.
"   Thomas, 245.

Wagner, Frank W., 1279.
Wakefield, Elmer E., 514.
"   Frances, 514.
"   Lavery, 514.
Wales, Elizabeth, 30.
Walker, Benjamin, 99.
"   Betsey, 99.
"   Content, 99.
"   Cynthia, 99.
"   Elizabeth, 210.

Walker, Hannah, 76, 96.
"   John, 99.
"   Lucy, 99.
"   Polly, 99.
"   Roxy, 99.
"   Rufus, 99.
"   Welcome, 99.
Wallace, Edward, 532.
"   Stella, 532.
Walsh, Lizzie, 1122.
Walsworth, Susan Malissa, 304.
Walworth, Theresa H., 628.
Ward, Eliza C., 139.
"   Henry A., 1103.
"   Henry D., 987.
"   Jessie, 987.
"   Mary A., 987.
Wardell, Emily, 99.
Warfield, Ithamar, 6.
"   John, 6.
Warner, Israel C., 640.
"   Sarah A., 438.
Watson, Daniel, 867.
"   Daniel Francis, 867.
"   John Valentine, 867.
"   Laura Irene, 867.
"   Olive, 387.
"   Samuel, 387.
"   William, 1000.
"   William Ansel, 867.
Wattles, Theano, 466.
Watts, Fred Madison, 702.
"   Harry Lorenzo, 702.
"   William B., 702.
Weatherwax, Frank, 539.
"   Lina, 539.
"   William A., 539.
Webb, Jane, 686.
Webber, Clara C., 814.
Webster, Prudence, 455.
Weeks, Adeline, 272.
"   Bertha Anna, 948.
Wells, Martha, 330.
"   Nettie, 100.
Wessels, ———, 191.
West, Ruth, 84.
Wetherell, Lyman, 95.
Wheaton, Ebenezer, 5.
"   Hannah, 5.
"   Jeremiah, 5.
"   John, 5.
"   Mehitable, 5.
"   Nathaniel, 5.
"   Sarah, 5.
Wheelock, Mary, 17.
"   Samuel, 17.
Whilt, Hilda J., 1253.
Whipple, Albert, 537.
"   Arminta, 537.
"   Emma, 504, 537.
"   Hattie, 610.
"   Mary, 537.
"   Mary Alberta, 537.
"   Orlan, 623.
Whitcomb, Mary E., 889.
White, Harriet, 411.
"   Lydia, 166.
"   Mary, 166.
Whitely, Ollie, 983.
Whiting, Alice, 283.
"   Henry, 138.
Whitney, Almira, 100, 103.
"   Almira Maria, 100, 323.

Whitney, Asa, 100.
" Chauncey John, 100.
" Chauncey L., 100.
" Clarence, 100.
" Ellen A., 100.
" Emily Francelia, 100.
" George W., 100.
" Harriet, 100.
" Harriet D., 100.
" Ira, 100, 103.
" Ira Jackson, 100.
" Jane Lucretia, 100.
" John, 103.
" Lawrence, 100.
" Lorenzo, 100.
" Lorenzo M., 100.
" Lucy Caroline, 100.
" McKendree, 100.
" Pliny, 103.
" Ruth A., 100.
" Ursula, 103.
" Warren, 100, 103.
" Waters, 103.
" Welcome, 103.
" Wesley, 100, 103.
" William, 103.
" Worthy, 103.
" W. V., 1111.
Whiton, Julia Sophia, 472.
Whitridge, R. B., 712.
Whitten, Mercy, 233.
Whyland, Alphonso, 379.
" Joseph, 379.
" Julia, 379.
" Mary, 379.
" Sarah, 379.
Wilcox, Asa, 665.
" Esther, 313.
" Eva B., 1533.
" Harriet C., 1427.
" Phoebe, 315.
" Rachel, 247.
" William H., 311.

Wilder, John, 176.
Willard, Mary, 590.
Williams, Alda, 1537.
" Blanche, 1537.
" Burdette, 1537.
" Corinne, 1537.
" Frank, 1537.
" Mildred, 1537.
Wilson, David, 1003.
" Elizabeth, 330.
" Emerine L., 330.
" Ruth Amidon, 1003.
Wing, Joseph, 74.
Winship, Ella, 380.
Wirth, William, 952.
" William Aaron, 952.
Woffendan, Frederick W., 99.
" Leon H., 99.
" Murray S., 99.
" Ruth E., 99.
" Samuel, 99.
Wolcott, Henry, 137.
" James, 137.
Wood, Ruth, 27.
Woodward, Ella S., 190.
" Mary L., 1461.
Woodworth, Mary Abby, 443.
" Monroe, 1128.
Wright, David, 219.
" Sarah Agnes, 811.

Yeadon, Emma M., 539.
" Halgerda, 539.
" Joshua, 539.
" Mary J., 539.
Yeomans, Louisa M., 635.
Young, Lewis C., 963.

CPSIA information can be obtained
at www.ICGtesting.com
Printed in the USA
BVHW040158060321
601610BV00005B/396